CRITICAL ACCLAIM FOR WALKER PERCY AND *THE THANATOS SYNDROME*

"Controversial. . . . Another of his distinguished ironic voyages across uncharted waters of good and evil, and the result is a happy contradiction in terms: a philosophical novel that will appeal to a broad readership. . . . You'll never be bored."

Chicago Sun-Times

"The stuff of a deliciously wacky comedy, orchestrated with a deft touch. . . . the book is constructed of a plot that moves quickly and unpredictably, dialogue that shimmers with intelligence and verve. . . . *The Thanatos Syndrome* is highbrow hilarity, all the more discerning for disguising its tears behind lots of laughs."

Newsday

"To read Walker Percy is to fall under his spell. It was Keats who said that 'poetry should surprise by a fine excess.' If that is a good definition, and I think it is, Percy has been writing novels which are poetry. *The Thanatos Syndrome* is surely one of his finest."

Chicago Tribune

"This sad, funny, antic, wonderful novel glows with radioactive sodium and genius. . . . In this grand, sardonic comedy, the author has forged a new genre, the theological-medical thriller, an enterprise fraught with literary risks boldly assumed and fully overcome. . . . The novel of ideas is alive and well."

The Philadelphia Inquirer

"Rockets along. . . . The book may serve up a bit of thriller here, a whiff of science fiction there, a hint of metaphysics and threat of rant, the occasional outburst of comedy, all in a highly readable manner."

The Boston Globe

"The novel has a . . . beautiful atmosphere (you can smell the river, taste the chicory) and some funny, tender scenes. Percy is not afraid of life's complexities either. He often touches on the quicksilver relationships between Southern blacks and whites, between men and women in love, between men and religion—and fresh, sometimes breathtaking, truths come gleaming through."

People

"Not since Norman Mailer's *American Dream* or E.L. Doctorow's *Ragtime* has a serious American work of fiction from one of the front-rank elder statesmen of our culture seemed so potentially popular and accessible. . . . We have here more of Percy's splendid American dreaming, tied to a plot that's as fast-moving as any thriller on the market. . . . One of the most suggestive and at the same time entertaining books that I have read in a long time."

The Houston Post

"[A] hilarious comedy of social interactions."
San Francisco Chronicle

"Although *The Thanatos Syndrome* might narrowly be called a novel of suspense, Percy writes with such clarity and on so many levels from wry comedy to moral eloquence that it escapes the classification in an explosion of ideas. . . . Percy has rendered his milieu as truly as Chekov did his in *The Cherry Orchard*."
Houston Chronicle

"*The Thanatos Syndrome* reads like a good thriller. . . . Percy controls his main narrative with great sureness; it is suspenseful, it is provocative, it is witty. Nobody presently writing has so keen an eye for the surreal quality of our cultural topography."
The New Republic

"Percy has a fine ear for behavior; he has a lot of fun catching different voices and body language gestures. . . . Percy's novels . . . do give one a lift."
The Christian Science Monitor

"This novel embodies Percy's most detailed, explicit attack on contemporary materialism and science. . . . Walker Percy scrupulously delivers all the promises his plot provides."
Time

THE THANATOS SYNDROME

Walker Percy

IVY BOOKS • NEW YORK

Ivy Books
Published by Ballantine Books
Copyright © 1987 by Walker Percy

Library of Congress Catalog Card Number: 86-29409

ISBN 0-8041-0220-1

This edition published by arrangement with Farrar, Straus & Giroux, Inc.

Manufactured in the United States of America

First Ballantine Books Edition: May 1988

To Robert Coles

The place where the strange events related in this book occur, Feliciana, is not imaginary. It was so named by the Spanish. It was and is part of Louisiana, a strip of pleasant pineland running from the Mississippi River to the Perdido, a curious region of a curious state. Never quite Creole or French or Anglo-Saxon or Catholic or Baptist like other parishes of Louisiana, it has served over the years as a refuge for all manner of malcontents. If America was settled by dissenters from various European propositions, Feliciana was settled by dissenters from the dissent, American Tories who had no use for the Revolution, disgruntled Huguenots and Cavaliers from the Carolinas, New Englanders fleeing from Puritanism, unionists who voted against secession, Confederate refugees from occupied New Orleans, deserters from the Confederate Army, smugglers from both sides, criminals holed up in the Honey Island Swamp.

Welcomed in the beginning by the hospitable and indolent Spanish of a decrepit empire, some of these assorted malcontents united long enough to throw out the Spanish and form an independent republic, complete with its own Declaration of Independence, flag, army, navy, constitution, and capital in St. Francisville. The new republic had no inclination to join French Louisiana to the south or the United States to the north and would as soon have been let alone. It lasted seventy-four days. Jefferson had bought Louisiana and that was that.

As pleasant a place as its name implies, it still harbors all manner of fractious folk, including Texans and recent refugees from unlikely places like Korea and Michigan, all of whom have learned to get along tolerably well, better than most in fact, who watch L.S.U. football and reruns of M*A*S*H, drink Dixie beer, and eat every sort of food imaginable, which is generally cooked in something called a roux.

The downside of Feliciana is that its pine forests have been mostly cut down, its bayous befouled, Lake Pontchartrain polluted, the Mississippi River turned into a sewer. It has too many malls, banks, hospitals, chiropractors, politicians, lawyers, realtors, and condos with names like Château Charmant.

Still and all, I wouldn't live anywhere else.

It is strange, but these Louisianians, for all their differences and contrariness, have an affection for one another. It is expressed by small signs and courtesies, even between strangers, as if they shared a secret.

In what follows, the geography of the place has been somewhat scrambled. All of the people in Feliciana have been made up. The only real persons are the German and Austrian professors and physicians who were active in both the Weimar Republic and the Third Reich—Drs. deCrinis, Villinger, Schneider, Nitsche, Heyde—and the Swiss psychiatrist Dr. C. G. Jung. For this information about the Nazi doctors and their academic precursors in the Weimar Republic, I am indebted to Dr. Frederic Wertham's remarkable book, A Sign for Cain.

WALKER PERCY

I

1. FOR SOME TIME NOW I HAVE NOTICED THAT SOME-
thing strange is occurring in our region. I have noticed
it both in the patients I have treated and in ordinary encoun-
ters with people. At first there were only suspicions. But yesterday my suspicions were confirmed. I was called to the
hospital for a consultation and there was an opportunity to
make an examination.

It began with little things, certain small clinical changes
which I observed. Little things can be important. Even more
important is the ability—call it knack, hunch, providence,
good luck, whatever—to know what you are looking for and
to put two and two together. A great scientist once said that
genius consists not in making great discoveries but in seeing
the connection between small discoveries.

For example, a physician I once knew—not a famous professor or even a very successful internist, but a natural diag-
nostician, one of those rare birds who sees things out of the
corner of his eye, so to speak, and gets a hunch—was going
about his practice in New Orleans. He noticed a couple of
little things most of us would have missed. He had two patients in the same neighborhood with moderate fever, enlarged lymph nodes, especially in the inguinal region. One
afternoon as he took his leave through the kitchen of a great

house in the Garden District—in those days one still made house calls!—the black cook whom he knew muttered something like: "I sho wish he wouldn't be putting out that poison where the chirren can get holt of it." Now most physicians would not even listen or, if they did, would not be curious and would leave with a pleasantry to humor old what's-hername. But a good physician or a lucky physician might prick up his ears. There *was* something about that inguinal node—"Poison? Poison for what? Rats?" "I mean rats." "You got rats?" "I mean. Look here." There in the garbage can, sure enough, a very dead rat with a drop of blood hanging like a ruby from its nose. The physician went his way, musing. Something nagged at the back of his head. Halfway down St. Charles, *click*, a connection was made. He parked, went to a pay phone, called the patient's father. "Did you put out rat poison in your house?" No, he had not. Is Anne okay? "She'll be fine but get her to Touro for a test." At the hospital he aspirated the suspicious inguinal node. Most doctors would have diagnosed mononucleosis, made jokes with the young lady about the kissing disease—So you're just back from Ole Miss, what do you expect, ha ha. He took the specimen to the lab and told the technician to make a smear and stain with carbol-fuchsin. He took one look. There they were, sure enough, the little bipolar dumbbells of *Pasteurella pestis*. The plague does in fact turn up from time to time in New Orleans, the nation's largest port. It's no big deal nowadays, caught in time. A massive shot of antibiotic and Anne went home.

This is not to suggest that I have stumbled onto another black plague. But if I am right, I have stumbled onto something. It is both a good deal more mysterious and perhaps even more ominous. The trouble is, unfortunately for us psychiatrists, that diagnoses in psychiatry are often more difficult—and less treatable. There is seldom a single cause, a little dumbbell bacillus one can point to, or a single magic bullet one can aim at the tiny villain. Believe it or not, psychiatrists still do not know the cause of the commonest of all human diseases, schizophrenia. They still argue about whether the genes are bad, the chemistry is bad, the psychology is bad, whether it's in the mind or the brain. In fact, they're still arguing about whether there is such a thing as the mind.

It began with little things. The other day, for example, I was seeing a patient I hadn't seen for two years. I've been away, but that's another story. She had a certain mannerism, as do we all, which was as uniquely hers as her fingerprints. If she said something in her usual bantering way and I had the good luck to get behind it, make a stab in the same bantering tone and get it right, she had a way of ducking her head and touching the nape of her neck the way women used to do years ago to check hairpins in a bun and, as a slight color rose in her cheek, cut her eyes toward me under lowered lids almost flirtatiously, then nod ironically. "Uh huh," she'd say with a smile. She monitored her eyes carefully. A look from her was never a casual thing.

An analyst who sees a patient several times a week for two years and who has his eyes and ears open—especially that third ear Reik talks about which hears what is not said—comes to know her, his patient, in some ways better than her husband, who probably hasn't taken a good look at her for years.

But last week, when I saw her in the hospital, her mannerism was gone. Her eyes were no longer monitored. A curious business. I'd have noticed it even if I were seeing her for the first time. Women are generally careful of their eyes. She simply gazed at me, not boldly, but with a mild, unfocused gaze. She responded readily enough, but in monosyllables and short phrases, and now and then gave a little start as if she had in some sense or other come to herself. Then she'd drift off again.

To summarize her history in a word or two: She was a New Englander, a Bennington graduate, a shy but assured person who married a high-born, freewheeling Louisiana Creole whom she met at Amherst, a high-roller later in oil leases and real estate. So here she found herself, set down in this spanking new Sunbelt exurb, in a new "plantation-style" house, in a new country club, next to number-six fairway. All at once she became afraid. She was afraid of people, places, things, dogs, the car; afraid to go out of her house, afraid of nothing at all. There are names for her disorder, of course—agoraphobia, free-floating anxiety—but they don't help much. What to do with herself? She did some painting, not very good, of swamps, cypresses, bayous, Spanish moss, egrets, and such. I thought of her as a housebound Emily Dickinson, but when I saw her on the couch in my office— she had made the supreme effort, gotten in her car, and driven to town—she looked more like Christina in Wyeth's painting, facing the window, back turned to me, hip making an angle, thin arm raised in a gesture of longing, a yearning toward— toward what?

In her case, the yearning was simple, deceptively simple. If only she could be back at her grandmother's farm in Vermont, where as a young girl she had been happy.

She had a recurring dream. Hardly a session went by without her mentioning it. It was worth working on. She was in the cellar of her grandmother's farmhouse, where there was a certain smell which she associated with the "winter apples" stored there and a view through the high dusty windows of the green hills. Though she was always alone in the dream, there was the conviction that she was waiting for something. For what? A visitor. A visitor was coming and would tell her a secret. It was something to work with. What was she, her visitor-self, trying to tell her solitary cellar-bound self? What part of herself was the deep winter-apple-bound self? What part of herself was the deep winter-apple-smelling cellar? The green hills? She was not sure, but she felt better. She was able to leave the house, not to take up golf or bridge with the country-club ladies, but to go abroad to paint, to meadows and bayous. Her painting got better. Her egrets began to look less like Audubon's elegant dead birds than like ghosts in the swamp.

I contrived that it crossed her mind that her terror might

not be altogether bad. What if it might be trying to tell her something, like the mysterious visitor in her dream? I seldom give anxious people drugs. If you do, they may feel better for a while, but they'll never find out what the terror is trying to tell them. At any rate, it set her wondering and made her life more tolerable. She wasn't afraid of being afraid. We were getting somewhere.

Now here she is two years later, back in the hospital, again facing the window. But no yearning Christina she. More like a satisfied Duchess of Alba, full round arm lying along sumptuous curve of hip.

"Mickey," I said.

She turned to face me with a fond, unsurprised gaze, eyes not quite focused, not quite converging.

"Well well well," said Mickey. "My old pal Doc."

Never, not in a state of terror or out of it, would she have called me that. She was one of the few patients who called me Tom.

"You're looking very well, Mickey."

I must have been leaning toward her, for my hand was propped on the edge of her bed. Her arm fell on my hand, the warm ventral flesh of her forearm imprisoning my fingers.

"Well, yes." She lay back, settling her body, giving the effect somehow of straddling a little under the covers.

I remember registering disappointment. The flatness of her gaze gave the effect one senses in some women who have given up on the mystery of themselves and taken somebody else's advice: Be bold, be assertive.

"Old Doc." Her chin settled into her full throat, luxuriating. "You really did it, didn't you?"

"Did what?"

"Blew it."

"You mean—"

"Do you think people don't know where you've been for two years?"

It is not necessary to reply. She has already drifted, eyes unconverged, gazing past me.

"Mickey, did you want this consultation, or was it Dr. Comeaux's idea?"

"Old Doc." My fingers are still imprisoned under her arm. "I was always on your side. I defended you."

"Thank you."

"I'm just fine, Doc."

"You mean you didn't send for me?"

"Mickey's glad to see you, Doc. Come by me."

"I'm by you." Come by me. That's Louisiana talk, not New England. "If you're feeling fine, Mickey, what are you doing here?" I look at her chart. She's not on medication.

"I got it all, Doc. Did you know I was a rich bitch?"

"Yes, I knew that."

"Did you know Durel and I own the biggest hunter-jumper ranch in the parish?"

"Yes, I knew that. Then why—"

"We got it made. You want to know the name?"

"The name?"

"Bar-in-Circle Ranch." She released my hand and showed me the bar and circle with her fingers. She winked at me, like a schoolchild who's just learned a dirty joke. "You like that?"

"Sure." I'm reading her chart. "Mickey, it doesn't seem that things are so fine here. It seems there was an incident at the ranch with a groom, a fire, your prize stallion destroyed in the fire."

"He was coming on to me," said Mickey idly.

"According to this, he was a thirteen-year-old boy and the complaint by his parents was that it was you coming on to him."

She shrugged, but was not really interested enough to argue. Am I mistaken or is there not a sort of horsewoman's swagger as she moves her legs under the covers? "That stallion was a killer, Doc. Now. How about you?"

"What about me?"

"You know where the ranch is."

"Yes."

6

"And you got your troubles."

"So?"

"So you come on out by me. Durel likes you too."

As I listen to her and flip through the chart, something pops into my head. For some reason—perhaps it is her disconnectedness—she reminds me of my daughter as a four-year-old. It is the age when children have caught on to language, do not stick to one subject, are open to any subject, would as soon be asked any question as long as one keeps playing the language game. A child does not need a context like you and me. Mickey LaFaye, like four-year-old Meg, is out of context.

"Mickey, what is today?"

"Monday," she says, unsurprised. I am right. She gives me the day and the date willingly.

Then it was that I had my wild idea, my piece of luck—perhaps it was part of my own nuttiness—which first put me on the track of this strange business.

"Mickey," I asked her, "what date will Easter fall on next year?"

Again no surprise, no shifting of gears from one context to another. There is no context. What I do notice is that for a split second her eyes go up into her eyebrows, as if she were reading a printout.

She gives me the date. I wouldn't know, of course. Later I looked it up. She was right.

She gives me other dates. They were right. I ask her where St. Louis is. She tells me where St. Louis is. Now everybody knows where St. Louis is, but people generally don't answer the question Where is St. Louis?, asked out of the blue, without wanting to know why you ask, unless they are playing Trivial Pursuit.

Then is she an idiot savant, one of those people who don't have sense enough to come out of the rain but can tell you what is 4,891 times 23,547 by reading off some computer inside their head? I did not know at the time, but I knew later. No, she was not.

7

I gaze down at her, my arms folded over the chart. What has happened to her? How can she be at once as innocent as a four-year-old and as blowsy as the Duchess of Alba? At the time I had no idea.

"Mickey, what about the dream?"

"Dream?"

"The dream of Vermont, your grandmother's cellar, the smell of winter apples, the visitor who was coming."

"The dream." For a moment she seemed to become her old self, to go deep, search inward. She seemed to reach for something, almost find it. She frowned and shrugged. "Dream of Jeannie, Doc. That's what Bobby calls me. Jean's my real name. Jeannie with the light brown hair. You like?"

"Yes. Bobby?"

"Bob Comeaux. *Doctor* Comeaux, Doc."

"I know." I turn to leave.

"Doc."

"Yes?"

"You call Bobby."

"I will."

"Bobby wants something."

"All right."

"And what Bobby wants—"

"All right," I say quickly, suddenly needing to leave. "So I ask Dr. Comeaux and he'll tell me?"

"Yes." Her legs thrash enthusiastically.

I leave, knowing very little, not even who called me for a consultation or why. I will ask Dr. Comeaux.

2.

A STRANGE CASE, YES, BUT NOTHING TO WRITE UP for the *JAMA*.

Indeed, I couldn't make head or tail of it at the time, the

bizarre business with the boy and the stallion, but mainly the change in Mickey LaFaye. But what physician has not had patients who don't make any sense at all? To tell the truth, they're our stock-in-trade. We talk and write about the ones we can make sense of.

Here's another mini-case, not even a case but a fifteen-second encounter with an acquaintance even as I left Mickey's room and started down the hall, musing over the change in Mickey. How much of the change, I was wondering, comes from my two years away and the change in me?

Here's old Frank Macon, polishing the terrazzo floor. I saw him a week ago, just after I returned. Frank Macon is a seventy-five-year-old black janitor. I have known him for forty years. He used to train bird dogs when there were still quail around here. Then as now he was polishing the terrazzo with a heavy rotary brush. From long practice he was using the machine well, holding back on one handle to give it a centripetal swing until it caromed off the concave angle of the wall to propel itself back by the torque of the brush. I broke his rhythm. He switched off the motor and eyed me. He clapped his hands softly and gave me one of his, a large meaty warm slab, callused but inert.

"Look who's back!" he cried, casting a muddy eye around and past me. He throws up an arm. "Whoa!"

"How you doing, Frank!"

"Fine! But look at you now! You looking good! You looking good in the face and slim, not poorly like you used to."

"You're looking good too, Frank."

"You must have been doing some yard work," says Frank, good eye gleaming slyly.

"Yes," I say, smiling. He's guying me. It's an old joke between us.

"I knowed they couldn't keep you! People talking about trouble. I say no way. No way Doc going to be in trouble. Ain't no police going to hold Doc for long. People got too much respect for Doc! I mean." Again he smote his hands together, not quite a clap but a horny brushing past, signifying polite amazement. He turned half away, but one eye still gleamed at me.

One would have to be a Southerner, white or black, to understand the complexities of this little exchange. Seemingly pleasant, it was not quite. Seemingly a friend in the old style, Frank was not quite. The glint of eye, seemingly a smile of greeting, was not. It was actually malignant. Frank was having a bit of fun with me, I knew, and he knew that I knew, using the old forms of civility to say what he pleased. What he was pleased to say was: So you got caught, didn't you, and you got out sooner than I would have, didn't you? Even his pronunciation of police as pó-lice was overdone and farcical, a parody of black speech, but a parody he calculated I would recognize. Actually he's a deacon and uses a kind of churchy English: Doctor, what we're gerng to do is soliciting contributions for a chicken-dinner benefit the ladies of the church gerng to have Sunday, and suchlike.

I value his honesty—even his jeering. He knew this and we parted amiably. We understand each other. He reminds me of the Russian serfs Tolstoy wrote about, who spoke bluntly to their masters, using the very infirmity of their serfdom as a warrant to scold: Stepan Stepanovitch, you're a sinful man! Mend your ways!

"How Miss Ellen doing?" he asked, playing out the game of Southern good manners.

"Just fine, and your family?" I said, watching him closely. Am I mistaken or is there not a glint of irony in his muddy eye at the mention of my wife's name?

That was my encounter with Frank Macon a week ago, a six-layered exchange beyond the compass of any known science of communication but plain as day to Frank and me.

This is my encounter with Frank this morning, in the same hospital, the same corridor, the same Frank swinging the same brush. He simply stepped aside, not switching off the machine, neither servile nor sullen, not ironical, not sly, not farcical, not in any way complex, but purely and simply perfunctory.

"How you doing, Frank?"

"Good morning, Doctor."

"Still featherbedding—" I begin in our old chaffing style, but he cuts me off with, of all things, "Have a nice day, Doctor"—and back to his polishing without missing the swing of the machine. I could have been any doctor, anybody.

Here again, a small thing. Nothing startling. He might simply have decided to dispose of me with standard U.S. politeness, which is indeed the easiest way to get rid of people. Have a nice day—

Or he might have decided that the ultimate putdown is this same American civility. What better dismissal than to treat someone you've known for forty years like a drive-up customer at Big Mac's?

Or: Feeling bad, tired, old, out of it, he might have drawn a blank.

Or: Something strange has happened to him.

3. THEN ALONG CAME MY SECOND CASE, WHICH GAVE me my first clue that something queer might be going on hereabouts, that Mickey LaFaye was not just a solitary nut.

Donna S——, a former patient, called to make an appointment.

It was last Wednesday afternoon. Downtown was deserted. The banks were closed. The other doctors were playing golf. They've mostly moved out to the malls and the hospital parks, where they've built pleasant plantation-style offices with white columns and roofs of cypress shakes.

* * *

Here I am, waiting for her, not exactly besieged by patients, sitting on the front porch of my office, my father's old coroner's building behind the courthouse, a pleasant little Cajun cottage of weathered board-and-batten and a rusty tin roof. It is October but it feels like late summer, the first hint of fall gentling the Louisiana heat, the gum leaves beginning to speckle. I am watching the sparrows who have taken over my father's martin hotel. The cicadas start up in the high rooms of the live oaks, fuguing one upon the other.

I am the only poor physician in town, the only one who doesn't drive a Mercedes or a BMW. I still drive the Chevrolet Caprice I owned before I went away. It is a bad time for psychiatrists. Old-fashioned shrinks are out of style and generally out of work. We, who like our mentor Dr. Freud believe there is a psyche, that it is born to trouble as the sparks fly up, that one gets at it, the root of trouble, the soul's own secret, by venturing into the heart of darkness, which is to say, by talking and listening, mostly listening, to another troubled human for months, years— we have been mostly superseded by brain engineers, neuropharmacologists, chemists of the synapses. And why not? If one can prescribe a chemical and overnight turn a haunted soul into a bustling little body, why take on such a quixotic quest as pursuing the secret of one's very self?

Anyhow, there I sat, waiting for Donna and making little paper P-51s and sailing them into the sparrows flocking at the martin house. I have had enough practice and gotten good enough with the control surfaces so that the little planes generally made a climbing turn, a chandelle, and came back.

Here comes Donna, swinging along under the oaks. A stray shaft of yellow sunlight touches fire to her coppery hair.

I watch her. She's a big girl but not fat anymore. Not even stout or "heavy," as one might say hereabouts. But certainly not fat in the sense that once it was the only word for her, even though physicians, who have an unerring knack for the wrong word, would describe her on her chart as a "young obese white female."

Then she was plain and simply fat. She was also, or so it

seemed, jolly and funny, the sort described by her friends as nice as she could be. If she were put up for a sorority in college, she would be recommended as a "darling girl." And if one of her sisters wanted to fix her up with a blind date, the word would be: She has a wonderful sense of humor. She was the sort of girl you'd have gotten stuck with at a dance and you'd have known it and she'd have known that you knew it and you'd have both felt rotten. Girls still have a rotten time of it, worse than boys, even fat boys.

I used to see her alone at Big Mac's: in midafternoon, I because I had forgotten to eat lunch, she because she had eaten lunch and was already hungry again; at four in the afternoon with a half-pounder, a large chocolate shake, and three paper boats of french fries lined up in front of her. Pigging out, as she called it.

She was referred to me by more successful physicians who'd finally thrown up their hands—What do I want with her, they'd tell me, the only trouble with her is she eats too damn much, I've got people in real trouble, and so on—as a surgeon might refer a low-back pain to a chiropractor: He may be a quack but he can't do you any harm. Maybe she's got a psychiatric problem, Doc.

Actually I helped her and ended up liking her and she me. Yes, she had always been "nice." "Nice" in her case had a quite definite meaning. It meant always doing what one was supposed to do, what her mamma and papa wanted her to do, what her teacher wanted her to do, what her boss wanted her to do. Surely if you do what you're supposed to do, things will turn out well for you, won't they? Not necessarily. In her case they didn't. She felt defrauded by the world, by God. So what did she do? She got fat.

She started out being nice as pie with me. She listened intently, spoke intelligently, read books on the psychiatry of fatness, used more psychiatric words than I did. She was the perfect patient, mistress of the couch, dreamer of perfect dreams, confirmer of all theories. All the more reason why she was startled when I asked her why she was so angry. She was, of course, and of course it came out. She couldn't stand her mother or father or herself or God—or me. For one thing, she had been sexually molested by her father, then blamed by her mother for doing the very thing her mother had told her to do: Be nice. So she couldn't stand the double bind of it, being nice to Daddy, doing what Daddy wanted, and believing him and liking it, oh yes, did she ever (yes, that's the worst of it, the part you don't read about), and then being called bad by Mamma and believing her too. A no-win game, for sure. So what to do? Eat. Why eat? To cover up the bad beautiful little girl in layers of fat so Daddy wouldn't want her? To make herself ugly for boys so nobody but Daddy would want her?

I couldn't say, nor could she, but I was getting somewhere with her. First, by giving her permission to give herself permission to turn loose her anger, not on them at first, but on me and here where she felt safe. She didn't know she was angry. There is a great difference between being angry and knowing that you are angry. We made progress. One day she turned over on the couch and looked at me with an expression of pure malevolence. Her lips moved. "Eh?" I said. "I said you're a son of a bitch too," she said. "Is that right? Why is that?" I asked. "You look a lot like him." "Is that so?" "That's so. A seedy but kindly gentle wise Atticus Finch who messed with Scout. Wouldn't Scout love that?" she asked me. "Would she?" I asked her. She told me.

She lost her taste for french fries, lost weight, took up aerobic dancing, began to have dates. She discovered she was a romantic. At first she talked tough, in what she took to be a liberated style. "I know what you people think—it all comes down to getting laid, doesn't it?—well, I've been laid like you wouldn't dream of," she said with, yes, a sneer. "You people?" I asked her mildly. "Who are you people?" "You shrinks," she said. "Don't think I don't know what you think and probably want." "All right," I said. But what she really believed in was nineteenth-century romantic love—perhaps even thirteenth-century. She believed in—what?—a knight?

14

Yes. Or rather a certain someone she would meet by chance. It was her secret hope that in the ordinary round of life there would occur a meeting of eyes across a room, a touch of hands, then a word or two from him. "Look, Donna," he would say, "it's very simple. I have to see you again"—the rich commerce of looks and words. It would occur inevitably, yet by chance. The very music of her heart told her so. She believed in love. Isn't it possible, she asked me, to meet someone like that—and I would know immediately by his eyes—who loved you and whom you loved? Well yes, I said. I agreed with her and suggested only that she might not leave it all to chance. In chance the arithmetic is bad. After all, there is no law against looking for a certain someone.

After hating me, her surrogate seedy Atticus Finch, she loved me, of course. I was the one who understood her and gave her leave. Our eyes met in love. It was a good transference. She came to understand it as such. She did well. She was working on her guilt and terror, the terror of suspecting it was her fault that Daddy had laid hands on her and that they'd had such a good time. She got a good job at a doctor's office—as a receptionist, did well—and got engaged.

I didn't share her faith in the inevitability of meeting a certain someone by chance, but I do have my beliefs about people. Otherwise I couldn't stand the terrible trouble people get themselves into and the little I can do for them. My science I got from Dr. Freud, a genius and a champion of the psyche—*Seele*, he called it, yes, soul—even though he spent his life pretending there was no such thing. I am one of the few left, yes, a psyche-iatrist, an old-fashioned physician of the soul, one of the last survivors in a horde of Texas brain mechanics, M.I.T. neurone circuitrists.

My psychiatric faith I got in the old days from Dr. Harry Stack Sullivan, perhaps this country's best psychiatrist, who, if not a genius, had a certain secret belief which he himself could not account for. Nor could it be scientifically proven. Yet he transmitted it to his residents. It seemed to him to be an article of faith, and to me it is as valuable as Freud's genius. "Here's the secret," he used to tell us, his residents. "You take that last patient we saw. Offhand, what would you say about him? A loser, right? A loser by all counts. You know what you're all thinking to yourself? You're thinking, No wonder that guy is depressed. He's entitled to be depressed. If I were he, I'd be depressed too. Right? Wrong. You're thinking the most we can do for him is make him feel a little better, give him a pill or two, a little pat or two. Right? Wrong. Here's the peculiar thing and I'll never understand why this is so: *Each patient this side of psychosis, and even some psychotics, has the means of obtaining what he needs, she needs, with a little help from you.*"

Now, I don't know where he got this, from Ramakrishna, Dr. Jung, or Matthew 13:44. Or from his own sardonic Irish soul. But there it is. "Okay, that patient may look like a loser to you—incidentally, Doctors, how do we know you don't look like losers to me, or I to you?" said Dr. Sullivan, a small ferret-faced man with many troubles. But there it was, to me the pearl of great price, the treasure buried in a field, that is to say, the patient's truest unique self which lies within his, the patient's, power to reach and which we, as little as we do, can help him reach.

Do you know that this is true? I don't know why or how, but it is true. People can get better, can come to themselves, without chemicals and with a little help from you. I believed him. Amazing! I'm amazed every time it happens.

Very well, I am an optimist. I was an optimist with Donna. I was willing to explore her romanticism with her. What I believed was not necessarily that her knight might show up— who knows? he could—but rather that talking and listening ventilates the dark cellars of romanticism. She needed to face the old two-faced Janus of sex: how could it be that she, one and the same person, could slip off of an afternoon with Daddy, her seedy Atticus Finch, do bad thrilling things with him, and at the same time long for one look from pure-hearted Galahad across a crowded room? Daddy had got to be put together with Galahad, because they belonged to the same

16

forlorn species, the same sad sex. She was putting it together in me, who was like her daddy but had no designs on her and whom she trusted. She could speak the unspeakable to me. Sometimes I think that is the best thing we shrinks do, render the unspeakable speakable.

So here she is two years later. I watch her curiously as she comes up the porch steps. She looks splendid, a big girl yes, but no fat girl she. She's wearing a light summery skirt of wrinkled cotton in the new style, slashed up the thigh and flared a little. Her hair is pulled up and back, giving the effect of tightening and shortening her cheek. With her short cheek, flared skirt, and thick Achilles tendon, she reminded me of one of Degas's ballet girls, who, if you've noticed, are strong working girls with big muscular legs.

I try to catch her eye, but she brushes past me, swinging her old drawstring bag, and strides into my office. She ignores the couch. Seated, we face each other across the desk.

Her gaze is pleasant. Her lips curve in a little smile, something new. Is she being ironic again?

"Well?" I say at last.

"Well what?" she replies equably.

"How have you been?"

"Oh, fine," she says, and falls silent. "How about you?" Yes, she is being ironic.

"I'm all right."

"I see"—and again falls silent but equably and with no sense of being at a loss.

"Do you wish to resume therapy?"

She shakes her head but goes on smiling.

"It was you who called me, Donna."

"I know."

I wait for her to start up. She doesn't. I decide to wait her out. Finally she says, "I knew you were back."

"And you wanted to wish me well."

"I saw you in the store."

"I see." Something stirs in the back of my head.

"I often see your wife in the store."

"Is that right?"

"She's your second wife, isn't she?"

"Yes."

"She is often with that famous scientist, or is he a bridge player, anyway a close friend, I'm sure." Again the lively look. Again the stirring just above my hairline.

"Donna, I'm sure you didn't come here to tell me you saw my second wife at the store."

"No." She opens her mouth and closes it.

When patients get stuck, you usually get them off dead center by asking standard questions, as if you were seeing them for the first time.

"Are you still working at the clinic?"

"Yes"—neutrally. Again she falls silent, but without a trace of the old unease or hostility.

"How does it go?"

"Oh, fine."

As we gaze at each other, the stirring at the back of my head comes up front. I have the same nutty idea.

"Where do you live now, Donna?"

"In Cut Off, Louisiana." Her reply is as prompt and triumphant as if I had at last hit on the right question.

"I see. Where is Cut Off, Donna?"

Her eyes move up a little as if she were consulting a map over my head. "Cut Off, Louisiana, is sixty-one miles southwest of New Orleans." There is no map over my head.

"Very good, Donna. Donna, where is Arkansas?"

Again the eyes going up into her eyebrows. "Arkansas is bounded on the north by—"

"That's fine, Donna, I see that you know. Give me your hand, Donna."

She gives me her right hand across the desk. I had thought she was right-handed, but needed to be sure. I look at it, the broad thumb, the short nail. I remember dreaming of her once, making much in the dream of a certain stubbiness of hand and foot. Her foot does in fact have an exaggerated

18

arch, like a dancer's. A broad quick little hoofed mare of a girl she was in the dream.

I look into her eyes, which are dilated and dark with pupil. Again she reminds me of Degas girls, with their big black eye dots.

"Are you taking any medicine, Donna?"

She shakes her head quickly. How do I know, as certainly as if she were a four-year-old, that she is telling the truth?

"Donna, make a circle with your thumb and forefinger like this and look at me through it, like so."

She does. She looks at me through the circle with her left eye. Ordinarily in a right-handed person, the right eye is dominant.

I am musing but rouse myself. I'll muse later.

"Donna, is there anything I can do for you?"

She shakes her head, almost merrily.

"Donna, why did you come to see me? What do you want?" Although I had not yet got onto this peculiar business, I already knew—with her as well as with Mickey La-Faye—that I could ask her any question in any context.

Her eyes are focused above me. She nods toward something. "That."

I turn around in my chair. There in the bookshelf, in a space between two bookends, squats a little pre-Columbian figurine, a mud-colored, sausage-shaped woman with a large abdomen. A patient with mystical expectations from a trip to Mexico and some Mayan ruins had given it to me. Her mystical Mexican expectations didn't pan out. They seldom do.

"You like that?" I ask Donna.

She nods.

"Would you like to have it?"

She nods eagerly, the same quick assent of a four-year-old.

"Why?" I am curious. Is it because it is fat and fertile? Because it is mine? Because it is Mexican? Does she have the Mexican itch?

"Something I need."

"It is something you need?"

19

"Yes, I need."

I need? A curious expression. I get up to get it to give it to her. Not hearing her chair scrape, I am startled when at the very moment I turn around, I run into her. She has come around my desk, barefoot and silent. She backs into me.

"Oh, sorry," I say automatically, moving sideways to my chair, but she has already reached behind her, seized my hands, brought them around her clasped in hers and against her. She presses the figurine in my hand against her body.

"What's this about, Donna?"

By way of answer, she cranes her head back into my neck and begins turning to and fro. I begin to free my hands. She tightens her grip. "You know."

"Know what?"

"Donna needs you."

"No, Donna doesn't. We've been through all that, remember? First the hatred, then the love, neither of which had anything to do with me. We got past it, remember?"

She's turning to and fro. "I always liked to smell you. You in your seersuckers, not young not old, but like—?"

"Like Atticus?"

"Yeah." She nods but is not heeding.

She is engaging me, so to speak. To describe her backward embrace, I can only use the word primatologists use, *presenting*. She was presenting rearward. Enough of this. What probably saved me from the erotic power of her move was its suddenness and oddness.

She reaches back for me, clasping her hands at the back of my neck.

"You smell like—"

"Like your father?"

That did it. As suddenly as she started, she stops and goes stiff.

"It's okay," I tell her, and turn her, not to face me, but to get her back to her chair with minimal embarrassment. She is not embarrassed. But her face is heavy and lengthened, mouth pulled down like a sulky child.

"It's okay, Donna."

"Okay." She's not badly put off.

I look at her for a while. Something crosses my mind.

"Donna, do you wish to come back next week?"

"Yes." An ordinary, perfunctory yes.

"All right. You come back. Meet me at the hospital. Same time. I want to run a few tests on you. Okay?"

"Okay."

She's up and off, swinging her bag, as carelessly as she came.

It is only after she's left that I discover I've broken out in a sweat. There's this business about seductive patients, known even to Hippocrates, and no credit to the physician—consider old funny-looking Hippocrates, who probably smelled stronger than I or Atticus Finch. But seductive is seductive, more or less, sometimes more than less. Ahem. What to do. One thing to do is open lower right desk drawer, remove fifth of Jack Daniel's from where it's been for two years, still half full and two years older, pour four fingers into a water glass, knock back. Ahem. That's better.

4. IS THERE A COMMONALITY BETWEEN THESE TWO CASES? Have I been away so long and lived so strangely that everyone else seems strange? No, there's something wrong with these women. And with Frank Macon. Two cases are too few even to suggest a syndrome, but I am struck by certain likenesses . . . In each there has occurred a sloughing away of the old terrors, worries, rages, a shedding of guilt like last year's snakeskin, and in its place is a mild fond vacancy, a species of unfocused animal good spirits. Then are they, my patients, not better rather than worse? The answer is unclear. They're not on medication. They are not hurting, they are not worrying the same old bone, but there is something missing, not merely the old terrors, but a sense in each of her—her what? her self? The main objective clue so far is language. Neither needs a context to talk or answer. They utter short two-word sentences. They remind me of the chimp Lana, who would happily answer any question anytime with a sign or two to get her banana. Both women will answer a question like Where is Chicago? agreeably and instantly and by consulting, so to speak, their own built-in computer readouts. You wouldn't. You'd want to know why I wanted to know. You'd want to relate the question to your—self.

I'm sitting on the porch again, not sailing airplanes but musing and keeping one eye on my watch—I have to meet Max and Bob, my "parole officers," at two—when suddenly I get a flash. Well, not quite a flash, but a notion. Could it be that—

Could it be that there has occurred in both Mickey and Donna some odd suppression of cortical function?

I am thinking of my sole contribution to medical science, a paper I wrote some years ago after an explosion in the physics lab at Tulane on the effect of a heavy-sodium fallout on the inhibitory function of the cerebral cortex on sexual behavior, which earned me a write-up in *Time* and some small local fame. I did in fact make a contribution toward the development of the present-day CORTscan, a scanning device for measuring localized cerebral functions. But there's no reason to suspect a heavy-sodium factor in these cases. There's been no explosion. It is true that the nuclear facility at Grand Mer has a sodium reactor, but there's been no accident—or even an "occurrence," as they call it.

But accident or not, are there not signs of a suppression of cortical function in Mickey and Donna? I'm thinking particularly of the posterior speech center, Wernicke's area, Brodmann 39 and 40, in the left brain of right-handed people. It is not only the major speech center but, according to neurologists, the locus of self-consciousness, the "I," the utterer, the "self"—whatever one chooses to call that peculiar trait of humans by which they utter sentences and which makes them curious about how they look in a mirror—when a chimp will look behind the mirror for another chimp.

Yes, I've been away, and yes, I've not been so well myself. But there's an advantage in absence and return. One notices changes which other people don't. Tommy has grown six inches, hadn't you noticed? Betty looks ill. Mickey and Donna? Maybe they, my patients, are not crazy, but something's going on here. What I need is objective evidence, more cases . . .

But first I must convince Max and Bob that I am not crazy myself, or at least no crazier than most doctors.

5. MEET BOB COMEAUX AND MAX IN BOB'S SPLENDID office in Fedville, the federal complex housing the qualitarian center, communicable diseases control, and the AIDS quarantine. He's at the top now, director of something or other—Quality of Life Division, or something like—in the penthouse of the monolith with a splendid panoramic view of the river in its great sweep from the haze of Baton Rouge to the south to the wooded loess hills of St. Francisville to the north. Except for the cooling tower of Grand Mer looming directly opposite and flying its plume of steam like Mt. St. Helens, it could be the same quaint lordly river of Mark Twain, its foul waters all gold and rose in the sunset. There's even a stern-wheeler, the new *Robert E. Lee*, huffing upstream, hauling tourists to the plantations.

Max and Bob are cordial and uneasy, having no stomach for this chore, riding herd on a colleague—what doctor would? Ordinarily we get along with standard medical jokes and doctors' horsing around, but this business is official, legal, and awkward.

Accordingly, they go out of their way to be easy, yawn and stretch a lot, sit anywhere but in chairs. Bob is dressed for riding, in flared stretch pants, field boots, and suede jacket, as if he had dropped in from the stables. There's a connection between us. We went to the same medical school in the East and so we talk about Murray's Bar and Grill on upper Broadway and old Doc So-and-so at Columbia-Presbyterian, as if we were classmates. In fact, we didn't even know each other. He was some years after me. He's from Long Island, but is very much the Southern horseman now, as handsome as Blake Carrington, with his steel-gray eyes and steel-gray sideburns brushed straight back like the rest of his hair, and his easy way of half sitting on his desk, swinging one leg and leaning over, hands in pockets. There is not a single wrinkle on his smooth tanned face except for a fold of skin at the corner of each eye, which gives him a slightly Oriental look.

There is a manila file on the desk next to his thigh.

Max doesn't do as good a job at acting casual. He's dressed too carefully in suit and vest, like a local doctor summoned before a congressional committee. He's concerned about me and seems at a loss—Max of all people—not knowing what to say except to express his concern. "You're okay, Tom?" he asks softly, keeping hold of my hand after the handshake. "Sure." "Are you sure?" he asks. "Sure."

For some reason I become aware of my seedy suit. Ellen is not around much and I pay no attention to what I wear. I haven't got around to buying clothes since my return. My cousin Lucy calls it my Bruno Hauptmann suit, a ten-year-old double-breasted broad-stripe seersucker, which I wasn't even aware I was wearing until suddenly it feels dank and heavy.

"Let's get this over with, guys," says Bob Comeaux briskly, leaning over his hands and swinging his leg. "So we can have a drink or something. I got to muck out a stall." This, we understand, is in a manner of speaking.

"Right," says Max. Max and I are now sitting like patients in two chairs facing Bob Comeaux's splendid desk.

"Oh, say, Tom," says Bob Comeaux.

"Yes?"

"Thanks for looking in on Mrs. LaFaye this morning. I appreciate it."

"Glad to. As a matter of fact, I'd like to speak to you, to both of you, about the clinical changes in her. I have an idea that—"

"Yeah, sure," says Bob, looking at his watch. "We'll do that."

"I'm also a bit confused about the consultation. It was never made clear to me who requested it."

"We'll get into that too. Right now, what say if we do the boiler plate and get the official crud out of the way."

"Fine" I say.

"Yes," says Max. "Here's what I suggest—"

"Let's do it by the book, guys," says Bob Comeaux, removing his hands from his pockets and clapping one softly into the other. "What I'm proposing is that, at least for the time being, Tom come aboard here in my division. It's not just a matter of my making room for him—hell, I've been after him for years and he can write his own ticket—and he won't need a license."

"Wait," says Max. "Hold it, Doctor." Max holds up a hand like the Tulane professor that he is, flagging down an errant intern on grand rounds. "Let's just hold it a second."

"Very well, Doctor," says Bob Comeaux gravely. "What's the problem?"

"No problem. Possibly a misunderstanding. My understanding is that Dr. More wants to return to private practice. Has, in fact. Isn't that so, Tom?"

"That's so," I say, thinking for some reason about an expression in Mickey LaFaye's eyes, in Donna's eyes. There was something about her, them—There was something like—

"I understand! I read you, Doctor! And believe me, there is nothing I admire more about us old-time clinicians, ha, than our concern for the traditional one-on-one doctor-patient relationship. But we got a little problem here.''

"What's the problem?" says Max in his old ironic style. Max is upset about something. I am noting that for some reason Bob Comeaux is striving for standard medical heartiness and not succeeding; is, in fact, doing very badly.

"The problem, fellows," says Bob Comeaux, looking up for the first time and smiling his rueful attractive smile, "is that Tom's license to practice is in bureaucratic limbo. Theoretically he has a probationary license, but that leaves him open to malpractice suits and any cop who wants to lean on him. What I'm saying is that I can take him aboard here and he can do what he pleases, licensed or not."

"That's ridiculous," says Max to me. "That's wrong!"

"What's ridiculous?" asks Bob Comeaux, puzzled.

"That he has to report to us on his practice."

Bob Comeaux leans forward over his pocketed hands, frowning but not unpleasantly. "I'm not clear, Max. Do you mean that we both agree that Tom should be practicing any kind of medicine he pleases? Or do you mean that he was wrongfully deprived of his license?"

"I mean it's wrong! The whole damn thing."

We fall silent. Max's defense of me is loud and lame.

I am thinking that I should be experiencing a sinking of heart at Max's lame defense of me but that I'm not. Instead, I find myself watching Bob Comeaux curiously. There is a new assurance about him. I observe that when he leans over, and now when he takes his hands out of his pockets and folds them across his chest, grasping his suede-clad arms, at the same time sitting-leaning gracefully, one haunch on the desk, he is doing so consciously and well. There is a space between what he is and what he is doing. He is graceful and conscious of his gracefulness, like an actor.

Max is nothing of the sort. He is upset and at a loss. Max suddenly looks tired and old. No longer the bright young Jesus among the elders, planes of his temples flashing light, amazing the older staff physicians with his knowledge, he sounds more like a Jewish mother. He moralizes: This is wrong, this isn't the way it's supposed to be.

But Max revives, perks up, sits erect. "Excuse me, Bob, but this is all a lot of humbug. The fact is that is why we are here: to review Dr. More's competence and integrity, which I'm assuming is not in question here, and as members of the ethics committee of the medical society to recommend to the state board that his license be reinstated in full, which will then occur as a matter of course, right?"

"Right. Except for one annoying little glitch like I told you," says Bob Comeaux patiently. He looks both genial and doleful.

"What glitch?"—Max, cocking his head.

"You know as well as I do, Max," says Bob Comeaux wearily. "In the case of a felony count, even with our recommendation, a license can only be reinstated after a year's probationary service under our supervision—which is exactly what I'm offering him, except that he'll be free and won't have to report to us."

"Felony?" Max spreads his hands, beseeches the four walls, the Mississippi River. "What felony?"

"Oh boy," says Bob Comeaux softly, shaking his head. He flips open the file next to his thigh on the desk where he's still lounging at ease, reads in a neutral clerk's voice, sighting past his folded arms. "These are the minutes of the first hearing before the State Medical Board. Dr. Thomas More charged by Agent Marcus Harris of the ATFA—let me see, blah blah—with the sale of one hundred prescriptions of Desoxyn tablets and two hundred prescriptions of Dalmane capsules at one dollar per dose for the purpose of resale at the Union 76 truck stop of I-12 near Hammond, Louisiana—blah, blah—look, guys, there is no need to go back over this stuff." He closes the file.

"That's entrapment!" Max cries, again to the world at large. "That narc guy was posing as a trucker."

"Right," says Bob Comeaux glumly. "A sting operation.

Could I ask you something, Tom—something I've never understood?''

"Sure."

"I've never understood why you didn't just charge those guys a medical fee. Why sell the damn prescriptions wholesale through a goddamn truck stop?''

"I needed the money. I knew the owner of the truck stop and had confidence in him, that he would only deal with truckers who needed them. You will note that the dosages were minimal, twenty-five milligrams of Desoxyn and thirty milligrams of Dalmane, just enough to get them up enough to keep awake and then down so they could sleep. You know those guys push those big double and triple tandems over crumbling interstates for up to eighteen hours a day. Then they're so tired they can't sleep.''

"Oh boy," says Bob Comeaux.

Max opens his hands again but says nothing. Doesn't have to. Tom, that was dumb, was what he would say.

"Okay," says Bob gently. "Here's our little problem. Desoxyn is an amphetamine, isn't it, Tom?''

"Yes."

"Dalmane is a hypnotic, right?''

"Yes."

"We're talking controlled substances, fellows, schedule three. We're talking a felony count under new state and federal statutes.''

"So what's the big deal?" asks Max, asking the space between me and Bob Comeaux. "So it was a dumb thing to do. Not dangerous, but dumb. As a matter of fact, he probably saved lives by keeping those poor bastards awake. Dumb, yes. But he's paid for his mistake. The feds are not interested in him. As far as we are concerned, the ethics committee, I don't see the problem. I'm sure Tom doesn't mind my saying that he was not at all himself at the time. I know because I was treating him.''

"No, Max," I say. "You were not treating me at the time.

28

That was earlier." For some reason I am having difficulty concentrating.

"Tom is a very creative person," says Max, "as we all know. Like all creative people he has periods of lying fallow."

"I wasn't lying fallow, Max. I was mostly lying drunk. My practice went to pot. I needed the money."

"But for a good cause!" exclaims Max, raising a finger. "You were thinking of your family. And what a lovely family!"

Bob Comeaux is shaking his hand, but tolerantly, even smiling. "Okay, how's this?" he asks briskly, again setting one hand softly into the other. "Let's just put this business on hold for a couple of weeks. I think there may be a way to beat this bum rap." He rises, stretches. Max rises.

"Let me just say one thing," says Max, not moving toward the door.

"Sure, Max," says Bob Comeaux, smiling. He is no longer ironic.

"I don't have to remind you of what Tom here has accomplished, by his breakthrough in the field of cortical scanning, for which he received national recognition. Furthermore—"

"No, Doctor, you don't have to remind me." Bob Comeaux is holding out both arms to us in a kind of herding gesture in the direction of the door. "What is more, I feel certain we can work something out. We're not about to lose Dr. More's services. Two things, Tom. One, Mrs. LaFaye. I'm going to need your help with her, okay?"

"Sure. As a matter of fact I have an idea—"

"Sure sure. I'll get back to you, there's plenty of time. The other is frankly a favor you could do me and also an old friend of yours."

"Sure. Who?"

One arm falls. Bob Comeaux's hand touches my shoulder. "Your old friend, Father Simon."

"Father Simon?"

"Father Simon Smith."

"Oh. Rinaldo."

"Yes. Father Simon Rinaldo Smith."

"What's wrong with him?"

"Well, he's not doing well." He moves closer, hand still on my shoulder. "It's a long story, but I was sure you'd be concerned. I'll call you in a day or so. Will you talk to his assistant, Father Placide?"

"Placide? Sure." What is Comeaux up to with the clergy? Whatever it is, I sense only that he wants me to talk them into something or other, probably something to do with Rinaldo's hospice, and I don't particularly want to. Don't want to talk to them, let alone talk them into something.

"Okay, Doctors," says Bob Comeaux, opening his arms again. "Meeting's adjourned—unless you have a question. Dr. Gottlieb?"

Max sighs and shakes his head.

"Dr. More?"

"Yes?" I can't stop thinking about Donna and Mickey.

"Any questions?" asks Bob Comeaux patiently.

"Well, we're here to review my present practice, aren't we?"

"Sure, fella, but we're not worried about—"

"As a matter of fact I'd like to discuss a couple of cases, one a patient of yours, Bob, Mickey LaFaye. There is something interesting—"

"Very!" cries Bob Comeaux, looking at his watch. He claps his hands softly. "Why don't we have lunch? I'll give you a buzz. Any further questions? Max? Tom?"

"Bob, where is Hammond?"

"What?" says Bob quickly.

"You mentioned Hammond, Louisiana. Where is it?"

"Where is Hammond," Bob repeats, looking at me. His eyes stray toward Max. "Okay, I give up. What's the gag?"

"Nothing. Forget it."

Now Max is doing the herding, smiling and herding me. He's like a guest trying to get a drunk friend out the front door before he throws up on the rug.

We're both anxious to leave. But first I'd better fix things up with Bob Comeaux. He's up to something, wants something, wants me to do something. What's he cooking up with this business about my license and with his smooth invitation—threat?—to hire me on here at Fedville? I don't know, but there is no need for me to look nuttier than I am.

"Thanks, Bob, for everything," I say warmly, shaking hands, matching his handshake for strength, his keen gray-eyed expression for its easy comradeliness—two proper Louisiana gents we are. "I'll let you in on a little secret."

"Yeah?"

"I just used you as a control."

"No kidding."

"Yeah. I've had a couple of patients who may show an interesting cortical deficit at Brodmann 39 and 40, you know, the Wernicke speech area. They answer questions out of context—and I'm thinking of using it as an informal clinical test. I needed a couple of normal controls. You wouldn't answer the Hammond question out of context. You're a control. Max is next."

"Gee thanks." But Bob Comeaux cocks a shrewd eye at me. "But who—Never mind."

"Max," I say, "where is Hammond?"

"I can't say I care," says Max. Max looks relieved.

"You guys get out of here," says Bob Comeaux. "Jesus, shrinks."

We're in the hall. Max is padding along faster than usual, but in his usual odd, duck-footed walk. Max waits until we hear Bob Comeaux's door close behind us. He moves nearer and speaks softly.

"You okay, Tom?"

"Sure."

"What was that stuff about Hammond?"

"I wasn't kidding. I really have picked up a couple of odd things lately, Max. And I wanted to check Comeaux out. Have you noticed anything unusual in your practice lately?"

"Unusual?" Max is attentive but still guarded. "Such as?"

31

"Oh, changes in sexual behavior in women patients—"

"Such as?"

"Oh, loss of inhibition and affect. Downright absence of superego. Loss of anxiety—"

Max laughs. "Well, don't forget my practice is not here but in New Orleans, the city that care forgot. It has never been noted for either its anxiety or its sexual inhibitions." Max is eyeing me. It is not his or my patients he's thinking about. "Tell me something, Tom."

"What?"

"What is Comeaux up to?"

"You noticed. I thought you might tell me."

"That business about your license was uncalled for. This so-called probation is pro forma, purely routine and up to us. There is no reason to have any trouble."

"I'm glad to hear it."

"Dr. Comeaux wants something," says Max thoughtfully.

"I know. Do you know what it is?"

"No, but it was interesting that Mrs. LaFaye, your wealthy patient, was mentioned."

"Why is that interesting?"

"The word is, he's got something going with her."

"Such as?"

"My wife, who knows everything around here because she is a realtor like your wife, says he has been very helpful to Mrs. LaFaye, his neighbor and fellow horseperson, rancher, whatever, and that he or Mrs. LaFaye or both are trying to buy up the adjoining land."

"That's the hospice he was talking about."

"Oh, you mean out at—"

"Yes."

We're standing at the elevators. I notice that Max is still preoccupied.

"Max, I'd like to talk to you about a couple of cases."

"Sure. Come on over to my place now. Sophie would be delighted to see you—and Ellen."

Max is always embarrassed to mention Ellen. Why? Because my first wife ran off with a fruity Englishman. No, two fruity Englishmen.

"I can't. I have to get home."

"I understand. How's Ellen and the kids?" he asks too casually. We're standing side by side gazing at the bronze elevator doors.

"They're fine."

"Is Ellen home?"

"Well, you know she went back to Georgia to stay with her mother when I was convicted and sent to—"

"I know, I know. But she's back now."

"Yes—though I haven't seen much of her. She just got back from a bridge tournament."

"Yes. I heard from—I heard she was some sort of prodigy at it."

"She just got back from Trinidad. The big annual Caribbean tournament. She and her partner, Dr. Van Dorn, won it."

"I see. Well, I know she's way out of our class, that is, mine and Sophie's. But do you think the two of you might come over one evening—"

"Sure. I'll ask her." We gaze at the bronze door one foot from our noses.

"How about next week?"

"She won't be in town."

"No?"

"No. She's been invited to the North American championships."

"I see. How long does it last?"

"I think about a week. It is being held at the Ramada Inn West in Fresno, California."

"I see."

The elevator doors open.

"John Van Dorn thinks she can compile a sufficient number of red points to become a master, I think they call it, in less than two years' time, starting from scratch, something of a record."

"Remarkable," says Max, concentrating on the arrow. Something—Ellen?—is making him uneasy again. He wants to get out of the elevator and go about his business. But then his worrying gets the better of him. "Look. Who's been watching Tommy and—ah—"

"Margaret. Well, we still have old Hudeen, you will remember—"

"Oh yes. Hudeen. Fine old woman."

"Yes. And a live-in person, Hudeen's granddaughter, who stays with the kids at night."

"Good. Very good. Very good," says Max absently. Max is torn, I notice, torn between his desire to welcome me back and his Jewish-mother disapproval. He worries about me. But as soon as we're out of the Fedville high-rise and into the parking lot, Max seems to recover his old briskness. He eyes my Caprice with mild interest, takes hold of my arm. "Now, Tom—"

"Yes?"

"I am concerned about—concerned that you get going again with your practice and back with your—ah—family."

"I know you are, Max."

"I think we can straighten out this license business. I'll take care of Comeaux."

"Good."

Max is examining his car keys intently. "You don't seem much interested."

"I'm interested."

"You're not depressed, are you?"

"No."

"Well, I do wish you would check in with me. You were, after all, my patient once, and I need all the patients I can get, ha." This is as close as Max ever comes to making a joke. "Just a little checkup."

"Sure. And I do want to discuss a couple of bizarre cases with you. I wasn't kidding about some sort of cortical deficit. But it's more radical than that."

"More radical?"

34

"There's not only a loss of cortical inhibitions, superego, anxiety which was once present. There's something else, a loss of—self—"

"Of self," Max repeats solemnly, concentrating on his ignition key. He looks worried again. He's thinking. There are worse things than depression, for example, paranoia, imagining a conspiracy, a stealing of people's selves, an invasion of body-snatchers.

"So you give me a call," says Max, frowning, eyes casting into the future.

"Right, Max."

"You need more cases, Tom," he says carefully.

"I know, Max."

"Two cases are not exactly a series."

"I know, Max."

He doesn't look up from his car keys. "What's this business about Father Smith?"

"Have you seen him since you got back?"

"Father Smith? No. Only a phone call."

"What did he want?" Max asks quickly.

I look at him. This quick, direct question is not like him.

"I'm not sure what he wanted. As a matter of fact, it was a very odd conversation."

What was odd was that Father Smith sounded as if he was calling from an outside phone, perhaps a booth in a windy place. I remember thinking at the time that he reminded me of those fellows who listen to radio talk shows in a car, decide to call in a nutty idea, stop at the first booth. The priest said he wanted to welcome me home. Thanks, Father. He also wanted to discuss something with me. Okay, Father. Did I know he had been to Germany? No, I didn't. Recently? No, when I was a boy. I see, Father. So he gets going on the Germans for a good half hour, in a rapid, distant voice blowing in the wind.

"What did he talk about?" asks Max, eyeing me curiously.

"The Germans."

"The Germans?"

"Yes."

"I see. By the way, Tom. Don't argue with Comeaux. It's a waste of time. And stop worrying about this. It's going to work out."

"I'm not worried." I'm not. Max is worried.

6. BOB COMEAUX LIKES TO ARGUE. I DON'T MUCH.

For two years I was caught between passionate liberals and conservatives among my fellow inmates at Fort Pelham. Most prisoners are ideologues. There is nothing else to do. Both sides had compelling arguments. Each could argue plausibly for and against religion, God, Israel, blacks, affirmative action, Nicaragua.

It was more natural for me, less boring, to listen than to argue. I was more interested in the rage than the arguments. After two years no one had convinced anyone else. Each side made the same points, the same rebuttals. Neither party listened to the other. They would come close as lovers, eyes glistening, shake fingers at each other, actually take hold of the other's clothes. There were even fistfights.

It crossed my mind that people at war have the same need of each other. What would a passionate liberal or conservative do without the other?

Bob Comeaux reminds me of them. He comes just as close when he argues, much closer than he would in ordinary conversation, his face, say, a foot from mine. He wants to argue about "pedeuthanasia" and the Supreme Court decision which permits the "termination by pedeuthanasia" of unwanted or afflicted infants, infants facing a life without quality.

I can tell he has hit on what he considers an unanswerable argument and can no more resist trying it out on me than a lover can resist giving his beloved a splendid gift.

"Can you honestly tell me," he says, coming even closer,

"that you would condemn a child to a life of rejection, suffering, poverty, and pain?"

"No."

"As you of all people know, as you in fact have written articles about"—he says triumphantly, and I can tell he has rehearsed these two clauses—"the human infant does not achieve personhood until some time in the second year for the simple reason, as you yourself have shown, that it is only with the acquisition of language and the activation of the language center of the brain that the child becomes conscious as a self, a person. Right?"

He waits expectantly, lips parted, ready, corners moist. His eyes search out mine, first one, then the other.

"Do you see what I mean?" he asks.

"I see what you mean," I answer.

He waits for the counter-arguments, which he already knows and is prepared to rebut.

He is disappointed when I don't argue.

Instead, I find myself wondering, just as I wondered at Fort Pelham, what it is the passionate arguer is afraid of. Is he afraid that he might be wrong? that he might be right? Is he afraid that if one does not argue there is nothing left? An abyss opens. Is it not the case that something is better than nothing, arguing, violent disagreement, even war?

More than once at Fort Pelham I noticed that passionate liberals, passionate on the race question, had no use for individual blacks, and that passionate conservatives could not stand one another. Can you imagine Jerry Falwell and Pat Robertson spending a friendly evening alone together?

One of life's little mysteries: an old-style Southern white and an old-style Southern black are more at ease talking to each other, even though one may be unjust to the other, than Ted Kennedy talking to Jesse Jackson—who are overly cordial, nervous as cats in their cordiality, and glad to be rid of each other.

In the first case—the old-style white and the old-style black— each knows exactly where he stands with the other. Each can handle the other, the first because he is in control, the second because he uses his wits. They both know this and can even enjoy each other.

In the second case—Ted Kennedy and Jesse Jackson—each is walking on eggshells. What to say next in this rarified atmosphere of perfect liberal agreement? What if one should violate the fragile liberal canon, let drop a racist remark, an anti-Irish Catholic slur? What if Jesse Jackson should mention Hymie? The world might end. They are glad to get it over with. What a relief! Whew!

Frowning and falling back, Bob Comeaux even gives possible arguments I might have used so that he can refute them.

"In using the word *infanticide*, you see, you are dealing not with the issue but in semantics, a loaded semantics at that."

"I didn't use the word."

Bob shrugs and turns away, his eyes suddenly distant and preoccupied, like an unsuccessful suitor.

7. HOME TO THE QUARTERS. WE'VE LIVED THERE FOR years. Sure enough slave quarters they were, from an old indigo plantation, twenty or so sturdy brick boxes with stoops and kitchen gardens, attached like row houses with chimneys in common, lined up under the cliff and along the bayou like old Natchez-under-the-hill, repossessed by vines and possums— where no white folks had dreamed of living for a hundred years.

Even when we were poor, Ellen fixed ours up with authentic iron hooks and pots for the fireplace. Then Ellen and my realtor mother, Marva, teamed up and between them became a real estate genius, my mother being naturally acquisitive, thinking money, Ellen having natural good taste. They bought the whole row for a song and during the time I was away borrowed money, added two stories painted in different pastels like the villas of Portofino, stuck on New Orleans balconies, put a tiny dock in front of each and a Jacuzzi behind, calculating the place would be as prized now as it was misprized then, for being too small, too close together, too near the water—and named it The Quarters. All this during the two years I was detained by the feds at the minimal security facility at Fort Pelham, Alabama. They, Ellen and my mother, were like those fragile Southern ladies who, when their men, brave and somewhat addled, went off to that war, suddenly turned into straw bosses, hucksters, fishwives, tallywomen, slickers.

Here is my mother, before she took to her bed in her own nursing home, pitching to a client, more likely than not a West Texas oilman or a Massachusetts account executive removed to New Orleans, frightened by the blacks, bugging out to the country, looking for a weekend place on the water and what he conceived to be authentic historical Louisiana quaintness. Mother: "Notice the walls, authentic slave brick, eighteen inches thick, handmade by the slaves—many were magnificent artisans, you know—from local clay from claypits right up the bayou—it's all gone now, the clay and the art, a lost art, notice that odd rosy glow. You hardly need air conditioning with these walls—they didn't live so badly, did they? You see that bootscrape by the steps? Do you know what that is? an authentic brick form hand-wrought by the slaves. We think The Quarters combines the utility of a New York townhouse with the charm of a French Quarter cottage, don't you?" As a matter of fact, they did.

This is the real thing, she told them—and it was—and it makes Château Isles, Belle-this, and Beau-that look phony, don't you agree? Yes, they did. The Quarters sold out at three hundred thousand per unit.

While I, a disgraced shrink, was doing time in Alabama, my wife and mother were getting rich selling slave quarters.

I am anxious to see Ellen. I've seen her once since she got back from Trinidad late last night, but she was so tired we hardly exchanged ten words. She slept like a child, on her stomach, mouth mashed open on the pillow, arm hanging off the bed. I put her arm up. It's still splendid, her arm, as perfectly round and firm as a country girl's.

There's noise above—the kitchen is upstairs. I go up the tight spiral of a staircase, heart beating, but not with effort. Ellen's not there. There's only the help and the kids.

Hudeen's at the stove. She's eighty and infirm and gets to the kitchen by an outside elevator. She likes to come to work for a few hours. Ellen has installed her in a tiny square bounded by stove, fridge, sink, table, and stereo-V mounted in a bracket so that she need never take more than two steps in any direction, mostly sits, need never take her eye from the daytime drama that unfolds for four hours, precisely the four hours she's here.

"Where's Miss Ellen?" I ask her.

"Miz Ellen she still piled up in the bed!" says Hudeen in a soft shout, doing me the courtesy of touching the volume control of the stereo-V but not turning it down. "You talk about tired," she says, still keeping an eye on the screen. "But she be down directly."

Chandra, a young, very black woman, is playing Monopoly at the breakfast table with Margaret. Neither looks up.

Tommy is standing in the middle of the room, hands at his side, standing in place but footing a soccer ball, toeing, slicing, ankling, caroming the ball from foot to foot, idly and without effort.

I give Margaret and Tommy a hug. My children don't know what to say to me. Margaret is still hot and sweaty from the school bus. She gives me her cheek and a swift sidelong look. She has straight black Ella Cinders hair and is secretive and knowing, twice as smart as a boy will ever be. In her thin brown body, sweet with the smell of hot cotton and schoolgirl sweat, there is both a yielding and a resistance. She's a swift brown blade of a girl.

"Why you standing around?" Chandra asks me. Chandra is abrupt and unmannerly, but is the only one who will speak to me. "Why don't you sit down?"

I sit down.

"You looking good, healthy for a change," says Chandra to me. "Roll, Margaret."

Tommy and Margaret are on an easy footing with old black

Hudeen and young black Chandra. They look and talk past me, as if I were still a drunk, a certain presence in the house which one takes account of, steps around, like a hole in the floor. Are all fathers treated so by their children, or only disgraced jailbird fathers?

"Hudeen, what time is Miss Ellen coming down?" I ask, wondering whether to go upstairs.

"She be fine!" cries Hudeen softly, shelling peas and keeping an eye on the stereo-V. "She be down!" Is she telling me not to go up?

Long ago Hudeen gave up ordinary conversation. Her response to any greeting, question, or request is not the substance of language but its form. She utters sounds which have the cadence of agreement or exclamation or demurrer. Uhn-ohn-oh (I don't know?); You say!, You say *now!*, Lawsymussyme (Lord have mercy on me?); Look out!—an all-purpose expression conveying both amazement and good will.

Hudeen is barely literate, but her daughter went to college and became a dental hygienist. She married a dentist. They are as industrious, conventional, honest, and unprofane as white people used to be. They have five children, three girls named Chandra, Sandra, and Lahandra, and twin boys named Sander and Sunder.

Chandra is smart, ill-mannered, discontent, but not malevolent. She graduated in media and newscasting at Loyola, interned at a local station, worked briefly as a street reporter. She wants to be an anchorperson. The trouble is, she hasn't the looks for it; she doesn't look like a tinted white person, what with her Swahili hair, nose, lips, and skin so black that local light seems to drain out into her. Said Hudeen once, talking back to the TV as usual when somebody mentions black—Hudeen, who still has not caught up with the current fashion in the proper race name: colored? Negro? black?—"Black?" she said to the TV. "What you talking about, black? That woman light. Sunder he light. Sandra bright; Chandra now—we *talking* black!"—hee hee hee, cackling at the TV.

At first it worried me, Chandra's anger and her rash goal,

aiming for anchorperson, perhaps even hoping someday, this being America, to replace good gray Dan Rather, and finding herself instead doing what? back in the kitchen feeding white children. Good Lord, such exactly might her remote ancestor have done, living in these very quarters—if she were lucky enough to get out of the indigo fields and up in the kitchen of the big house. Mightn't Chandra blow up one of these days, I used to think, change one diaper too many and pitch Margaret into the bayou?

As a matter of fact, no. So much for the wisdom of psychiatrists. Maybe this is what I might have done in her place, but not Chandra. Having observed them carefully, Chandra and Margaret, I long ago concluded that women don't work that way. At least Chandra doesn't. Chandra has nothing but good nature and patience and—dare a white Southerner say it?—affection for Margaret. Margaret loves Chandra.

Instead, she, Chandra, takes it out on me. She goes out of her way to be pert with me, perter than I'm used to from people black or white. At first I took it for sass and felt the old white gut tighten: one more piece of lip and you're out on your ass, and so on.

Right now, for example:

I: "How've you been, Chandra?"

Chandra, frowning as she lands on Park Place with her little token, a flat iron: "Nothing wrong with me! Anything wrong with you?"

Shocked murmurings from Hudeen, who overhears this—not real shock but conventional, socially obligatory shock: "Lawlaw ainowaytawpeepuh," eyes not leaving the TV. Translation: Lord, Lord, that ain't no way to talk to people, that is, white people.

The other day Chandra gave me a lecture: "You want to know your trouble, Doc?"

"What's my trouble, Chandra?"

"You too much up in your head. You don't even pay attention to folks when they talking to you. How you act in your office?

Psychiatrists are supposed to be sensitive to the emotional needs of their patients, aren't they?''

"That's true."

Chandra's speech is a strange mixture of black Louisiana country and Indiana anchorperson. It's because she was brought up by Hudeen when her super middle-class mother was going to college, and then took courses at Loyola in standard U.S. TV speech. She sounds like Jane Pauley fresh out of a cotton patch.

"Doc, you know what you do?"

"No, what do I do?"

"You walk around like this, hands in your pockets, your eyes rolled back in your head like this. Somebody asks you something and you don't even ack like you hear. You just nod like this." Chandra has gotten up and is walking around, eyes rolled back. Hudeen is making deprecating sounds but is laughing despite herself. Tommy and Margaret laugh outright. I have to laugh too. Note that she says *asks*—with effort—not *aks*. But then says *ack*.

"No, Doc, I'm kidding. I know you're a highly trained psychiatrist, the best around here. I know some of your patients and what you've done for them. I know you're people-oriented in your practice."

People-oriented! Only from an Indiana anchorperson.

Ed Dupre, a proctologist colleague, heard Chandra talk pert to me one day when we came in for a drink after fishing.

"You know what I would do if she worked for me and talked to me like that?"

"I think I do."

"I would lay one right upside her head."

"I know you would."

Once when she was particularly sassy with me and my shortcomings—though by then I knew it wasn't sass, it was directness—I told her as directly, "Chandra, you know what you ought to do?"

"No, what I ought to do?" she asked quickly, frowning.

"You ought to go to charm school."

"What you talking about, charm school?" She looked at me

sharply, thinking at first I'm getting even, sassing her back, then seeing that maybe I'm not.

"No, I'm serious. You're a very smart professional woman but you lack certain social skills." I can get away with saying that but not "bad manners." "You have to have these skills to get ahead in your profession. You can't walk into a studio and talk to a program director or producer, white or black, the way you talk to me."

"Uhmmhmm!"—fervent noises of agreement from Hudeen.

"What it is, this charm school?" Chandra wanted to know. She knew I was leveling.

I told her. She listened. Of course there are such places where you go to get coached for job interviews, how to walk, sit, carry on a conversation, eat.

"Chandra"—I told her to get away from the old black-white business—"it's the current equivalent of the old finishing school."

"Finished is right," she said, but she was eyeing me shrewdly. "No kidding?"

"No kidding."

Thoughtfully she spooned stuff into Margaret—and went to charm school, and got a job—for a while.

Who knows? She might make it yet. As the Howard Cosell of anchorpersons.

"Tell Miss Ellen I'll be downstairs," I tell Hudeen.

"She be down!" cries Hudeen softly, inattentively.

"Chandra," I say, "where is St. Louis?"

"What you talking about, where is St. Louis!" cries Chandra, eyeing me suspiciously.

"Tell Doctor where is St. Louis!" says Hudeen, hardly listening.

"St. Louis is on the Mississippi River between Chicago and New Orleans," says Margaret, my daughter, Miss Priss, smartest girl in class, first to put up her hand.

"Right," I say.

They're all right.

"My other daughter, she live in Detroit," says Hudeen to the TV.

Two strange thoughts occur to me in the ten seconds it takes to spiral down the iron staircase.

One: how strange it is that we love our children and can't stand them or they us. Love them? Yes, for true. Think of the worst thing that could happen to you. It is that something should happen to your little son or daughter, he get hurt or killed or die of leukemia; that she be raped, kidnapped, get hooked on drugs. This is past bearing. Can't stand them? Right. When we're with them, we're not with them, not in the very present but casting ahead of them and the very present, planning tomorrow, regretting yesterday, worrying about money and next year.

Counselors counsel parents: Communicate! Communicate with your kids! Communication is the key!

This is ninety percent psycho-crap and ten percent truth, but truth of a peculiar sort.

I don't communicate with Tommy and he doesn't with me, beyond a single flick of eye, a nod, and a downpull of lip. If I sat Tommy down and said, Son, let's have a little talk, it would curdle him and curdle me, and it should.

Imagine Dr. Sarah Smart, popular syndicated columnist and apostle of total communication, showing up one night and saying to her daughter, Let's have a little talk. I hope daughter would tell Mom to shove off.

Second thought on last iron step: It occurs to me that, except for the drink I took after Donna's visit, I haven't had a drink or a pill for two years, except for the drink at the Little Napoleon on the way home.

I sit down. I am able to sit still and notice things, like a man just out of prison, which I am, and glad of it. I sit in a chair, feet on the floor, arms on the arms of the chair, and watch the reflection of the late-afternoon sun off the bayou. I had never noticed it before. It makes parabolas of light on the ceiling which move and intersect each other.

I've gotten healthy. For two years I was greenskeeper of the officers' golf course at the Fort Pelham air base. They made use of my history as a golfer. But instead of worrying about putting and chipping, hooking and slicing, I ran a huge John Deere tractor with a gang of floating cutters fore and aft, raked the sand traps, swung down the rough, manned the sprinklers, kept the greens like billiard tables.

Here's the mystery: Why does it take two years of prison for a man to be able to sit still, listen, notice his children, watch the sunlight on the ceiling?

8. *DIXIE* MAGAZINE IS ON THE COFFEE TABLE NEXT TO the fireplace, which bristles with wrought-iron hooks and pots.

Van Dorn is on the cover.

I pick it up and hold it in the sunlight. Under Van Dorn's picture is a list of captions:

> RENAISSANCE MAN
> NEW OWNER AND RESTORER OF BELLE AME
> NUCLEAR WIZARD
> MITSY'S TROUBLESHOOTER
> INTERNATIONAL BRIDGE CHAMPION
> OLYMPIC SOCCER COACH AND EDUCATOR

Van Dorn is wearing a yellow safety helmet and holding rolled-up blueprints in one hand and socking the end of the roll with the other. He's standing in front of the house at Belle Ame and gazing at the great cooling tower of Mitsy. He's a bit thick in the neck, but quite handsome, handsomer in the picture than in fact he is. His expression as he looks at the cooling tower is condescending, if not contemptuous. In his helmet he reminds me of a German officer standing in the open hatch of a tank and looking down at the Maginot Line.

There's a noise above me, a breath of air? I look up.

Ellen comes whirling down the staircase. She's wearing her Trinidad outfit, a bright orange-and-black print wound around her like a sari. It flares as she descends, showing her strong bare brown legs. She's gained weight. The muscle on her shin curves out like a dancer's. In her hair she's woven a bit of the same cloth in a bright corona of color.

She's effusive, gives me a hug and a kiss, as if she hadn't seen me since Trinidad. Maybe she was too sleepy to remember me last night.

"Good God," she says, frowning and backing off, eyeing me up and down in her old canny Presbyterian style. "Where did you get that suit? Throw it away. Burn it."

Her skin is as clear as ever, almost translucent, transmitting a peach glow of health, her skin faintly crimsoned, like flesh over light. She's put on weight but not too much. Her tightly wrapped Trinidad sari becomes her.

An idea occurs to me.

"You're looking extremely well."

"Well, thank you."

"The tan is very becoming. Moreover—"

"It ought to be. I worked on it. I usually peel."

"Do you remember how nice it used to be in the afternoon?"

"What? Oh, for heaven's sake."

"What do you say if we go in there for a while?" I nod to the downstairs bedroom.

"That's the best proposal I've had all week!" she says, too heartily.

"Well?"

"Dummy, we've got to go to the awards dinner in thirty minutes."

"This will only take fifteen."

"Oh, for—! That's Chandra's bedroom now."

"Chandra won't mind. Do you remember the Sears Best?" Sears Best was a king-size mattress on a big brass bedstead.

47

"What? Oh, I certainly do. And it certainly was!"

I look at her. She is both hearty and preoccupied. She taps her tooth.

"Do you remember standing at the sink and being approached from behind?"

"What? Oh." She blushes. For half a second I could swear she remembered love in the afternoon and was on the very point of heading for Sears Best. But she frowns, looks at her watch, makes her clucking sound. "Oh, God, I forgot. I have to call Sheri Comeaux about tonight. What—a—pain!"

"I don't think I can make it."

"Why the hell not?" Her fists are on her hips.

"I'm not much for school functions—" I begin.

"Well, hear this. You damn well better be. This happens to be important to Tommy and for his future. It just so happens that Tommy is getting an award for summer soccer, *the* award, and that he is Olympic material. It also just so happens that if Tommy and Margaret are going to Belle Ame Academy, an honor in itself, you had damn well better show some interest, because Van is already breaking the rules taking them this late."

And so on. Instead of letting me lay her properly on a king-size bed, she picks a king-size argument. Van Dorn, it seems, has started up a private school at Belle Ame on the English model, with tutors, proctors, forms, and suchlike. Ellen has yanked Tommy and Margaret out of St. Michael's—it's possible because school has just started. It's all right with me, I've already agreed, but for some reason she wants to pick a religious argument. This is, in a sense, funny. It is as if I were still a Catholic and she a Presbyterian, when in fact I am only a Catholic in the remotest sense of the word—I haven't given religion two thoughts or been to Mass for years, except when Rinaldo said Mass on the Gulf Coast, and then I went because it was a chance to get out of the clink—and Ellen is now an Episcopalian. She's become one of those Southern Anglicans who dislike Catholics—Romans, she calls them—and love all thing English.

I won't argue. She can send them to Eton if she likes. Mainly I'm glad to have her back. Very well, I'll go to the awards dinner. There's something else on my mind. But my acquiescence only makes her angrier.

"And not only that," she says, fists still on hips.

"Yes?" I say, thinking how nice it would be, what with all this anger, flushed face, flashing eyes, if—and in fact say as much. "It certainly would be nice if we could fight it out in there."

"And not only that," she repeats.

"Yes?"

"For Tommy's sake, you better remember you promised to take Van fishing."

"I remember," I say gloomily.

"All right." Again she looks me up and down, me in my Bruno Hauptmann suit. "And get dressed, for heaven's sake. And keep in mind about Van."

What I keep in mind is her voluptuousness and distractedness. It is odd. At the height of her anger she's both voluptuous and distracted, preoccupied by something. Her eyes do not quite focus on me.

9. THE AWARDS BANQUET IS SHORTER AND LESS PAINFUL than I had feared. I manage not to drink. What is surprising is that Ellen does—does drink—something she seldom did, and not merely drink but in the end gets so drunk I have to take her home. Sheri Comeaux explains why. Van Dorn let her down, did not invite her to the North Americans at Fresno.

John Van Dorn is doing a very graceful job emceeing the banquet and passing out trophies. He is talking about the summer soccer camp and plans for the soccer "program" during the academic year at Belle Ame. Afterward he passes out trophies. When he hands Tommy his trophy, a gold-colored statuette, he doesn't let go, so there are the two of them holding the trophy while Van Dorn speaks. Tommy is embarrassed. He doesn't know whether to keep holding on to the trophy or what to do with his eyes.

"I have one little suggestion for you moms and dads," says Van Dorn, who is not embarrassed. "What would you say to giving up your sons and daughters to this program for four years? That's all I ask. And what do I promise in return?" He pauses, looks at the moms and dads, looks at Tommy, speaks in a soft voice. "What I promise is a good shot at the Junior Olympic gold for this team four years from now in Olympia, Greece, where the original Olympics were held."

Applause, cheering. From Tommy only relief when Van Dorn lets go of the trophy and he can sit down.

Ellen, surprisingly, is already drinking a lot. Ordinarily she'd be the proud mom, but she polishes off her third Absolut, smiles and applauds, and goes to the ladies' room.

"Listen, Tom," says Sheri Comeaux, pulling me close. We're sitting at a table for four in the rear of the Camellia Room of the Holiday Inn. Bob Comeaux is silent and distant, as if we had had no dealings this morning. Their son Ricky also got a trophy, but a smaller, silver-colored one. "I have to talk fast. Ellen just found out Van's not going to the North Americans and she's taking it hard. She had her heart set on it. They'd have won for sure."

Sheri's a good sort. "Welcome home, Tom," she had said earlier. "You have friends, you know—more than you know." Sheri was a New Orleans nurse when she married Bob Comeaux. She's not uptown New Orleans or Garden District, but she's not Irish Channel or Ninth Ward either. French-Irish-Italian, she'd have gone to school at Sacred Heart, not with the Mesdames of the Sacred Heart Academy on St. Charles Avenue but at Sacred Heart parochial school on Canal Street. She and Ellen both married doctors, both took up duplicate bridge at the same time, neither having to work—Sheri because Bob was a successful doctor, Ellen because she and Marva made a lot of money in real estate. Sheri has the fond, slightly dazed look of many doctors' wives.

"I better talk fast before she comes back," says Sheri.

"Okay, talk fast." Sheri is making me nervous because she's drinking too, hanging on my arm, talking a lot, mentioning names, and making a point of it as if she knew about Bob and Mickey LaFaye. But she always comes back to Ellen.

"That girl is loaded! With talent I mean. I mean, she is some kind of genius and doesn't even know it. Do you know what she did?"

"No."

"We were playing in this dinky little sectional over at Biloxi—this was before we met Van Dorn. It was good for nothing but black points of course. So there we were, two little bridge ladies with a bunch of other bridge ladies. It's about four women to one man, and what men. And here *he* comes—surprise, surprise—God knows what they paid him to make an appearance. We were playing women's pairs the first day and there he is, strolling around the tables watching the play. We were all nervous and giggling. I know you don't know anything about the strange world of duplicate bridge, but having John Van Dorn show up at a sectional tournament is like Ivan Lendl turning up at the local tennis club. I mean, we're talking world-class, Tom." She finishes her drink. Bob Comeaux, to my relief, has gotten up and is talking to Van Dorn in the aisle. He's listening intently to Van Dorn, looking down, arms folded, ear cocked. Van Dorn catches my eye, winks, makes a casting motion with his wrist. I nod.

"Yes, Sheri?"

"You got the picture? Us little bridge ladies trying to keep our minds on the game and him walking around, kibitzing. Got it?"

"Yes."

"So next day, it's mixed pairs. And we're resigned to anybody we draw. We're standing at the customers' desk to get our partners and wondering who we're going to end up with—you talk about dogs—I mean, you wouldn't believe who I got. But anyway. There were a few professionals hanging around as usual. You know, you can get a life master or a professional, but you have to pay—personally I think the system stinks—it's like a bunch of middle-aged ladies looking over the gigolos. But there we were, counting our little money to see if we can afford one of the L.M.s or professionals at least. Actually it's the best way to learn, but I think it's degrading. I look up and there *he* is. Oh, he's a charmer. He introduces himself to both of us as if we were the famous ones. 'You're Mrs. More, I believe, and you're Mrs. Comeaux?' I nearly drop my teeth, but you know Ellen, laid back and cool. 'Yes?' she says.'' Sheri mocks Ellen's coolness. ''He bows, I swear I think he even clicked his heels like a Prussian general, you know? He's the perfect gentleman, but it's obvious it's not me he had in mind. Oh, he knew all about you too. 'I know your husband's work,' he says to Ellen. 'Magnificent!' Ellen still hasn't got the message. 'But I've also seen your work—oh, I can tell in about thirty seconds,' he tells Ellen. 'I saw you pull that Steknauer finesse not once but twice.' Then he turns to me as if Ellen's not there. 'Mrs. Comeaux,' he says, 'there's such a thing as card sense and there's such a thing as a sixth sense. This lady *knows* where the cards are. I don't know how she knows but she knows. I don't think she knows how she knows either. It is as if she had a little computer stored in her head.' Then he turns to Ellen and there's Ellen going, Ah—uh— ahem, and so forth. So he says to Ellen, 'Would you do me the honor of being my partner in mixed pairs today?' 'Well, ah uh,' goes Ellen. 'I don't believe I have the—ah—' And she's actually going through her purse. I give her a nudge: Dummy! So he says, with another bow, 'The fee is waived. The honor is mine.' Well, let me tell you, I have to give Ellen credit. That gal's got class. Without turning a hair she shrugs and says, 'Very well.' Very well, I'm thinking, Jesus. Of course, some of the old biddies were jealous, said he was interested in Ellen's money, but that's a lie. She's a natural-born bridge genius.''

''Did they win?'' I ask. I look at my watch. What is keeping Ellen?

''Win! They haven't lost since. And now they're not going to Fresno. I don't get it. Old charmer turns into old asshole. Right, Tom?'' She's got another Tanqueray.

"Right. But why don't you go see if Ellen's—"

"Sure." Her son Ricky comes up and shows her his trophy. She gives him a hug and me a wink. "Wonderful, darling." After Ricky's gone, she says, "You want to know what those trophies look like?"

"What?"

"Like K.C. bowling trophies, right?"

"Right. Now—"

"You want to know something, Tom?"

"What?"

"You really screwed up, didn't you?"

"I suppose I did."

"But you know something?"

"What?"

"I always thought you were the best around here, the most honest and understanding—unlike some I could mention, namely Dr. Perfect here." And here in fact is Bob Comeaux, who pays no attention to her even though she hasn't lowered her voice. Instead, he leans past me, ear cocked with the same intensity, and speaks to the table: "I hope you've given some serious thought to our conversation this morning. Okay, Tom?" His hand rests heavily on my shoulder.

"Sure, Bob," I say, not sure what part of the conversation he means. Probably Father Smith. "Sheri—" I turn to her, but she's gone—to fetch Ellen, I hope.

Van Dorn, passing behind Bob Comeaux, makes a sign to me as if he did not want to talk to Bob. He holds up one hand open and a forefinger.

"Okay," I say. "Six o'clock."

Ellen comes back, seeming all right, and drinks two more Absoluts. She smiles and nods in her new unfocused way at nothing. She's getting somewhat dreamy but seems on the whole composed and pleasant.

10. ELLEN IS NOT SO DRUNK THAT SHE CANNOT GET UP the spiral staircase. But it is well that I am behind her, because I can assist her without seeming to, moving up behind her and in step, knee behind her knee, hands up the rail and almost around her. I fear she might fall.

Our new bedroom is on the third floor across a tiny hall from the children's. Ellen bought two iron convent beds, now in high fashion, when the convent closed. What short narrow nuns. My feet stick out through the bars.

How to sleep with her? There's no spoon-nesting on these cots. And she's already flopped on one, dressed, filling it. She's not passed out or even drunk, but open-eyed, dreamy, placative, and still smiling in the same moony way.

Well then, turn out the light and—

I turn out the light.

"Lights!" says Ellen.

I turn on the light. True, drink and dark can make you sick. I know. But she's smiling.

I have an idea. "I have an idea."

She waits, smiling.

"Let's go downstairs to our old room."

"Chandra."

"Chandra's not here."

"How?"

"How to get down? We can go down to the kitchen and take the elevator."

"All right."

She seems agreeable. I am pleased.

She's not too drunk to back down the stairs to the kitchen exactly as we came up, smiling at the joke of me keeping her safe.

54

Chandra's room, our old bedroom, is spick and span. The Sears Best bed takes up half the room. There's a photograph on the bed table of Chandra receiving the Loyola broadcast journalism award from Howard K. Smith.

"Undress," says Ellen.

I begin undressing.

"Me."

"What? Oh." She's leaning over toward me, arms outstretched, pullover blouse pulled half up. The neck drags across her short wiry wheat-colored hair, but it springs back into place.

She waits for me to undress her, smiling and cooperative, standing when standing is required, sitting, lifting herself. I finish undressing her; she is standing, naked, smiling and turning. She is tanned all over. There are no white areas. Compared to the convent beds, the Sears Best mattress looks as big as a soccer field.

Ellen starts for the bed. I start for the wall switch and turn out the light and head back.

"Lights!" says Ellen.

Very well. By the time I've turned on the light and come back, Ellen is in bed but is, to my surprise, not lying on her side as she used to but is on all fours.

Very well, if that's—

"Well, bucko?"

Bucko?

"Cover," says Ellen.

"You mean—" I say, taking the sheet.

"No."

"I understand," I say, and cover.

"All right," says Ellen.

It is all right, though surprising, because we have never made love so. Her head is turned and I miss seeing her face. There is only a tousle of wiry hair, a glimpse of cheek and eyes, now closed, and mouth mashed open. She utters sounds.

Afterward as we spoon-nest in our old style, she drowses off but goes on talking. It's a light, dreaming sleep, because the words I can understand are uttered with that peculiar emphasis people use when they talk in their sleep. It's REM sleep. I can see her eyes move under her lids. I'm afraid to turn out the light.

"Schenken or K.S.?" she asks in her dream.

"Schenken?"

"Blackwood shmackwood."

"All right." I think she's using contract bridge words. She's playing in a tournament.

"Mud," she says.

"Mud?"

"Bermuda Bowl, but no Fresno."

I am curious. I think these are places where bridge tournaments are held. Why no Fresno? I give her a shake, enough to bring her up into a waking dream, enough to talk. It's like talking to a patient under light hypnosis.

"Why not Fresno?" I ask her, using the same quirky tone of her sleep-talking.

"You want me to stand around at the partnership table with all those other women?"

"Well, no," I say. I didn't think she'd been invited.

"I'd feel like a dance-hall hostess. For open pairing you just stand there while they look you over."

"I see."

"No way."

I am silent. After a while her eyes stop moving. She's going to sleep but still talking.

"Schenken?" she murmurs, asking a question, I think.

"No," I say, not liking the sound of it.

"K.S.?"

"No."

"Roth-Steiner?"

"No."

"Azalea?"

"Yes." Azalea sounds better, whatever it is.

"Azalea," she murmurs drowsily, smiling, and as drowsily she straightens and turns on her stomach. Before I know what she's doing, she has swung around on the bed like a compass needle, dreamily but nonetheless expertly done a one-eighty, buckled and folded herself into me, her wiry head between my thighs.

We've not done this before either, but by now I'm not surprised and I'd just as soon.

When we've finished, she's quite content to nestle again and go to sleep. "No Fresno," she murmurs, does another one-eighty, settles into me.

"Very well," I say. "No Fresno."

I have an idea.

"Listen, Ellen. This is important." I drop the dream voice and get down to business—just as you talk to a patient after fifty minutes on the couch when she swings around ready to leave. "Are you listening?"

She's listening. She's turned her head enough to free up her good ear from the pillow. She's deaf in the other.

It happened at Leroy Ledbetter's bar. I tell her about it.

On the way home I stopped at the Little Napoleon, but not, I thought at the time, for a drink.

The Little Napoleon is the oldest cottage in town. It hails from the days when lake boatmen used to drink with the drovers who loaded up the pianos and chandeliers on their ox carts bound from France via New Orleans to the rich upcountry plantations. It is the only all-wood bar in the parish, wood floor worn to scallops, a carved wood reredos behind the bar—a complex affair of minarets and mirrors. Two-hundred-year-old wood dust flies up your nostrils. The only metal is the brass rail and a fifty-year-old neon clock advertising Dixie beer. I decided I needed a drink after talking to Bob Comeaux.

The straight bourbon slides into my stomach as gently as a blessing. Things ease. It is one condition of my "parole" that I not drink. But things ease nevertheless.

I buy Leroy Ledbetter a drink. He drinks like a bartender: as one item in the motion of tending bar, wiping, arranging glasses, pouring the drink from the measuring spout as if it were for a customer, the actual drinking occurring almost invisibly, as if he had rubbed his nose, a magician's pass.

There is one other customer in the bar, sitting in his usual place at the ell, James Earl Johnson. He's been sitting there for forty years, never appearing drunk or even drinking, his long acromegalic Lincoln-like face inclined thoughtfully. He always appears sunk in thought. His face is wooden, fixed. It might be taken to be stiff and mean with drink, but it is not. Actually he's good-natured. In fact, he's nodding all the time, almost imperceptibly but solemnly, a grave and steadfast affirmation. He's got Parkinsonism and it gives him the nods, both hands rolling pills, and a mask of a face. He smiles, but it's under the mask.

"What seh, Doc," says James, as if he had seen me yesterday and not two years ago.

"All right. How you doing, James?"

"All right now!"

James comes from Hell's Kitchen, a neighborhood in New York City. He was once a vaudeville acrobat and knew Houdini, Durante, and Cagney. He was with a Buff Hottle carnival that got stranded here fifty years ago. He liked it in Feliciana. So he stayed.

"What about Ben Gazzara?" I asked him years ago about an actor I admired, knowing that he too came from Hell's Kitchen.

James would always shrug Gazzara off. "He's all right. But Cagney was the one. There was nobody like Cagney." He nods away, affirming Cagney. "Do you want to know what Cagney was, what he really was?"

"What?" I would reply, though he had told me many times.

"Cagney was a hoofer."

"What about his acting, his gangster roles?"

"All right! But what he was was a hoofer, the best I ever saw."

The only movie of Cagney's he had any use for was the one about George M. Cohan. "Did you see that, Doc?"

"Yes."

"Did you see him dance 'Yankee Doodle Dandy'?"

"Yes."

"You see!"

"You looking good, Doc," says Leroy. "A little thin but

good. All you need is a little red beans and rice. But you in good shape. You been playing golf?''

"Not exactly. I've been taking care of a golf course, riding a tractor, cutting fairway and rough.''

Leroy nods a quick acknowledgment of the courtesy of my oblique reply, which requires no comment from him and also relieves him of having to pretend I've not been away.

"You going to a funeral, Doc?'' asks James, his face like a stone.

"Why no.''

"You mighty dressed up for Saturday afternoon.''

I catch a glimpse of myself in the mirror of the reredos, whose silvering is as pocked as a moonscape. It's true. I'm dressed up in my Bruno Hauptmann double-breasted seersucker. Why do I remind myself of an ungainly German executed fifty years ago?

Leroy buys me a drink and pours himself one. I knock mine back. It feels even better, warmth overlaying warmth. His disappears in a twinkling, hand brushing nose.

Leroy feels better too. He leans over and tells me about his safari. He owns a motor home, and he and his wife belong to a club of motor-home owners, ten other couples. They've just got back from Alaska. Last year, Disney World. Year before, Big Bend.

"Tell you what you do, Doc. You need a vacation, you and the missus. Ya'll take my Bluebird and head out west or to Disney World. Do you both a world of good. Take the kids. Here are the keys.''

"Thank you, Leroy.'' I'm touched. He means it. His Bluebird is a top-of-the-line motor home, the apple of his eye. It cost more than his home, which is the second floor of the Little Napoleon. "I might take you up.''

I tell Ellen about the Bluebird. I know she's listening because her head is turned, good ear clearing the pillow.

"Why don't we get in Leroy's Bluebird and drive out to Jackson Hole? The aspens will be turning. Do you remember camping at Jenny Lake?''

"I'm not going to Fresno alone.''

59

I didn't think she was going to Fresno.

"We'll drive to Fresno and then come back by Jenny Lake."

"Not time."

"Not time enough? Why not?"

"Fresno is—twenty-one hundred miles." I look at her. I can see the slight bulge of her cornea move up like a marble under the soft pouch of her eyelid. "Jackson Hole is nine hundred miles northeast of Fresno."

"I see."

"Fresno is almost exactly in the geographical center of California."

"I see."

I turn out the light.

11. VAN DORN SHOWS UP BRIGHT AND EARLY SUNDAY morning, dressed in a Day-Glo jacket, a sun helmet in which he has stuck colorful flies. He's wearing waders.

"You won't need that jacket."

"Right. The bream might mind?"

"Yes. And you won't need the waders."

"Why not?"

"If you try to wade in one of these bayous, you'll sink out of sight in the muck. I'll get you some tennis shoes."

We spin down the bayou in my ancient Arkansas Traveler, a fourteen-foot, olive-drab aluminum skiff with square ends and a midship well. My twenty-year-old Evinrude kicks off first yank.

A bass club is having a rodeo. Identical boats, of new grass-green fiberglass, nose along the bank. Fishermen wearing identical red caps sit on high swivel seats in the bow.

"You sure you want to fish for bream?" I ask Van Dorn.

"I figured you might know places those guys don't know. I've been with them. They're mostly Baton Rouge lawyers."

Down the Bogue Falaya past country clubs, marinas, villages, *bocages, beaux condeaux.* I turn into the bushes, through a scarcely noticeable gap in the swamp cyrilla, and we're in Pontchatolawa, a narrow meander of a bayou, unspoiled because there's too much swamp for developers and it's too narrow for yachts and water-skiers. It is not even known to the bass rodeo.

I cut the motor. Pontchatolawa hasn't changed since the Choctaws named it. The silence is sudden. There is only the ring of a kingfisher. The sun is just clearing the cypresses and striking shafts into the tea-colored water. Mullet jump. Cicadas tune up. There is a dusting of gold on the water. The cypresses are so big their knees march halfway across the bayou. Their tender green is just beginning to go russet.

"My Lord," says Van Dorn, almost whispering. "We're back in the Mesozoic. Look at the fucking ferns."

Van Dorn is busy with his tackle. I watch him. There is as usual in him the sense both of his delight and of his taking pleasure in rehearsing it.

There is a huge swirl of water under his nose. He gives a visible unrehearsed start.

"Good God, what was that, an alligator?"

"Probably not, though they're here. Probably a gar."

"Gators won't bother you, will they?"

"No, gators won't bother you."

I try to place his speech. Despite its Southernness, the occasional drawled vowel, it is curiously unplaced. He sounds like Marlon Brando talking Southern.

We are drifting. I keep a paddle in the water.

"Can we try for bream?" Van asks.

"All right, though it's late. The best time is when they nest in April and July. But some of them will be hanging around. You see those cypress knees over there."

"Sho now."

"You see the two big ones?"

"Yeah."

"Just beyond is a bed. It's been there for years. They use the same bed. My father showed me that one fifty years ago."

"Well, I be."

"You see that birch and cyrilla hanging out over it from the swamp?"

"Those two limbs? Yeah."

"What you got to do is come in sideways with your line so you won't get hung up."

"Sho. But wouldn't it be a good idea to cut those limbs off? That's pretty tight."

"Then all the sunfish would leave. You don't mess with light and shade."

"No kidding."

Van Dorn has opened his triple-tiered tackle box. He takes out a little collapsed graphite rod and reel, presses a button, and out it springs, six or seven feet. He shows me the jeweled reel, which is spring-loaded to suck back line.

"Very nice."

"You can keep this in your glove compartment. Once I was driving through Idaho, saw a nice little stream, pulled over. Six rainbows."

"What type of line you got there?"

"It's a tapered TP5S."

His equipment probably cost him five hundred dollars.

"You not fishing, Tom?"

"No. I'll hold the boat off for you."

"You don't want to fish!"

"No." What I want to do is watch him.

He takes off his helmet and selects a fly. "I thought I'd try a dry yellowtail."

"Would you like something better?"

"What's better?"

"Something that's here and alive. Green grasshoppers, wasps. Catalpa worms are the best."

"Fine, but—"

"Wait a minute. I remember something."

62

We drift silently past the bed and under a catalpa tree. The perfect heart-shaped leaves are like small elephant ears. A few black pods from last year hang down like beef jerky. This year's pods look like oversized string beans. I stand up, cut a leaf carefully at the stem. "Hold out your hands." I roll the leaf into a funnel, shake down the worms, small white ones that immediately ball up like roly-polies. "Sunfish are fond of these."

"Well, I be. What now?"

"Take off that fly and put on a bream hook."

"This little bitty job?"

"Right. Even big sunfish have tiny mouths."

"How about just nigger-fishing with worms?"

"Earthworms are all right, but these are better." It is hard to tell whether he is trying to say "nigger-fishing" in a natural Southern way or in a complicated liberal way, as if he were Richard Pryor's best friend.

"Okay, you're set," I tell him. "You see the beds close to the bank, a dozen or so?" Bream beds are pale shallow craters in the muck made by the fish fanning the eggs.

"I see."

Van Dorn is surprisingly good. He slings his hundred-dollar line under the cyrilla on second try. Even more surprising, he catches a fish. I thought they'd be gone. A big male pound-and-a-half sunfish feels like a marlin on a fly line.

"Well, I be goddamned," says Van Dorn, landing him, his pleasure now as simple as a boy's. We gaze at the fish, fat, round as a plate, sinewy, fine-scaled, and silvered, the amazing color spot at his throat catching the sun like a topaz set in amethyst. The colors will fade in minutes, but for now the fish looks both perfectly alive yet metallic, handwrought in Byzantium and bejeweled beyond price, all the more amazing to have come perfect from the muck.

But the beds are mostly empty. Van Dorn catches a couple more bream and a half dozen bass. "For y'all," he says. Y'all? Hudeen will be pleased. Into the ice well go the fish, out comes the beer.

It is getting on to noon and hot in the sun. We drink beer and watch the gnats swarm. The cicadas are fuguing away. I watch him.

"That was sump'n, cud'n," says Van Dorn.

Cud'n?

"You want to know something, Tom?"

"What?"

"I'll make you a little confession. I think at long last I'm back where I belong. Among my own people. And a way of life."

"I see."

"Do you understand? What do you think?"

"Yes." What I'm thinking is that Louisiana fishermen would not dream of speaking of such things, of my own people, of a way of life. If there is such a thing as a Southern way of life, part of it has to do with not speaking of it.

"Tom, I'm what you call a jack-of-all-trades, master of none. I do all right, but I'm not really first-rate. I've been a pretty good physiologist, computer hacker, soccer bum, bridge bum, realtor, you name it. I went to Harvard and M.I.T. and did all right—I was a real hacker at M.I.T. and not bad at Harvard, but they were not for me, too many nerds at one, too many wimps at the other. So I cut out and headed for the territory like Huck. I chucked it all—except the kids."

"Don't you run the computer division at Mitsy?"

"Yeah, but it's routine, checking out systems and trying to keep the local yokels from messing up—we don't need another T.M.I. No, if I'd been first-rate I'd have gone from hacking to A.I."

"A.I.?"

"Artificial intelligence, Tom. That's where it's at. As you well know—don't think I don't know your work on localizing cortical function."

"I've gotten away from that."

"Tom, you've no idea what's around the corner. It's a scientific revolution to end all revolutions. But I'm out of it now—quite content to be back where I started from."

"Where are you from originally, Van?"

"Not a hundred miles from here. Port Gibson. Did you know the general was born there?"

"What general?"

"Earl Van Dorn."

"You related?"

"How can there be two Van Dorns from Port Gibson without being kinfolks?"

"I see."

I watch Van Dorn as he lounges at his ease, head cocked, eyes squinted up at the cypresses. He's not as handsome as his picture in *Dixie*. His handsomeness is spoiled by the heaviness of his face and jaw, his pocked skin, the coldness of his blue eyes in the shadow of his sun helmet, humorless even when he is smiling. But he does remind me of an Afrika Corps officer, the heavy handsome face, helmeted, the steel-blue eyes, even the skin so heavily pocked on the cheeks that it looks like a saber scar.

"Do you enjoy bridge?" I ask, watching him.

"Let me put it this way, Tom. It was fun, I was good at it, and I made a living. Now I don't have to. Do you play?"

"No. A little in college. All I remember is the Blackwood convention. When you bid four no-trump you're asking for aces."

He laughs. "Still do—with modifications."

"Tell me something, Van," I say, watching him over my beer can. "What is mud?"

"Mud?" He takes a long swig, holds the can against his forehead. "You mean as in drilling mud?"

"No, a bridge term."

"Oh." He laughs. "You mean mud as in M.U.D. You do know something. That means the middle of three cards in an unbid suit. It's an opening lead and tells your partner something."

"I see. How about Schenken?"

"Schenken? Oh, I get it. Ellen must be talking bridge. That's an Italian bidding system."

"K.S.?"

"Same thing."

65

"Roth-Steiner?"

"Same, though it sounds German. Ellen goes for the Italian systems—and she's good. Say, what—"

"How about Azalea?"

Van Dorn frowns. "Azalea?"

"The Azalea convention."

"Oh." He smiles as he shakes his head slowly, rolling his forehead against the beer can. "That's a wild one. Not Azalea—you had me confused. Azazel. The Azazel convention. After the fallen angel."

"What is the Azazel convention?"

"It means you're in a hell of a mess. It is a way of minimizing loss."

"How does it work?"

"It's in the bidding. If you discover that you and your partner are bidding different suits and are at cross purposes and over your heads, you signal to her that it is better for her to go down in her suit. We'll lose less that way. You do it by bidding your opponents' suit for one round."

"You mean if your opponents are bidding hearts, and your partner is raising you in your suit, hoping for a slam, you wave her off by bidding hearts for one round, signaling to her: You go back to your suit and go down."

"You got it."

"I see."

"I think you've played more bridge than you're letting on, Tom."

"Why do you think that?"

"You know the jargon and you're even on to their harmless little double entendres."

"Double entendres?"

"You made one yourself—bidding hearts and going down."

"So I did." Azazel. "So Azazel can be more than one kind of invitation."

"You got it, cud'n."

* * *

When we round our grand canal of a bayou and come in sight of The Quarters, Van Dorn makes a sign to me.

I cup my ear to hear over the motor.

"Cut the motor."

I cut the motor.

"It's about Ellen, Tom."

"Yes?"

"There's something I want you to do."

"What's that?"

"I want you to go to Fresno with Ellen, Tom."

"You're not going?"

"No way. I got these kids starting up school and soccer. First things first."

"She seemed disappointed."

"She'll do fine! True, we've done well, won some tournaments, but what she doesn't know is that I'm not indispensable. She's the one. That's why I wanted you to go."

"I couldn't play tournament bridge."

"No. I mean to watch her."

"Watch her?"

"Tom, you got to see it to believe it. And I think you'd be interested even if it weren't Ellen." As the boat drifts, Van Dorn takes off his Wehrmacht helmet, leans forward, and gives me a keen blue-eyed look.

"See what?"

"I can only give you the facts. You're the brain man, the psychologist. Maybe you've got an explanation."

"Of what?"

"Tom, it's not her bidding—which is okay, better than okay, somewhat shaky but highly proficient—after all, bidding is nothing more than a code for exchanging information. No, it's in the play. Tom, *she knows where all the cards are*. Do you hear what I'm saying? She knows what cards her opponents are holding. Now, most of us can make an educated guess after a few rounds of play, but *she knows*!"

"So?"

"Tom, let me ask you a question."

"All right."

"Do you set any store in ESP, clairvoyance, and suchlike?"

"No."

"Neither did I. But how else do you explain it? She's not cheating. So either she is reading the cards, which is clairvoyance, or she's reading the minds of the players, which is telepathy, right?"

"Yes."

"What do you think, Tom?"

"You did mention A.I. earlier. Artificial intelligence."

"Yes."

"If, as you say, brain circuitry can be understood as a fifth-generation computer, maybe she's able to use hers as such and after a few rounds of play calculate the exact probabilities of where the cards are."

Van Dorn gives me his keenest look. "And that would be even more amazing than ESP, wouldn't it? You mean like an idiot savant. Don't you think that hasn't occurred to me? But Ellen is no idiot."

"No."

"Tom, look."

"Yes?"

"You're a very intuitive therapist—on top of having made an early breakthrough in cortical function. But we're not talking about brain circuitry. We're talking about something else. We're talking about someone who may be able to *use* her own brain circuitry. How about that? Think of the implications."

"All right."

"Tom."

"Yes?"

"I think you should go to Fresno with Ellen."

"I see."

"Tom?"

"Yes?"

"I really think you ought to do something about this."

"I will, Van. I will."

* * *

Azazel is, according to Hebrew and Canaanite belief, a demon who lived in the Syrian desert, a particularly barren region where even God's life-giving force was in short supply. God told Moses to tell Aaron to obtain two goats for a sacrifice, draw lots, and allot one goat to Yahweh as a sacrifice for sin, the other goat to be marked for Azazel and sent out into the desert, a place of wantonness and freedom from God's commandments, as a gift for Azazel.

Mohammedans believe that Azazel is a jinn of the desert, formerly an angel. When God commanded the angels to worship Adam, Azazel replied, "Why should a son of fire fall down before a son of clay?" Whereupon God threw him out of heaven and down into the Syrian desert, a hell on earth. At that very moment his name was changed from Azazel to Eblis, which means despair.

Milton made Azazel the standard-bearer of all the rebel angels.

II

1. MONDAY MORNING. SITTING ON THE FRONT PORCH of my office waiting for a patient, sailing paper P-51s, and watching the sparrows flock around the martin hotel.

I am not paranoid by nature, but I think someone is following me. Several times this week I've seen a Cox Cable van, sometimes following, sometimes ahead of me, sometimes parked and fixing a cable.

Ellen's gone to Fresno alone. She seemed sober this morning, unhungover, cheerful, and in her right mind, full of practical plans. Van Dorn, she said, may join her later. How could he not? They have never lost a tournament. If not, at least he had promised to save her from the humiliating ordeal of the partnership desk, would fix her up with a worthy partner in the Mixed Pairs competition.

Worried about Ellen. Call home to try to reach Chandra.

Chandra answers, offhandedly, "Yeah?"

"Chandra, I want you to do me a favor. Would you?"

Chandra, alerted, voice suddenly serious: "I will."

"Chandra, I am counting on you to help me with the kids while my wife is gone. Can I depend on you to be there after three when the kids get home from school?"

"You certainly can," says Chandra in her new Indiana voice but not sounding put-on.

"Thank you." I can count on her.

"But—"

"Yes?"

"Mrs. More said she made other arrangements."

"What other arrangements?"

"I don't know."

Other arrangements. "Chandra, don't worry about the other arrangements. I need you there when the children get home."

"I'll be here."

A note in the mail and a recorded message on the machine, both from my cousin Lucy, Dr. Lucy Lipscomb.

The note, dashed off on a prescription pad: "Tom" (not Dear Cousin Tom, though we are cousins, certainly not cud'n): "I need to see you. Important. Bob C. and Van Dorn are up to something. It concerns you, dope. Call me. L."

That's her laconic style all right, maybe slightly overdone, what with her new doctoring manner. She's completed her residency at Tulane and is back here as house physician at the local hospital.

I call. Can't reach her at Pantherburn, where she lives, or at the hospital, but leave message: I'll be at the hospital later to see Mickey LaFaye.

The sweet-gum leaves are speckled with fall but the morning sun is already hot. Sparrows flock. The martins are long gone for the Amazon. My nose has stopped running.

Taking stock.

Time was when the patients I saw suffered mainly from depression and anxiety: prosperous, attractive housewives terrified for no apparent reason; rich oilmen in a funk after striking it rich; in a funk after going broke; students, the best and the brightest, attempting suicide for reasons unknown to themselves; live-in couples turning on each other with termagant hatred.

I had some success with them. Though I admired and respected Dr. Freud more than Dr. Jung, I thought Dr. Jung

71

was right in encouraging his patients to believe that their anxiety and depression might be trying to tell them something of value. They are not just symptoms. It helps enormously when a patient can make friends with her terror, plumb the depths of her depression. "There's gold down there in the darkness," said Dr. Jung. True, in the end Dr. Jung turned out to be something of a nut, the source of all manner of occult nonsense. Dr. Freud was not. He was a scientist, wrong at times, but a scientist nonetheless.

Two years in the clink have taught me a thing or two.

I don't have to be in a demonic hurry as I used to be.

I don't have to plumb the depths of "modern man" as I used to think I had to. Nor worry about "the human condition" and suchlike. My scale is smaller.

In prison I learned a certain detachment and cultivated a mild, low-grade curiosity. At one time I thought the world was going mad and that it was up to me to diagnose the madness and treat it. I became grandiose, even Faustian.

Prison does wonders for megalomania. Instead of striking pacts with the Devil to save the world—yes, I was nuts—I spent two years driving a tractor pulling a gang mower over sunny fairways and at night chatting with my fellow con men and watching reruns of *Barnaby Jones*.

Living a small life gave me leave to notice small things—like certain off-color spots in the St. Augustine grass which I correctly diagnosed as an early sign of chinch-bug infestation. Instead of saving the world, I saved the eighteen holes at Fort Pelham and felt surprisingly good about it.

Small disconnected facts, if you take note of them, have a way of becoming connected.

* * *

The great American philosopher, Charles Sanders Peirce, said that the most amazing thing about the universe is that apparently disconnected events are in fact not, that one can connect them. Amazing!

Here are a few disconnected facts, as untidy as these pesky English sparrows buzzing around the martin house.

Ellen.

Is she sick?

There is this:

Change in personality: from a thrifty albeit lusty, abstemious albeit merry, Presbyterian girl to a hard-drinking, free-style duplicate-bridge fanatic.

Her sexual behavior.

Her gift for bridge: Van Dorn says that after three rounds of play she can calculate the probabilities of distribution of cards in individual hands as accurately as a computer.

Her relationship with Van Dorn.

The Azazel convention.

Bob Comeaux and John Van Dorn. Lucy says they are "up to something." The only evidence so far: Both are overly friendly toward me. Both want something. What? Bob wants me to work with him at Fedville. Why? Van Dorn wanted me to go to Fresno with Ellen. Why?

Three new patients (short case histories follow) who couldn't be more different, yet there is a certain eerie similarity, certain signs and symptoms in common, such as

Change of personality: From the familiar anxieties, terrors, panics, phobias I used to treat to a curious flatness of tone. Their old symptoms are in a sense "cured," but are they better? Worse?

Change in sexuality: Sexual feelings more openly, yet more casually, expressed. Less monogamous? More promiscuous? Or simply more honest, part and parcel of the sexual revolution?

Plus certain clues to changes in sexual behavior in women: less missionary positioning, front to front, and more front to rear, six to nine, Donna backing into me. Also a hint of estrus-like behavior in Mickey LaFaye, who speaks of her "times," not meaning her menses. Check menses in future histories.

Language behavior: Change from ordinary talk in more or less complete sentences—"I feel awful today," "I am plain and simply terrified," "The truth is, Doc, I can't stand that woman"—to two- or three-word fragments—"Feel good," "Come by me," "Over here," "Donna like Doc"—reminiscent of the early fragmentary telepathic sentences of a three-year-old, or perhaps the two-word chimp utterances described by primatologists—"Tickle Washoe," "More bananas."

Context loss: They respond to any learned stimulus like any other creature but not like an encultured creature, that is, any human in any culture. Example: Ask them out of the blue, Where is Schenectady? and if they know, they'll tell you—without asking you why you want to know.

Idiot-savant response: They're not idiots but they're savants in the narrow sense of being able to recall any information they have ever received—unlike you and me, whose memory is subject to all manner of lapses, repressions, errors, but, rather, like a computer ordered to scan its memory banks. An ocular sign: eyes rolling up behind closed lids as if they were "seeing" a map when asked, Where is St. Louis?

Is this a syndrome? If so, what is its etiology? Exogenous? Bacterial? Viral? Chemical?

In a word, what's going on here?

Can't say. My series of patients is far too short. Three patients. I need fifty. I need blood chemistry, seven different kinds of brain scans, especially CORTscans.

* * *

Here comes a patient. Enrique Busch. I spy him a block away and hurry to get inside. Wouldn't do for a shrink to be caught sitting on the porch zinging paper P-51s at a martin hotel. Ellen taught me that when she was my receptionist-nurse. Act like a respectable physician. Wish I had her back.

Inside, just time enough to call Lucy Lipscomb. Nothing doing. I leave a message at the hospital that I'll see her around noon after I see more patients.

Here is Enrique.

CASE HISTORY #1

Enrique Busch is an old, chronically enraged ex-Salvador-an. Although he was not a member of one of the fourteen families who owned that unfortunate little country, he married into one and had the good fortune to get out with most of his money and his family and remove to Feliciana, where he bought up thousands of acres of cutover pineland, which he converted to Kentucky bluegrass country with horse farms, handsome barns, hunter-jumper courses, and even a polo field.

His presenting complaint two years ago: insomnia. His real complaint: rage. Every night he lay stiff with rage. He spent the day abusing people. I have never seen such an angry man. There is nothing like an angry Hispanic. It was killing him, this rage, with hypertension, sleeplessness, pills, and booze. He hated Communists, Salvadoran liberals, Salvadoran moderates, Salvadoran Indians, nuns, priests, fundamentalists, Cubans, Mexicans (!), blacks. He hated Americans, even though he had gone to Texas A&M, chosen this country, and done well here. Why did he hate the U.S.? Because we were suckers, weren't tough enough, were appeasing Communists, and sooner or later would find ourselves face to face with Soviet troops across the Rio Grande. And so on.

I couldn't do much for him beyond helping him recognize his anger and to suggest less booze and barbiturates, and outlets for his energy less destructive than death squads. Take up a sport. Beat up something besides people. Beat up a golf ball. Shoot something besides people. He took my suggestion. The upshot: Too old for polo, he took up hunting and golf, joined the ROBs (Retired Old Bastards), a genial group of senior golfers at the country club. The golf, eighteen holes a day, tournaments at other clubs, helped. He competed ferociously and successfully, his blood pressure went down, he slept better, but in the end he blew it and either withdrew or got kicked out. Why? Because he never caught on to the trick of Louisiana civility, the knack of banter and horsing around, easing up, joshing and joking—in a word, the American social contract, in virtue of which ideology is mitigated by manners and humor if not friendship. He could not help himself. On the links he could hack up the fairway, hook and slice and curse with the best of them, but afterward in the clubhouse he could not suppress his Central American rage. One doesn't do this. His fellow ROBs didn't like Communists or liberals or blacks any more than he did. But one doesn't launch tirades over bourbon in the locker room. One vents dislikes by jokes. But Enrique could never see the connection between anger and jokes (unlike Freud and the ROBs). He never caught on to the subtle but inviolable American freemasonry of civility. And so he got kicked out.

So here he is two years later. And how is he? Why, he's as easygoing and fun-loving as Lee Trevino. Not only is he back in the ROBs, he's just won the Sunbelt Seniors at Point Clear. Blood pressure: 120/80.

He even tells me a joke, not a very good joke. Here is the joke:

There was this old Southern planter who had bad heart trouble. So his doctor tells him, Colonel, you got to have a heart transplant. He says, Okay, Doc, go right ahead. But what the planter doesn't know is that the only heart the doctor can find is the heart of a young black who's been killed in a razor fight. So when the old planter wakes up, the doctor comes in and tells him, Colonel, I got bad news and good news. The bad news is that I had to give you a nigger's heart. Good God, says the old planter, that's terrible; maybe you better tell me the good news. So the doctor says, the good news is your deek is ten centimeters long.

"You get it, Doc?" says Enrique, laughing.

"Yes, I get it, Enrique," I say. "But it should be ten inches, I think, not ten centimeters."

"You right, Doc! Ten inches!" says Enrique, slapping his leg, laughing all the harder, not caring that he's screwed up the joke.

So what has happened to Enrique? I don't know.

Why is he here?

He needs something. And in fact I can help him. It's about his daughter Carmela, a nice girl, a thoroughly American, Southern U.S. girl. It seems she has enrolled at the University of Mississippi as a freshman. She loves it. Her heart is set on being pledged by the Gammas, a sorority. All her friends are Gammas. If she does not make Gamma, her life will be ruined. There would be little doubt she would make it, but it seems there is a little hitch, says Enrique, and it is because her complexion is quite brunette like mine, and you know how it is in Mississippi, even though she is pure Castilian-German. Now here it is, the end of rush week, and she has not been pledged.

Enrique in fact looks like an Indian.

"That's too bad, Enrique," I say, still wondering why he's here.

"Here's the thing, Doc. I understand that the Gamma rush captain is a young kinswoman of yours, the granddaughter in fact of the distinguished lady from the Mississippi Delta who was the foundress of this very chapter of Gammas. Now here it is at the end of rush week—" He looks down at his diamond-studded Rolex watch as if minutes counted.

I look at him in astonishment. How does he know such things? I had forgotten myself, if I ever knew, that Jo Ann had gone to Ole Miss, let alone that she was rush captain of Gamma.

"Come inside, Enrique." I remember all too well what it is to have an unhappy daughter.

It takes ten minutes. I call Aunt Birdie in Vicksburg and Jo Ann at Oxford. Two or three words about Carmela being a darling girl, member of an ancient aristocratic Castilian and Prussian family, indeed one of the first fourteen families of El Salvador, a prime prospect whom they can't afford to lose to the Chi O's, and so on.

I hang up. "She'll get her invitation this afternoon," I tell Enrique.

"Oh, my dear friend! Jesus!" cries Enrique, leaping to his feet. There are actually tears in his eyes. I'm afraid he's going to embrace me, so I shake hands quickly. He shakes with both of his. "You name it, Doctor! Anything!"

"My pleasure, Enrique." It is. Such matters can be serious. I can't stand to see a child, any child who sets her heart on it, get blackballed by the sisters, who can in fact be as mean to one another as yard dogs.

But my interest in Enrique lies elsewhere. It is the change in him. Imagine a Central American who's lost interest in politics! Who knows all about Ole Miss sororities!

On the way out I ask him casually where San Cristóbal is— San Cristóbal, the town in Chiapas, Mexico, where his family first settled. If I'd asked him two years ago, asked him anything about Mexico, he'd have got going on the Mexicans, whom he dislikes, but now he merely closes his eyes.

"Oh, I'd say it's about three hundred miles northwest of Santa Anna." Santa Anna is the place where he lived on his finca in El Salvador. He doesn't even ask me why I wanted to know. He'll tell me anything, give me anything.

I ask him if he will come in next week for a couple of tests—I tell him I want to see if he's as healthy as he looks. What I really want is a CORTscan.

"My pleasure, Doc," says Enrique, trying out his interlocking grip on an imaginary club, swinging as easily as Sam Snead.

CASE HISTORY #2

Here is Ella Murdoch Smith.

Her problem used to be failure and fright. "I can't cope," she once told me quietly. "It's too much. What happens when people can't cope? Is there a place to go, some government program for people who just can't cope any longer?" she asked ironically but seriously. I told her I didn't know of any such program. "But this is ridiculous," she said. "Have you ever heard of a card game where you're dealt a hand, a losing hand, and you're stuck with it, can't turn it in, can't fold and draw a new card, and you're stuck with it the rest of your life?" I admitted I had never heard of such a game. "You're right," she said. "There is no such game. I want to fold this hand." I took her threat of suicide, of folding her hand for good, seriously.

Her husband had left her with two small children. She had to go to work. An educated woman, she had no particular skills and had a hard time holding down a job, taking care of the children, running the house. She became frightened.

I looked at her. That was three years ago. What was remarkable about her was that here she was, a handsome, formidable woman with heavy breasts, youngish but with hair gone prematurely iron-gray and done up in two heavy braids— and shaking like a leaf. She had been frightened for months.

Frightened of what? Failure? Not according to her. One might have thought she had enough ordinary troubles to frighten anybody. But she had her own theory. She read books on psychology. She misread Freud. Her theory was that she had a strong sexual drive, that it was not being satisfied, and that in consequence she became anxious. So anxious she couldn't cope.

As the older Freud would have told you, it's not that simple.

I think I helped her. I only saw her a few weeks. There was not enough time or money for a proper analysis. But we made some progress.

The young Freud might have partly agreed with her—of course, it was the other way around, she was agreeing with Freud. Suppressed or unfulfilled sexual needs translate into anxiety, etc. Now I don't know how it was with the middle-class Viennese *Hausfrauen* Freud saw as patients. Maybe he was right about them. But he was not right about Ella. As a matter of fact, she satisfied her needs and drives, as she called them, had an affair with one of her bosses, a chicken farmer—and became more frightened than ever. She actually wrung her hands and cried, her face going red as a child's between her heavy iron-gray braids.

I began to notice something about her. The only times she was not frightened were when she carried off some little performance, a gesture which seemed to her to be "right," that is, sufficiently graceful, clever, savvy, warranted, that it pleased her and me. I never cease to be amazed at the number of patients who are at a loss or feel crazy because they don't know what to do from one minute to the next, don't think they do things right—I don't mean right in the moral sense, but right in the way that people on TV or in books or movies always do things right. Even when such actor-people do wrong, go nuts, they do it in a proper, rounded-off way, like Jane Fonda having a breakdown on TV. "I can't even have a successful nervous breakdown!" cried Ella, wringing her hands. She thought she had to go nuts in a poetic way, like Ophelia singing sad songs and jumping in the creek with flowers in her hair. How do I know what to do, Doctor? Why can't you tell me? What I want to tell them is, this is not the Age of Enlightenment but the Age of Not Knowing What to Do.

One day she carried off a charming little gesture and I noticed that it pleased her very much. She showed up with copies of *Feliciana Farewell*, the yearbook of our high school—yes, she had discovered that we had attended the same high school here and the same university in North Carolina. She opened the two books to show me her picture and mine—yes, we had both been editor of the yearbook. She gave me the yearbooks. It pleased her. She stopped trembling.

We talked about failure. What is failure? Failure is what people do ninety-nine percent of the time. Even in the movies: ninety-nine outtakes for one print. But in the movies they don't show the failures. What you see are the takes that work. So it looks as if every action, even going crazy, is carried off in a proper, rounded-off way. It looks as if real failure is unspeakable. TV has screwed up millions of people with their little rounded-off stories. Because that is not the way life is. Life is fits and starts, mostly fits. Life doesn't have to stop with failure. Not only do you not have to jump in the creek, you can even take pleasure in the general fecklessness of life, as I do, a doctor without patients sailing paper P-51s at a martin house. I am a failed but not unhappy doctor.

I took her hints of suicide—"I don't have to play this hand," etc.—seriously. We spoke of failure and she got better. I can't claim a cure, but she got better. She showed some initiative, stopped wringing her hands, moved to Nags Head on the Outer Banks of North Carolina, got a job teaching school, put her children in the excellent public school system of North Carolina, and even began writing poetry. She sent me a postcard showing the beach and the dunes of Kitty Hawk. It read: "Did you ever walk on a beach in December in a gale. The winter beach is lovely." Later she sent me a poem she wrote called "Spindrift," about the spindrift of the waves being like the spindrift of the heart, etc.

Now, admittedly there is still some cause for alarm here: Ella setting too much store by walking on a winter beach and writing a poem about spindrift. There are at least a thousand women poets in America, mostly in California and New England, who walk on beaches and write poems about spindrift, spindrift of the waves, spindrift of the heart. Beware of women poets who write about spindrift. There is a certain peril in this enterprise. She could easily shoot herself down. The winter beach and the spindrift, relied on too much, could let you down. But at least I understood her and she me. We transmit on the same wavelength. She was functioning, living, not trembling, taking herself less seriously, had come to terms with failure. Her children were doing well in school, were happy, had not yet fallen prey to the miseries of adulthood.

Cure? No. What's a cure in this day and age? Maybe a cure is knowing there is no cure. But I helped her and she me. She gave me a gift which I liked. I still have her two volumes of *Feliciana Farewell* on my shelf.

So here she is two years later.

She had called earlier, saying she needed my testimony in an industrial liability case, that it meant big bucks.

Big bucks? That didn't sound like Ella.

I am waiting on the porch when she shows up. She arrives in a Nissan pickup with gun racks in the rear window. She's wearing an elbow cast. The driver stays in the truck, a fellow in a yellow hardhat. I ask her if he's going to wait for her.

She laughs. "Don't worry about Mel. Let's go inside."

I follow her in. The change in her is startling. Her hair is cut short, dyed pinkish-blond, as crimped and stiff as steel wool. She's wearing long shorts, the kind that pull up over the stomach, and she's got a stomach, but the bottoms are rolled up high on her thigh. Her clear plastic shoes have openwork over the toes. Jellies, I think they're called. About two dollars a pair from K-Mart. She looks like a Westwego bingo player.

It seems she has returned to Louisiana, gotten a job with Mitsy, the local nuclear utility at Grand Mer.

Now I've got nothing against Westwego types—they can be, often are, canny, shrewd, generous women, good folks. But there's something about the way she plays the part—yes, that's it, she's playing it and not too well, somewhat absentmindedly.

But I'm fond of her. When she makes as if to give me a hug, I give her a hug. She's bigger.

"How you doing, Doc?"

"I'm fine. I'm glad to see you."

"I hear you been having trouble."

"Yes. But I'm all right now. Do you have trouble?"

"Old Doc. You always been my bud."

"Thanks, Ella." It's time she let go, but she hugs me tight, a jolly, nonsexual hug, like a good old Westwego girl.

"Dear old Doc. Tell me something."

"All right."

"You getting much, Doc?"

"What? Oh." Well, so much for the spindrift of the heart. "What happened to your arm, Ella?" I ask, holding her off to take a look.

"You're not going to believe this, Doc."

Maybe I won't, but it's a relief to get her into a chair, aggrieved and telling me her troubles.

I am wondering about Mel out in the truck.

She goes into a long rigmarole about getting abused by her superior at Mitsy, a person named Fat Alice, who beat her up and broke her arm—and then getting fired. She wants to sue Mitsy for a million dollars and wants me to testify about her mental health.

"The real boss, who is also her boss, says he knows you," she concludes.

"Who is that?"

"Mr. Beck. Albert J. Beck."

"Bubba Beck? Yes, we went to high school together. Don't you remember him? He was all-state quarterback."

"Will you call him?"

"Yes. What is it you really want, Ella?"

"I want my old job back and I want him to tell Fat Alice to leave me alone."

"All right."

"Tell him also that thanks to Fat Alice I was also exposed to radioactive sodium and have been rendered sterile."

"All right."

I reach Bubba at home. Although I haven't spoken to him for twenty years he doesn't seem surprised.

"How you doing, Ace?" asks Bubba.

"I'm fine. I have a patient here with a problem. You might be able to help."

"Let's have it, Ace."

I summarize Ella's complaint.

Bubba speaks at some length.

"Thanks, Bubba. I'll get back to you."

I hang up and take a look at Ella. She's got one leg crossed over the other, is frowning mightily at her thigh, squeezing it from the bottom to make the top, which is somewhat quilted, tight. She plucks something on her skin.

"Ella," I say.

"Yes?" she says, looking up with mild interest.

"Why didn't you tell me that Fat Alice is FA413-T, a rather low-grade robot which vacuums the floor and monitors the room air for particles?"

"So what?" cries Ella. "She still got me cornered and broke my arm and subjected me to radiation poisoning."

"Ella, you were not even in the primary coolant unit. You worked in the secondary unit with non-radioactive sodium."

"She still pushed me!"

"Ella, listen. You've got your job back if you want it. What is more, you've been promoted. You are now Fat Alice's superior." What Bubba told me was that Ella, whose job was hardly more demanding than Fat Alice's—reading dials and noting molar concentrations of chemicals—could now periodically remove Alice's software cassette and run it through the magnetic cleaner. "Do you want your job back?"

Ella claps her hands. "Wow," she says, and starts around the desk. "You were always my bud."

"Okay, hold it, Ella. I want to show you something."

An idea occurs to me just in time, and I get a book and hold the book between me and Ella. "I want you to look at something."

"Anything, Doc! Anything at all!"

The book is *Feliciana Farewell*, her gift of three years ago, the yearbook and our year. I open it to the group picture of our class, only twenty or so boys and girls standing in a tight little trapezoid, each with the fixed, self-obsessed expression of high-school seniors. The world lies ahead, the expression says, and who am I?

It is by way of being a quick study, a little test, as crude and inconclusive as palpating an abdomen for liver cancer.

I've used it before. Most people, I daresay nearly all "normal" people, will seek out themselves in the photograph, usually covertly, but I can watch their eye movements. As a matter of fact, there is a laser device which can track and print out the eye movements until the eye settles on its prey. Which is me? How do I look? People are generally self-conscious, either shy or vain, like General Jeb Stuart, whose last words were "How do I look in the face?"

I wish I had my Mackworth head camera, which actually traces out eye movements. I need the records.

The point of the test, of course, is that self-consciousness implies that there is a self.

The book is open under my chin, facing her, her eyes on the book, my eyes on her eyes. They are looking at the picture, yes; focused? perhaps; interested? mildly. But there is no seeking herself out. A laser trace would show not a zig-zag, cat chasing mouse of self, but a fond little moseying, cow-grazing. Maybe she's looking for me.

"Okay, Ella," I say, closing the book and putting it on the shelf. "You've got your job back and been promoted. You come back here next week after work." I don't have to ask her. I want a tracing, medical evidence.

"Oh boy." She claps her hands. "Thanks, Doc. Wait till I tell Mel."

"All right."

CASE HISTORY #3

Here come Kev Kevin and Debbie Boudreaux, old friends, patients now, married couple: Kev, an ex-Jesuit; Debbie, an ex-Maryknoll nun.

They've had their troubles. I see them for marriage counseling. I don't do much of that, but they are old friends.

The trouble is that Debbie, who had taken over her father's Oldsmobile agency in New Orleans, was quite competent and happy as the young woman executive, named Woman of the Year by the C. of C., in fact, as happy as she had been as Sister Thérèse teaching at the Ortega Institute in Managua. But Kev was unhappy as personnel director of Boudreaux Olds, even though there had been every reason to expect that his experience as counselor at the Love Clinic at Fedville should stand him in good stead in dealing with salesmen and servicemen.

This dispute was acrimonious. They fought even more than non-ex-religious couples.

Here is a sample:

Debbie: The trouble with you is you're still a closet Jesuit. Even though you've taken up transcendental meditation and teach it to the salespeople at your little ashram and play tapes of the Bhagwan and the Maharishi, supposedly to increase their selling potential, what you're really running is a closet-Jesuit retreat. Next you'll have them saying the rosary and making the stations of the cross. You don't want to sell Oldsmobiles, you want to convert people. And the truth is, like the Bhagwan and most Orientals—and most Jesuits—you have contempt for women.

Kev: The trouble with you is you've turned into the worst kind of man-eating bitchy feminist. You're known as the Bella Abzug of the LADA (Louisiana Automobile Dealers Association). You pretend you're the belle of the ball at the C. of C., but deep down you hate men. And if you want to know the truth, that's the reason you and all the other nuns quit, not because of politics or the Church, but because you don't know who in the hell you are and you copped out, and so you take it out on men from the pope on down. You still hate their guts and you still don't know who in the hell you are or what you are doing.

Debbie: Speak for yourself.

Kev: Doc, you wouldn't believe what she's into now.

"What?"

"Wicca."

"Wicker?" I'm thinking, Good, she's doing handcrafts.

"Witchcraft."

Debbie: Don't bad-mouth what you don't understand. Wicca bears no relation to your stereotypical witchcraft, witches on brooms. It is extremely positive and loving, because it is the old nature religion, a nonsexist pre-Judeo-Christian belief. No guilt trips. It is nothing less than becoming one with nature and with yourself.

Kev: Plus a little hex here and there.

And so on.

To tell the truth, at the time I didn't have much use for either of them, though they were my friends and my patients. I confess certain sardonic feelings toward both of them. There was Kev's faddish Hinduism, his new voice, which has suddenly become hushed and melodious like the Maharishi's, his casual but mysterious allusions to his siddhi. What's a siddhi? I asked. A spiritual gift. Like what? Like levitation, no big deal, he said. Yes, during meditation he was often six inches off the floor. And there was Debbie's new lingo, her everlasting talk about dialoguing, creativity, community, intersubjectivity, centeredness (her favorite word, *centeredness*). And her new word, *empowerment*.

What would happen, I wonder, if I asked them what they thought about God and sin?

I thought they did better, looked better, felt better as Father Kev and Sister Thérèse in the old days, as priest and nun, than as siddha Kev in his new soft Maharishi voice and a NOW Wicca Debbie in her stretch pants. If you set out to be a priest and a nun, then be a priest and a nun, instead of a fake Hindu or a big-assed lady Olds dealer who is into Wicca—this from me, who had not had two thoughts about God for years, let alone sin. Sin?

That meeting was before I went to prison. Prison works wonders for vanity in general and for the secret sardonic derisiveness of doctors in particular. All doctors should spend two years in prison. They'd treat their patients better, as fellow flawed humans. In a word, prison restored my humanity if not my faith. I still don't know what to make of God, don't give Him, Her, It a second thought, but I make a good deal of people, give them considerable thought. Not because I'm more virtuous, but because I'm more curious. I listen to them carefully, amazed at the trouble they get into and how few quit. People are braver than one might expect.

This was three years ago.

Anyhow, after listening to this marital warfare for a few weeks, I had an idea which might help them. I made a semi-serious suggestion. Yes, I confess it, my suggestion had its origins both in a wish to help them and in a certain derisiveness and a desire to be rid of them. Yet it worked! Why not, I asked them, why not put your talents to better use? After all, you've both had extensive experience in counseling. You both have superior—er—intersubjective and social skills (they used words like that, worse than shrinks). Why don't you start your own counseling center, perhaps couples' counseling. You could do it and you'd be helping yourselves while helping others. Was I being sarcastic? Not altogether. They'd been battling so long, they knew all the tactics of marital warfare. Ex-soldiers, after all, keep the peace better than politicians. Look at MacArthur in Japan, Eisenhower in Washington.

We laughed. And they did! And they got so involved in other couples' fights, they stopped fighting each other. They started something called Beta House out in the country. I talked Enrique Busch into letting them have a great barn with stables at the time Enrique was quitting polo and taking up golf. I did it by lying, that is, by not telling Enrique who

Debbie was, that is, an ex-Maryknoller from El Salvador, or telling Debbie who Enrique was, a member of the famous fourteen families—they would have wanted to shoot each other on the spot—but by telling Enrique that Debbie's father had founded the White Citizens' Council in Feliciana, which he had, and by telling Debbie that Enrique had deep feelings for the people of El Salvador, which he did.

So Beta House was founded in a barn, the stables converted to intimate bedrooms for estranged couples, the loft to an encounter room. Painted on the side of the barn was the logo they'd agreed upon, a yin-yang centered between two hearts, the yin-yang a concession to Kev's Eastern leanings, the two hearts expressing Debbie's notions about dialoguing and centeredness. Two hearts centered on a yin-yang.

So here they are three years later:

They're pleased to see me and I them. There is no space of irony between us. I wish them well and they me. They're as lovey now as they were fractious before. They sit side by side on my couch, holding hands and feeling each other up—which generally gives me a pain but doesn't now because it's an improvement over the mayhem.

"How does it go?" I ask them.

"Wow," they say; both, I think. They look at each other and laugh. Then, putting on serious faces, they utter little noises of gratitude, not sentences, but exclamations: "Dear Doc," "Our Doc," "Oh boy, Almond Joy," and suchlike. It seems I saved their marriage. It seems I get credit for the barn and Beta House, even though I only made a single, not quite serious suggestion, mainly to get rid of them. No more talk of Wicca.

"Very good," I say presently. "I'm glad things are going so well. You both look fine. But what can I do for you? I can't imagine that you need anything further from me."

Secret looks between them, more laughter, again an instant sobering up, and they make their request.

Do you know what they want from me? A prescription for Alanone, the new Smith, Kline & French polyvalent vaccine which confers some immunity against both the lymphadenopathy virus of LAV-III and the glycoprotein D of Herpes II.

Without turning a hair and in the same smiling voice of our newfound friendship, I ask them why they need it. "I thought you were running a couples' retreat."

"Couples' community," they both correct me. Kev makes certain noises of demurral, but Debbie says quickly and as if she were reading it, "It is also an open community. We do not discourage creative relationships across stereotypical bonding. We find that open relationships, entered into maturely, enrich rather than impoverish the traditional one-on-one bonding."

I do not say something derisive as I might have two years ago, but merely reflect a moment, sigh, and reach for my PDR, the physicians' big red book—what do I know about creative relationships or pills and vaccines?—and write them a prescription for—How many do you want? "Three hundred," says Kev; "Four hundred," says Debbie. I make it four hundred. After all, better not to have than to have LAV-AIDS and Herpes II.

Somewhat abstracted, I forget to run the simplest test on them, a dominant-eye test or an out-of-context language test, like: Where is Ketchum, Idaho? (They'd know, because the Bhagwan had hung out there.) I have no doubt that either would have told me instantly and as merrily as a four-year-old, eyes rolled up to consult their interior brain maps. I'll test them later.

Absently, I receive their hugs and thanking noises and watch from the windows as they depart in their old Econoline van with its flaming yin-yang logo centered between two dialoguing hearts.

2. WHAT TO MAKE OF THESE PATIENTS? WHAT'S IN COMMON?

Nothing? Something? Enough for a syndrome?

Here's Mickey LaFaye, formerly anxious and agoraphobic, terrified of her own shadow, now a sleek, sleepy, horsewoman Duchess of Alba straddling under the sheets. Plus some peculiar business about a stallion and a stable boy. Plus Dr. Comeaux's special interest in her.

Here's Donna S———, formerly a fat girl, abused as a child, but a deep-down romantic, waiting for Galahad. Now she's jolly, lithe, and forward, or rather backward, presenting rearward.

Here's Enrique, once an enraged Salvadoran, now a happy golfer with no worries except his daughter making Gamma.

Here's Ella Murdoch Smith, once failed and frightened, guilt-ridden, couldn't cope, a solitary poet of the winter beach and spindrift. Now Rosy the Riveter, hardhat lady at Mitsy, with her boyfriend in a standard Louisiana pickup, getting beat up by a robot.

And Kev and Debbie, old friends, ex-Jesuit and ex-Maryknoller, a quarrelsome, political, ideological couple. Now content, happy as bugs in a rug; no, not happy so much as fat-witted and absorbed. Running some sort of encounter group out in the pines which sounds less like a couples' retreat than a chimp colony.

Don't forget Frank Macon, old hunting pal, once a complex old-style sardonic black man, as compact of friendship and ironies as Prince Hamlet, as faithful and abusive as a Russian peasant. Now as distant and ironed out as a bank teller: Have a nice day.

And Ellen.

What's going on? What do they have in common? Are they

better or worse? Well, better in the sense that they do not have the old symptoms, as we shrinks called them, the ancient anxiety, guilt, obsessions, rage repressed, sex suppressed. Happy is better than unhappy, right? But—But what? They're somehow—diminished. Diminished how?

Well, in language, for one thing. They sound like Gardner's chimps in Oklahoma: Mickey like—Donna want—Touch me—Ask them anything out of context as you would ask chimp Washoe or chimp Lana: Where's stick? and they'll tell you, get it, point it out. Then: Tickle me, hug me. Okay, Doc?

Then there's the loss of something. What? A certain sort of self-awareness? the old ache of self? Ella doesn't even bother to look at her own photograph, doesn't care.

Bad or good?

For another thing, a certain curious disinterest. Example: Take the current news item: Soviets invited to occupy Baluchistan, their client state in southern Iran to restore order, reported advancing on Bandar Abbas on the Persian Gulf. What to do? Let them have it? Confront them? Ultimatum? Two years ago people would be huddled around the tube listening to Rather and Brokaw. My patients? My acquaintances? No arguments, no fright, no rage, no cursing the Communists, no blaming the networks, no interest. Enrique doesn't mention liberals anymore. Debbie does not revile Jerry Falwell anymore.

There's a sameness here, a flatness of affect. There was more excitement in prison, more argument, more clash of ideology. In Alabama we were polarized every which way, into pro-nukes and anti-nukes, liberals and conservatives, atheists and believers, anti-Communists and anti-anti-Communists, born-again Christians, old-style relaxed Catholics, lapsed Catholics, Barbara Walters haters, Barbara Walters lovers.

Nothing like Alabama!

The warfare in that quonset hut at Fort Pelham!

We inmates, or rather detainees—assorted con men, politicians, ex–Presidential aides, white-collar crooks, impaired physicians pushing pills, mercy killers, EPA inspectors on the take from lumber and oil barons—criminals all, but on the whole engaging and nonmurderous. And next door, Hope Haven, a community of impaired priests, burned-out ministers and rabbis, none criminal, none detained, but all depressed, nutty, or alcoholic, generally all three, who had not run afoul of the law as we had but had just conked out, and so had great sympathy for us and made themselves available. One of them, my old pal and ex-parish priest, Rinaldo, Father Simon Rinaldo Smith, sojourned next door to me on the Alabama Gulf Coast for a year to recover from his solitary drinking. (I must call him. Has he gone nuts again?)

At Fort Pelham we had discussion groups, seminars, screaming political arguments over meals, fistfights. In prison, ideas are worth fighting for. One also gets paranoid. There is a tendency to suspect that So-and-so has it in for you, to read hostile meanings into the most casual glance.

I witnessed such a fight between an anti-Communist Italian Republican dentist from Birmingham who had patented a new anesthetic and more or less inadvertently killed half a dozen patients and an anti-anti-Communist Jewish lawyer from New York, my cellmate Ben Solomon, recently removed to New Orleans, where he had been convicted of laundering Mafia-teamster money for a black mayoral candidate.

This pair and I were sitting in the prison library one afternoon, the Birmingham dentist reading *Stars and Bars*, a new New Right magazine published at Fort Sumter, South Carolina; the New York lawyer reading *The New York Review of Books*. I was reading a new history of the Battle of the Somme, a battle which, with the concurrent Battle of Verdun, seemed to me to be events marking the beginning of a new age, an age not yet named. In the course of these two battles, two million young men were killed toward no discernible end. As Dr. Freud might have said, the age of thanatos had begun.

These two fellows had argued violently at table about racism in the South and the crypto-communism of Northern liberals. Now in the library I looked up from the Battle of the Somme and began to watch them. Both were gazing down at their magazines but neither was reading. Not a page was turned for twenty minutes. It was clear from his expression that Ben Solomon, the lawyer, was festering, nurturing some real or fancied slight, which was being rapidly magnified in his head to a mortal insult. I knew the signs. Perhaps he had lost the last argument and was thinking of what he might have said, a killing remark. But it was too late for talk. His fists clenched and unclenched on the table. The dentist, I perceived, was aware of the lawyer's mounting rage. Then why didn't they steer clear of each other? Why didn't one just get up and leave? But no. They were bound, wedded, by hatred. They were like lovers. Finally the lawyer rose slowly and stood over the dentist, looking down at him, fists clenched at his sides. In a trembling voice he said, "Did you or did you not imply that as a supporter of Israel I was a second-class and unpatriotic American?"

The dentist, surprised or not, did not look up from his *Stars and Bars*. "Only after that crack, addressed to others but intended for me, about rednecks, crackers, yahoos, and gritspitters. I only replied in kind."

"You mentioned something about Yankee kikes."

"Only after you used the expression 'Southron fascist rednecks.' "

"Take it back," said the lawyer, clenching and unclenching.

Take it back! I am marveling. Like my five-year-old Tommy: Take it back. Well then, why not?

"Look, Doctor," I said mildly, "if the word offends him—" Both ignore me.

"You take it back," said the dentist, rising.

"Look, Ben," I say, rising, "why not take—"

"Who in the fuck asked you?" says Ben, not taking his eyes from the dentist.

Neither would take anything back. I am rising from the Battle of the Somme to say something like "Hold it, fellows." Actually I'm fond of both of them.

"Tell him to take back 'redneck,' " says the Italian (redneck!) dentist to me, without taking his eyes from the lawyer.

"Take back 'redneck,' " I tell Ben. "Then he'll—"

"Tell him to take back 'Yankee kike.' "

"Okay. Take back—" I begin, relaying messages two feet. But before I can utter another word, they have actually hurled themselves at each other, and now they are actually rolling on the floor, grappling and punching, two middle-aged gents grunting and straining, their bald scalps turning scarlet. Neither can hurt the other, but they're apt to have a stroke.

I am straddling them, trying to wedge them apart. Good God: a New York–New Orleans Democrat Jew fighting it out with a Birmingham Italian Confederate Republican.

"Cut it out, goddamn it!" I yell at them, straddling both. "You're going to have a stroke!"

I did get in between and did stop the fight, easily, because both wanted an excuse to quit with their Jewish and Confederate honor intact. For my pains I got punched and elbowed, my glasses knocked across the room. "Somebody hit Doc!" one of them cries.

They both set about taking care of me, the lawyer fetching my glasses, the dentist staunching my bleeding lip. I go limp to give them something to do, carry me to the infirmary.

A discovery: A shrink accomplishes more these days by his fecklessness than by his lordliness in the great days of Freud.

What, then, to make of my patients?

Time was when I'd have tested their neurones with my lapsometer. But there's more to it than neurones. There's such a thing as the psyche, I discovered. I became a psyche-iatrist, as I've said, a doctor of the soul, an old-style Freudian analyst, plus a dose of Adler and Jung. I discovered that it is not sex that terrifies people. It is that they are stuck with themselves. It is not knowing who they are or what to do with themselves. They are frightened out of their wits that they are not doing what, according to experts, books, films, TV, they are supposed to be doing. *They*, the experts, know, don't they?

Then I became somewhat simpleminded. I developed a private classification of people, a not exactly scientific taxonomy which I find useful in working with people. It fits or fitted nearly all the people I knew, patients, neurotic people, so-called normal people.

According to my private classification, people are either bluebirds or jaybirds. Most women, it turns out, are bluebirds. Most men, by no means all, are jaybirds.

Mickey LaFaye, for example, is, or was, clearly a bluebird. She dreamed of being happy as a child in Vermont, of waiting for a visitor, a certain someone, of finding the bluebird of happiness.

Enrique Busch was a jaybird if ever I saw one. He wanted to shoot everybody in El Salvador except the generals and the fourteen families.

It is a question of being or doing. Most of the women patients I saw were unhappy and wanted to be happy. They never doubted there was such a creature as the bluebird of happiness. Most men wanted to do this or that, take this or that, beat So-and-so out of a promotion, seduce Miss Smith, beat the Steelers, meet their quota, win the trip to Oahu, win an argument—just like a noisy jaybird. The trouble is, once you've set out to be a jaybird, there's nothing more pitiful than an unsuccessful jaybird. In my experience, that is, with patients who are not actually crazy (and even with some who are), people generally make themselves miserable for one of two reasons: They have either failed to find the bluebird of happiness or they're failed jaybirds.

It is not for me to say whether one should try to *be* happy—though it always struck me as an odd pursuit, like trying to be blue-eyed—or whether one should try to beat all the other jaybirds on the block. But it is my observation that neither pursuit succeeds very well. I only know that people who set their hearts on either usually end up seeing me or somebody like me, or having heart attacks, or climbing into a bottle.

Take a woman—and some men—who think thus: If only I could *be* with that person, or away from this person, or be in another job, or be free, or be in the South of France or on the Outer Banks, or *be* an artist or God knows what—then I'll be happy. Such a person is a bluebird in my book.

Or consider this person: What am I going to do with my no-good son, who is driving me crazy—what I want to do is knock him in the head. Or, what is the best way to take on that son of a bitch who is my boss or to get even with that other son of a bitch who slighted me? Wasn't it President Kennedy who said, Don't get mad, get even?—now, there was a royal jaybird for you. Or, I've got to have that woman— how do I get her without getting caught? Or, I think I can make a hundred thousand almost legally, and so on. Jaybirds all. B. F. Skinner, the jaybird of psychologists, put it this way: The object of life is to gratify yourself without getting arrested. Not exactly the noblest sentiment expressed in two thousand years of Western civilization, but it has a certain elementary validity. True jaybird wisdom.

But what has happened to all the bluebirds and jaybirds I knew so well?

They've all turned into chickens.

Here I am out of the clink and back in the normal law-abiding world, the Russians are coming, the war, if there's a war, is going to make the Somme look like Agincourt, and here are all these people tranquillized, stoned out on something, grinning and patting one another, presenting rearward. What happened to the bluebird of happiness or the jaybird ruckus? These folks act more like Rhode Island Reds scratching in the barnyard or those sparrows befouling the martin house.

Are they better or worse?

I think it's a syndrome, but I am not sure. I aim to find out.

First call Cousin Lucy. She's an M.D., Vassar smart and Southern shrewd, a sane person, perhaps the only one around. And she knows me.

Maybe she can tell me who's crazy and who's not.

She calls me between Ella Murdoch Smith and Kev 'n' Debbie.

She's at the hospital, in the doctors' lounge, taking a break. Can she see me?

Sure, I'll be there around twelve, to see Mickey LaFaye.

Good. She's got an impaction in the same room. An intern screwed up and she's got to do it. Do I have a few minutes now? she asks.

Sure. Kev 'n' Debbie haven't arrived. They wouldn't mind waiting anyhow. But what's this all about?

Can't tell me now. Later.

Well then, I have something to tell her. Okay? Okay. I can hear the crinkle of the plastic of the chair in the doctors' lounge as she settles back. There's a click and a long, hissing exhalation. She's still smoking.

We're in luck. She doesn't get called for twenty minutes. There's time to tell her about my "syndrome." I don't get into case histories but summarize the symptoms and signs, the odd language behavior and sexual behavior. There are some things you don't forget, like riding a bicycle or teaching interns. I don't mention Ellen.

It takes fifteen minutes.

When I finish, there's a long silence.

"Well?" I say at last.

She clears her throat and makes a small spitting noise. I can see her touch the tip of her tongue for a grain of tobacco, spit it out.

"What I need to know," I tell her, "is whether the two years away have warped my perspective, whether it is me, not they, who has become strange—in a word, whether I'm seeing things."

"Yes," she says in a changed voice.

"Yes what?"

"Yes, you've changed. Yes, the cases are real. You're not seeing things."

"What do you think?"

"About you or them?"

"Them."

"I might have an idea. And about you too."

"I'll look for you at the hospital around noon," I tell her. Kev and Debbie are at the door.

"Don't worry. I'll find you."

98

3. SECOND CONSULTATION WITH MICKEY LaFAYE.
There is a slight unpleasantness about doing a psychiatric consultation in a small general hospital. Here a psychiatrist is ranked somewhere between a clergyman and an undertaker. One is tolerated. One sees the patient only if the patient has nothing else to do.

In your office you are in control. You control where you sit, where the patient sits or lies, who speaks, what is said. You even control the silences. Here it is the patient who controls while you stand about on one foot, then the other; here it is Mickey lying at her ease among the pastel Kleenexes and Whitman Samplers, chin at rest in her full, sumptuous throat, her tawny eyes watching me incuriously while I stand just clear of her bed as wary as a preacher.

It is hardly an ideal setting for an interview, but I know what I want and do not intend to waste time.

It is a double room in the medical wing. Mickey LaFaye is in the bed next to the window. I stand at her bed but not touching it, facing the window. Behind me, not six feet away, is the curtained-off bed of the second patient. Lucy is attending the patient. I recognized her legs under the curtain, the same strong calves and laced-up oxfords I remember from when she was interning in pathology and I used to see her standing on tiptoe, calves bunched, to get at the cadaver.

Lucy is doing some procedure, no doubt clearing an impaction. The old woman is making querulous sounds of protest. She is not cooperating. Lucy's murmur is soothing, but there is in it a note of rising impatience.

Directly opposite me, not thirty feet away, through the window, across a completely enclosed quadrangle of grass, beyond another window, stands Bob Comeaux in the glass box of the nurses' station. I caught his eye. He is dressed in his riding clothes, turtleneck sweater, suede jacket. His office is not here at the hospital or close by but at the federal complex on the river. Dressed as he is, he is probably dropping by after his morning ride and before going to work. It is clear that he is doing just that, dropping by an ordinary small general hospital in his riding clothes, as much as to say that his real work as neurologist is elsewhere.

Standing next to him is Sue Brown, the floor nurse, a pleasant woman and an excellent nurse, who was glad to see me and made me welcome. She cheerfully entered the test I ordered in Mickey's chart, which is no doubt the chart Bob Comeaux is holding.

"How do you feel, Mickey?"

"Oh, fine! Fine!" Her legs move under the covers. Again she somehow gives the effect of straddling.

"What are your plans when you leave here?"

"Vermont!" she says in the same mild exclamatory voice.

"You're going back to your grandmother's farm?"

"Yes!"

"Why are you going?"

"Cool! Too hot here! Vandals and police and all!"

"Where are the vandals?"

"Out at the ranch!"

"There has been some trouble out there?"

"Oh yes! Terrible!"

"I see. Who's going to look after the ranch while you're gone?"

"Dr. Comeaux!"

"Does going back to Vermont remind you of your dream?"

"Dream?" It is not so much a question as the puzzled repetition of the word.

"You remember. The dream you used to have about the cellar, the smell of winter apples, the expectation of something important about to happen which would tell you the secret of your life."

"Apples? Oh yes. In the hamper next to the chimney."

"That's right. What are you going to do after you get to Vermont?" I am curious to know how she will answer a question which requires making a plan and telling of the plan in sentences.

"So much better there! Not to worry. Dr. Comeaux—"

"Dr. Comeaux says you'll feel much better there?" Almost despite myself, I find myself repeating and filling out her utterances as one would with a child.

She nods emphatically. "Right. Power of attorney!"

"I see. Now, Mickey, I'll tell you what we're going to do. I'm going to do two quick little tests right now. All you have to do is follow along with me. Then I'm going to take you down to the PETscan room and they're going to do another test. All you have to do is sit in a chair and they'll put a funny cap on your head and let you listen to music and words—like a radio headset, okay?"

She nods eagerly. Now you're talking! This is what she's good at. Taking directions, cooperating—not like that bad old woman in the next bed!—playing the game.

"I'm going to crank you up straight. Now."

I sit on the bed, leaning almost athwart her, and, taking her face in both hands, turn her directly toward me. I cover her left eye.

"What do you see?"

"You."

"Am I moving?"

"No."

"Now." With a forefinger I depress the fundus, the eyeball, of the open eye through the eyelid. "Am I moving now?"

"Yes."

I take my hand away. "Now, with both eyes open, look back and forth as fast as you can."

She does it, then looks at me hopefully, to see if she has done well.

"That's fine. What happened?"

"What—"

"Did I move?"

"Yes! You—everything—the room—"

"That's fine, Mickey."

She looks pleased.

It is not fine. What is amazing is that with a normal eye and a normal brain, no matter how violent the movement of the eyes, the room—and I—will be perceived by you as what they are, stationary.

"Okay, Mickey. Now let's do this. I'm going to roll the bed table right up here, give you pencil and paper, okay? Now, what I want you to do is make X's and O's like this." I show her and she makes some X's and O's and looks up for approval.

"That's fine, Mickey. Now here's what I want you to do. Make an X and an O, then two X's and O's, then three X's and three O's and so on. Do you understand?"

She nods eagerly and starts making X's and O's. She makes an X and an O, two X's and an O, then a series of X's with an occasional O.

"That's fine, Mickey. Now I want you to come along with me and we'll—"

Before I get any further, she has obediently folded back the covers and swung her legs out without, I notice, taking the universal woman's precaution of minding her gown, which rides up her not thin thighs.

"Just a moment, Mickey. I'll get you a wheelchair."

I become aware of a silence behind me, a silence, I realize, which has gone on for some time.

I turn. Lucy Lipscomb has come out of her curtained-off bedroom. I thought at first it was to give me a hand.

"Hello, Tom." She smiles, then hesitates, mouth open, as if she wanted to tell me something.

"Lucy."

"Could I have a word with you?" She is not smiling. "Wait a minute." She peels off her gloves and goes into the bathroom.

I haven't seen her for a year or so. She's better-looking. Perhaps it's the gleaming white coat, so starched that it rustles with every movement, against her dark skin. Perhaps she's lost weight. Perhaps it's the way her haircut doesn't look butch anymore. She used to cut it herself, I thought. It was as rough-cut as a farmer's—she is a farmer as well as a doctor. But instead of looking like a Buster Brown, it looks French, straight dark bangs come down her forehead at angles. No butch she. There is a reflex hammer and an ophthalmoscope in her breast pocket.

"Sorry about the ward conditions, Tom."

"It didn't matter."

"I noticed that. It seems you have an audience, or rather an onlooker." She speaks in an easy but guarded voice, looking over my shoulder.

"Who? Oh." I turn around. Across the tiny quadrangle, still holding the steel chart in both hands, Bob Comeaux is looking straight at me.

"Yeah. He's waiting to see me when I finish."

"Hm. So it seems. Could I also?"

"Also what?"

"Have a word with you."

"Sure."

Mickey is thrashing impatiently. Lucy is spoiling her game.

I'm out the door and down the hall, looking for a wheelchair for Mickey.

"Doctor!" A sharp peremptory un-Southern man's voice. "Just hold it right there."

It's Bob Comeaux, with Sue Brown holding a chart. He's angry, I see at once, so angry that he's past prudence, to the point of showing his anger toward another doctor in the presence of a nurse—which for a doctor is angry indeed. He's lost his temper. His nostrils flare and have actually whitened where they join the lip. Sue Brown gives me a frightened smile.

Bob Comeaux is not smiling. His eyes are up in his eyebrows, mouth tight like a chief of surgery on grand rounds.

"Doctor, would you mind stepping over here?" We walk back, past the open door of the room, presumably to get a little away from Sue Brown. We don't want a nurse to see doctors fight. But Sue Brown has vanished into thin air. For a split second I am aware of Lucy through the doorway, standing still, her brown eyes rounded.

Bob Comeaux and I find ourselves standing side by side, backed against the wall, hands in pockets, looking down at our toes in a studious exercise of control, of not facing each other, not confronting, not yelling, not fistfighting. We could be a couple of horsy docs discussing the hunter-jumper show. I notice that his field boots are muddy. He's wearing short spurs. I remember wondering at that very moment if his coming to the hospital in riding clothes is simply a matter of convenience or whether it is more than that.

"Doctor, what the fuck do you think you're doing?" asks Bob Comeaux pleasantly, smiling—white around the mouth with rage—down at his boots.

"I was doing the consultation on Mickey you asked for."

"I saw what you were doing."

"You did?"

"You ran a Tauber test, then some Luria X's and O's. I saw you."

"So?"

"What the fuck for?"

"I—"

"And you were about to wheel her out."

"Yes."

"Where were you taking her?"

"Down to get a PETscan. That's the best I can do in this hospital. You must have seen the order on the chart."

"I sure as hell did. But to what end, for Christ's sake?"—smiling, taking a deep breath, examining each muddy boot carefully. He's getting it back, his lost temper. "Oh, I know you, old buddy!"—now smiling brilliantly, even nudging me. He has recovered himself and can wipe the smile and come close with a comradely seriousness. "God knows, I understand your intellectual curiosity, Tom—such is the stuff of great discoveries—but I'm just an ordinary clinician and must think first of my patient.''

"I think she's got a cortical deficit, probably prefrontal.''

"Very interesting. Okay, okay. Let's skip the metaphysics. You get into the prefrontal, you get into metaphysics. In any case it's academic when it comes to managing her. That's not why I asked you in on this.''

"Why did you ask me in, Bob?''

"I thought for one thing to do you a fucking favor. Believe it or not, I thought we were friends, and as a friend I wanted you back on your feet as a working physician—entirely apart from my role as one of your probationers. As such, I don't mind telling you it was I who got the Board of Medical Examiners to move you from a Class Three to a Class Two offense.''

"What is that?''

"It means, Doctor, that your license is not revoked or suspended but that you are on probation. Do you think that happened by accident? We are hoping to get it down to Class One, reprimand. Tom, we want you doctoring here and not greenskeeping in Alabama. A good idea for all concerned, wouldn't you say?''

"Yes.''

"Okay. Now as far as LaFaye is concerned, my point is that she is neurological and not psychiatric, which puts her on my turf, right? So all we need to commit her to my program over at NIMH is your co-signature as consultant.''

"I see.''

Things have eased between us. Hands in slant pockets, he's pushing himself off the wall by nodding his head. His spurs clink against the terrazzo. We've fallen into our standard medical comradeship, having gone to the same medical school, years apart. We did not know each other there but we remember the old Columbia joke which has almost become a password, a greeting, between us:

"Just keep in mind, Tom, the two most overrated things in the world."

"I will."

"Sexual intercourse and—"

"Johns Hopkins University."

Bob Comeaux likes this because he knows I interned at Hopkins.

The anger is gone, the threat withdrawn. Or did I imagine the threat? The threat: That if I don't behave I could find myself back in the pine barrens of Alabama, driving the big John Deere.

Bob Comeaux has always been skittish with me. The anger over Mickey LaFaye is something new and puzzling. The skittishness is old. It comes from something in his past which he is almost, but not absolutely, certain that I don't know, can't know. There is no reason why I should know, but the tiny possibility makes him skittish. Sometimes I catch him appraising me, wondering. It is a very small thing that I might know and it needn't worry him, but it does. In fact I do know it, this curious little thing, and by the merest chance. It came from my reading the *P & S Alumni News* two years ago. You know a physician is not doing well when he has nothing better to do during office hours than read the alumni news. One's eye skims down the listed names for someone familiar in "Necrology"—who died?—in reunions, newsy notes from alumni, honors. What my eye caught was not a name but a town, this town, in "Alumni Notes," and opposite the name of the physician, a Dr. Robert D'Angelo Como, and the breezy note: "Bob doing yeoman work in the brain pharmacology of radioactive ions at NIH's Feliciana Qualitarian Life Center—an appropriate name for a Qualitarian satellite, reports Bob, who describes himself as a converted Johnny Reb with his own hound dawgs, hosses, and ham hocks." Hm. The familiar mixture here of professional seriousness and the always slightly deplorable tone of medical bonhomie. But Como? Not Comeaux? That's what worries Bob. I can imagine what happened. It was his twenty-fifth class reunion and the secretary got his name not from his letter but from his class roster—yes, there he is on the reunion list, Dr. Robert D'Angelo Como. A small matter certainly, especially in Louisiana, where name changes were commonplace to accommodate whatever nation prevailed. German Zweig and Weiss often became La Branche and Le Blanc. Le Blanc and Weiss have been known to become White. No one cares. I know a man named Harry Threefoot whose family changed their name from Dreyfus. From French-Jewish to Choctaw. Why? Who knows? And in Louisiana who cares? Harry laughed about it. No, the little pique of interest comes from another small scrap of memory. A couple of years ago Mickey LaFaye, not then a horsewoman, lying on my couch, was going on in her old derisive tone about her husband, Durel, and his exclusive Feliciana Hunt Club, the old-line names and the old money it took to get in, the snobbery of it, the silliness and cruelty of fox hunting and so on, then less derisively about an attractive doctor she'd met at the Hunt Club, Dr. Robert Comeaux, newly arrived at Fedville but not one of your D.C. bureaucrats, no, he was old-line Delaware Huguenot stock. Voted into the club on the first ballot. Something occurred to me. Two years ago. My eyes went up to my bookshelves. My father subscribed to a yearly tome, the *U.S. Medical Directory*. I took down the most recent, ten years old. There he was: Dr. Robert D'Angelo Como, b. Long Island City, N.Y., C.C.N.Y., Columbia University's College of Physicians & Surgeons . . .

A small thing, but puzzling. Why would anybody want to change Como to Comeaux nowadays? Why would anyone prefer to be thought Huguenot and not Italian? I've known plenty of both, and frankly—

A small thing, but enough to make him skittish with me. But he's very much at his ease now, clicking his spurs against the terrazzo and pushing off the wall by ducking his dark head just graying at the temples, neither Sicilian nor Huguenot now but very much the English gent in his muddy field boots. He smiles his new, brilliant smile.

"Bob, what's this about a fire and vandalism out at Mickey's ranch? Did something happen out there? Something about a groom?"

"Oh boy." Bob's face goes grave, showing white around the eyes inside the tan. With his deep tan and flashing white smile suddenly going grave, Bob is as handsome as a young George Hamilton. "Oh boy, it was more than that. The fire was the least of it. Tom, Mickey took it into her head one day last week to remove her husband's .45 automatic from the closet shelf, drive out to the ranch, and begin shooting her thoroughbreds, beginning with the least valuable, fortunately—you know, she's got over two million in horseflesh out there—until she was stopped and disarmed by a groom. Those horses weren't burned. She shot them. Then she deceived the groom by pretending contrition, talked him out of the gun, headed back to the house. Tom, I'm afraid she intended harm to herself or her children or both."

"How do you know that?"

"She told me."

"How did she tell you? In her present state I can't see her telling a story, relating an event."

"You noticed that." Bob Comeaux gives me a keen-eyed look. "You would. You're quite right. You get it out of her by questioning her like a child. But she'll tell you!"

"What's this about some sort of sexual business between her and the groom? Did the groom attack her?"

Bob looks grave. "I fear not, Tom." He stands quite close, facing me, head down, talking so low that not even Sue Brown, who's back, now six feet away, can hear. "She was coming on to him, Tom."

"That's the groom's story?"

"Yes, and I didn't believe it at first. But she told me herself, quite openly."

We fall silent, pondering. Now Bob is back against the wall, speaking in our old offhand style.

"Tom, you asked me earlier, with your typical Freudian skepticism, just how did I propose to modify her behavior and what sort of behavior I wanted from her." Actually I didn't ask him any such question. "Well, you've seen for yourself. Wouldn't you say that such behavior needs modifying—entirely apart from whatever is going on in her subconscious mind, as I believe you call it."

"Yes."

"You know, Doctor, you and I might just be the ones to achieve a meeting of minds over the old mind-body problem, that ancient senseless quarrel. What do you think?"

"Our minds might."

"Ha ha. Never quit, do you?" By way of leave-taking he gives me a warm, horse-smelling, shoulder jostle. "Oh, Tom—"

"Yes?"

"I know I can count on you to help me see to it that Mrs. LaFaye gets the best care we can give her."

"You can."

"Thanks, hoss. What say to the Ein und Zwanzig and a flick?" That's old P & S talk for let's go to Twenty-One to eat and then to the movies at Radio City.

"Thanks, but I got a junior dog." I got a date with a student nurse.

"Oh shit. Tom?"

"Yes?"

"I almost forgot. This is not a favor. This is something I'm sure you'd want to do because it involves an old friend of yours."

"Who's that?"

"I spoke to you about Father Smith and Father Placide over at St. Michael's?"

"Yes?"

"Well, it seems the good fathers have a problem. Father Placide called me a couple of weeks ago. Incidentally, he's a hell of a nice guy—we served on a couple of committees together. He's got a little problem and frankly I think you're in a better position to handle it than I."

"What's the problem?"

"The problem is Father Smith. It has to do with his behavior. Ha ha, I'm sorry, Tom, but I'm quoting Father Placide. Frankly, Tom, I'm a little out of my element here. I believe you've known Father Smith for some time, that you knew him well in, ah, Alabama."

"Yes. What's wrong with him?"

"I'm not clear on that—something about him flipping out, not coming down from a fire tower. Anyhow, I'd appreciate it if you would talk to Placide. I'd take it as a personal favor."

"All right."

He looks at his watch, a curved gold wafer. "Could you drop by there this afternoon?"

"Well—"

"Tom, just hear what Father Placide has to say. Then I want you to take a look at Father Smith and give me a DX. Okay?"

"All right," I say, looking around for Lucy.

"Great," says Bob, giving me a strong pronated handshake and a long level-eyed look. "You know something, hoss. If the creek don't rise, I think we're going to make it. Right?"

"Right," I say, wishing he'd let go of my hand and wondering what he wants from Father Placide.

4. LUCY CATCHES ME IN THE PARKING LOT. SHE'S GOT two sandwiches and two Cokes. We sit in her old pickup, a true farm vehicle spattered to the windows with cream-colored mud. The truck bed is loaded with a tractor tire and a cutter blade from a combine.

My two-toned Caprice, even older, is alongside. Beyond, in the far corner of the lot, a Cox Cable van is parked facing out. Later I remember wondering what a cable van was doing here. The hospital has a dish antenna.

"You look underfed. Eat," says Lucy, eating. She still wears her white coat.

But I don't eat. I sit hands on knees. The hot October sun pours through the windshield. The vinyl seat is torn. Stuffing extrudes through the tear.

Lucy lights up one of her Picayunes, plucks a grain of tobacco from the tip of her tongue, pointing her tongue. I remember her doing this before.

"You and Bob seem to have patched things up," says Lucy, watching me. She is sitting in the corner, half facing me, white coat open, bare knee folded on the seat. A splendid knee.

"What? Yes." A *déjà vu* has overtaken me. It began when she unlocked her door, got in, and I, waiting at the other door, watched her lean almost horizontally, holding the wheel with her left hand and with two fingers of her right, palm up, lift the latch. She's done this before for me, hasn't she?

It is the smell of hot Chevy metal and the molecules of seat stuffing rising in my nostrils and the rustling of her starched coat. I've been here before.

"You were testing her for a cortical deficit, weren't you?"

"Yes. I'm glad you were there."

"I made it my business to be there. Did you find it?"

"What? Oh, the deficit. Yes, I think so."

"I wanted to tell you why Bob Comeaux was so angry."

Lucy is telling me something about Comeaux and his interest in Mickey LaFaye and her ranch. It is difficult to listen.

The *déjà vu* has to do with sitting in a car with a girl, woman, with her swiveled around, bare knee cocked on the seat, with the smell of hot Chevy metal. We'll sit there for a while, then we'll—

She touches my arm. I give a start. She is leaning toward me. "Are you all right?"

"Sure. Why?"

"You've been sitting there for five minutes, not saying a word."

"I'm all right."

"My God." She has made a sharp cluck in her teeth, pulling back the corner of her mouth like a country woman, leaned over, and taken hold of the lapel of my jacket. "Did they give you that suit when you got out of jail?" With a curious rough gesture, like a housewife fingering goods, she rubs the seersucker between thumb and forefinger, gives it a yank and a brush back. "You're very pale. I'd like to have a look."

"A look?"

"With this." She's taken her ophthalmoscope from her breast pocket. "I've gotten very good with eyegrounds. I can tell more about you with one quick look than with a complete physical."

"I believe you. All right."

"Not here. Too much sun. In my office."

Her office in the hospital has a small desk, two chairs, and an examining table. I sit on the table, knees apart. With me sitting and her standing we're of a height. I make as if to get my knees out of her way, but she's already between them. She examines my eyegrounds. The lance of the brilliant blue-white light seems to probe my brain. When she changes from my right eye to my left, we are face to face. Her coat rustles. I feel the radiation of heat from her cheek and once the touch of down. She doesn't wear perfume. Her breath is sweet. She smells like a farm girl, not a doctor.

"All right," she says, with a slight blush, I think, and backs away. "Your arteries look good. No narrowing, no plaques, no pigment, no hypertension, I would suppose."

"Did you think I'd had a stroke?"

"You were absolutely motionless."

I look at her. I don't think I'd ever taken a good look at her before. I used to think of her as a convent-school type, St. Mary's-of-the-Woods, good-looking in a hearty Midwestern way, good legs, black bobbed hair, handsome squarish face with a bruised ripe freckled effect under the eyes—the sort who might become a nun or marry a Notre Dame boy, and live in Evanston. But of course she's not. She's none of these. She's old local Episcopal gentry. She went not to St. Mary's in Indiana but to St. Elizabeth's in Virginia.

A lot happened to her. She married, not a Notre Dame boy, but Buddy Dupre, Ed's brother, a pleasant Tulane DKE, not merely pleasant but charming, the sort of Southern charmer who drinks too much. He had that sweetness and funniness which alcoholic Southern men often have, as if they cannot bear for the world not to be as charming as they are. He farmed a little at Pantherburn, Lucy's family's place, charmed everybody, got elected to the state legislature, began to spend most of his time at the Capitol Motel in Baton Rouge, did not so much separate from Lucy as drift pleasantly away, got investigated by the house ethics committee for taking a bribe from a waste-disposal contractor, got exonerated by the legislature ethics committee, which has never found a legislator unethical, drifted farther, to New Orleans, where he divorced Lucy and married the contractor's daughter, leaving Lucy high and dry at Pantherburn, but intact, herself intact, and Pantherburn and its two thousand acres intact. She farmed it herself, planted and harvested soybeans in the not so rich loess loam, with only day labor. Then out of the blue and in her late twenties she went to medical school. She still farms Pantherburn, not with the two hundred slaves who used to pick the indigo or cut the sugar cane, or the one hundred sharecroppers who used to pick the cotton, but with two tractor drivers and two John Deeres and a leased combine for harvesting the soybeans.

I take a good look at her. She's sitting at her desk, clicking thumbnail to tooth, not looking at me. She is somehow both stronger-looking and more feminine. There's this odd dash of gamin French about her face, bruised cheek, and almost black boy's hair. She reminds me of Southern women in old novels: "a splendid vivacious girl, not beautiful, but full of teasing, high spirits."

It is as if she had only just now decided to become a woman, but not entirely seriously. Having failed at marriage, she has succeeded in farming and doctoring and has discovered that succeeding at anything is a trick, a lark. She's enjoying herself. She is also exhilarated by my failure and disgrace. Now she can "take care" of me with her brisk tugs and brushings. We are kin; I am old enough to be her father, yet she's more like a mother, might any moment spit on her thumb and smooth my eyebrows. She feels safe and can give herself leave with me.

She cocks her head. "Are you coming out to Pantherburn this afternoon?"

"If you want me to."

"Do you remember coming out to Pantherburn years ago and examining my uncle? and committing him to Mandeville? when he was hiding out in the woods or the attic and wouldn't talk to anyone?"

"Yes. How is he?"

"He's all right. I remember how you talked to him and got him to talk. I remember how you listened to him. You looked as if you knew everything there was to know about him."

"As it turned out I didn't, did I?"

She cocks her head. "You know what?"

"What?"

"I think you got yourself in trouble on purpose."

"Why would I do that?"

"I think you wanted out of here, even if it meant going to prison. It wasn't bad, was it?"

"I'm glad to be out. I've got to go now."

"I know. To Father Placide about your old friend Father Smith."

"You seem to know what's going on around here."

"And you seem not to."

"Maybe you'd better tell me."

"About Bob Comeaux? He wants Mrs. LaFaye's place, her horses and probably her money, and will even take Mrs. LaFaye to get them."

"You told me that. What does he want from Father Placide?"

She explains patiently. "It's no secret. Bob Comeaux wants to buy old St. Margaret's—you know, where Father Smith's hospice is, or was. He wants it for a private nursing home, a real moneymaker, you know. Actually that building would be a marvelous investment. Imagine a hundred nuns living out there! And it just so happens the hospice has folded up and Father Smith has too, he's not at all well. The bishop would like to get rid of it, he needs the money. Placide would like to get rid of it so Father Smith can come back and help him with the parish. You're supposed to talk Father Smith out of the fire tower and into coming back to St. Michael's. Then the bishop can sell the place to Bob Comeaux and everybody will be happy. Do you understand?"

"No." I am thinking about the *déjà vu*. I think I know what it was about. It was about cars, women, girls, youth, the past, the old U.S.A., about remembering what it was like to be sitting in a car with a girl swiveled around to face you, her bare knee cocked up on the vinyl, with four wheels under you, free to go anywhere, to the Gulf Coast, to Wyoming. It, the *déjà vu*, came from the smell of hot Chevy metal and vinyl and seat stuffing tingling in the nostrils and radiating up into the hippocampus of the old brain and into the sights and sounds of the new cortex, which gathers into itself a forgotten world, bits and pieces of cortical memory like old snapshots scattered through an abandoned house.

I rise. She takes hold of my lapel again. "You come on out to Pantherburn later. I have something to show you. I know you can come. Your wife's gone."

I laugh. "I'm not surprised. You know everything else."

"You don't have much luck with women, do you?"

"What does that mean?"

"Nothing. Only that you could use somebody right now to look after you."

"And you're going to look after me."

"Somebody had better."

"Why is that?"

"You're a mess. Look at you. You may be smart, but you're a mess."

"That's true."

"Eat your BLT. I put it and the Coke in your car."

"All right."

"Eat."

She grabs my lapel again, both lapels. We are almost face to face.

"You're coming out to Pantherburn later?"

"Yes."

"I've got an idea."

"What?"

"How many cases have you got of this—ah—syndrome?"

"Oh, a dozen, I guess."

"Could you bring the case histories with you?"

"I know the case histories."

"Okay. Then bring their social security numbers."

"What for?"

"Trust me."

"All right."

5. I FIND FATHER PLACIDE IN THE RECTORY OF ST. MIchael's. Mrs. Saia, the housekeeper, lets me in. It is his living quarters, but the living room looks like an untidy business office. There are desks, file cabinets, typewriters, a photocopier, a computer, stacks of bulletins and collection envelopes, and a coin-counting machine.

A man dressed in a business suit, probably a deacon, is seated at a desk in the hall sorting out different-colored cards. He greets me amiably. I try to remember his name.

St. Michael himself is still there, a three-foot bronze archangel brandishing a loose sword, bent at the tip, which I used to fiddle with while attending meetings of the St. Vincent de Paul Society years ago. The sword got lost. They must have found it. I seem to remember that—

Father Placide is nowhere to be seen. The next room, connected by an arched doorway, is a kind of parlor furnished with old-fashioned mohair sofas. Half a dozen women are sitting there. It is some kind of meeting, perhaps the altar society, perhaps the Blue Army, perhaps the Legion of Mary. I recognize three of them: Mrs. Saia, a plump, cheerful, middle-aged woman with perfect dark satiny skin; Mrs. Ernestine Kelly, wife of councilman Jack Kelly, an old fisherman friend of mine and sometime barmate at the Little Napoleon, a very pretty gray-haired woman with a solemn, even sad, expression, whom one thinks of as pious in the old sense, who still observes the old Catholic devotions, still makes First Fridays, sends vials of Lourdes water to sick friends, and from time to time mails me a holy card with a saint's picture and always the same note: Praying for you and your intentions, on which occasions I always wonder what she is praying for, my doing time in Alabama? mine and Jack's drinking? my loss of faith? Ellen's neglect of me for duplicate bridge? And Jan Greene, a youngish, intense blade of a brunette, ex–New Orleanian, wife of a gynecologist colleague and an old-style Catholic who wants to rescue the Church from its messing in politics and revolution, from nutty nuns and ex-nuns, from antipapal priests and malignant heterodox Dutch theologians, and so revive the best of the old Church, that is, orthodox theology, without its pious excesses, meaning Ernestine's holy pictures and First Fridays.

The women see me and give me guarded greetings, with half nods, smiling. They can't decide how disgraced I am, so charitably give me the benefit of the doubt.

Perhaps Father Placide is at the meeting, but no, here he comes breezing in behind me. He greets me cordially, paying no attention to the meeting.

Father is a thin, young, pale, harassed priest. Except for

his black dickey with clerical collar attached, which he wears over a T-shirt, he looks like an overworked intern. His face has a greenish pallor and the speckling of a stubble, the look of a man who has forgotten to shave. There is a rash where the collar irritates his neck.

Though I hardly know him, he greets me as warmly as if I were a faithful parishioner, but it may be that he is too harried to remember. He takes the easy confidential tone of one professional consulting another: Look, Dr. More, we have a little problem here—

We are sitting side by side at a broad table holding the coin counter and covered by papers and cloth coin bags. He speaks easily, alternately rubbing and widening his eyes like a surgeon who has finished a six-hour operation and has flopped in a chair to discuss the case.

The women in the parlor resume their meeting.

The case is Father Smith. He, Father Placide, has his troubles. The main trouble is that the pastor, Monsignor Schleifkopf, has departed, returned to the Midwest, some say to join the conservative schismatics in Cicero, some say to join the liberal Dutch schismatics in South Bend. St. Michael's Church here is still Roman Catholic; that is, it still recognizes the authority of the pope as the lawful successor to St. Peter. Young Father Placide was left with the burden of running the parish until a replacement could be found. This would not have been a problem since the other assistant, Father Smith, though not a young man, was a vigorous one. And he seemed well when he came back from Alabama, no longer a boozer. Between the two of them they could and did take up the slack. Father Smith ran the hospice out by the fire tower and the little mission "under the hill" and helped out at St. Michael's with Masses, meetings, confessions, CYO, and such. Now, it seems, Father Smith has conked out, leaving Placide holding the bag.

"Doctor," says the priest, his hollow white eyes not quite focused, "I can't do it all. We've been promised a pastor this month. We were promised a pastor last month and the month before. It would be very helpful if Father Smith would help out here. I understand y'all are old friends, so I was wondering if you might see him, talk to him, give him—ah—whatever therapy he might need, tell him I need him. The deacons here, they're fine, they're doing a tremendous job, but they can't do Masses, confessions, funerals, weddings, and suchlike. Doc, I'm going to tell you something, listen: I'll serve the good Lord and His people as long as I can, but, Doc, I'm going to tell you, they 'bout to run this little priest into the ground.''

"What's wrong with Father Smith? Has he started drinking?''

"No." Father Placide gives a great shrug, holds it, looks right and left. "Who knows? He says he'd like nothing better than to help out but he can't.''

"Why can't he?''

"I'll tell you the truth. I don't know.''

"Is he sick?''

"Not that I know of. Not in the usual sense. Maybe in your sense." He taps his temple. "That's why I need you to talk to him.''

"How do you mean?''

"I'm not quite sure. Father Smith is a remarkable man, a gifted priest, as you well know. He's always been a role model for me. In fact, he's gotten me past some bad moments. But—" Again he shrugs and falls silent.

"I don't think I understand what the problem is," I say, wondering whether we're supposed to be out of earshot of the women and whether they're waiting for Father Placide. But he speaks in an ordinary voice and pays no attention to the women or to the deacon in the hall.

"Look, Doctor, you're an old friend of Father Smith's, right?''

"Right.''

"You know that for years he has lived out in the woods at the hospice near the fire tower and that he has never given up his part-time job as fire watcher for the forestry service.''

"Yes."

"Not that I don't sympathize with him. I mean, how would you like to live here? Ainh?" He opens his hands to the cluttered office and the oval print of the Sacred Heart with a dried-up palm frond stuck behind it.

"Not much."

"Look, Doc," says the priest, rubbing both eyes with the heels of his hands. "Look, I'm not the best and the brightest. I finished in the bottom third of my seminary class. I don't know whether Father Smith is a nut or a genius, or whether he has some special religious calling. It's out of my league, but I can tell you this, Doc, I need help. Me, I'm not going to be much help to the Lord if they have to peel me off the wall and carry me off, ainh Doc?"

Father Placide talks in an easy colloquial style, hardly distinguishable from any other U.S. priest or minister, except that now and then one hears a trace of his French Cajun origins. It is when he shrugs and cocks a merry eye, hollow but nonetheless merry, and says *ainh? ainh?* His *three* is just noticeably *t'ree.*

"I understand, Father. What do you want me to do?"

"I ask you, my friend, to speak to Father Smith, persuade him to come down and help me out. For just a few weeks."

"Come down?"

"From the fire tower."

"In a manner of speaking, you mean."

"Not in a manner of speaking, *cher.* He won't come down."

"Won't come down from what?"

"From the fire tower."

"Literally?"

"Literally. He has a man bring up his groceries and empty his camp toilet."

"How long has he been up there?"

"Three weeks. Since the hospice was closed."

"Why was the hospice closed?"

120

A shrug. "The government. You know, they cut Medicare for hospices but not for Qualitarian centers."

"Then is he staying up there as a kind of protest?"

A big French shrug, eyes going left, then right. "Who knows? Maybe, but it's more than that."

"How do you mean?"

"He told me that he had—ah—discovered a mathematical proof of what God's will is, that is, what we must do in these dangerous times."

"I see."

"Now, he may be right. It's out of my league. Me, I'm a very ordinary guy and have to baptize babies and run the school and suchlike. I'd like to preach the good news of the Lord, but it seems like I don't have the time. Ask him if he can take off a little time from saving the world to help one po' li'l priest."

"All right, Father."

"One more little thing—" He is shuffling papers on the table.

"Yes?"

"I'm supposed to be organizing an ecumenical meeting here—" He sighs. One more thing to do. "I got to find five of our laymen who are willing to— Would you be interested?"

"No, thanks."

"Okeydoke," says the priest absently, unoffended, shuffling more papers. Is he looking for something else I can do? I get up.

The doorbell rings. Mrs. Saia starts out from the meeting. Father Placide jumps up. "I'll get it, Sarah! Hold the fort." I think he is avoiding the meeting.

While Father Placide is gone, I am wondering how best to get out of here. The front door is blocked by the deacon, who likes to talk. I find myself remembering that during the race riots here years ago I once escaped through the ducts of the air-conditioning system. Now I remember. I used St. Michael's sword to unscrew the Phillips screws of the intake grille of the air-conditioner—to escape during the riots.

One of the ladies is saying, "—and I heard that he wouldn't even come down when he had a heart attack and wouldn't let anybody come up to treat him except Dr. Gottlieb. And the only reason he let him come up was that he, Father Smith, had converted to the Jewish religion."

"Oh no," says Mrs. Saia sharply. "He's peculiar, but he wouldn't do that. I know him well—after all, he lived here. Peculiar, yes. Why, you wouldn't believe—"

Ernestine Kelly breaks in with her low-pitched but querulous voice. I can see her sweet, sad face. "I don't know about that, but I can tell you this on good authority because I know the people it happened to. Both desperate cases. One had a tumor of the womb which was diagnosed as malignant. The other, a close friend of mine, had a son working for Texaco who fell off a rig during a hurricane. After three days the Coast Guard gave up on him. Both of these people had the same impulse the same night, the exact same time, to get up and go for help from Father Smith. They did. Of course they couldn't get up the tower, so they both wrote their intentions on notes and pinned the notes to the steps of the tower. The very next day the first person's tumor had gone down—the doctors could not find a trace of it—and the other person's son was found clinging to a board—for three days and three nights."

Jan Greene snorts. "For God's sake. Like Jonah. I mean, really. Has it ever occurred to anybody that he might be up there for a much simpler, more obvious reason?" Her voice is impatient, even ill-tempered. I can see her lean forward in her chair, eyes flashing, face thrusting like a blade.

Silence, then Ernestine Kelly's injured voice: "Are you suggesting miracles cannot occur?"

"I am not. But why not look for simpler explanations?"

"Hmph. Such as."

"Such as the tumor was a fibroid and went down spontaneously—they often do. The boy's life was preserved because he hung on to the raft or whatever. And Father Smith could be staying up there for the oldest reason in the world."

122

The other women wait. Finally someone says, "What's that?"

"He could be doing vicarious penance for the awful state of the world. It is, after all, good Catholic practice," says Jan sarcastically. "The Carmelites and the Desert Fathers have been doing it for centuries. This really slays me. Here we are on the very brink of World War Three, on the brink of destruction, and nobody gives it a second thought. Well, maybe somebody is. After all, how do you think the siege of Poitiers was lifted? How do you think Lucca was saved from the Black Plague in the fourteenth century?"

Hm. Poitiers? Lucca? Nobody knows how they were saved. The Desert Fathers. The other ladies are floored. But not for long. "I still say—" tolls Ernestine, her voice a soft little bell.

Father Placide is back. "Sorry, Doc. Another dharma bum. Trying to get out to California. Looking for a handout. One more thing, Doc—"

"Look, Father," I say, lowering my voice, "I think those ladies are waiting for you to run the meeting. Hadn't you better—"

Father Placide laughs. "You kidding, *cher*?" For once he does lean close and almost whisper. "Me run that gang? I don't tell them. They tell me."

"Well—" I stand up. "I have to see Father Smith."

"Good luck, *ma fren*," says Father Placide, shaking hands, hollow-eyed but merry. "Tell Simon to phone home." He laughs. Tired as he is, he doesn't seem to bear a grudge.

"I will."

Dan—yes, that's his name—looks up from his index cards as I pass and addresses not me, it seems, but there's no one else in the hall.

"Why make it complicated?" he says, not quite to me and not quite as a question. "It's just a cop-out. There is such a thing. He quit, period. Who wouldn't like to quit and take to the woods? But somebody has to do the scut work. Some people—" he says vaguely, and goes back to spinning his Rolodex.

"Right," I say as vaguely as I close the door.

6. THE FIRE-TOWER ROAD WINDS THROUGH A LONG-leaf-pine forest to a gentle knoll perhaps fifty feet above the surrounding countryside. Beyond, fronting a meadow, stretches a spacious low building with a small central steeple, which looks stuck on, and far-flung brick wings. The building looks deserted. The meadow is overgrown. Half a dozen Holstein cows graze, all facing away from the bright afternoon sun.

There is a single metal utility shed straddled by the legs of the tower, fitted with two aluminum windows. A chimney pipe of bluish metal sticks through the roof.

Not a soul is in sight. I roll down the Caprice window and listen. There is no sound, not even cicadas. No breeze stirs the pines, which glitter in the sunlight like steel knitting needles.

Getting out, I walk backward, the better to see the tower. It is an old but sturdy structure of braced steel, perhaps a hundred feet tall. The cubicle perched on top looks like a dollhouse. One window is propped open. Shading my eyes against the sun, I yell. My voice is muffled. The air is dense and yellow as butter.

A bare hand and arm appear at the window. It is not a clear gesture. It could be a greeting or summons or nothing. I will take it that he is waving me up. I climb a dozen steep flights of green wooden steps smelling of paint. Presently the crowns of the longleafs are beside me, then below me. The heavy shook sheaves of needles, each clasping a secret yellow stamen, seem to secrete a dense vapor in which the sunlight refracts.

Thumbtacked to a post at the foot of the tower are three cards, two ordinary business cards and an old-fashioned holy picture of the Sacred Heart, each with the scribbled note: "Thanks for favors granted." On the metal upright of the tower I notice several penciled crosses, like the plus signs a child would make.

The stairs run smack into the floor of the tiny house. The trapdoor is open. Father Smith gives me a hand.

I haven't seen him in months. We were both in Alabama, he almost next door on the Gulf Coast at a place named Hope Haven for impaired priests, mostly drunks. I used to attend his Mass, not for religious reasons, but to get away from Fort Pelham, the golf course, the tin-roofed rec hall, the political arguments, and the eternal stereo-V.

He has aged. He still looks like an old Ricardo Montalban with a handsome seamed face as tanned as cordovan leather, hair like Brillo, and the same hairy *futbol* wrists. His chest is a barrel suspended by tendons in his neck. Emphysema. As he pulls me up past him, his breath has an old-man's-nose smell. But he is freshly shaven and wears a clean polo shirt, unpressed chinos, and old-fashioned sneakers.

He is different. It comes to me that the difference is that he is unsmiling and puzzled. He inclines his head to the tiny room. The gesture is not clear. It could mean make yourself at home.

Home is exactly (I find out) six feet square. He is more than six feet tall. I see a bedroll against the wall. I reckon he sleeps on the floor catercornered.

The room is furnished with a high table in the center, two chairs like barstools, in one corner a chemical toilet, and nothing more. Mounted on the table is a bronze disk azimuth, larger than a dinner plate, fitted with two sighting posts and divided into 360 degrees. The four sides of the cubicle are glass above the wainscot except for a wall space covered by a map. Hanging from the map are strings weighted by fish sinkers. Next to the map is a wall telephone.

Outside, the gently rolling terrain stretches away, covered by pines as far as the eye can see. In the slanting afternoon sun the crowns of the pines are bluish and rough as the pile of a shag rug. The countryside seems strangely silent and unpopulated except toward the south, where the condos and high-rises on the lakefront stick up like a broken picket fence.

"It's good to see you, Father." I offer my hand, but he does not seem to notice. Perhaps he regarded his pulling me up through the trapdoor as a handshake. Then I see that something is wrong with him. He is standing indecisively, fists in his pockets, brows knitted in a preoccupied expression. He does not look crazy but excessively sane, like a busy man of the world, with a thousand things on his mind, waiting for an elevator. Then suddenly he snaps his fingers softly as if he had just remembered something, seems on the very point of mentioning it, and as suddenly falls silent.

We stand so for a while. I wait for him to tell me to sit. But he's in a brown study, frowning, hands deep in pockets, making and unmaking fists. So, why not, I invite him to have a seat. He does.

We sit on the high stools opposite each other, the azimuth between us.

"Allow me to state my business, Father. Two pieces of business. Father Placide wanted to know how you were and wanted me to inquire whether you might help him out. Dr. Comeaux wanted to know whether you have decided to recommend his purchase of the buildings and property of St. Margaret's."

Again he gives every sign of understanding, seems on the point of replying, but again falls silent and gazes down at the azimuth with terrific concentration, as if he were studying a chess board.

"Father," I say presently, "I know you must be upset about the hospice closing."

Nodding agreeably, but then frowning, studying the table.

126

"I know how you feel about the Qualitarian program taking over, the pedeuthanasia, the gereuthanasia, but—"

"No no," he says suddenly, but not raising his eyes. "No no."

"No no what?"

"It wasn't that."

"Wasn't what?"

"They have their reasons. Not bad reasons, are they? They make considerable sense, wouldn't you agree? They're not bad fellows. They make some sense," he says, nodding and repeating himself several times in the careless musing voice of a bridge player studying his hand. "Well, don't they?" he asks, almost slyly, cocking his head and almost meeting my eyes.

"It could be argued," I say, studying him. "Then are you going to approve the sale to Dr. Comeaux?"

"Hm." Now he's drumming his fingers and tucking in his upper lip as if he had almost decided on his next play. "But here's the question," he says in a different, livelier voice—and then hangs fire.

"Yes?"

"Tom," he says, nodding, almost himself now, but concentrating terrifically on each word, "what would you say was wrong with a person who is otherwise in good health but who has difficulties going about his daily duties, that is—say—when he is supposed to go to a meeting, a parish-council meeting, a school-board meeting, visit the nursing home, say Mass—his feet seem to be in glue. He can hardly set one foot in front of the other, can hardly pick up the telephone, can hardly collect his thoughts, has to struggle to answer the simplest question. What would you say was wrong with such a person?"

"I'd say he was depressed."

"Hm. Yes. Depressed."

I wait for him to go on, but he doesn't.

"Were you, are you, able to say Mass?"

"Mass," he repeats, frowning mightily. "Yes," he says at last in his musing voice. "Oh yes."

"Could you preach?"

"Preach." Again the cocked head, the sly near-smile. "No no."

"No? Why not?"

"Why not? A good question. Because—it doesn't signify."

"What doesn't signify?"

"The words."

"The words of the sermon, of the Mass, don't signify?"

"That's well put, Tom," he says, not ironically. "But the action does."

"Why don't the words signify?"

"Let me ask you a question as a scientist and a student of human nature," he says, almost in his old priest-friend-colleague voice.

"Sure."

"Do you think it is possible that words could be deprived of their meaning?"

"Deprived of their meaning. What words?"

"Name it! Any words. Tom, U.S.A., God, Simon, prayer, sin, heaven, world."

"I'm afraid I don't understand the question."

"Here's the question," he says in a brisk rehearsed voice. Again, for some reason, he reminds me of a caller calling in to a radio talk show. He almost raises his eyes. "If it is a fact that words are deprived of their meaning, does it not follow that there is a depriver?"

"A depriver. I'm afraid—"

"What other explanation is there?" he asks in a rush, as if he already knew what I would say.

I always answer patients honestly. "One explanation, if I understand you correctly, is that a person can stop believing in the things the words signify."

"Ah ha," he says at once, smiling as if I had taken the bait. "But that's the point, isn't it?"

"What's the point?"

"Don't you see?" he asks in a stronger voice, eyes still lowered, but hitching closer over the azimuth.

"Not quite."

"It is not a question of belief or unbelief. Even if such things were all proved, if the existence of God, heaven, hell, sin were all proved as certainly as the distance to the sun is proved, it would make no difference, would it?"

"To whom?"

"To people! To unbelievers and to so-called believers."

"Why wouldn't it?"

"Because the words no longer signify."

"Why is that?"

"Because the words have been deprived of their meaning."

"By a depriver."

"Right. Once, everyone admits, such signs signified. Now they do not."

"How do you mean, once such signs signified?"

Again he smiles. Again it seems I have fallen into his trap. He rises, stands to one side, hands in pockets making fists. "I'll show you. Do you see that?" He nods to the horizon.

I look. There is nothing but the shaggy sea of bluish pines. My nose has started running. The air is yellow with pollen.

"Right there." He nods, hands still in pockets.

I look again. There is a straight wisp of smoke in the middle distance, as insignificant-looking as a pile of leaves burning in a gutter.

"Yes."

"As a matter of fact, would you help me report it? My hands are a bit unsteady."

Perhaps that is why he keeps his hands in his pockets, to hide a tremor.

"Sure. What do I do?"

"Line up the sights on the smoke."

I rotate the azimuth and sight along the upright posts to the wisp of smoke. "I make it eighty-two degrees."

"Very good. Wouldn't you agree that there is no question about what the smoke is a sign of?"

"Yes, I would."

"What is it a sign of?"

"Fire."

"Right!"—triumphantly. "Now would you hang up the reading?"

I turn to the wall map, which is encircled by pins like the Wheel of Fortune. I pick up a weighted string and hang it over pin number 82.

"Very good!" says the priest. He's looking over my shoulder. "Now what do we have here?"

"We have the direction of—"

"Right! We have one coordinate, don't we?"

"Yes."

"But that's not enough to locate the fire, is it?"

"No, it isn't."

"What else do we need?"

"We need another coordinate."

"All *right*! And how do you suppose we get it?"

All at once I know what he reminds me of. He's the patient priest-teacher teaching the dumb section at Holy Cross Prep.

I am willing to play dumb. "I don't know. I don't see how we can get a triangulation fix from here."

"And you're right! So we need a little help, don't we? So—" He picks up the wall phone and dials a number. "Emmy," he says in a different voice, "give me a reading on that brush job in 5-9. Okay, Blondie, I read. How goes it in Waldheim? All *right*. That's a fiver-niner. You call it in. Over."

He speaks easily, good-humoredly. No, he's not a priest-teacher. He's a ham operator, one of those fellows who are shy up close but chummy-technical with a stranger in Bangkok.

He turns to me. "Her reading is 2-9-2. She's in the Waldheim tower." He shows me a pin. "Here. Now, what are you going to do about it?"

I pick up the string and the Waldheim sinker and hang it over pin 292. The weighted strings intersect at a crossroad on the map. The priest, I can see, is pleased by the elegance of the tight intersected strings. So am I.

The priest is pushing one fist into the other hand, hard, taking turns. I realize he is doing isometric exercises. Now he is pulling against interlocked fingers.

"We know what the smoke is a sign of. We have located the sign," he says between pushes and pulls. "Now we are going to act accordingly. That's a sign for you. Unlike word signs."

"Right." I look at my watch. I'm afraid he's going to get going on the Germans. "It's good to see you, Father, but I have an appointment. Do you wish me to tell Father Placide or Dr. Comeaux anything?"

"Sure," says the priest, who is back in his place across the azimuth. "Now here is the question." There's a lively light in his eye. He's out to catch me again. He has the super-sane chipperness of the true nut.

"Can you name one word sign which has not been evacuated of meaning, that is, deprived?"

"I don't think I can. As a matter of fact, I'm afraid that—" Again I look at my watch.

Two things have become clear to me in the last few seconds.

One thing is that Father Smith has gone batty, but batty in a way I recognize. He belongs to that category of nut who can do his job competently enough, quite well in fact, but given one minute of free time latches on to an obsession like a tongue seeking a sore tooth. He called in the forest fire like a pro, but now he's back at me with a mad chipper light in his eye.

The second thing is that I promised Father Placide to make an "evaluation" of Father Smith's mental condition. Can he do priestly work?

No, three things.

The third thing is that all at once I want badly to get out of here and see Lucy Lipscomb.

"Can you name the one word sign," Father Smith asks

131

me, leaning close over the azimuth, "that has not been evacuated of meaning, that is, deprived by a depriver?"

"I'm not sure what the question means. Later perhaps—"

"Will you allow me to demonstrate," says the priest triumphantly, as if he had already demonstrated.

"Of course," I say with fake psychiatric cordiality.

"The signs out there"—he nods to the shaggy forest—"refer to something, don't they?"

"Right."

"The smoke was a sign of fire."

"That is correct."

"There is no doubt about the existence of the fire."

"True."

"Words are signs, aren't they?"

"You could say so."

"But unlike the signs out there, words have been evacuated, haven't they?"

"Evacuated?"

"They don't signify anymore."

"How do you mean?" From long practice I can keep my
voice attentive without paying close attention. I wonder if
Lucy—

"What if I were to turn the tables on you, ha ha, and play
the psychoanalyst?"

"Very good," I say gloomily.

"You psychoanalysts encourage your patients to practice
free association with words, true?"

"Yes." Actually it's not true.

"Let me turn the tables on you and give you a couple of
word signs and you give me your free associations."

"Fine."

"Clouds."

"Sky, fleecy, puffy, floating, white—"

"Okay. Irish."

"Bogs, Notre Dame, Pat O'Brien, begorra—"

"Okay. Blacks."

"Blacks?"

"Negroes."

"Blacks, Africa, niggers, minority, civil rights—"

"Okay. Jew."

"Israel, Bible, Max, Sam, Julius, Hebrew, Hebe, Ben—"

"Right! You see!" He is smiling and nodding and making fists in his pockets. I realize that he is doing isometrics in his pockets.

"See what?"

"Jews!"

"What about Jews?" I say after a moment.

"Precisely!"

"Precisely what?"

"What do you mean?"

"What about Jews?"

"What do you think about Jews?" he asks, cocking an eye.

"Nothing much one way or the other."

"May I continue my demonstration, Doctor?"

"For one minute." I look at my watch, but he doesn't seem to notice.

"May I ask who Max, Sam, Julius, and Ben are?"

"Max Gottlieb is my closest friend and personal physician. Sam Aaronson was my roommate in medical school. Julius Freund was my training analyst at Hopkins. Ben Solomon was my fellow detainee and cellmate at Fort Pelham, Alabama."

"Very interesting."

"How's that?"

"Don't you see?"

"No."

"Unlike the other test words, what you associated with the word *Jew* was Jews, Jews you have known. Isn't that interesting?"

"Yes," I say, pursing my mouth in a show of interest.

"What you associated with the word sign *Irish* were certain connotations, stereotypical Irish stuff in your head. Same for Negro. If I had said Spanish, you'd have said something like guitar, castanets, bullfights, and such. I have done the test on dozens. Thus, these word signs have been evacuated, deprived of meaning something real. Real persons. Not so with Jews.''

"So?"

He's feeling so much better that he's doing foot exercises, balancing on the ball of one foot, then the other. Now, to my astonishment, he is doing a bit of shadowboxing, weaving and throwing a few punches.

"That's the only sign of God which has not been evacuated by an evacuator," he says, moving his shoulders.

"What sign is that?"

"Jews."

"Jews?"

"You got it, Doc." He sits, gives the azimuth a spin like a croupier who has raked in all the chips.

"Got what?"

"You see the point."

"What's the point?"

He leans close, eyes alight, "The Jews—cannot—be—subsumed.''

"Can't be what?"

"Subsumed."

"I see."

"Since the Jews were the original chosen people of God, a tribe of people who are still here, they are a sign of God's presence which cannot be evacuated. Try to find a hole in that proof!''

I try—that is, I act as if I am trying.

"You can't find a hole, can you?" he says triumphantly.

"But, Father, the Jews I know are not religious. They either do not believe in God or, like me, they don't attach any significance beyond—"

"Precisely!"

"Precisely?"

"Precisely. *Probatur conclusio*, as St. Thomas would say." He seems to have finished.

"Right," I say, reaching for the rung of the trapdoor. I think I know what to tell Father Placide.

"Hold it!" He waves an arm out to the wide world. "Name one other thing out there which cannot be subsumed."

"I can't."

"Pine tree?"

"How do you mean, pine tree?"

"That pine tree can be subsumed under the classes of trees called conifers, right?"

"Right."

"Try to subsume Jews under the classes of mankind, Caucasians, Semites, whatever. Go ahead, try it."

"Excuse me, Father, but I really—"

"Do your friends still consider themselves Jews?"

"Yes."

"You see. It does not matter whether they believe. Believe or not, they are still Jews. And what are Jews if not the actual people originally chosen by God?"

"Excuse me, Father, but is it not also part of Christian belief that the Jews did not accept Jesus as the Messiah and that therefore—"

"Makes no difference!" exclaims the priest, throwing a punch as if this were the very objection he had been waiting for.

"It doesn't?"

"Read St. Paul! It is clear that their inability to accept Jesus was not only foreordained but altogether reasonable and is not to be held against them. Salvation comes from the Jews, as holy scripture tells us. They remain the beloved, originally chosen people of God."

"Right. Now I—"

"It is also psychologically provable."

"It is?"

"Jews are naturally skeptical, hardheaded, and, after all, what Jesus was proposing to them was a tall order."

"Yes. Well—" He's standing on the trapdoor and I can't lift it until he gets off.

"What do you think Peres would say if Begin claimed to be the Messiah?"

I have to laugh.

"No no." The priest hunches forward, almost clearing the trapdoor. "You're missing the point."

"I am?"

"How many times in your work have you encountered someone who claims to be Napoleon, the Messiah, Hitler, the Devil?"

"Often."

"How often have you encountered a Jewish patient who claimed to be the Messiah or Napoleon?"

"Not often."

"You see?"

"Yes."

"No, you don't."

"I don't?"

"You still don't see the bottom line psychologically speaking?" My nose has started running seriously. He is standing on the trapdoor and my nose is dripping.

"One, a Jew will not believe another Jew making such a preposterous claim, right? But—But—!" Now he has come to the bottom line sure enough. For he has stopped doing isometrics and throwing punches and has instead placed both hands on the azimuth and lined me up in the sights. He speaks in a low intense voice, pausing between each word. "Is it not the case, Doctor, that if a Jew speaks to a Gentile, speaks with authority, with sobriety, as a friend—*the Gentile—will—believe—him!* Think about it!" He has leaned over so close I can see the white fiber, the arcus senilis, around his pupil.

I give every appearance of thinking about it.

"Even an anti-Semite! Did you ever notice that an anti-Semite who despises Jews actually believes them deep down—that's why he hates them!—and isn't that the reason he despises them?"

I eye him curiously. "May I ask you something, Father?"

"Fire away."

"Do you still regard yourself as a Catholic priest?"

For the first time he seems surprised. He stops his isometrics, cocks his head. "How do you mean, Tom?"

"Why are you?"

"Why am I what? Oh. You mean why am I a Catholic— Tom, may I ask you a question?"

"Sure."

"Do you remember what a sacrament is?"

I smile. "A sensible sign instituted by Christ to produce grace. I can still rattle it off."

The priest laughs. "Those sisters did a job on us, didn't they?"

"Yes. Maybe too good."

"What? Oh. Yes, yes. Do you remember the scriptural example they always gave?"

"Sure. Unless you eat my body and drink my blood, you will not have life in you."

"Same one!" says the priest, again laughing, then falls to musing. "Life," he murmurs absently and under his breath. "Life. But that's the trouble, the words—"

"What's that?" I ask the priest, wondering if he's still talking to me.

"Oh," he says, giving a start. "I'm sorry. To answer your question—" He frowns mightily.

What question?

"Are you forgetting about the ancient Romans?"

The ancient Romans. My nose is running badly. I have to go.

"Aren't you forgetting that the ancient Romans, who were, after all, not stupid people and were right about most things though not very creative, were also right about us."

"I suppose I had forgotten."

"The historians say they mistook us for a Jewish sect, didn't they?"

"Sure."

"Was it a mistake?"

Now he's clear of the trapdoor. I give the rung a yank.

"The Jews as a word sign cannot be assimilated under a class, category, or theory. No subsuming Jews! Not even by the Romans."

"Right." I yank again. What's wrong with this damn thing?

"No subsuming Jews, Tom!"

"Okay, I won't."

"This offends people, even the most talented people, people of the loftiest sentiments, the highest scientific achievements, and the purest humanitarian ideals."

"Right."

"You have to turn it," he says, noticing my efforts to open the trapdoor.

"Thank you." No, that doesn't work either.

"The Holocaust was a consequence of the sign which could not be evacuated."

"Right."

"Who remembers the Ukrainians?"

"True."

"Let me tell you something, Tom. People have the wrong idea about the Holocaust. The Holocaust, as people see it, is a myth."

Oh my. My heart sinks. On top of everything else, is he one of those? I try harder to open the damn door.

While he is talking, he has taken hold of my arm.

I remove his hand. "Goodbye, Father."

"What's the matter Tom?"

"Are you telling me that the Nazis did not kill six million Jews?"

"No."

"They did kill six million Jews."

"Yes."

"Then what are you saying?"

"What I'm trying to tell you is that the origins of the Holocaust are a myth—"

"Never mind. I'm leaving."

"Very well. What are you going to tell Father Placide and Dr. Comeaux?"

"I am going to tell Father Placide that you are too disturbed to be of any use to him at St. Michael's. I am going to tell Dr. Comeaux that you are also too disturbed to operate the hospice and that I hope you will sell it to him. Now will you let me out of here?"

"I appreciate your frankness," says the priest, nodding vigorously, hands making and unmaking fists in his pockets. "Shall I be frank with you?"

"Sure, if you'll open this damn door."

"I will. But please allow me to tell you something about yourself for your own good."

"Please do."

"You are an able psychiatrist, on the whole a decent, generous, humanitarian person in the abstract sense of the word. You know what is going to happen to you?"

"What?"

"You are a member of the first generation of doctors in the history of medicine to turn their backs on the oath of Hippocrates and kill millions of old useless people, unborn children, born malformed children, for the good of mankind—and to do so without a single murmur from one of you. Not a single letter of protest in the august *New England Journal of Medicine*. And do you know what you're going to end up doing? You a graduate of Harvard and a reader of *The New York Times* and a member of the Ford Foundation's Program for the Third World? Do you know what is going to happen to you?"

"No," I say, relieved to be on a footing of simple hostility, "—even though I did not graduate from Harvard, do not read *The New York Times*, and do not belong to the Ford Foundation."

The priest aims the azimuth at me, but then appears to lose his train of thought. Again his preoccupied frown comes back.

"What is going to happen to me, Father?" I ask before he gets away altogether.

"Oh," he says absently, appearing to be thinking of something else, "you're going to end up killing Jews."

139

"Okay," I say. Somehow I knew he was going to say this.

Somehow also he knows that we've finished with each other. He reaches for the trapdoor, turns the rung. "Give my love to Ellen and the kids."

"Sure."

At the very moment of his touching the rung, there is a tapping on the door from below. The door lifts against his hand.

"That's Milton," says Father Smith in his workaday ham-operator voice and lifts the door.

A head of close-cropped iron-gray hair pops up through the opening and a man springs into the room.

To my astonishment the priest pays no attention to the new arrival, even though the three of us are now as close as three men in a small elevator. He takes my arm again.

"Yes, Father?"

"Even if you were a combination of Edward R. Murrow, Walter Cronkite, and Charles Kuralt rolled into one—no, *especially* if you were those guys—"

"As a matter of fact, I happen to know Charlie Kuralt, and there is not a sweeter guy, a more tenderhearted person—"

"Right," says the priest ironically, still paying not the slightest attention to the stranger, and then, with his sly expression, asks, "Do you know where tenderness always leads?"

"No, where?" I ask, watching the stranger with curiosity.

"To the gas chamber."

"I see."

"Tenderness is the first disguise of the murderer."

"Right."

The stranger has sprung up through the opening with no assistance, even though he's carrying a plastic pail of water in one hand and an A&P shopping bag in the other. Evidently he's used to doing this.

"Well—" I say, stepping down. We needn't shake hands.

"Here's the final word," says the priest, taking hold of my arm.

"Good," I say.

Now we three are standing facing in the same direction, the stranger evidently waiting for me to leave, not even having room to set down pail and shopping bag.

"If you are a lover of Mankind in the abstract like Walt Whitman, who wished the best for Mankind, you will probably do no harm and might even write good poetry and give pleasure, right?"

"Right."

"If you are a theorist of Mankind like Rousseau or Skinner, who believes he understands man's brain and in the solitariness of his study or laboratory writes books on the subject, you are also probably harmless and might even contribute to human knowledge, right?"

"Right."

"But if you put the two together, a lover of Mankind and a theorist of Mankind, what you've got now is Robespierre or Stalin or Hitler and the Terror, and millions dead for the good of Mankind. Right?"

"Right," I say indifferently.

Now the stranger places the pail in a corner and lines up items from the bag on the table next to the azimuth: two bars of soap, a pack of small Hefty bags, a double roll of Charmin toilet paper, three large boxes of Sunkist raisins, half a dozen cans of food, including, I notice, Vienna sausage and Bartlett pears.

The priest introduces me. "Dr. Thomas More, this is Milton Guidry, my indispensable friend and assistant. He keeps me in business, brings me the essentials, removes wastes, serves Mass. Unlike me, he is able to live a normal life down there in the world. He used to run the hospice almost single-handedly, plus milk the cows. He still milks the cows. Now he works as a janitor at the A&P. Between his small salary there and my small salary from the forestry service and selling the milk, we make out very well, don't we, Milton?"

The newcomer nods cheerfully and stands almost at attention, as if waiting for an order. Milton Guidry is a very thin but wiry man of an uncertain age. He could be a young-looking middle-aged man or a gray-haired young man. His face is unlined. His neat flat-top crewcut, squared at the temples, frames his octagonal rimless glasses, which flash in the sun. The bare spot at the top of his head could be the result of a beginning of balding or a too-close haircut. He wears a striped, long-sleeved shirt and a bow tie—he could have bought both at the A&P—neatly pressed jeans, and pull-on canvas shoes. He is of a type once found in many rectories who are pleased to hang around and help the priest. In another time, I suppose, he would be called a sacristan. He listens intently while the priest gives him instructions. It does not seem to strike him as in the least unusual that Father Smith is perched atop a hundred-foot tower in the middle of nowhere and giving him complicated instructions about getting cruets, hosts, and wine. This, Milton's attentive attitude seems to say, is what Father does.

"Do you say Mass here?" I ask the priest. We stand at close quarters, our eyes squinted against the sun now blazing in the west.

"Oh yes. Every morning at six. And Milton has not been late yet, have you, Milton?"

Milton nods seriously, hands at his sides. "It is easy," Milton explains to me, "because I have an alarm clock and I live in the shed below." He points to the floor. "I set the alarm for five-thirty."

"I see."

"I used to set my alarm for five-forty-five, but I felt rushed. I like to give myself time."

"I see." I really have to get out of here.

"Milton has to work mornings next week," says the priest, eyeing me. "Would you like to assist?"

"No thanks."

The priest seems not to mind. In the best of humors now, he holds the trapdoor open for me and again sends his love to Ellen and the children.

"Tom," he says, holding the door in one hand and shaking my hand with the other, "take care of yourself."

"I will."

"Let me say this, Tom," he says in a low voice, not letting go of my hand, pulling me close.

"What?"

"I think you're on to something extremely important. I know more than you think."

I look at him. The white fiber around his pupils seems to be spinning.

"I have great confidence in you, Tom. I shall pray for you."

"Thanks." I am working my hand free.

"Did I ever tell you that I had spent a year in Germany before the war in the household of an eminent psychiatrist whose son was a colonel in the Schutzstaffel?"

"Yes, you did. Goodbye, Father."

"Last night I dreamed of lying in bed in Tübingen and listening to church bells. German church bells make a high-pitched, silvery sound."

"Goodbye, Father."

"Goodbye, Tom." He lets go. Both he and Milton stand clear. They are smiling and nodding cheerfully. "There are dangers down there, Tom, you may not be aware of. Be careful."

"I will," I say, stepping down, wanting only to be on my way.

III

1. OUT OLD I-12 AND INTO THE SUN TOWARD BATON Rouge and the river. A short hop, but the old interstate, broken and rough as it is, is nevertheless clogged with truckers of all kinds, great triple tandems and twenty-six-wheelers thundering along at eighty who like nothing better than terrorizing private cars like my ancient Caprice. There are many hitchhikers, mostly black and Hispanic. The rest stops are crowded by pitched tents, seedy Winnebagos, and Michigan jalopies heading west from the cold smokestacks and the dried-up oil wells.

I fancy I catch sight of the Cox Cable van, but he is ahead of me, so how could he be following? But just in case. Just in case, I squeeze in between two tandems in the right lane, duck past the trucker and into an exit so fast that he gives me the bird and an angry air-horn blast.

Take to the blue highways, skirting Baton Rouge and the deserted Exxon and Ethyl refineries, picking my way through a wasted countryside of tank farms, chemical dumps, befouled bayous. The flat delta land becomes ever greener with a pitch-dark green as if the swamp grass had been nourished by oil slicks. The air smells like a crankcase.

Upriver and into West Feliciana, the first low loess bluffs of St. Francisville, and into the pleasant deciduous hills where Audubon lived with rich English planters, painted the birds, and taught dancing for a living. Out of the hills and back toward the river and Grand Mer, the great widening of the river into a gulf where the English landed with their slaves from the Indies, took up indigo farming, and lived the happy life of Feliciana, free of the seditious Americans to the north, the corrupt French to the south, and in the end free even to get rid of the indolent Spanish and form their own republic.

Down to the old river and the great house, Pantherburn, once on Grand Mer itself, left high and dry by one of the twists and turns of the river now some miles to the west, leaving behind not a worn-out plantation but a fecund bottomland, Lucy's two thousand acres of soybeans, straight clean rows now in full leaf gray-green as new money. A tractor pulling a silver tank trails a rooster tail of dust. The tractor stops. The driver dismounts and picks up one end of the tank.

The alley of great oaks which used to run from house to landing now ends in the middle of a field. The first house inside the gate is not Pantherburn but a new mobile home propped on cinder blocks and fenced by white plastic pickets. A Ford Galaxy, older than my Caprice, is parked under a chinaberry tree.

Pantherburn is a graceful box, a perfect cube flanked all around by wide galleries and Doric columns. Some colonial architect knew what he was doing. The plastered columns, as thick as oak trunks, are worn to the pink of the bricks and from a distance look as rosy as stick candy. The siding is unpainted, silvery lapped cypress. The house, lived in by Lipscombs for two hundred years, looks hard used but serviceable. It has not been restored like the showplaces on the River Road. An old-fashioned Sears chest freezer, big enough to hold a steer, hums away on the side gallery.

Inside, the house is simple and not large. The great galleries and columns give it its loom and spread. There are four rooms downstairs and up, divided by a hall as wide as a dogtrot.

Lucy and her uncle are waiting for me on the lower gallery, Lucy is in shirt-sleeves and jeans, hands in pockets, eyeing me, lip tucked. She reaches up and gives me a hug and, to my surprise, a frank kiss on the mouth. What a splendid, by no means small, woman. Again the smell of her cotton gives me a *déjà vu*. I know if I choose to know, but don't of course, what will happen next. And yet I do.

The uncle shakes hands, giving one pump country-fashion, not meeting my eye, and stands off a ways, snapping his fingers and socking fist into hand. He is silent but agreeable. His face is as narrow and brown as a piece of slab bark. He wears an old duck-hunting cap and a loose bloodstained camouflage army jacket, with special pockets for shells and game. The cap is folded like a little tent on his narrow head.

We stroll around the front yard and to the back, which contains a tiny graveyard. The sun has reached the trees. It is cooler. Lucy walks like a housewife going abroad, arms folded, stooping with each step. The uncle keeps up, but in a flanking position, some twenty feet away. His old liver-and-white pointer, Maggie, follows at his heel, her nose covered with warts, nuzzling him when he stops, burrowing under his hand. He talks, I think, to us. He speaks of his bird boxes and points them out. "Ain't been a bluebird in these parts for forty years. I got six pair this summer. I got me twenty pair of wood ducks down in the flats. You want to see them?"

"Sure," I say.

"Not now, Uncle," says Lucy, stooping over her folded arms as she walks.

The uncle, flanking, keeps talking, paying no attention to Lucy nor she to him. "Most folks don't know how the ducklings get out of the boxes twenty feet high. Some say they climb down the bark using a special toenail. Some say mamma duck helps them down. Not so. I saw them. You know what those little sapsuckers do? They climb out of the hole and fall, flat fall out and hit the ground *pow*, bounce like a rubber ball, and head for the water."

The graveyard is a tiny enclosure, fenced by rusty iron spikes and chest-high in weeds. "I can't cut in there with a tractor, so it doesn't get cut," says Lucy.

"I heard they used to cut it with scissors," says the uncle.

"Did you know once there were forty people here not counting field people?" By "they" and "people," he means slaves.

Lucy, paying no attention, shows me the grave of our common ancestor, an English army officer on the wrong side of the Revolution. It is a blackened granite block surmounted by an angel holding an urn.

"Do you remember that in his will he left his daughter, who was thirteen, an eleven-year-old mulatto girl named Laura for her personal use." Lucy jostles me. "I wish somebody would leave me one."

"You seem to be doing fine."

"He suffered spells of terrible melancholy and harbored the delusion that certain unnamed enemies were after him, all around him, coming down the river and up the river to put an end to the happy life in Feliciana."

"It was probably the Americans."

"We come from a melancholy family. Are you melancholy?" she asks. "No, you don't look melancholy; me either." I notice that her cheeks are flushed. "He married a beautiful American girl half his age, only to have his first, English wife show up. Both women lived here at Pantherburn for a while." Lucy gives me a sideways look.

"No wonder he jumped in the river. Which wife are we descended from?" I ask her.

"I'm from the English, the legitimate side; you from the American."

"Then we're not close kin."

"Hardly kin at all. I'm glad," says Lucy.

We are walking again, the uncle in his outrider position. "I got me a pair of woodies right there," he says, shaking two loose fingers toward the woods. "You ought to see that little sucker fly into the hole."

"I'd like to."

"They've long since left the boxes, Uncle," says Lucy wearily.

"Do you know how he does that? Some people say he lights on the edge and goes in, but no. He flies in. I saw him. I'm talking about, he flies right in that hole. Do you know how he does it?''

Lucy, stooping and walking, is paying no attention.

"No, I don't," I say.

"He's only got about a foot of room inside, right?"

"Right."

"You know what he does—I saw him."

"No."

"That sucker flies right in and brakes in the one foot of room inside, like this," says the uncle, suddenly flaring out his elbows like braking wings. "I've seen him! You want to see him? Let's go."

"All right."

"Not now, Uncle," says Lucy.

2. LUCY AND I SIT ON THE GALLERY WATCHING THE SUN go down across the levee through the oaks of the alley, making winks and gleams and casting long shafts of foggy yellow light. She smokes too much, long Picayunes, often plucks a tobacco grain from the tip of her tongue, looks at it.

Lucy fixes toddies of nearly straight bourbon in crystal goblets the size of a mason jar. My nose is running. Perhaps the toddies will help. I haven't had a toddy for years. An eighteenth-century traveler once wrote of Feliciana and Pantherburn: "There is always at one's elbow a smiling retainer ready with a toddy or a comfit." What's a comfit?

Beyond the oaks, the truncated cone of the Grand Mer facility rises as insubstantial as a cloud in the sunset. A pennant of vapor is fastened to its summit like the cloud on Everest.

We sit in rocking chairs.

"Well now," I say after a long drink of the strong, sweet bourbon. My nose stops running.

"Yes indeed," says Lucy.

A duck is calling overhead.

"Is that the uncle?"

"Yes."

Footsteps go back and forth on the upper gallery. The quacking is followed by a chuckling sound.

"Is he talking to somebody?"

"No, he's practicing his duck calls. He was runner-up in the Arkansas nationals last year. That's the feeding call he's doing now. He does it with his fingers. He's been doing it six hours a day since January."

"I see." I take another long pull. The bourbon is so good it doesn't need sugar. "I was wondering why you wanted me to come."

"I want you to stay here while Ellen's gone. It's all right with Ellen. I asked her."

I look at her quickly. Is she trying to tell me something? She is. She rocks forward in her chair to look back at me, shading her eyes against the sun. "What if I were to tell you that it is absolutely all right for you to be here? Would you take that on faith without further explanation?"

"No."

"Do you want me to explain further?"

"No."

She looks at me along her cheek, eyes hooded.

I take another drink. "I appreciate it, but I'm fine. Hudeen's taking good care of me."

"Not as good as I could."

"I'm sure of that."

"No, I'm also selfish. Just now I think I can help you with your syndrome. I have an idea about it. And just now I also need you. You're my only relative besides him"—her eyes go up—"and he's driving me nuts. He needs you too. It's all right for you to stay. Vergil thought you were my father."

"Vergil?"

"You remember Vergil. He's my only help on the farm, he and Carrie, his mother. You remember him. He remembers you.

149

He drives the tractor, does everything. Unfortunately, I have to pay him a fortune. Nobody gave him to me. Will you stay?"

"You mean tonight or—?"

"Speak of the devil."

Vergil has come onto the gallery behind us.

I had known him as a child, but do not recognize him. His father, laid up in a mobile home by the gate and living on the Medicaid Lucy got him, I remember as a hale, golden-skinned Ezio Pinza, fisherman and trapper, hearty and big-chested, too big—he had emphysema even then. They, the Bons, are known hereabouts as freejacks, meaning free persons of color, freed, the story goes, by Andrew Jackson for services rendered in the Battle of New Orleans. More likely, they're simply descendants of the quadroons and octoroons of New Orleans. A proud and reticent people, often blue-eyed and whiter than white, many could "pass" if they chose but mainly choose not to, choose, rather, to stay put in small contained bayou communities.

Vergil Bon, Jr., is another cup of tea. He's got the off-white skin, black eyes, and straight black Indian hair of his mother, but he wears, somewhat oddly, a Tom Selleck mustache. His body is rounded, drawn in simple lines, as if he still had his baby fat, but he's very strong. It was his large simple arm I saw lifting the silver tractor tank. When we shake hands, he smiles but doesn't look at me. His hand is large and inert. He thinks he's being polite by not squeezing. He speaks softly to Lucy, shows her a greasy machine part. Lucy says, "You can? Okay, fix it and I'll get a new one tomorrow. Write down what it is.

"He can fix anything," Lucy tells me when he's gone. "I pay him a fortune, but he's worth it. Do you know he's going to finish up at L.S.U. next semester with two degrees in geology and chemical engineering? He worked on the rigs for years, made toolpusher at age twenty-three, at four thousand a month. He's thirty-five now and is going to end up owning Texaco. He helps me as a favor. I take care of his father. How about it?"

"How about what?"

"Staying."

"I'll stay tonight. As a matter of fact, I need your help."

"With your syndrome?"

"It's not mine. I think I'm on to something. But you're going to have to tell me whether I'm as crazy as our ancestor. Furthermore, you're an epidemiologist and this is up your alley. You saw what I found in Mickey LaFaye's case."

"Yes," says Lucy solemnly. "I don't think you're crazy. I saw Mrs. LaFaye. You've got something. Perhaps we could help each other. Did you bring a list of patients with their social security numbers?"

"Yes. Why do you need them?"

"You'll see. I've got a little surprise for you. A couple, in fact."

Half the toddy is gone. She is drinking with me, drink for drink, and shows no sign of it, save perhaps a widening of the pupils in her dark gold-flecked eyes. But that could be because the sun is behind the levee and no longer in our eyes. The sweet strong bourbon seems to fork in my throat, branching up the back of my head and sending a warm probe into my heart.

"Ahem," I say.

"Yes indeed," says Lucy, smiling.

"Tell me—ah—about the syndrome," says Lucy, pulling up close.

"Yes, certainly." I do, at length, all I know, and with the pleasure of telling her and of her close listening, head cocked, tapping her lips with two fingers, brown gold-flecked eyes fixed on me above plum-bruised cheeks. It is a pleasure telling her, talking easily, she listening, smoking, and plucking tobacco grains from her tongue, we ducking our heads just enough to set the rockers rocking. I take an hour. She fixes us another toddy. She drinks like a man and shows no sign of it except in her eyes. Her eyes change like the sunlight, now lively A-plus smart-doctor's eyes, now a woman's eyes. Beyond peradventure a woman's eyes. Above us the uncle is calling the ducks home for feeding and now and then gives a high-ball, a loud drake's honk. We don't mind.

It is dusk dark. In the west a red light, probably atop the Grand Mer cooling tower, blinks in the mauve sky.

When I finish, Lucy stops rocking and watches me for a long time, fingers on her lips. She puts her hand lightly on my arm.

"I'll tell you what. Here's what we're going to do. Let's go have supper. I brought some Popeyes fried chicken and Carrie cooked us some of her own greens. Then I want to show you something upstairs. What do you say?"

"Yes, certainly."

"By the way."

"Yes?"

"Do you know what Blue Boy means?"

"Blue Boy? No."

"I heard someone at the Fedville hospital talking to Van Dorn about Blue Boy. I wasn't supposed to hear. He looked annoyed."

We finish our toddies and go inside. The old house is dim and cool. There is a smell in the hall as wrenching as memory, of last winter, a hundred winters, wet dogs, Octagon soap, scoured wood. The weak light in the crystal chandelier is lost in the darkness above. The uncle appears from nowhere, flanking us, slides back the twelve-foot-high doors. Light winks on the silver inset handles polished by two hundred years of use.

"Is it true, Uncle," I ask him, "that all the hardware of the doors, even the hinges, are silver?"

"That's true. The Yankees were too dumb to notice. They stole everything else, but missed the silver. You see those handles?"

"Yes."

"Not a white hand touched those handles until the war."

"Is that so?"

"That's so. All you had to do was walk to a door and it would open; go through and it would close."

"Is that right?"

"The people around here were thick as fleas."

Lucy makes a sound in her throat.

"You can't hardly get one of them to do anything these days," says the uncle.

We eat at one end of the long table in the dark dining room,

152

taking fried chicken from the Popeyes bags. There is a pitcher of buttermilk, cornbread, and a tub of unsalted butter. The greens are thick and tender and strong as meat. The one light bulb winks red and violet in the beveled crystal of the chandelier. Dark paintings the size of a barn door are propped against the walls. They seem to be landscapes and bonneted French ladies swinging in a formal garden. They've been propped there since the war, too heavy to hang from the weakened molding. They must have been too big for the Yankees to steal.

I ask the uncle about different duck calls. Lucy makes a sound in her throat. He begins to tell me, but she interrupts him.

"You can have Dupre's room," says Lucy. "I cleaned all his stuff out."

"Fine."

"He had his own room here his last year here," she adds without looking at me.

"I see."

"Do you know who slept in that room?" asks the uncle.

"No."

"General Earl Van Dorn."

"Is that right?"

"That's right. You knew he was from Mississippi—right up the river. One of our people. You know what he did, don't you?"

"What?"

"After those frogs in New Orleans and those coonasses in Baton Rouge gave up without a fight, the Yankees occupied this place. Beast Butler made his headquarters right here. Buck Van Dorn came in with the Second Cavalry from Texas and ran them off. He stayed here until they ordered him to Arkansas. He slept in that room. He was a fighting fool and the women were crazy about him. Miss Bett's grandma, the one they called Aunt Bett, like to have run off with him."

"That's a lot of foolishness," says Lucy absently. "Come on upstairs, I have something to show you," says Lucy, and leaves abruptly.

But the uncle leans close and won't let me go.

"You know what they're always saying about war being hell?" he asks.

"Yes."

He leans closer. "That's a lot of horseshit."

"Is that right?"

"Let me tell you something. I never had a better time in my life than in World War Two. When I was at Fort Benning I lived for six months in a trailer with the sweetest little woman in south Georgia. She was an armful of heaven. When I was at Fort Sill, I had two women, one a full-blooded Indian, a real wildcat. She like to have clawed me to death. Do you know who were the finest soldiers in the history of warfare?"

"No."

"The Roman legionnaire, the Confederate, and the German. I read up on it. The Germans were like us. They beat the shit out of us at Kasserine. Don't tell me, I was there. We shouldn't have been fighting them. Patton gave me a field commission. I made colonel by the time we got to Trier. When I was at Trier I lived with a German girl for three weeks. They were putting out for anything you'd give them, but she was crazy about me. A fine woman! But Patton was a fighting fool. We whipped the Germans in the end, but it was because they'd rather us than the Russians. Patton took seven hundred thousand prisoners. I was in the 3d Armored Division of the Third Army. He wanted to take Berlin and Prague and drive to the Oder—the Germans would have helped us—but Roosevelt wouldn't turn us loose. That son of a bitch Patton was a fighting fool. We could have gone to the Volga."

"Tom!" Lucy calls angrily from the dim hall.

"If Roosevelt hadn't stopped us, we'd have gone to the Volga and wouldn't be in the mess we're in now. We were fighting the wrong people."

"Tom!"

Lucy takes me upstairs.

"How much of that was true?" I ask her.

"What? Oh, God, I don't know. Very little. I stopped listening ten years ago. He made himself a colonel last year. But if I have to listen to that damn duck call another day, and then about Rommel and Patton and Buck Van Dorn another night, I'm going to shoot him. I'm so glad you're here! Do you know what he's done in the fifty years since that war?"

"No."

"Nothing. I mean nothing. But shoot birds and animals and blow that duck call. The only thing he's learned in fifty years is how to do it with your fingers."

Upstairs in the hall Lucy hands me a pair of folded blue jeans, a light flannel L. L. Bean shirt, and pajamas. They're new. The pajamas are still pinned.

"I got these for Uncle Hugh, but they're too big." For some reason she blushes.

"Thank you."

"Get out of that smelly suit," she says brusquely, gives the lapel a yank. "I'm going to burn it."

There are four rooms upstairs and a wide hall, arranged exactly as below.

"You stay in here. Did you bring anything?"

"No."

"I thought so. Tch." She seizes my coat again between thumb and forefinger, gives it a hard tweak, brushes it back like somebody's mamma. "Look at you. You look like a jailbird. Thin as a rake. I'll fatten you up." She begins to close the door. "You knock on my door right there in exactly fifteen minutes. That's my office."

"All right."

The door closes. The room is empty of everything but a bed and an armoire, which is empty. Buddy Dupre has been cleaned out, all right.

I take a shower and put on my new jeans and Bean shirt. In exactly fifteen minutes I knock on her door. "Come in!" comes her cool hospital voice.

I blink at the fluorescent light. The room could be an office in Fedville. There are desks, data processors, terminals, keyboards, screens, cables, shelves of medical texts and journals, cabinets of discs and cassettes, the whole as brilliantly lit as a laboratory.

We sit side by side at a large particle-board table bare except for a keyboard, screen, black box, telephone.

"How do you like it?"

"It looks expensive."

"It is, but it's mostly federal equipment. As their epidemiologist I rate a terminal."

"Does that mean you're hooked up to—"

"Everything. All networks. To CDC in Atlanta, NIH in D.C., Bureau of the Census, State Department of Health in Baton Rouge, AT & T, GM, Joe Blow, you name it."

"I see."

The fluorescent light is unsuitable. I wish we were having a drink on the gallery.

"I think we have a lead."

"What's that?"

Lucy pushes a button. The room goes dusk dark.

"Well," I say.

"We have to wait for our eyes. We have to read the screens."

"All right."

She has both hands on my arm. "You want to know something?"

"Yes."

"I think you're on to something."

"I see."

"And I think we have a lead."

"Good."

"Okay. Let's boot up."

"Okay. What's the lead?"

"Correct me, but aren't the symptoms you describe in your syndrome similar to the findings in your paper about the heavy-sodium accident at Tulane years ago?"

"Somewhat. I've thought of that, but—"

"Do you think your syndrome could be a form of heavy-sodium intoxication?"

"It had occurred to me, but there's been no accident, no yellow cloud—"

"Did you know that thing over there"—she nods toward Grand Mer—"has a sodium reactor?"

"Sure, but there's been no accident."

"They call it an incident. Or an event. Or an unusual occurrence. An incident is worse than an event."

"But there's been no event."

She smiles. "How do you know?"

"I don't."

"Would you like to find out?" We're side by side on a piano bench. She settles herself, straightens her back, touches fingers to keys like a concert pianist getting to work.

"Sure." I am pleased she remembers my paper, my last scientific article written perhaps ten years ago.

"Something occurs to me." Now she's settled back again, tapping fingernail to tooth. "Did you know that when Grand Mer was licensed, the EPA required as a condition of licensure the monitoring of blood levels of heavy sodium in both Feliciana Parish and Pointe Coupée across the river?"

"How would they go about that?"

She shrugs. "Whenever a routine blood workup was ordered in a hospital, heavy sodium and chloride levels were checked as routinely as blood sugar or NPN."

"So?"

"So I'm wondering if they still do it."

"I wouldn't know. I haven't ordered much lab work lately."

"Let's find out."

"All right."

"Come over here by me now."

"I'm by you. Is that a terminal?"

"Yes. Now then—" She consults a little book, punches keys on the keyboard, punches other keys on a small black box, humming a tune, musing and busy. She reminds me of a chatelaine, the ole miss of Pantherburn. Red lights begin to blink on the black box.

The screen lights up with an arcane readout: LaDptPbH and a flashing question mark.

"Do you know what that is?" she asks me.

"Louisiana Department of Public Health?"

"Right, I use 'em all the time. Now"—humming—"let me get the access and user codes."

"Aren't they closed now?"

"They don't close, dummy. I'm not talking to people. I'm talking to their data bank." She's hitting more keys. The bank must be pleased, lights up with a merry flashing ACCESSED.

"You're in?"

"We're in. Now to ask the question. What's the question?"

"We want the mean plasma level of heavy sodium of hospital admissions in Feliciana Parish, say, for this year."

"Well expressed, well—" she muses, hitting keys.

The computer utters a sour bleat, flashes SnError.

"What does that mean? That is, doesn't know or won't tell?"

"It means we asked a dumb question."

"I feel like I flunked a test."

"That particular bank has a personality."

"Like Hal."

"No no. It's on our side. Hm. Tom, what did we do wrong?"

"How did you write heavy sodium?"

"As heavy sodium."

"Try Na-24."

"That's the atomic weight?"

"Yes."

"Smart." She hits keys. The thing is pleased, flashes a smiling ACCESS ACCESS ACCESS, then, as if it were thinking things over, waits a second and reads out: 6 mmg., meaning 6 micrograms. The symbol is really 6 μ but I figure this was not practical typographically. We gaze at it blinking. "Jesus," I say.

Lucy looks at me. "What does that mean?"

"Six micrograms. That is very little, but any is too much. I suppose it means the mean value of heavy-sodium levels in all hospital blood workups, including positives and negatives."

"Is it too high?"

"Any number would be too high."

"But that's very little, isn't it?"

"Yes, but too much." I feel a prickling under the collar of my new Bean shirt. I look at her musing. "What else can we ask?"

"We can ask any terminal any question. It's just a matter of framing the question."

"Well?" She looks at me, hands on keyboard. She's shifted now, from chatelaine to girl-Friday secretary, Della Street waiting for Perry to make up his mind.

"What we need is a control."

"Right." She waits, smiling.

"Let's do yours and mine. Have you had a complete physical lately?"

"Sure. I had to get one to get this job."

"You got it at Fedville?"

"Right. How about you?"

"Me too."

"At Fedville?"

"Yes."

"When was that?"

"When I was arrested by the feds."

"Of course. I wanted to come see you."

"It was not a good time. Can you talk to Fedville now?"

"Sure. I'm on intimate terms with their mainframe. Let's see. Yours would be about two years ago, right?"

"Right."

"Two years. What a waste."

"Waste of what?"

"Give me your SS number."

I give it. "Can we get individual readings?"

"We can get anything we ask for. I have Class One clearance."

More black book, more punching out the big keyboard, little box, more queries, accesses, OKs. The thing doesn't even pause to think it over this time. Back come the answers. I have the feeling the thing is sitting pleased, waiting to be patted.

LL   NA24—0   CI37—0
TM   NA24—0   CI37—0

We gaze and blink some more.

"Does that mean what I think it means?" Lucy asks me.

"It means you and I are negative, zero levels of heavy sodium and chloride."

"I don't get it," says Lucy at last. "We both live here."

I look at her. "Have you heard anything about an accident over there? Or an incident? Or event?"

"Not a word."

"Would you hear if there had been one?"

"I don't know. But I live next to the damn thing. So if anybody got sick, it would be me, wouldn't it?"

"One would think so. If, that is, it—" I fall silent. "You're feeling all right, aren't you?"

She cocks an eye. "Wouldn't you have to test me to find out?"

"Test you for what?"

"Presenting rearward. Think about that."

"That's true," I say, thinking about that.

"Okay," she says, not smiling, but eyes round and risible. "How many patients in your series?"

"Maybe twenty or so."

"How many were hospitalized or had blood work?"

"Maybe half a dozen."

"Do you know who and where?"

"Sure."

"Let's try a couple."

"Okay. How about Mickey LaFaye? Here's her SS number. But her workup was done at the local hospital."

"No problem. They have a terminal and I've got their number. Now, she's the one who—"

"New England lady, married Durel LaFaye—you know him—high roller—ended up as a starveling Christina with free-floating anxiety, panic, unnamed longing—"

"Me too."

"What? You don't look much like Christina."

160

"Aren't you glad?"

"—now a complete turnaround: a voluptuous Duchess of Alba pigging out on Whitman's Sampler, goes berserk, shoots half her thoroughbreds, perhaps fooling around with groom—"

"I got it!" She takes my arm in both hands, eyes bright. "Let's run her! No, wait. Oh shoot. Their little terminal would be down. No, wait. They would have to report to Baton Rouge, wouldn't they? Let's try the mainframe again."

"Just ask for sodium. It's the active ion."

Long colloquy, nixes, queries, Sn errors; then: okay, access; then: Na-24—18mmg.

"What do you know." I am gazing at the screen. Again there's a tingle under my Bean collar. There's more. There's the heavy, secret, lidded, almost sexual excitement of the scientific hit— like the chemist Kekule looking for the benzene ring and dreaming of six snakes eating one another's tails—like: I've got you, benzene, I'm closing in on you.

Lucy feels the same excitement. She pulls up close, round-eyed. Her exultation gives her leave. She can say things, ask things she couldn't ordinarily.

"We've got something big, Tom," she says, pulling close.

"I know."

"I'm sorry about Ellen," she says, still holding my arm, flushed with six emotions, happy enough to afford sorrow.

"Thanks."

"What are you going to do about—" She stops, eyes searching my face.

"About what?"

"About Ellen and—? About Ellen and—your life."

I don't say anything.

Another searching look, hands still on my arm, then a squeeze and a brisk yank at my sleeve, a brushing off. She lights up a cigarette, plucks a tobacco grain from her tongue.

"Let's do another one, Tom."

"All right. Donna S———. That's Donna Stubbs. Fat girl. Molested by father. A romantic at heart, expected a certain someone—"

"Me too."

"—did well in therapy, took up aerobic dancing, lost weight, dated, but when I saw her last week, she exhibited an unusual erotic response."

"Unusual?" asks Lucy, hands on the keyboard. "How?"

"I told you about her. Presenting rearward—like estrus behavior in a pongid."

"How would you know?"

"She also had the peculiar language response I told you about. Mention a place name, like her hometown Cut Off, and they seem to consult a map in their heads, a graphic like your computer here. They seem to look over my head as if they were following a cursor on a map."

"Did you say Cut Off?"

"She's gone back to Cut Off. I know she saw a doctor there and went to a hospital with symptoms of hypertension."

"Hm." I give her Donna's number. "No hospital in Cut off."

"Try Golden Meadow."

She found Donna in Golden Meadow: Na-24—12.

"Wow," says Lucy.

"Right."

"Give me another one."

"Let's try Frank Macon. You know him. Janitor at Highland Park, should be on employees' health records. Old friend, ambivalent black, love-hate, we understood each other, very funny and wise about hunting dogs. Now talks like Bryant Gumbel: Have a nice day."

"Number? Okay, easy. Got him."

Frank: Na-24—7.

"Jesus."

"Right."

"Give me another one."

"Let's try Enrique Busch. Ex-Salvadoran. Married into one of the fourteen families. Probably involved in the death squads. Ferociously anti-Communist and anti-clerical. Now has only two interests: golf and getting his daughter into Gamma sorority."

"I'll take the death squads."

"You can probably find him at East Feliciana Proctology Clinic. He has intractable large bowel complaints."

"No wonder."

She gets him.

Enrique: negative! Nominal! Normal!

Lucy looks at me. "What does that mean?" She's more excited than I am.

I shrug. "Presumably that it's normal, not a toxic reaction, for a rich Hispanic removed to this country to progress from death squads to golf and sororities."

"What does that mean?"

"It means, Lucy, that we've got an epidemiological element here and that it's up your alley and that I want to find it."

"I know! I know!" Excited, she grabs me, with both hands again, then grabs Hal the computer. "We have to find a pattern. A vector. Another one?"

"Well, here's Ella Murdoch Smith's number. Classmate at East Feliciana High, diehard segregationist in the old days, yet intelligent, Ayn Rand type, left town when schools were integrated so her children wouldn't be ruined, went to Outer Banks of Carolina, lived in a shack, taught school, educated her children, wrote poetry about spindrift and the winter beach. Returned last year, rages and Ayn Rand ideology gone, got menial cleaning job right here at Mitsy, came to me complaining of plots of fellow employees against her, particularly one Fat Alice. My impression: paranoia, until I talked to her supervisor and found out Fat Alice was a robot. My impression: though Fat Alice was programmed to 'speak,' Ella couldn't tell that she was not human. She was responding to Fat Alice's speech like another robot. No more poems about spindrift."

Ella rolls out like a rug on the screen: Na-24—21, C-137—121.

"Are you writing these down?" I ask her.

"Honey, I'm doing better than that. I got them taped right here. If we get enough, we can run them through and see if we can come up with a vector, a commonality."

"How many do we need?"

"The more the better. I'll tell you what." She grabs me and gives me a jerk.

"What?"

"Give me a few more, then I've got an idea. Tom, we're missing something. It's under our noses and we're missing it!"

"Yeah."

"Well, let's see." I'm looking at my list. "Well, there's Kev and Debbie. Father Kev Kevin, ex-Jesuit, and Sister Thérèse, ex-Maryknoller, now Debbie Boudreaux. Both radicalized, joined Guatemalan guerrillas, Debbie radical feminist, used to talk about dialoguing, then began to talk tough, about having balls, cojones—now both retired to a sort of commune retreat house in pine trees, marital problems: Kev accusing Debbie of being into Wicca and having out-of-body experiences with a local guru which are not exactly out of body, Debbie accusing Kev of becoming overly active as participant therapist in a gay encounter group—"

"That's enough. How do we get a handle on them?"

"Try American Society of Psychotherapists."

"Got you. Give me the numbers. Okay. Okay. Got them."

Kev: zero. Normal!

Debbie: zero. Normal!

Lucy: "I'm confused. Talk about flakes. What do you make of them?"

"One of three things. One, they're acting like normal married couples. Two, they're pathological, but the pathogen is not heavy sodium."

"Three?"

"Father Smith would say the pathogen is demonic."

"Demonic. I see. What do you say?"

"I say let's run some more."

We run a dozen more. We've got three negatives, the rest positive.

Lucy turns off all machines. Lights stop blinking. There are no sounds but the hum of lights. A screech owl's whimpers. It is three o'clock.

164

"I'm going to bed," I say. "Let's sleep on it."

"Wait wait wait."

"All right."

"I've got an idea."

"Okay."

"Do you know where these people live?"

"Sure."

"Okay. I'm going to give you a graphic, a map. Let's see how many we can locate. Maybe we can get a pattern."

"Let's do it tomorrow."

"It'll only take a second. Watch this."

She pops in a cassette and there's old Louisiana herself, a satellite view, color-coded, with blue lakes and bayous, silver towns and cities, rust-red for plowed fields, greens for trees— and the great coiling snake of the Mississippi.

"Now watch this."

The satellite zooms down. Here's Feliciana, from the Mississippi to the Pearl, from the thirty-first parallel to the Crayola blue of Lake Pontchartrain. I can even see the Bogue Falaya and Bayou Pontchatolawa, where I fished yesterday—was it yesterday?—with John Van Dorn.

"Here's your wand. Locate as many patients as you can."

Like Tinker Bell, I can touch the screen and make a star. I make a constellation. We gaze at it. It has no shape. It is a skimpy, ill-formed star cluster.

"How many questions will this thing answer?" I ask finally, hoping to stump it so I can go to bed.

"Almost any. It is a matter of framing the question."

"I can frame the question."

"Well?"

"It is a preposterous question."

"Ask it."

"There is no way it can be answered."

"Ask Hal. He's good."

"I want the computer to locate on this graphic every person in Feliciana Parish and adjoining parishes who has an elevated plasma level of heavy sodium—which is to say, any level of heavy sodium.''

"Good Lord,'' says Lucy. She gazes at me. I seem to hear her own circuits firing away like Hal thinking things over. She taps her teeth with a pencil. She tugs absently at my Bean collar, brushes me off. She slaps the desk. "Well, why the hell not? It's a challenge. There are data banks which have the information. It's just a matter of latching on to it, right?''

"Right," I say wearily. Why did I ask?

"As a matter of fact,'' she muses, plucking a grain of tobacco from her tongue and taking my arm again, "there just might be a chance.''

"There might be?''

"Sure. We got a five-thousand-baud system here.''

"That ought to do it. What is a baud?''

"Never mind. There just might be a chance.''

"Good.''

"You know why?'' She pulls close.

"Why?''

"Because. I seem to recall that when the Grand Mer unit was finished, it was after T.M.I. Then after Chernobyl NIH called for an EIS to placate the anti-nukes.''

"What's an EIS?''

"Environmental Impact Study.''

"Meaning?''

"Meaning a parish-wide sampling was done for radioactivity.''

"You mean people were tested?''

"Sure. Urinalyses almost certainly. And it's just possible that they could have—'' She jerks me. "Sodium would show up in the urine, wouldn't it?''

"Sure.''

"It is just possible—'' She searches my right eye, then my left. "Tell you what?''

"What?''

"Let's hit the mainframe in Baton Rouge and ask it to do the work. By God, there is just a chance.''

166

"Let's do that."

She gazes, taps her teeth, plucks at her tongue. "Here's what we'll do. We'll do some networking. We'll use State Public Health and if necessary the Census Bureau and if necessary NIH in D.C. And we'll ask the mainframe in Baton Rouge to do the asking. I've got the authority."

"Okay."

"Now understand this. It won't be entirely accurate, because if there's a John Hebert who's positive, the census will give us half a dozen John Heberts right here in Feliciana. You understand?"

"I understand."

"But we'll get some sort of distribution."

"Great."

Another half hour of phone work, little-black-box work, page flipping, key hitting, user names, user codes, access codes, logging in, PIVs, Hal's initial outrage, user authorization denied, SNERROR, QUERY QUERY QUERY, NIX—Hal relenting, until finally there is a single meek little green-for-go OK.

"Okay what?" I ask.

"Cross your fingers."

"Okay."

She takes a breath. "Here we go."

"Well?"

"I'm afraid to hit the key," says Lucy, grabbing me, eyes round.

"Show me the key and I'll hit it."

She shows me the key, turns her face.

I hit the key.

Something is wrong.

It looks like a weather map. It looks like what happens when the TV weatherman switches to his satellite map of Louisiana streaked with cold fronts, upper level clouds, clear black sunshine.

"I don't get it, Lucy. What are we looking at?"

Lucy is laughing, eyes rounded, triumphant. She grabs me. "You don't get it. Okay, let's zoom in. What do you see now?"

167

"It looks like a weather front right on top of Feliciana. But there is no front.

"Look again." Zooming closer.

There is Feliciana as before and there are the clouds, closer, grainier. Now I see it. But surely not. It can't be. The clouds are particulate, galactic clouds of tiny twinkling stars, as if the screen had been hit by a handful of Christmas glitter. Part of Baton Rouge is a regular snowfield.

"Do you mean to tell me—" I begin, hardly believing what I see.

"I mean to tell you," says Lucy, face close, big-eyed, holding on to me like a ten-year-old.

"—that each dot is—"

"—a case of heavy sodium. I only asked for sodium. Every dot on that graphic is a person. You're looking at the actual geographical distribution of your syndrome."

There is nothing to do but gaze. "That's beautiful," I say finally. "You're beautiful."

"I know! I know!" She hugs me. "Oh, I'm so sorry about— but I'm also so glad about—"

I say nothing, gaze at the screen.

"Zoom back."

"Okay."

A single rack of clouds hangs over Feliciana like a warm front backed up from the Gulf. Strange: the lakefront is mostly clear, even though it's high-density population. Baton Rouge? Northwest quadrant of the city cloudy, central and south lightly speckled, a scattering of star clusters over Feliciana.

"What's the factor?" I ask Lucy. "You're the epidemiologist."

"I know, I know. It's under our noses. We're looking right at it and can't see it."

"Look harder."

"Look at that." She points to Baton Rouge. "It's a starry yin embracing a clear yang. It's telling us. It's practically shouting."

"You listen." I get up. The toddies and the time have caught up with me.

"You okay?" she asks, pulling me down, staring into one eye, then the other.

"I'm tired. Let's sleep on it."

"Don't leave." She takes my arm.

"I'm not going anywhere. See you in the morning. We'll talk about this stuff. Interesting."

"One thing," she says. We're standing in the dim hall.

"Yes?"

"I want you to take these." She puts something in my hand. Two capsules.

"What are these?"

"Alanone."

"Why should I take them?"

"Tom," she says. "Do you trust me?"

"Sure." I try to see her face, but the dim light of the chandelier is behind her.

"Would you trust me now and take those without asking whys and wherefores?"

"No."

"Oh dear." She sighs. "I didn't think you would."

"I think you'd better tell what this is about."

"Oh my. Very well. I guess I have to." She was touching me but now she's moved away a little. Her face, in the light now, is tender and grave.

Another *déjà vu*. The tragic tingle of bad news, the sweet sorrow to come. Her hand is on my arm. It is like the touch of a friend at a funeral.

"It's this." It must have been in her pocket. She hands it to me, a slip of paper. Her eyes are in shadow. "You'll hate my guts but I had no choice."

"What's this?"

I hold it up to the slit of light from her office. "A lab slip?"

She's silent.

I read aloud. "A Schoen-Beck test? On who?"

She's silent.

"On Ely Culbertson? Come on. What's this? A joke?"

"Schoen-Beck is for Herpes IV antibodies." She could be

169

talking to the lab. "That's the new one. Genito-urinary and neural."

"I know, I know. So what?"

"The name is Ellie Culbertson, Tom."

"He's dead."

"Ellie, Tom. Not Ely."

"I see. So what?"

"That's what Van Dorn calls Ellen, isn't it, as a compliment to her bridge playing. You've told me yourself. She's his Ellie Culbertson."

"Yes, but—"

"Dear," she says, taking my arm. "People don't use their real names for this test."

"True, but you still don't know who this is."

"Honey, George Cutrer told me." Her voice is sorrowful.

"Who in the fuck is he to know?"

"Honey, he's chief of ob-gyn. And he has to tell me. I'm the epidemiologist, remember?"

"Who else did he tell?"

"No one. I swear."

"Let's see the date. Where's the date?" I can't seem to read the date.

She's beside me, reading past my shoulder in the slit of light.

"The date was six weeks ago."

"How do you know it wasn't me?"

She has another slip. She's the good intern. "Here. Six months ago she was negative. Six months ago you were in prison in Alabama. Six weeks ago she's positive. Six weeks ago you were still in prison in Alabama. Now, unless they allow conjugal visits in federal prisons—"

"That was uncalled for."

"You're right. Jesus, I'm sorry."

"Good night."

She plucks my sleeve.

"Do you hold it against me?"

"No." I don't.

170

"I feel rotten. But you see that I had to tell you. I'm sorry. I know you feel rotten too."

"I don't." I don't. I don't feel anything. "Good night."

"If there is anything at all you need. Anything."

"Thanks. I think I'll have a drink and go to bed."

"I'll get you one. You go on upstairs. I'll bring you one."

I remember where it's always been kept. In the sideboard in the dining room.

"Thanks."

She folds my hand on the capsules. "I'll get you a drink to chase them."

I don't move.

"Tom—"

"Yes?"

"You see, I had no way of knowing whether you and Ellen— that is, since you got back—and I don't intend to ask."

"Good."

"I think I'll go on up. You remember where—"

"Yes, in the sideboard. I remember."

"One more thing, Tom." She's half turned away.

"Yes?"

"I've taken two too."

"Two too," I repeat.

"There's nothing wrong with me, Tom. Do you understand?"

"Yes," I say, not understanding.

"Are you all right?"

"I'm fine."

"So I'll say good night."

"All right."

She gives me a kiss on the mouth, eyes open, searching mine.

3. I HAVE A FEW DRINKS STANDING AT THE SIDEBOARD IN the dim dark of the dining room. There is a single gleam from the hall chandelier on the polished table. It's been twenty years since I stood here. Yet I remember exactly where the decanter is, an expensive silver-and-crystal affair, and the child's silver cup Uncle Rylan used for a jigger, and that he filled it, the decanter, with a cheap bourbon named Two Natural. It's the same bourbon and twenty years haven't helped it. Several times I fill the cup, keeping a thumb at the rim to feel the cup fill. I stand in the dark.

Uncle Rylan would stand at the sideboard making a toddy for Miss Bett, first stirring sugar into three fingers of water. The silver spoon made a tinkling sound against the crystal. The stirring went on much longer than was required to dissolve the sugar. There was always talk of politics during the stirring.

Even here with the freshly polished furniture there is the old smell of the house, of scoured wood and bird dogs.

It is not bad standing in the dark drinking.

There is this to be said for drinking. It frees one from the necessities of time, like: now it is time to sit down, stand up. One would as soon do one thing as another.

* * *

Time passes, but one need not tell oneself: take heed, time is passing.

Lucy finds me either standing at the sideboard or sitting at the table.

"Are you all right?"

"Sure."

She is wearing a heavy belted terry-cloth robe as short as a car coat. Her hair is wet.

She turns on the light and looks up at me. I'm not sitting. I'm still standing at the sideboard.

"You are all right, aren't you? I can tell."

"Sure."

She looks at the decanter but she does not ask me: did you drink all that?

"Well?" she asks after a moment.

"Well what?"

"Wouldn't you like to go to bed?"

"Sure."

I take another drink from Uncle Rylan's child's cup. It was the sugar of the toddy which made this lousy bourbon tolerable.

"I'll tell you what," she says, looking down at me. I'm sitting.

"What?"

"I'll help you up."

"All right."

I used to come here as a child for Christmas parties and blackberry hunts and later for the dove shoots at the opening of the season every November. It was a famous dove hunt.

The tinkle of spoon against glass was the occasion of a certain kind of talk. The talk was of bad news, even of approaching disaster—what Roosevelt was doing at Yalta, what Truman was doing at Potsdam, what Kennedy was doing at Oxford (Mississippi)—but there was a conviviality and a certain pleasure to be taken in the doom talk. As a child I associated the pleasure of doom with the tinkle of silver against crystal.

"I know how you feel," says Lucy. "Did you ever know how I always felt about you?"

"No."

She's wrong. I don't feel anything but the bird-dog reek of memory.

"I'll tell you what," says Lucy.

"What?"

"Put your arm around my shoulders." She puts my arm around her shoulders. "Put your weight on me. I'm a strong girl."

"All right." She is a strong girl.

"God, you're heavy."

"Then I'll not put my weight on you," I say, not putting my weight on her.

She laughs. "Come on. Up the stairs."

They, the English Lipscombs, must have spoken exactly the same way, with the same doomed conviviality and the same steady tinkle of silver against crystal, when the Americans came down the river two hundred years ago in 1796 and up the river with Silver Spoons Butler in 1862.

In the bedroom Lucy says, "Do you need any help?"

"No, I'm fine."

"You are, aren't you?" She smiles, absently spits on her thumb, smooths my eyebrows. "But I'll help you anyhow."

"All right."

"What's the matter?" asks Lucy.

"Nothing."

"You look uncomfortable."

"It's this collar. No doubt it's the newness."

We had to take pins out of the pajamas. "Maybe another pin."

"Tch. My word. It's the stupid price tag. Hold still."

"All right."

The mattress is new and hard but not uncomfortable. It used to be a feather bed. The bottom sheet is fitted and snapped on tight as a drum. The top sheet harbors trapped cold air. But the patchwork quilt is old and warm. The pillow slip is new, but the pillow is old and goose down.

The silence and darkness and smell of the house is like a presence.

"You're okay," says Lucy.

"Yes."

"You seem all right but somewhat—distant."

"I'm not distant."

"You're not even drunk."

"That's true."

"You're shivering."

"I'm fine."

"I think I'll stay here for a while, if you don't mind."

"All right."

In Freiburg they have feather beds too. But instead of a quilt comforter, they have something like a bolster, a long narrow pillow to cover the gap on top. I wake early in the morning to the sound of church bells, not like the solemn tolling of our church bells, but a high-pitched crystalline sound, *eine Klingel*, yes, almost a tinkling.

We were hiking out of Waldkirch in the Schwarzwald. Though we had just met, we were both from the South, she from Montgomery, far from home and lonely, a girl named Alice Pratt. This was before young Americans bummed around Europe free and easy, sleeping in tents and hostels. We both wanted the same thing, to touch, laugh, be easy with each other, kiss perhaps—

175

who knows!—even love! Yet we were shy and didn't know what to do. What to do? What to say? We made conversation. We thought of things to say. We spoke of mutual friends at Agnes Scott and Tulane. We were caught, trapped between the happy, safe, Wiener-waltz musical security of the Grand Tour of the 1870s and the shacked-up, stoned-out ease of the 1970s. What if we could not think of something to say?

"I'll cover you up," says Lucy.
  "All right."
  "Better still, I'll warm you up."
  "All right."

What if I touched Alice Pratt? But how? We're hiking along, brows furrowed, casting about for topics of conversation, when all of a sudden and dead ahead, rounding the bend of the narrow blacktop road not two hundred yards away, appears a Tiger tank leading a column of tanks, a Wehrmacht officer standing in the open forward hatch. Maneuvers! I don't think we're supposed to be here. I grab Alice Pratt and yank her into the dark fir forest. We lie on a soft bed of needles and watch an entire panzer division pass. I am Robert Jordan lying on the pine needles. I hold her. She wants me to. When the panzers are gone, we look at each other and laugh. We have been given leave by the German Army and Robert Jordan.

Her mouth is on mine. She, Alabama-German-Lucy-Alice, is under the comforter and I under her, she a sweet heavy incubus but not quite centered. Her hair is still damp. She needs centering.

* * *

Miss Bett reads from her grandmother's journal:

> Later we worked on a silken quilt comforter. Mr. Siegel, our new German tutor, went riding with us. We can't stop giggling at him. Everyone was in stitches when he thanked us for our "horsepitality."

> For Christmas Daddy gave a little darky to all seven brothers, each to become a body servant. Rylan took his to Virginia.

We are kissing. Her short heavy hair tickles my cheek, first on one side then the other, as she turns to and fro in her kissing. She needs centering.

I move her a bit to center her. There is no not centering her. Now.

"Now," Lucy says.

The sweet heaviness and centeredness of her, I think, is no more or less than it should be.

Now.

Rylan Lipscomb, b. 1840, volunteered 1861 for the Crescent Rifles, Company B, Seventh Louisiana Regiment. Killed in Cross Keys, Virginia, 1862.

At Fort Pelham, Harry Epps, in for counterfeiting credit cards, knows how to beat the pay phone with a phony charge card. He knows a dial-a-girl number in Pensacola and how to get not a recording but a woman. "Now, why don't we both relax and tell each other what we like. I have all the time in the world," says a woman's voice in a soft Alabama accent, softer and farther south than Birmingham, but not countrified like a waitress at an I-10 truck stop.

* * *

I recognize the Picayune taste.

"I remember this feather bed," I tell her.

She pushes herself up to see me by straightening her elbows. "This is not a feather bed."

"It used to be a feather bed."

"It's not now and I'm glad. It's just fine."

"Why?"

"You're just fine too. Go to sleep."

"All right, but not right now."

"All right."

The feather bed flows up and around me, but something is missing. The bolster? A cold bluish dark fills the room. It must be early morning. Colly is laying a fire in the grate. I can smell the fat pine kindling. His starched white coat creaks. The match scratches on the slate hearth. He starts a blaze of pine first. The pine is so fat it can be lit by a match. As he sets the coals from the scuttle one by one, he holds his breath, lets it out in a hiss after each coal is placed. His hand passes unhurriedly through the blue-yellow flame. Colly is said to be the great-grandson of the faithful slave and body servant of Rylan Lipscomb.

The uncle is walking up and down the gallery outside, blowing duck calls. It's a high-ball, a bugling *hoanh hoanh* to get the attention of high-flying mallards so they'll cock a green head and come circling down for a look. "That's a lot of crap about war being hell," he says. "I never had a better time in my life."

Miss Bett reads from her grandmother's journal:

I never saw men so happy as Rylan and his brothers when they marched off with the Crescent Rifles.

Finished *Rob Roy*. What a delight after Horace Greeley!

A couple is in for marriage counseling, facing me across the desk.

He to her: I like the explicit VCR in the bedroom, in 3-D and living color. We both get excited. You have to admit you do too. Doc, you ought to hear her.

She to him: Yes, but you're really screwing her not me.

He to both of us: It's better than nothing, isn't it?

I: (silent, flummoxed).

There is a honking on the gallery. The French doors are open. The uncle walks in. He has the flaps of his hunting cap down over his ears. "And I'll tell you something else they're wrong about. A little pussy never hurt anybody."

"What?"

"Get up!"

It is Lucy for sure, shaking me.

"What?"

Alarmed, I'm up, having jumped clean out of bed.

"Are you all right?" asks Lucy, taking hold of me. She's still wearing her terry-cloth car coat. The ceiling light is on. There is the disagreeable oh-no feel of a duck-hunting morning, dawn-dark, lights on, and leaving the warmth of a feather bed.

Lucy is eyeing me curiously, lip tucked. I am wearing pajama bottoms.

"Are you all right?"

"Yes."

"You sure are."

"Sure."

"I've got something to show you."

"What time is it?"

"Six."

"Six."

"Six. Get up. It's important." She's excited.

"All right. Do you mind if I dress?"

"No." She turns, pauses. "What?"

"What?"

"You were about to say something, weren't you?"

"Yes."

"What was it?"

"I've never been in Germany."

"Is that so. Well, it's been a strange night all around. Wonderful, in fact. Please hurry. This is important."

"All right."

"I want to tell you something else too."

"All right."

"About you and me."

"All right."

I have never been to Germany.

There is no coal fire in the grate.

Colly has been dead for forty years.

Miss Bett has been dead for fifty years, Aunt Bett for a hundred years.

The uncle did not come in my room. The French windows are locked. But now he is walking up and down the gallery calling ducks.

There is a Picayune taste in my mouth.

4. WE SIT SIDE BY SIDE AT HER TERMINAL, SHE STILL TERRY-clothed and bare-kneed. She's been here awhile. The seat is warm from her. We are gazing at Feliciana on the screen twinkling away like a nebula crowded with stars.

"Do you see what I see?"

"No."

She pulls me close, her eye next to my eye, as if I could see better.

"I've been looking at it for two hours and all of a sudden it hit me. Don't you see?"

"No."

"Water."

"Water," I repeat.

"It's the water supply, dummy. Don't you see?"

"No."

She spells it out. "Where does the water people drink come from now?"

I am silent for a long time. Water?

"Where does the water come from?" I say. "Well, now that the water table has fallen out of sight and the aquifer is low, it comes from deep wells and the river."

"Right. And where in the river does it come from?"

"Well, there's an intake around here. Between here and Baton Rouge."

"Right here." She puts a pencil point on a westerly loop of the river. "This is the Ratliff intake installed five years ago to be above the chemicals—you know, it's the Ruhr Valley from here to New Orleans. It supplies most of western Feliciana and the northeast sector of Baton Rouge. Now watch closely, I'm going to show you something."

"I'm watching."

"Okay. Now what we're looking at is the distribution of all known positives for heavy sodium or chloride, right?"

"Right."

"Take a good look and remember the distribution—for example, here in northeast Baton Rouge, running across here in most of the smaller towns and countryside back of the lake. With clear areas here, here, and along the lake. Okay?"

"Okay. Now I'm going to show you another graphic. Another brainstorm!" She rubs her hands together, pleased with herself, "I got this from the S and WB."

"What's that?"

"The state Sewerage and Water Board. All I had to do was ask them for a graphic showing the areas supplied by Ratliff number one, that's what they call it. Now watch this."

She hits a key. A pretty map rolls out, a Miró watercolor of red swatches, bands, and blocks.

"You got it? You oriented?"

"I think."

"Now watch." She hits keys, back and forth from twinkling star-clustered Feliciana to Miró-red Feliciana. "What do you see?"

"They're roughly the same."

"Roughly, my foot. They're almost exactly the same. Look. Same clear areas. Lakefront, small enclaves here, here, a town here and here. I don't know why."

I say slowly, "The lakefront condos and high-rises use treated lake water. These clear areas are large new developments with their own deep wells. Towns like these, Covington, Kentwood, Abita Springs, have their own deep wells." I look at her curiously. "What do you drink here?"

"Would you believe cistern water?"

"Cistern? I knew this place had an old cistern, but—"

"Carrie and Vergil swear by it. Carrie says it's softer and Vergil says it's healthier. No metal ions. He had it analyzed. What about you?"

I recollect. "Ellen is a nut on bottled water. Abita Springs water for ordinary use and Perrier for parties. Wait a minute."

"Yes?"

"You're saying that stuff got into the main water supply."

"Got into it or was put into it."

"Put into it." We look at each other.

"I think I'll fix us some coffee," says Lucy.

We drink black coffee from old cups the size of small soup bowls. The coffee is chicoried and strong as Turkish.

"Look," I say at last. "Here's what we're going to do."

"What?"

"Put Feliciana back up there."

"All right."

"Now here we are here. A mile or so from the old river."

"Right."

"Here's the Grand Mer facility on Tunica Island."

182

"Right, and here's the Ratliff intake here."

"Not a mile from Grand Mer."

"Right."

"Lucy, you're telling me that the drinking water from here is contaminated by heavy-sodium ions."

"Obviously."

"And I'm telling you that this facility here at Grand Mer has a heavy-sodium reactor."

"I know."

"Then clearly there is a leak from this source here to this intake here."

"A leak or something."

"Or something. Here's what we're going to do."

"What?"

"If you can spare Vergil, he and I will go take a look."

"And I. I'll fix you some breakfast and—"

"Call in sick."

"Call in sick. Let's go back to bed. I'll wake you at nine."

I go back to bed dressed. I go back to ordinary sleep, as if I had dreamed the whole thing, panzers, nukes, bad water, Alice Pratt—but not Lucy.

5. BREAKFAST IN THE OLD DINING ROOM IS A MEAL OF quail, grits, beaten biscuits, fried apple rings, and the same bowl-size cups of chicoried coffee. I don't know whether Lucy or the uncle or Carrie Bon cooked it. The uncle is proud of the quail—they're his, he's got a freezerful—half a dozen hot little heart-shaped morsels per plate, six tender-spicy, gamy-gladdening mouthfuls.

Lucy is half finished. She gives me a single quick look, head down, through her eyebrows. She and the uncle watch in silence

183

while I eat. I am starved! Lucy smiles, smokes, and drinks her coffee. Satisfied, the uncle leaves.

We move to the other end of the table, where Lucy spreads out a geodetic survey map, weights the corners with cups and cellars. She summons Vergil.

When she stands, I see she's wearing jeans too, worn and gray and soft as velvet. They fit her admirably. She sits at the head, Vergil and I flanking her; Vergil, arms folded on the table, eyes fixed on the map.

"I think we got trouble," says Lucy, plucking tobacco from her tongue. "I think there's been a Grade Two incident at Grand Mer. Either a spill or a leak. Vergil knows the plumbing—maybe he can help us. What I can't understand is how in the hell it could get into the Ratliff intake upriver. In any case, it's my business. When people get sick, etiology unknown, it becomes my business. What do you think?"

Vergil and I look at each other, "One question, Lucy," I say. "What?"

"You know those queries you made of the data banks last night?"

"Yes?"

"Do they know they've been queried by you?"

"Why?" She looks at me strangely.

"Just curious."

"It's routine epidemiology. I'm entitled. They wouldn't red-flag it—as they might if the query were suspicious, some hacker fishing around. They know me. I did the same thing with the Jap encephalitis, though not on such a grand scale as last night."

"I see. Lucy, are you going to notify the feds, EPA or NRC?"

"Of course. This is heavy-duty stuff—and you found it. We found it. We'll both report it, okay? But before the stampede of bureaucrats, I'd like to have a look for myself. Want to come? I think you better come. You're the guy that blew the whistle. I should think you'd be interested."

"I'm interested." She's forgotten it is my idea.

"Vergil's going to come. He knows the territory and the technology. He's our resource person. Okay, Vergil?"

"Sure," says Vergil without looking up.

"Okay, now look." Lucy weights the map with more crystal goblets and salt cellars. "Here we are at Pantherburn. Here's old Grand Mer, now a blind loop of the river, a lake. Up here is Angola, the state pen, a plantation with ten thousand inmates—which incidentally is supplied by the Ratliff number-one water district. Here's Fedville—"

"Is that in the water district?" I ask.

"No, it's not. They've got their own intake half a mile upriver."

"I see."

"You see what?"

"Nothing."

"Here's Tunica Island, not really an island, as you see, but part of the great Tunica Swamp. Here's the Grand Mer facility, reactor and cooling tower. Here's Raccourci Chute, the New River, and here upriver, less than a mile from the facility, is the Ratliff intake. And next to it, over the levee, is the pumping station which supplies the area of the occurrence of your syndrome. Here, not three hundred yards upriver, is Ratliff number-two intake, which supplies all of Fedville. Now here's the question. You already know, don't you?" She cocks an eye at me.

"Sure. The question is how what you call an incident can affect number-one intake, which is upriver, and not affect number two."

"Right," she says, eyeing me. "Why do you say 'what you call an incident'?"

"That's what you call it. I don't know what it is."

"Let's go look." She pushes back her chair.

"Do you just drive up to the gate and announce your business?"

"I sure as hell do. Because it is my business. And I've got both federal and state passes. I can go to the facility or the water district number-one station or the Fedville station. I can go anywhere. You, Tom, are coming along because it is also your business. You discovered it. What we don't know and mean to find out is whether it is a one-shot spill and we've seen the worst or whether it's an ongoing contamination. Vergil is coming because he knows pipes. What we've got here, both in the facility and in the water district, is essentially nothing more than a system of pipes. And Vergil is majoring in pipes, aren't you, Vergil?"

Vergil smiles and nods.

"What we got here is a pipe problem," Lucy tells us. "A busted pipe. Got to be. Let's go."

"Lucy," I say, taking her arm, "before we go I'd like to check one more reading upstairs. Could Vergil meet us at the truck in, say, fifteen minutes?"

"No problem." Vergil nods and is gone.

6. LUCY WAITS, SMILING, AT HER KEYBOARD. "WHO DO you want to run?"

"Ellen."

"Ellen." One swift, hooded glance, but her voice doesn't change. "Okay. How do we get a handle?"

"Easy. She's a volunteer nurse at Belle Ame Academy. So she takes the same physical all schoolteachers and staff take. Try State Public Health."

"Right. That's—ah—Van Dorn's outfit, isn't it?" she asks carefully.

"Yes."

"You got her SS number?"

"Yes." It's with mine in my wallet. I read it out to her.

She hits keys without comment.

The screen nixes. She looks at me neutrally.

"What name did you use?"

"Ellen More."

"Try Ellen Oglethorpe. That's her maiden name and tournament name."

A nod, no comment, not an eye flicker. She hits keys. "There she is."

NA-24—2.

We look in silence.

"That's not much, Tom."

"No, not much. But too much. Let's try Van Dorn. I don't have his number."

"No problem," she says, as neutrally as I. "I can get it from Fedville file."

She gets it, hits more keys. The screen answers laconically.

NA-24—0.

"How could that be?" I ask nobody in particular.

Lucy waits, like a stenographer, watching the keyboard. After a while she looks up at me. "What's the matter?"

"Nothing. Let's go," I say. "Vergil will be waiting."

We pile into Lucy's big pickup, Vergil standing aside so I'll sit in the middle next to Lucy. The uncle is nowhere in sight. Maggie, the pointer, thinking she's going hunting, jumps clear over the tailgate into the truck bed.

"We're not going to have any trouble," Vergil tells us in a soft voice. "There's only one fellow at the intake gate. I know him. He used to fish with my daddy. He's from Baton Rouge." The only sign that Vergil is black is the way he pronounces Baton Rouge, with a rough g, *Roodge*.

He's right. There is no trouble. We swing off the Angola road to a chain link gate, Lucy not even showing her pass to the uniformed guard in his booth, who probably recognizes her truck, out and over the Tunica flats between the high-rises of Fedville on the right and the barbed-wire chain link fence of the Grand Mer facility on the left. The gravel road slants up and over the levee. There across the still waters of old Grand Mer, now Lake Mary, and not half a mile away looms the great lopped-off cone of the cooling tower, looking for all the world like a child's drawing of Mt. St. Helens after it blew its top. The thin flag of vapor flies from its crater. From the pumping station below a brace of great pipes strapped together like the blood vessels in the thigh humps directly up and over the levee, making an arch high enough for a truck to pass under. Across the upper blind end of Lake Mary is the old revetment, great mattresses of concrete, old, moldering, lichened, laid down years ago in a vain attempt to thwart the river's capricious decision to jump the neck of the loop and take a shortcut south—to no avail. Ol' Man River done made up his mind.

Lake Mary, once the broad gulf of the river where stern-wheelers made their stops at plantation landings, stretches peaceably beyond the willows. Directly in front of us the new river booms past down Raccourci Chute as if it had just discovered the shortcut, half a mile wide, foam-flecked in excitement, sparkling brown wavelets crisscrossing in angry sucks and boils. A powerful towboat pushing an acre of barges labors upstream. There is no easy water here.

A short concrete L-shaped pier sticks out into the river. A privy-size guardhouse houses a guard not even uniformed and listening to his headset. He waves us past.

"I don't know what we're looking for," says Lucy.

In fact, there is not much to see. The concrete ell encloses the intake, a grid of steel bars some twenty feet square. It is girded around by a protective strainer of steel fins like whale teeth in which is lodged river junk, driftwood, beer cans, chunks of Styrofoam, the whole mess coated in yellow froth.

We stand looking down. "Well, that's it," says Lucy. "The grossly strained water goes down there, then up there in that pipe—how big is that pipe, Vergil?"

"Seventy-two-inch diameter."

"—then over to the pumping station and purification plant. Actually, it's good water when you drink it. We're above the big chemical plants. For the life of me"—she nods to the tower—

"I don't see how a spill down there could get into the water here."

We gaze some more. There is nothing to see.

But as we drift up the levee and back to the truck, Vergil calls us aside. We're on top of the levee. He is standing casually, hands in pockets, looking down as usual. "You want to see something?" he asks nobody in particular.

"Yes," we say.

"Look over there." He nods toward the south without looking up.

We look. There is nothing to see but the fence and, beyond, the batture which widens into the Tunica Swamp and is mostly grown up in willows.

"What do you see?" I ask Vergil finally.

"Look at the willows."

"I'm looking at the willows."

"Look at the color."

"The color of willows is green," says Lucy.

"That's right. So what do you see. Look where I'm looking." He looks.

We look. "Do you mean that couple of sick willows?" I ask at last.

"It's a track," says Vergil. "A faint yellowing which crosses the batture toward the tower."

"I see!" cries Lucy. "Damned if it isn't! But what does—"

"Let's go," I say. "We got company."

A small white pickup is moseying along the narrow roadway atop the levee.

"That's just the levee board patrol," says Lucy. "Now what do you think that yellow means?"

"Let's go, Lucy," I say, taking her arm.

We walk slowly down the slanting gravel road. The white truck seems to pay us no attention, bumps across the access road, under the pipe arch, and goes its way.

"Now would you mind telling me—" begins Lucy when we are in the truck.

"Let's wait till we get home," I say. Vergil and I are looking straight ahead. "Drive the truck, Lucy."

"Okay okay."

7. FOR SOME REASON NOBODY SAYS ANYTHING UNTIL we're back at the dining-room table gazing down at the map.

"Now what's all this about, Vergil?" asks Lucy.

"They have a line there."

"A line?"

"A pipe."

"Where?"

Vergil's forefinger with its glossy nail and large half-moon rests on the green neck between the river and lake.

"How do you know?"

"I used to run leaks for Continental all the way from Golden Meadow to Tennessee. That's how we spotted leaks by chopper."

"How?"

"By yellowing. Grass and leaf yellowing over the pipeline. I got so I could spot the slightest off-green."

We look hard at the map as if we could see it.

"I don't understand," says Lucy. "Couldn't it be a gas pipeline supplying Grand Mer?"

"No. It wouldn't be there. This runs from Grand Mer to Ratliff number one."

Again we look at the map.

"Well, if there's a pipeline there," says Lucy slowly, "wouldn't there be a cleared right-of-way with signs and so forth?"

Vergil smiles and shrugs. Ask me about pipes but don't ask me why folks do what they do.

Lucy looks at me. "Am I being stupid? Ya'll seem to know something I don't know. What does he mean?"

"He means that there would be a right-of-way and signs only if they wanted you to know the pipeline was there."

"What are you saying?"

"Vergil is suggesting that there is a pipeline there and that it is hidden."

"I see. You mean that if there is contamination of the water supply, it is deliberate."

"That's right."

She muses, eyes blinking and not leaving my face. "Why do I have the feeling that you are not only not surprised but that you know a lot more about this than you let on?"

I don't say anything.

She looks back at Vergil. His face is blank.

"What kind of contaminant are we talking about?" asks Lucy.

I shrug and tap the pencil on the cone on Tunica Island. "This is an old heavy-sodium reactor, one of the first and, I believe, one of the few still around. Right, Vergil?"

"Right," says Vergil, taking the pencil and warming to it. The subject is pipes. "Dr. More is right about the heavy sodium, but it's not the core, the reactor, it's the coolant. Okay?" He corrects me gently. He begins to sketch. "Okay, this is an old LMFBR, liquid metal fast breeder reactor. You've got your core here, a mixture of oxides of plutonium and uranium, and around it you've got your blanket of uranium, U-238. Now here's your primary coolant loop of liquid Na-24, used because of its heat-transfer properties—it's liquid over a large range of temperatures. Here is your secondary nonradioactive sodium loop, which cooks the steam, which in turn drives the turbines. And here is your water loop, which cools your condenser and turbine." With an odd little deprecatory gesture, Vergil both offers the drawing and shakes his head at it.

We gaze at the loops and the small tidy blacked-in core.

"I still don't get it," says Lucy. "Are you telling me that stuff from here"—she taps the primary coolant loop—"gets over to here?" She taps the Ratliff intake an inch away.

Vergil is silent. His eyes are black and blank.

"How?" Lucy asks both of us.

"By a pipe," I say, watching Vergil. He nods.

"But who—?" she begins.

We are silent.

"By a pipe, you say. But if that stuff was in a pipe in the willows here, it would be a liquid, wouldn't it? So how—"

We're back in Vergil's territory. "That's right. It would have to be treated, converted to a water-soluble salt, probably a chloride—like this." He picks up a crystal cellar from a corner of the map.

"But somebody has to *do* this!" Lucy accuses him. Vergil cuts his eyes, passes her to me.

"That's right, Lucy. Somebody designed it and built it."

We think it over. Now Lucy has the import.

"You mean to tell me," says Lucy in a measured voice, tapping pencil on table with each word, "that somebody has deliberately diverted heavy sodium from here, through a pipe, through the Tunica Swamp here, to put it in the water supply at Ratliff number one here?"

Vergil gazes at the map as if the answer were there.

"That's what we mean to tell you, Lucy."

"Does that mean it is something done officially, with NRC approval, perhaps by NRC, or could someone have done it surreptitiously?"

Lucy looks at me. I look at Vergil. Vergil shrugs.

Lucy puts her head down, raises a finger. "We're talking about somebody official, right? Nobody could have slipped in there and done it."

We both shrug.

"Well, I'll be goddamned."

"Yes."

"But why?"

"A good question."

"Now wait," says Lucy.

We wait for her.

"Assuming there is a pipe there, why is it leaking? Why the yellowing?"

I look at Vergil—he shrugs. "It don't take much of a leak—especially if somebody was doing the plumbing in secret without routine pipe checks."

Lucy is gazing at me. "We don't know this," she says at last. "We're guessing."

"That's right."

"We need more to go on, Tom, Vergil. Hard evidence. A piece of pipe. Let's go back and look. But look for what?"

Vergil clears his throat. "We could check out the pumping station."

We both look at him.

"Pumping station?" I say.

"Right here." He puts the point of the pencil on the stippled green of the Tunica Swamp between the tower and the intake.

"Pumping station?" says Lucy. "What for?"

Vergil is almost apologetic. "Well, your liquid here is not going to run by gravity upriver to your intake here."

"It's not going to run by gravity upriver," Lucy tells me.

"That's right, Lucy."

"I don't believe it. Who would put a pumping station there?"

Vergil smiles for the first time. "Ask him," he says, nodding to the window. There's the uncle, trudging across the overgrown yard, headed for the woods, down shoulder angled forward leading the way, the pointer at his heels. Vergil, smiling and good-humored, has allowed himself to lapse into local freejack talk. "He the one showed it to me. We went hunting birds last Christmas, you remember, Miss Lucy?"

"I remember," says Lucy absently. "We still got some of those quail frozen. We had some this morning."

"Mist' Hugh think it's an electric substation. I didn't say nothing. But there no wires except a little line to run the pump, no insulators. No signs, except a radioactive warning. I told him it is not a substation. But you not going to tell Mist' Hugh anything."

"There is something I don't understand," I tell Vergil.

193

"What's that, Doc-tor?" He almost said Doc.

"You say you and the uncle went quail hunting there."

"Yes, suh. My daddy evermore love quail and my mamma can evermore cook them, idn't that right, Miss Lucy?"

Lucy nods absently.

"Mist' Hugh, he some kind of hunter. A dead shot. I've seen him shoot two birds crossing with one shot. He and old Maggie." Vergil laughs.

We can see Maggie's tail stiff and high moving through the Johnson grass like a periscope.

"He loan me his automatic and kept his old double-barreled .12 and got more birds than I did. The reason we went to the island was to get woodcock. He claims they like it there, but we didn't see any. He say he can tell by the way Maggie points whether it's birds or woodcock."

"How did you get in there?"

"How you mean?"

"I mean whoever put in that pipeline and pumping station is not going to want people to see it—and there's that eight-foot fence plus barbed wire up here next to the intake."

"That's right. But they don't watch the other end of the island. Here." He touches the lower blind end of Lake Mary. "The fence goes right across Lake Mary, but except at very high water you can ease right under it. They don't care. Nobody bothered us."

"How would you go about getting in there now?"

"Mist' Hugh got an old skiff hid up in the willows by Bear Bayou here. You welcome to take it. He happy to take you. You just put into the lake here and ease up under the fence and put in here and walk half a mile on this old jeep trail, used to be a hog trail."

"How about you?" I ask him.

"Me? I got to work. Ax Miss Lucy."

"Ya'll three go," says Lucy testily. "I'll get Uncle Hugh to be the guide. You two take a look and see if you can figure out what in the hell is going on."

"Mist' Hugh be happy," says Vergil, laughing.

Lucy can't or won't go. She has to collect her thoughts—this is a different ball game; do you mean somebody is doing this on purpose? This calls for different queries, a different epidemiology.

"Tom," she says, tapping her teeth, "I'm looking for effects, symptoms, a correlation between high Na-24 levels and the attendant symptoms. What are you looking for?"

"Actually it would be the abatement of symptoms—of such peculiarly human symptoms as anxiety, depression, stress, insomnia, suicidal tendencies, chemical dependence. Think of it as a regression from a stressful human existence to a peaceable animal existence."

"That's a big help. How in hell can I frame a question in those terms?"

"Try for cases of mindless violence—like a rogue elephant—like Mickey LaFaye shooting her horses—or a serial killer, the fellow who killed thirty Florida coeds. Theoretically the pharmacological effect of Na-24 on some cortices should produce cases of pure angelism-bestialism; that is, people who either consider themselves above conscience and the law or don't care."

"Hm. Then I might turn up something from criminal data banks."

"Try it."

She watches us, frowning thoughtfully from the great open front door of Pantherburn.

The uncle is delighted to take us. He's got it into his head that it is some kind of fishing trip, for when we pile into my Caprice, he has a short casting rod with him.

Maggie thinks it's a hunt and wants to go, nudges her iron head into my crotch, but is not allowed.

We take the Angola road south and at the uncle's direction two or three turns onto gravel roads and dirt tracks, dip down out of the loess hills onto the flats of the Tunica Swamp. The willows here, often under water, still have dusty skirts from the dried mud of the spring rise.

The uncle leads the way through the willows, fishing pole

trailing, right shoulder leading the way, creeper and potato vines singing and popping around his wide, sidling hips.

Bear Bayou is no more than a creek's mouth. An old cypress skiff, hard and heavy but not waterlogged, is pulled up under bushes and, though even atop it, one can't see it. Even so, it is locked. With surprising agility the uncle has the boat in the water in no time, hops in it, and works it around to a tiny beach.

"Uncle," I tell him, "why don't I row? I feel like it. You sit in the stern and tell me where to go."

We're in Lake Mary almost at once. What a beneficence, popping out of the bayou funky with anise and root rot into warm sunshine and open water. Believe it or not, this quiet, almost clear stretch of water, peaceable as a Wisconsin lake, was once Grand Mer, the great muddy sea where the river came booming down into a curve, carving a broad gulf from the mealy loess hills, the roiling water teeming with packets and show-boats, loading cotton and indigo and offloading grand pianos, Sheraton furniture, Sheffield silver, Scots whiskey, port wine, cases of English fowling pieces, and even a book or two—Shake-speare, John Bunyan, and later Sir Walter Scott by the hundreds, Sir Walter in every plantation house as inevitable as the King James Bible and the Audubon prints; Sir Walter sending all these English-Americans to war against the Yankees as if they were the Catholic knights in *Ivanhoe* gone off to fight the infidel.

Now it's empty and quiet as Lake Champlain: old canny Natty Bumppo facing me in the stern and behind me Vergil Bon, the sure-enough Hawkeye of this age, one foot in the past with his old quadroon beauty and wisdom, yet smart as Georgia Tech; the other foot in the future, a creature of the nuclear age, the best of black and white. But is he? Good as he is, the best of black or white, does he know which he is? And who am I? the last of the Mohicans? the fag end of the English Catholics here, queer birds indeed in these parts.

It feels good pulling the oars, the sun on my back.

The uncle thinks he's going fishing. He's telling me about his rig.

"You see this little Omega spinning reel?"

"Looks like a toy."

"That's right! That's why it's light enough to cast a fly. This little sucker cost me two hundred dollars. You see this?" Tied to the line is a crude-looking wet fly weighted with a single shot.

"What kind of a fly is that?"

"That's a no-name fly. You want one? I'll make you one. I showed Verge, his daddy, this, and he said you can't cast a fly on spinning tackle and I said the shit you can't. So I thowed it out like this—but it's got to be this light Omega reel—and he said, Well, I be dog. He thought he knew it all about fishing." Vergil Junior behind me is silent. The uncle and Vergil Senior were fishing companions. "You see that gum tree there that's fallen down in the water?"

"I see it."

"You know what's up under there, don't you?"

"Sac au lait."

"You right! White perch. You know what you do, you take and hold us off with a paddle about this far out, circle the tree, and I thow this little sucker right to the edge of the leaves and let it sink. It never misses. I ain't had nobody to do that since his daddy got sick. We'd take turns holding each other off just right. You got to have another man with the paddle. You talk about *sac au lait!* But you got to have two. I mean shit, it's hard to do it by yourself. You want to hold up here a little bit and let me hold you off and you try this little sucker?"

"He goes out fishing by himself now," says Vergil behind me. "Ever' day."

The uncle's only sorrow these days, I see, is that he has no one to go hunting and fishing with.

"We can't stop now, Uncle. Maybe later. I'd like to go later. Right now I want you to show me that substation."

"Shitfire," says the uncle, disappointed, "and save matches. What in hail for?"

"I just want to see it. It's important."

"All right," says the uncle, pretending to be grudging but in fact glad enough to be going anywhere with anybody. "Just go on up the lake to the narrows."

A breeze springs up. The lake sparkles. It's good to pull the heavy skiff against the wavelets. The lake narrows. I watch the uncle for directions, and presently we duck and slide under the fence which used to cross dry land before the old blind end of the lake, fed by the rainy years, began to creep back toward the river. The river is not as low as we thought. The rise from the northern rains has begun.

The uncle goes on about his fishing with Vergil Senior in the old days and the great hunts. He decides to get irritated with Vergil Junior, who, however, has said nothing.

"I mean, shit," says the uncle. "I can't even get some folks to go woodcock hunting with me, even when they the one going to get the woodcock to take to their daddy, and I'm telling you it's the best eating of all, and right here in Tunica Island is the center of all the woodcock in the world. He don't even like to eat woodcock after we taken him with us. You know why? You remember, Vergil, when you was little I showed you the wood-cock—I had just shot him and he had worms coming out of his mouth—they do that—the woodcock is not wormy, he's been eating worms, he's full of worms, they swallow worms whole, and when you shoot them, hell, the worms going to come out, why not. Well, this boy takes one look at the worms coming out of the woodcock and ain't ever touched a woodcock since. Ain't that right, Vergil?" There's an edge in the uncle's voice which embarrasses me.

But Vergil is not offended. "That's right, Mist' Hugh." I can tell he's smiling behind me.

"The thing about a woodcock is, all you got to do is just graze him with one little bird shot and he'll fall down dead—just brush him, like"—the uncle shows us, brushing one hand lightly against the other—"and that sapsucker will fall down dead." The uncle frowns and decides to get irritated with Vergil again. He becomes more irritated. "Some folks," he tells me, as if Vergil can't hear, "get their nose in a book and they think they stuff on a stick. Ain't that right, Tom?"

Past the fence, for some reason we fall silent. I look around. There is no one and nothing to see except the vast looming geometry of the cooling tower and a bass boat uplake and across, the fishermen featureless except for their long-billed orange caps.

"Pull in right here at this towhead."

"Let's get this thing out of sight," I tell them. We pull the skiff onto a sandbar under the willows.

"Who you hiding from?" asks the uncle.

"I don't rightly know."

"Ain't nobody going to bother you at this end of the island. I ain't ever seen a guard but once and he was a fellow I knew. He knew I was after woodcock."

"I wish you had your shotgun now."

"Shit, they out of season, Tom. You want to get me in trouble?"

Just beyond the willows we hit an old jeep trail, one of the many that crisscross the island. It doesn't look recently used. We're trespassing. I'm thinking of patrols. Vergil hangs back, walking head down, hands in pockets. Perhaps he is offended by the uncle, after all.

The uncle looks back and moves close to tell me something. He is still angry with Vergil. His feelings are hurt because neither Vergil nor his father will go fishing with him anymore. "Do you know what you get when you cross a nigger with a groundhog?" He lowers his voice, but maybe not enough, I think, for Vergil not to overhear.

"No."

"Six more weeks of basketball." He gives me an elbow. "Get it?"

"Yes. Uncle, do you know where we're going?"

"Sho I know. I know ever' damn foot of this island."

We cross other jeep trails, one with fresh tire tracks.

Presently the uncle stops. We're at another fence, an enclosure. In the middle of the weeds there is a nondescript structure, a concrete cube fitted with a hatch on top like a diving bell.

"There's a sign here," I tell Vergil. Fixed to the gate is a small metal placard, the standard NRC sign, warning: RADIATION DANGER KEEP OUT.

"I never noticed that," says the uncle.

We gaze. There is nothing to see, less than nothing. It is the sort of thing, a public-service-utility-government fenced-off sort of thing to which ordinarily and of its very nature one pays not the slightest attention.

"This is what you wanted to see?" asks the uncle, his head slanted ironically, a dark blade. We could be fishing for *sac au lait*.

"Two things," says Vergil presently in a matter-of-fact voice. "You can see the pipeline in both directions, toward the tower and toward the intake, by the faint yellowing. See?"

"Yes."

"You see the hatch?"

"Yes."

"I judge the pump is waterproofed against high water, which can get up to six feet here."

"I see."

"I don't see any nipples or caps like over at the intake."

"Nipples? Caps?"

"You didn't notice it?"

"No, I didn't, Vergil."

"Next to the intake. A three-inch fiberglass nipple stubbed off and capped. Not something you would notice unless you were looking for it."

"You mean there was a pipe sticking out of the ground?"

"Yes. Probably with a valve just below ground, coming off a T. As if they might be taking samples from whatever is in the pipe."

"Shit, let's go," says the uncle.

"Right," I say, following them down the trail, thinking of nothing in particular. "Right."

"We got time to catch a mess of *sac au lait* before dinner," says the uncle.

"No, we haven't," says Vergil, pulling up short.

Blocking the jeep trail are two men. I recognize the red fishing caps.

But they're not fishermen. They're police, uniformed in brown, green-yoked shirts. Each carries a holstered revolver. I

200

recognize the six-pointed star of the shoulder patch. They're parish police, sheriff's deputies. One is youngish, slim and crewcut. The other is even younger, but bolder and fatter. Both are wooden-faced. I am relieved. What did I expect, some secret nuclear police?

"You fellows looking for us?" I say, smiling.

They nod, not smiling. The younger, husky one has his hand on the holster strap.

"Could we see some identification, please," says the older, wirier one.

Vergil and I reach for our wallets, hand them over.

"Shit, I didn't bring anything but my fishing license. We were going fishing. Will this do?"

The older one looks at it, doesn't take it. "What were you doing here?"

"I wanted to show them the best place in the parish for wood-cock," says the uncle. "But we ain't hunting! Y'all from Wild-life and Fisheries? The doctor here is a birdwatcher."

"You gentlemen better come with us," says the older cop.

"What for?" asks the uncle.

"What's the charge, Officer?" I ask.

"A fellow escaped from Angola last night," says young and stocky.

"Do you think it's one of us?" asks the indignant uncle.

"These two fellows have identification," says old and wiry.

"Jesus Christ, are you fellows telling me you think I escaped from Angola?" asks the uncle. "Wait a minute. Y'all from the sheriff's office in Clinton, ain't you? Wait a minute. Don't I know you?" he says to the younger. "Ain't you Artois Hebert's boy?"

"Yes, sir."

"Then you know me. Everybody knows me. Hugh Bob Lipscomb. Ask Sheriff Sharp. I been knowing Cooter Sharp." The uncle holds out his hand.

But the older deputy says only, "Let's go," and leads the way. The younger falls in behind us.

"There's something funny about this," says the uncle to me. "Those guys are from the sheriff's office."

"I know. Shut up."

"They're not NRC guards or federals! They didn't even mention trespassing!"

"I know. Shut up."

The lead deputy kicks up a woodcock. It squeals and goes caroming off in its nutty corkscrew flight, eyes in the back of its head. Once, the uncle told me why woodcock have eyes in the back of the head: "So they can stick that long beak, head and all, all the way down in the wet ground—and *still* see you."

"Let's go to Clinton," says the older deputy.

8. BOB COMEAUX SPRINGS US FROM JAIL ALMOST BEFORE we're booked. Who called him? Nobody, he explains, a routine telex which flags him down whenever one of his federal parolees runs afoul of the law. Aren't you glad I'm your parole officer? he asks amiably, shaking hands all around and even giving me a medical-fraternal hug.

Clinton has a new jail, or rather a carefully restored old jail done up in columns and shutters to match the colonial courthouse and the neat little shotgun cottage-offices of lawyers' row. The jail is strangely silent, with only a black vagrant and a white couple in the squad room who are being released even as we are booked. Unlikely inmates they are, the couple, a solemn, respectable-looking man and wife who could be a Baptist deacon and deaconess, almost formally dressed, he in a somber but stylish charcoal-colored suit and tie, she too in suit and tie, she with handsome unplucked black eyebrows and black hair whirled up like an old-fashioned Gibson girl. He wears oversize horn-rimmed specs, which give him an incongruous impish Harold Lloyd look.

The uncle of course knows everyone. We are received and booked amiably. Some mistake must have been made, we are assured. It will soon be straightened out. The deputy and jailer stand about swinging their arms. They kid the uncle: "Looks like they finally caught up with you, Hugh Bob," etc. Vergil is acutely embarrassed. He sees nothing amusing about jail.

There prevails the tolerable boredom and gossip of all police stations, tolerable because of the gossip. Something always turns up, the latest outrage and the headshaking, not without pleasure, of the cops who thought they'd seen it all and now here's the latest. The uncle, who has just got it from the deputy, passes it along to Vergil and me in the same low voice quickened by interest: a crime against nature, many crimes against nature, against children, by none other than this same couple, it is alleged, who run some sort of day camp, the very sort of child-care business these people get into to get at children, you know—alleged because this couple is being sprung for lack of evidence, but the deputy says we'll get them sooner or later, they always repeat. But children! The couple's name I remember as the very byword of somber, sober caring: Mr. and Mrs. Brunette.

"That's one thing I wouldn't put up with, messing with children," says the uncle cheerfully. "I'd cut their nuts out."

Bob Comeaux is all rueful smiles, chaffing and headshaking. "You old booger, you jumped the gun on us," he says in a low voice, pressing me toward the door. "Another twenty-four hours and you'd have been aboard and on the team."

His hand is touching my back as he escorts us out to his car, a mud-spattered, high-mounted, big-wheeled Mercedes Duck, a forty-thousand-dollar amphibian good for bird hunting in the pines or duck hunting in the swamp. Bob is dressed, if not for hunting, at least for a weekend at his lodge, safari tans and low-quarter boots, cashmere turtleneck. The uncle is impressed. Vergil is impassive. Our truck, I tell Bob, is parked on the Angola road. No problem, he says, and he's genial as can be, but I notice that he drops off Vergil and the uncle at Pantherburn first, even though it's out of the way.

We're sailing through the pines, the morning sun warm on

our backs. There is a pleasant sense of openness and of riding high and seeing all around, so unlike being sunk in my old spavined Caprice. The Mercedes smells like leather and oiled wood.

"Now, do you think you can get home without getting in any more trouble," says Bob, smiling at the road, "and make it to our meeting tomorrow when we're going to wind up this parole foolishness, spring you for good, and then make you an offer you can't refuse?"

"I haven't forgotten. I thank you for getting us out of jail, but frankly I'm a little confused."

"What's the problem, Doctor?" he asks, cocking an attentive ear, but I notice he's frowning at the wood dashboard, wipes the grain with his handkerchief.

"I don't understand what's going on at Grand Mer and the Ratliff intake and what your part in it is."

Bob Comeaux shakes his head fondly, socks the wheel. "Same old Tom! You always did lay it right out, didn't you?" All smiles, he goes suddenly serious. "Good question, Tom!" he says crisply.

To emphasize the seriousness—this is too important to talk about while sailing along in his Duck—we pull off at an overlook, the loess hills dropping away to a panorama of Grand Mer, the cooling tower with its single pennant of cloud, the river beyond, and upriver the monolith of Fedville.

Bob swings around to face me, so solemnly his smiling crow-feet are ironed out white. Again he socks the steering wheel softly. The windows of the Duck go down, the sunroof slides back without a sound, letting in sunlight and the fragrance of pines warming. But there is still the smell of leather, oiled wood, and pipe tobacco.

"You old rascal." He's shaking his head again. "You jumped the gun on us. I told those guys! I told them!"

"Told them what?"

"Take a look." From his suede jacket he takes a paper and hands it to me. It is stationery folded letter-size.

"So?"

204

"Take a look at the date!"

I take a look at the date. "So?"

"The date is the day before yesterday. It's already in your mail. The original, that is."

"Do you want me to read it?"

"At your leisure. It's a job offer—a proposition you can't refuse—employment to begin in"—he consults his wafer-thin Patek-Philippe—"exactly twenty-six hours, contingent only upon your clearing the formality of probation tomorrow. It's official. We even have the brass down from Bethesda, a couple of wheels from NIH. They want you aboard too."

"Job offer?"

"Tom," says Bob, his eyes both solemn and fond, "we want you aboard as senior consultant for NRC's ACMUI."

"What's that?"

He smites my knee. "You're right. That goddamn bureaucratese. Okay, try this. You're being offered a position as senior consultant on the Nuclear Regulatory Commission's Advisory Committee for the Medical Uses of Isotopes."

"Why?"

"Why? Because you know more about the brain pharmacology of isotopes than anyone else. You broke the ground. You're our man. Starting tomorrow you're on the team."

"What team?" I notice a broken V of ibis lowering on Tunica Island.

"There." He nods toward Fedville. "Your office is waiting for you. Your salary of $85,000—chickenshit, if you ask me, but it was the best I could do, so I went on the assumption that you're like me and that the service counts for something—will be supplemented by local QLC funding, which is mostly foundation money—I'm in with those guys—so you'll be making about $135,000—not up to a big-shot shrink, ha, but we figure it will free you up to do your own research, plus you'll have all the facilities of the center rent-free, as they say."

The wings of the ibis, not great flyers, are out of sync and flutter in the sunlight like confetti.

Bob pops in a cassette and soon the Mercedes is filled with Strauss waltzes coming from all directions.

"God, don't you love that," murmurs Bob, lilting along with "Artist's Life." "Doesn't that take you back to P&S, where we'd catch the Philharmonic, then hoist a tad of bourbon and branch at the Ein und Zwanzig?"

"Actually I'd be more apt to catch the flicks at Loew's State 175th Street and hoist a beer at Murray's Bar and Grill."

"Same old Tom," says Bob absently, but adjusting the four speakers, ear cocked for the right balance, listening with a frown. Satisfied, he settles back.

I take a good look at him. He has aged well. In his safari jacket, he's as handsome as Eric Sevareid, as mellow as Walter Cronkite. We two have come a long way, he as much as says, seen the follies of the world, and here we are. Like Eric and Walter he has grown both grave and amiable.

"Any questions, Tom?" asks Bob, moving his head in time with Strauss.

"What is that heavy-sodium shunt at Ratliff all about?"

Bob nods gravely, eyes going fine and gazing past me at the looming, lopped cone of Grand Mer.

"Good question. Very good question. And if you don't mind, I'll answer it in my own way with a couple of Socratic questions of my own, shrinkwise, you might say. Okay?"

"Okay." The wings of the ibis flash like shook foil and drop into the willows.

Bob leans back, puts forefinger to lips. "I'm assuming, Tom," he says, and pauses, as the strains of "Artist's Life" die away, "that we live by the same lights, share certain basic assumptions and goals."

"Yes?"

"Healing the sick, ministering to the suffering, improving the quality of life for the individual regardless of race, creed, or national origin. Right?"

"Right. But what does that have to do with heavy sodium in the water supply?"

"What does that have to do with heavy sodium in the water

206

supply," he repeats gravely. "Good question, Tom. One might have asked a similar question fifty years ago: What does it have to do with fluoride in the water supply? And if we'd asked it, we'd have gotten the same sort of flak from the Kluxers and knotheads—as you of all people know. Hence our little cloak-and-dagger secrecy. Frankly, I saw no need of it."

"So?"

"What would you say, Tom—" Bob, who has been lilting along with Strauss, leans forward and, turning down the music, fixes me with a smiling, keen-eyed look. "What would you say if I gave you a magic wand you could wave over there"—he nods over his shoulder toward Baton Rouge and New Orleans— "and overnight you could reduce crime in the streets by eighty-five percent?"

I wait, knowing there is more.

"Child abuse by eighty-seven percent?"

"You mean you've done it by—"

He waves me off. "We've done it—the numbers will be out next month—but let me finish. Teenage suicide by ninety-five percent. Ninety-five percent, Tom."

"Yes?"

"Wife battering by seventy-three percent."

"Yes?"

"Teenage pregnancy by eighty-five percent."

"Yes?"

"And here's some bad news for us shrinks." He winks at me. "Hospital admissions for depression, chemical dependence, anxiety reduced by seventy-nine percent."

"Yes?"

"And get this." He leans close. "AIDS by seventy-six percent."

"You've reduced AIDS by a heavy-sodium additive?"

"Not directly, but the numbers are there."

"How, if not directly?"

He sinks back, eyes me speculatively, turns up "Wiener Blut."

"I'll give you the easy answer first."

"All right."

"By reducing anal intercourse and drug use, shooting up with needles. That's how the LAV-HTLV-III virus is mainly transmitted, right?"

"Right. But—"

"Here comes the interesting part. Why we need you. Tom, hear this. We don't have stats for obvious reasons, but in the sodium treatment areas we've mentioned, the incidence of homosexuality has declined dramatically."

"How could you know such a thing?"

Bob shrugs. "Clinical impressions. How many homosexuals have you treated lately? And a couple of interesting items. The Gay and Lesbian Club at L.S.U. has disbanded. Voluntarily. Tom, every gay bar and bathhouse in Baton Rouge is out of business, and not from police pressure. And a tiny but telling little item: The sale of gay and S.M. video cassettes is down almost to zero. Not from censorship, Tom! From lack of interest."

"How does that come to pass, Bob?"

He appraises me. "I think you might have an idea, Tom, but I'm asking the questions, remember?"

"Then ask."

"Tom, how much do you know about chimpanzees?"

"Not much. Some. I did some work with them."

"I know. Tom, how many homosexual chimpanzees did you run across?"

"Then are you saying that you're zapping homosexuals with heavy sodium and regressing them to lower primates?"

He shakes his head, wags a finger. "You know better, Doctor. That's why we want you. For one thing, these same subjects have an average twenty percent increase in I.Q.—plus an almost total memory recall which makes you and me look like dummies. We ain't talking chimps, Tom."

"I know," I say absently. "They can tell you where St. Louis and Cut Off are."

"What?" he says sharply. "Oh, map and graphic recall. Yes, sir, they've got it. We're not zapping them. No zombies here. Far from it."

"Then what are you doing?"

He turns down "Wiener Blut." "You know what?"

"What?"

"I have an idea you might know more than we."

"Is that so?"

"That's so, but I'll tell you how much we do know."

"All right."

"We know that the heavy ion inhibits dopamine production in the prefrontal cortex—which as you know is probably the chemical basis of schizophrenia. We know it increases endorphin production, which as you know gives you a drug-free natural high. We know it suppresses the cortical response to bombardment from the limbic system, which again you know is the main source of anxiety. Tom, we can see it! In a PET-scanner! We can see the glucose metabolism of the limbic system raising all kinds of hell and getting turned off like a switch by the cortex. We can see the locus ceruleus and the hypothalamus kicking in, libido increasing—healthy heterosexual libido—and depression decreasing—we can see it! And here's the damnedest thing, Tom!—here's where we need your help—we need your help because of your expertise with the CORTscan, your baby—we know and you know that there are certain inhibitory functions in the cortex—you call it superego, Freudian forgetting—which wipe out most memory recall from the temporal lobe. Tom—!" He's as exhilarated now as "Wiener Blut."

"Those suckers can remember everything. We can see it both on PET and SPECT. Ask them a question: What did you do on your fifth birthday? and, Tom, I'm telling you, it's like watching the mainframe at NIH scanning its data bank. They retrieve it! If it's in the neurones, they get it! What do you think?"

"I'm impressed."

"Then be the devil's advocate. Attack us from your own expertise. Name one thing wrong we're doing." Both Bob and "Wiener Blut" wind up with a triumphant chord.

"Well, there's the technicality of civil rights. You're assaulting the cortex of an individual without the knowledge or consent of the assaultee."

"Assault!" He leans forward again, eyes blazing. "Let me tell you about assault and who's assaulted!"

"All right."

He points north, past Grand Mer. "Do you know what's up the river fifteen miles or so?"

"Sure. Angola."

"Right. Angola. The Louisiana State Prison Farm. Ten thousand murderers, rapists, armed robbers, society's assholes, who would as soon kill you as spit on you. That's where the assault comes from."

"So?"

"So, two little numbers, Tom. One: The admissions to Angola for violent crime from the treatment area have declined seventy-two percent since Blue Boy began."

"Blue Boy?"

"The name of our little pilot program."

"I see."

"Two: The incidence of murder, knifings, and homosexual rape in Angola, which is of course in the treatment area, has—declined—to—zero." He pauses. "Zero," he whispers.

"So why do you need me? It sounds like your pilot has succeeded."

"I'll tell you why we need you." He turns over the cassette. Here comes "Tales from the Vienna Woods." "First, you know as much about the action of radioactive isotopes on neurones as anyone—you're the pioneer. But I need you for something else."

"Yes?"

"Tom, as you intimated a moment ago, we've got an interesting philosophical question here. Both my colleagues and I need some dialoguing on the subject and we think you could contribute a very creative input."

The Strauss is very lovely. The Feliciana woods here, bathed as they are in the gold autumn sunlight, are surely as lovely as the Vienna woods. "What creative input do you have in mind, Bob?"

"Okay, try this for size. What we have here is a philosophical question. Yes, you're right, though your language was pejorative. Yes, we're treating cortical neurones by a water-soluble additive, just as we treated dental enamel by fluoride in the water fifty years ago—without the permission or knowledge of the treated. The courts upheld us then, probably will again. But that's not the question. The real, the fascinating, question is this. What do you think of this hypothesis, which is gaining ground among psychologists, anthropologists, neurologists, to mention a few disciplines—as well as among academics and in liberal-arts circles—even among our best novelists!—Kurt Vonnegut wrote a book setting forth this very thesis." He eyes me. "You already know, don't you?"

"Tell me."

"The hypothesis, Tom," says Bob, speaking slowly, "is that at least a segment of the human neocortex and of consciousness itself is not only an aberration of evolution but is also the scourge and curse of life on this earth, the source of wars, insanities, perversions—in short, those very pathologies which are peculiar to *Homo sapiens*. As Vonnegut put it"—his arm is on the back of the seat; I feel his pointy, jokey finger sticking into my shoulder—"the only trouble with *Homo sapiens* is that parts of our brains are too fucking big. What do you say to that?"

I don't say anything. He has gone elegaic. We're in the golden woods of old Vienna.

"*Homo sapiens sapiens*," he murmurs, lilting. "Or *Homo sap sap*." Reviving, he pokes me again. "We're not zapping the big brain, Tom. To put it in your terms, what we're doing is cooling the superego which, as you of all people know, can make you pretty miserable, and strengthening the ego by increasing endorphin production. No drugs, Tom—except our own—we're talking natural highs. Energies are freed up instead of being inhibited!" Here comes another poke. "News item: L.S.U. has not lost a football game in three years, has not had a point scored against them, and get this, old Tom, has not given up a single first down this season. As you well know, nobody talks in Louisiana about anything else." A final poke. "News item, Tom—not as well known but quite as significant: L.S.U.

engineering students no longer use calculators. They're as obsolete as slide rules. They've got their own built-in calculators.''

I look at him. "Do you mean to tell me—"

"All I mean to tell you is that cortical control has unlimited possibilities, once cortical hang-ups are eliminated. Just imagine a team that is always psyched up but never psyched out."

When Bob Comeaux says "hang-ups," there is just a faint echo of his Long Island City origins in "hang-gups."

"That is remarkable."

"Any questions, Doctor?" He's made his case and looks at his watch even as I'm looking at mine.

"Why don't you use some?" I ask him.

He looks right and left for eavesdroppers. "Between you and me I have—in my own family, Tom."

"I see."

"You got it, Doc?"

"I was just wondering about the decline in teen pregnancies. The mechanism of that escapes me."

He lights up. "Tom, it's beautiful. It's beautiful because it's so simple. All great scientific breakthroughs are simple. One change and presto, all the old hassles, twelve-year-olds getting knocked up, contraceptives in school, abortion, child abuse—all the old political and religious hassles are simply bypassed, left behind. Did you ever notice that the great controversies in history are never settled, that they are simply left behind? Somebody has a new idea and the old quarrels become irrelevant."

"What's the new idea?"

"It's been under our nose, so close we couldn't see it for looking. You'll kick yourself for asking."

"Tell me anyway."

"We simply change cycles, Tom."

"Change cycles."

"Sure, from menstrual to estrus. Look, Tom—"

"Yes?"

He rattles off the answer like a talk-show guest who's used to the question. "You know and I know the difference between a woman's cycle and most of female mammals'.''

"Yes."

"The human female can conceive during twenty of the twenty-eight days of her cycle. Any other female mammal can only conceive during estrus—say, eight days out of a hundred and eighty."

"So?"

"As I like to say, our sister *Homo saps*, God bless them, are in heat seventy-five percent of the time, and what I say is hurray for them and hurray for us. But any other lady mammal is in heat, say, nine percent of the time. Tom, the numbers tell the story. All you have to do with the hypothalamus is kick it into the estrus cycle and you've got a marvelous built-in natural population control. Then it's merely a matter of controlling a few days of estrus—hell, all you have to do is add one dose of progesterone twice a year to the school cafeteria diet and that's the end of it—goodbye hassles, goodbye pills, rubbers, your friendly abortionist. Goodbye promiscuity, goodbye sex ed—who needs it? Mom and Dad love it, the kids love it, and the state saves millions. Family life is improved, Tom."

"You mean you've tried it?"

"In one junior high school in Baton Rouge, five hundred black girls, year before last forty percent knocked up by age thirteen, last year one girl pregnant—one girl!—and why? because her mamma was packing her lunch box and she missed her progesterone during estrus. And, Tom, get this: a one hundred percent improvement in ACT scores in computation and memory recall in these very subjects."

"How about language?"

"Language?"

"You know, reading and writing. Like reading a book. Like writing a sentence."

"You son of a gun." Bob gives me another poke. "You don't miss much, do you? You're quite right. And for a good reason, as you must also know. We're in a different age of communication—out of McGuffey Readers and writing a theme on 'what I did last summer.' Tom, these kids are way past comic books and *Star Wars*. They're into graphic and binary communication—which after all is a lot more accurate than once upon a time there lived a wicked queen.''

"You mean they use two-word sentences.''

"You got it. And using a two-word sentence, you know what you can get out of them?''

"What?''

"They can rattle off the total exports and imports of the port of Baton Rouge—like a spread sheet—or give 'em pencil and paper and they'll give you a graphic of the tributaries of the Red River.''

"How about the drop in crime and unemployment?''

Bob smiles radiantly. "Tom, would you laugh at me if I told you what we've done is restore the best of the Southern Way of Life? Would you think that too corny?''

"Well—''

"Well, never mind. Just the facts, ma'am. Here are the facts: Instead of a thousand young punks hanging around the streets in northwest Baton Rouge, looking for trouble, stoned out, ready to mug you, break into your house, rape your daughter, packed off to Angola where they cost you twenty-five thousand a year, do you want to know what they're doing? Doing not because somebody forces them—we ain't talking Simon Legree here, boss—but doing of their own accord?''

"What?''

"Cottage industries, garden plots, but mainly apprentice-ships.''

"Apprenticeships?''

"Plumber's helpers, mechanic's helpers, gardeners, cook's helpers, waiters, handymen, fishermen—Tom, Baton Rouge is the only city in the U.S. where young blacks are outperforming the Vietnamese and Hispanics.''

"You're not talking about vo-tech training.''

"I'm talking apprenticeship. What would you do if you're running an Exxon station and a young man or woman shows up and makes himself useful for gratis, keeps the place clean, is obviously honest and industrious and willing. I'll tell you what you'd do, because I know. You'd hire him. You want to know what we're talking about?''

"What?''

"We're not talking about old massa and his niggers. We're not talking about Uncle Tom. We're talking about Uncle Tom Jefferson and his yeoman farmer and yeoman craftsman. You wouldn't believe what they can do with half an acre of no good batture land. And look at this.'' He shows me the key chain of the Mercedes. It is made of finely wrought wooden links. "Carved from one piece of driftwood.''

"Very nice.''

"Nice! You try to do it! And, Tom—''

"Yes?''

"Have you driven by the old project in Baton Rouge lately?''

"No.''

"Well, you know what they were like—monuments of bare ugliness, excrement in the stairwells, and God knows what. You know what you'd see now?''

"No.''

"Green! Trees, shrubs, flowers, garden plots—one of the anthropologists on our board noted a striking resemblance to the decorative vegetation of the Masai tribesmen—and guess what they've done with the old cinder-block entrances?''

"What?''

"They're now mosaics, bits of colored glass from Anacin bottles, taillights, whatever, for all the world like—can't you guess?''

"No.''

"The African bower bird, Tom. Lovely!''

"I see.''

"Do you remember the colorful bottle trees darkies used to make in the old days?''

"Yes,'' I say, wondering how Bob Como of Long Island City knows about bottle trees.

"We got some in the Desire project. Yes, Blue Boy's there.''

"I see.''

"Would you deny that is superior to the old fuck-you graffiti?"

"No." I look at my watch. "I've got to go home. Two questions."

"Shoot. Make them hard questions."

"Are you still disposing of infants and old people in your Qualitarian Centers?"

Bob Comeaux looks reproachful. "That's unfair, Tom."

"I didn't say I disapproved. I was just asking."

"Ah ha. All right! What you're talking about is pedeuthanasia and gereuthanasia. What we're doing, as you well know, is following the laws of the Supreme Court, respecting the rights of the family, the consensus of child psychologists, the rights of the unwanted child not to have to suffer a life of suffering and abuse, the right of the unwanted aged to a life with dignity and a death with dignity. Toward this end we—to use your word—dispose of those neonates and euthanates who are entitled to the Right to Death provision in the recent court decisions."

"Neonate? Euthanate?"

"I think you're having me on, Tom. We've spoken of this before. But I'll answer you straight, anyhow. A neonate is a human infant who according to the American Psychological Association does not attain its individuality until the acquisition of language and according to the Supreme Court does not acquire its legal rights until the age of eighteen months—an arbitrary age to be sure, but one which, as you well know, is a good ballpark figure. You of all people know this. Consult your fellow shrinks."

"I see."

"Next question?"

"How does Van Dorn figure in this?"

He laughs. "Ah, Van. Van the man, the Renaissance man. I'll tell you the truth. That guy makes me uncomfortable. I'm just an ordinary clinician, Tom. Just a guy out to improve a little bit the quality of life for all Americans. He does too many things well: tournament bridge, Olympic soccer, headmaster, computer hacker—he runs the computer division at Mitsy. In a word, he's the Mitsy end of the sodium shunt and is a consultant to NRC besides. He's to NRC what I am to NIH. He's project manager of the coolant division at Grand Mer—which means it's up to him to dispose of waste heavy sodium. No problem! Without him there'd be no goodies coming down the pipe. He not only set up the entire computer program for Mitsy but also the follow-up program for the beneficiaries of our little pilot program—some one hundred thousand or so subjects. We know how they're performing as individuals and as a class. If you want to know the medical status of Joe Blow, a hairdresser in Denham Springs, he'll hit a key and tell you. If you want to know the incidence of AIDS in all the hairdressers and interior decorators in the treatment area, he'll hit a key and tell you. As a matter of fact, he mainly credits you with his success. He says you're going down in history as the father of isotope brain pharmacology."

"I see."

"So for better or worse, Doctor, it appears you're one of us."

"So it seems."

"Van Dorn." He shakes his head. "What a character. I think he's a bit of a spook myself, but he does think in large terms. This little project is small potatoes to him. He's got bigger fish to fry."

"What are they?"

"A little item which he calls the sexual liberation of Western civilization. According to Van, the entire Western world has been hung up on sex since St. Paul."

"I see."

"We call him our Dr. Ruth, Dr. Ruth of the bayous."

"Dr. Ruth?"

"Dr. Ruth Westheimer, the good-sex lady. A little joke."

"I see. Okay, would you mind taking me to my car?"

We're sailing through the sunlit pines, "The Beautiful Blue Danube" all around us. Bob is enjoying himself. He puts a soft fist on my knee.

"Tom, we need you. We want you on the team. We need your

old sour, sardonic savvy to keep us honest. You understand, don't you?''

''Yes.''

''Okay, one thing. Tell me honestly. Don't pull punches. Has anything you've heard in the last few minutes about the behavioral effects of the sodium additive struck you as socially undesirable?''

''Not offhand, though it's hard to say. I'll have to think it over.''

''There you go!'' Again the soft congratulatory fist on my knee. ''That's the answer we're looking for. Be hard on us! Be our Dutch uncle!''

''What about the cases of gratuitous violence—Mickey La-Faye shooting all her horses—the rogue violence of that postal worker in St. Francisville who shot everybody in the post office?''

Now he socks himself. ''You've already put your finger on it!'' he cries aloud. ''That's why we need you.''

''I have?''

''Rogue. You said it. You know what happens once in a while with elephants, which, as you know, have the largest brain of all land mammals and the best memory scansion?''

''Rogue elephants?''

''Once in a great while. We don't know why with them and we don't know why with us. Oh, we got bugs, Tom. Why do you think we're bothering with you?''

''I understand.'' I see my Caprice pulled off the road at the Ratliff gate. After the Mercedes it looks as if it had been junked and abandoned.

We shake hands. ''One last thing, Tom,'' Bob says in a different voice, not letting go of my hand. ''I know that you'll respect the confidentiality of what we've been talking about. But there's a little legal hook to it too.''

''Legal?''

''It's a formality, but by virtue of the fact that you know about Project Blue Boy, you are now in the Grade Three section of the

National Security Act and are subject to the jurisdiction of the ATFA security guys.''

"It sounds like you're reading me my rights."

"I am! That's what comes from messing with feds."

"Are those the guys who busted us over there?" I nod toward Lake Mary.

"Oh no. Those were county mounties. We've got a working arrangement with them. The ATFA guys keep a low profile. But I'm afraid they'll be watching you—just as they watch me. It's a small price, Tom.''

"What is ATFA?"

"Alcohol, Tobacco, and Firearms. Tom, those guys make the FBI look like Keystone Kops."

A final firm handshake. "Tomorrow morning nine o'clock, my office at Fedville. I want you to meet my colleagues in Blue Boy. Tom, they're good guys. You'll like them. They're the best of two worlds."

"What two worlds?"

"Try to imagine a Harvard and M.I.T. brain who is not an asshole and try to imagine a Texas Humana can-do surgeon who is not an airhead."

"I'll try."

9. ELLEN IS GONE. MARGARET AND TOMMY ARE GONE. Hudeen and Chandra are in an uproar. It is hard to get the story.

A Cox Cable van is parked two blocks from The Quarters. A man in the cherry picker is working on the line. He and the driver pay no attention to me.

Chandra has a new job and a car to go with it, a white compact with WOW-TV in large black letters. She's the Feliciana correspondent and will do her first assignment this afternoon, the horse show at the Feliciana Free Fair. She's full of it. She uses words like "major market," "doing a remote," "feature segment."

Where is Ellen?

Hudeen, who long ago gave up ordinary talk except for exclamations and demurrers, can't seem to relate the sequence of events.

Chandra, excited and nervous about her new job, is not much better.

I have to get the story by a series of questions, sitting facing Chandra at the breakfast table, Hudeen standing as usual at the sink, shelling peas and cooking greens, one eye cocked on the old Sony Trinitron. Watching *As the World Turns*, which has been on for fifty years. There's young, now old, Chris Hughes. Over thirty years ago I was watching Grandpa Hughes counseling Ellen when the first bulletin came on that Kennedy had been plugged. Hudeen, sensing my alarm, is willing to turn down the sound and answer questions.

Ellen, it seems, has gone to Fresno, after all.

She left this morning.

With Dr. Van Dorn?

No, but he picked her up and took her to the Baton Rouge airport.

Tommy and Margaret went to school as usual, right?

Yes, he took them and they going to stay there as boarders while Miss Ellen gone.

What? What do you mean they're staying there? Why aren't they staying here?

Hudeen: I own no. Like I tole Miss Ellen, we take care them, ain't that right, Chandra?

Chandra, sobering up from being a TV personality: Yes, that's perfectly true. We're perfectly capable of taking care of them. Hudeen is here during the afternoon and I'm here at night. In fact, I offered to take them to the fair and they wanted to go. But after Dr. Van Dorn talked to your wife, they decided it would be better if they stayed at the school with the boarders.

For the whole week?

220

Yes.

I see.

"He done give her a whole big box of Go Diver," says Hudeen, hand on the volume control.

"What?"

Chandra: "After they talked in there," Chandra nods toward the living room, "more like arguing at first, while we were keeping Tommy and Margaret in here. Yes, he did give her a five-pound box of Godiva chocolates, which she ate while I was packing for her and the children. And about that time I get my call from WOW—"

"You say she ate them all?"

"I mean all," says Hudeen.

They get into a discussion of Godiva chocolates.

"She already a little heavy, I tole her!" Hudeen exclaims into the sink. "And I had her breakfast ready, her and the chirren, some fried grits and gravy, which don't put no weight on nobody."

Chandra is shaking her head at me and rolling her eyes up.

Hudeen, who doesn't miss much, sees her.

"Don't you mock me, girl!"

"I'm not mocking you." Chandra turns to me. "It's not the calories so much as the sugar metabolism and known carcinogens in chocolate."

Sugar metabolism. Carcinogens. I'm not following this.

"Just a minute." I hold out a hand to each. "Hold it. Let me get this straight. You, ya'll, are saying that Ellen had an argument with Dr. Van Dorn, that he gave her a box of candy, that you had to pack for her and the children, that she's gone to Fresno by herself, and that the children are going to stay at Belle Ame with the boarders?"

"Sho," says Hudeen, keeping an eye on Chris Hughes's granddaughter, a girl in deep trouble.

"She was quite upset about something," explains Chandra, again shaking her head at Hudeen, "which was why I helped with the packing—"

"Wasn't studyin' any packing," says Hudeen. "I tell her, I say, Miss Ellen, you got to pack."

"But she was fine, don't worry," says Chandra, as sober and sensible as I could want. "She polishes off that box of candy, which would have polished me off, and is perfectly fine. I don't like that man," she adds thoughtfully.

"Who, Dr. Van Dorn? Why not?"

"He's manipulative. I don't trust him," says Chandra.

"He biggety too," says Hudeen.

"How do you mean?"

"Telling me to call Carrie Bon and tell her Claude he staying out there too. Didn't ax, told, like I'm working for him."

"Wait. You're telling me that Dr. Van Dorn asked you to call Carrie Bon, Vergil and Claude's mother, at Pantherburn and tell her that Claude was going to be staying at Belle Ame too?"

"That what I'm telling you."

I look at Chandra. She shrugs. "That was after I left. I had got my call."

"What did you do, Hudeen?" Hudeen doesn't turn around but holds up both hands, pale salmon-colored palms turned up. "What I'm going to do, he standing right there holding out the phone. So I told her he be staying on with Tommy and Margaret and she say all right."

"I see."

"I sent him some clothes too, but he big."

"I know."

"I sent him your sweater and pajamas."

"Good."

"Dr. Tom—" For the first time Hudeen turns to face me, drying her hands with her apron, eyes almost meeting mine, then falling away. "I sho wish you'd— Ain't no way I can—" She turns back to the sink.

I look at Chandra. She too opens her hands. "She means that Tommy and Margaret need more parenting and that Mrs. More is preoccupied with her bridge or with—" She too falls silent.

Parenting. True, I could use more parenting skills.

We all fall silent.

I'm thinking about the argument and the Godiva chocolates. Then I think of nothing. Then something occurs to me.

"Chandra, I want you to do me a favor."

"Ask it." There is something alarming about her new gravity, her attentiveness to me. I think I liked her smart-aleckness better. "I got a few minutes before I have to do this remote. I'm meeting the camera crew and the remote unit."

"This won't take long. I want you to make a phone call for me."

"No problem." She picks up the wall phone.

"No. Don't you have a cellular phone in your car?"

"I surely do." She looks both pleased and puzzled.

"Okay, but first hand me that phone and I'll make a call."

Hudeen and Chandra make an effort to appear not to listen as I make my call. But they don't talk. Hudeen turns off the sink tap.

I call Belle Ame. A woman's voice answers. I ask for Van Dorn. He's not there.

"This is Dr. Thomas More. With whom am I speaking?"

"Oh, Dr. More! This is Mrs. Cheney from homeroom. You remember me!"

"I sure do."

"Dr. Van Dorn will be back in a few minutes. He's down at the soccer field."

"Very good, Mrs. Cheney." She has the sweet-lady voice of a sorority housemother. "I am calling to tell you I am picking up Tommy and Margaret and Claude Bon in about an hour. You can tell Dr. Van Dorn when he gets back."

"Well surely, Doctor, but I thought—"

"Plans have been changed. I'm picking them up. Please have them ready, Mrs. Cheney."

"I surely will, Doctor. But—"

But I've hung up. I pass the phone to Chandra. She looks at me.

"Chandra, I can't explain now—we have to move fast—but will you make a call for me from your cellular phone in your car?"

"Of course."

"You were leaving anyway."

"Yes, I—"

"Can you leave this instant?"

"Sure." She gets up. She hears something in my voice. "What's the call?" She's good. She doesn't ask why.

"Do this please. Go to your car, but don't make the call until you've driven ten blocks past those Cox Cable linemen. Then park and make this call. Call Belle Ame, here's the number. Ask for a Mr. or Mrs. Brunette. All I want to find out is if they're at the school. You don't need to talk to them. Mrs. Cheney will probably answer the phone. You will learn right away either that they're with the school or that she never heard of them. Hang up. You understand?"

"I understand," she says, watching me like a hawk.

"Then call me. If Mr. and Mrs. Brunette are with the school, say this: Dr. More, I just called to say I can make it tonight. If Mrs. Cheney never heard of them, say: Dr. More, I'm sorry, but I'm going to be tied up at work. Do you understand?"

"I understand." What she hears in my voice is the urgency. She's halfway to the door.

"I appreciate this, Chandra. We have to be careful, even with a cellular phone. I'll explain later."

"No problem." She's gone.

After Chandra leaves, Hudeen and I are silent. Finally Hudeen says "Shew!" and then after a while she says, I think, "Humbug."

I move to Chandra's chair next to the wall phone. The seat is still warm from Chandra.

Before I know it, Hudeen has given me a plate of Tennessee ham, collard greens, black-eyed peas, two corn sticks which she makes in an iron mold, and a slab of sweet butter. "You ain't going nowhere till you eat this. You looking poor. You *been* looking poor." By poor Hudeen means I'm not fat. "You want some buttermilk?"

"Yes."

I eat fast, watching the stove clock. It takes four minutes for the phone to ring. Hudeen jumps and says "Lawd." I let the phone ring twice. I pick it up.

"Hello"—with a mouth full of collards.

"Dr. More?"

"Yes?"

"Chandra Wilson."

"Yes, Chandra?"

"I just called in to the station and I can make it tonight."

"Thank you for calling, Chandra. I hope you'll feel better." I hang up.

I eat it all. The ham is strong and salty. The collards are even stronger than Carrie's mustards, stronger than the meat. Hudeen nods. She is pleased. She wants me fat.

I look at my watch and call Lucy at Pantherburn.

"Lucy—" I begin.

"Oh, my Lord, I've been worried to death. There's something I've got to—"

I cut her off. "Lucy, I appreciate your concern for your uncle and I'm on my way."

"What?" she says. "What?"

"I most deeply appreciate your concern for your uncle. I'm leaving now, okay?"

"Okay, but—" She understands that something is up and I can't talk.

"I need you to help me make a professional call, okay?"

"Okay"—baffled, but she'll go along.

"I'll see you in half an hour, okay?"

"Half an hour," she repeats in a neutral voice; then collecting herself: "Fine, I appreciate it!"

I finish the last of the buttermilk. "Thanks, Hudeen. They'll be back tonight."

"Bless God! I sho be glad."

"Hudeen, don't call Carrie Bon about Claude. Don't call anybody."

"Bless God, I'm not calling a soul."

10. THE COX CABLE VAN IS STILL IN PLACE, THE LINE-
man still in his bucket, the driver still behind the
wheel. Neither man looks at me.

A pickup follows me through town, but it passes me on the
boulevard, a new four-door Ranger. The passenger on the right
wears a new denim jacket, a long-billed, mesh Texaco cap. He
does not look at me. There is a nodding toy dog on top of the
dash and a gun rack in the rear window. There is only one gun
in the rack, an under-and-over rifle-shotgun. For a mile or so
the Ranger stays a couple of blocks ahead. But when I pull into
a service station it keeps going.

I call Lucy at the pay phone. Her "hello" is guarded.

"I'm at a service station in town. I can talk. I'm on my way
to pick up Margaret and Tommy and Claude at Belle Ame. I'll
explain. Since you are making a professional call there, why
don't I pick you up? That way I could drop you and Claude off.
To save time, meet me at Popeyes. Okay?"

"Sure." She is still cautious, knowing only that something is
up.

No sign of the van or the Ranger on I-12 or the River Road.

Lucy's truck is parked at the rear of Popeyes, backed in under
a magnolia heading out. It is two-forty-five. I park close, heading in, make a motion for her to stay put, and open the driver's
door. She slides over. She wears her white clinician's coat—
good, she picked up on the "professional call"—and has her
doctor's bag. She places the bag precisely on her lap, her hands
precisely on top of the bag. She gives me a single ironic look
under her heavy eyebrows but says nothing.

"We don't have much time," I say. We are spinning up River
Road. I feel her eyes on me as I drive. "I have something to tell
you. I think you have something to tell me. I'll go first."

226

"You go first," Lucy says.

"Ellen has gone to a bridge tournament in Fresno for the rest of the week. Without Van Dorn. I have reason to believe she is not well. I also have reason to believe there is something going on at Belle Ame, possibly involving the sexual abuse of children. For some reason Van Dorn has arranged for Tom and Margaret and Claude Bon to stay there with the boarders. I am going to pick them up after school. I don't think there is anything to worry about—with them. What I would like to do is have a word with Van Dorn, and while I'm talking to him, I'd like for you to look around, preferably in a professional capacity, maybe some sort of routine epidemiological check, talk to children and staff, whoever, see what you can see."

She hangs fire, eyes still on me, not altogether gravely. "Is that it?"

"For the present."

"As it happens, I can do better than that. I was over there last week checking on a little salmonella outbreak. Nothing serious, but it would make sense for me to make a follow-up call, collect a couple of smears. In fact, I ought to."

"Good."

"May I say something now?"

"Sure. Till we get there. Which is right up the road."

River Road is sunny and quiet. The traffic is light: two tourist buses, three cars with Midwest plates, half a dozen standard Louisiana pickups, three hauling boats. No new Ranger or van.

She speaks rapidly and clearly. "Comeaux is on to you. Their mainframe flagged down all our inquiries last night. They know what we know and that we know, even the individual cases. I've been at my terminal and telephone for the last two hours."

"That's okay. I've already spoken to Comeaux."

"Here's something that's not okay." Her voice slows. "Neither NIH nor NRS nor ACMUI ever heard of a sodium pilot by the name of Blue Boy or any other name. What do you think of that?"

"Maybe they don't want to tell you."

"Tom, I've got Grade Four clearance. I can access all three of them. Furthermore, I talked to Jesse Land himself."

"Who's he?"

"The director of ACMUI, and a friend and classmate at Vanderbilt. He would know and he would tell me."

"That is strange, but right now all I want to do is—"

"Tom."

"Yes?"

"Listen, please. This is stranger than you think. This means that Blue Boy is unauthorized officially and must have been put together by some sort of dissident coalition from NRC and NIH with some foundation money, probably Ford—I think I picked up something from them—plus an interesting local political connection."

"Very interesting, but what are you worried about? Evidently you've already blown the whistle, told Jesse whoever."

"It don't work that way, Tom."

"It don't?"

"You don't keep up with politics, do you?"

"No."

"The way it is in politics, Tom, is that if you're head of an agency you generally like to keep your job."

"I see."

"Tom, may I give you a couple of elementary political facts?"

"Sure. You've got a couple of minutes."

She speaks patiently, patting my thigh to make her points. "Number one: Tom, you are aware that the presidential election will occur next month?"

"I was aware of that."

"You're aware that the incumbent ticket is a shoo-in, almost certain winners?"

"I suppose." I am thinking of all the politcal arguments at Fort Pelham, which were endless and boring and often inflamed to the point of fights.

"Tom, if this Blue Boy outfit can make it until November 7, they've got it made for good. Blue Boy can be presented as a *fait accompli*. They've got the clinical results, Tom, the numbers. And the numbers are going to be irresistible. And, Tom, they're not only going to be authorized if they can make it by then, they're going to be heavily funded. NIH can't turn them down. You know that, don't you?''

"Well—" I look at my watch. School is out.

This time Lucy's hand stays on my thigh. "But there's one fly in the ointment, Tom."

"Is that so?"

"That's so. Guess who?"

"Who?"

"You."

"Me."

"Tom, you're the one thing they're worried about. You're the danger. They even have a name for you—or what they're afraid you might become."

"What's that?"

"An intervener. Which is to say, the deadliest sort of whistleblower. Tom, they have to do something about you."

"I know. They offered me a job. On the team."

"Are you taking it?"

"I haven't decided."

"Tom, for Christ's sake, they can send you back to Alabama, or—"

"Or?"

"Nothing."

"How could they send me back to Alabama?"

"Tom, you busted your parole when you crashed into the shunt site on Tunica Island. They have you."

"I see. So?"

"He thinks you've already blown the whistle on them."

"How's that?"

"It seems the deal between your pal Bob and your Father Smith has fallen through. Father Smith is not only not going to sell his hospice to them, he called the wrath of God down on him. Bob thinks you told him about the pilot and that you're going to turn loose the Catholics and fundamentalists on him. That would blow it."

"I suppose."

"Fortunately, you've got one thing going for you. No, two things."

"Yes?"

"One, Father Smith is crazy as a jaybird and everyone knows it. He spoke to Bob through a bullhorn."

"What's the other?"

"The other is, you're not exactly the type to get involved in religious crusades, and everybody knows that."

"So?"

"Tom." She has come close. There's half the seat left beyond her. We're spinning down River Road in the pickup like Louisiana lovers.

"Yes?"

"Bob Comeaux laid it out for me one, two, three. He was perfectly open and aboveboard and, Tom—"

"Yes?"

"He's got a good case."

"He has?"

"May I tell you?"

"Tell me later." I can see the widow's walk of Belle Ame over a cypress break.

"We're here. Let's get the kids." We're through the great iron gates of Belle Ame and into an English park.

Nothing could look less sinister than the gentle golden light of Louisiana autumn, which is both sociable and sad, casting shadows from humpy oaks across a peopled park, boys and girls in running suits gold and green, a bus loading up with day students, and the playing fields beyond, youth in all the rinsing sadness of its happiness, bare-legged pep-squad girls flourishing in sync banners as big as Camelot, boys in a pickup game of touch coming close to the girls both heedless and mindful.

Lucy speaks quickly, one hand creasing the flesh of my thigh to fold the words in.

"Take the job with Comeaux. You have no choice."

"I probably will. Look out for a couple named Brunette, a Mr. and Mrs. Brunette."

"Okay. You and the kids better spend the night at Pantherburn."

"Why?"

"Your phone's bugged, for one thing. Hal told me."

"So is yours, probably."

"Not now."

"Why not?"

"I fixed a device on my modem."

"You have a lovely one."

"What?"

"I said you have a lovely modem."

"You're crazy."

"Come back in half an hour. Head for the rec room over there."

I'm not looking at her now but at Van Dorn. He's coming down the outside staircase of Belle Ame, which hangs like a necklace from this lovely old lady of a house. Belle Ame, lovely lady. He's smiling, his arms outstretched. He's expecting us.

11. BELLE AME IS NESTLED UNDER THE LEVEE IN A magnolia grove, which hides most of the tank farm which surrounds it on three sides and the towers and pipery of the refinery which used to hum night and day like twenty dynamos before the oil wells dried up.

This is no hard-used, working plantation house like Pantherburn. There are no Sears freezers on the gallery, no bird dogs scrabbling in the hall. Belle Ame has been restored to its 1857 splendor, a slightly vulgar splendor, showy and ritzy even then, with its florid Corinthian columns from late rich Rome and the late rich South. It is even more showy and ritzy now, as much now the creature of Texaco and Hollywood as of King Cotton then. Texaco, which owned it, wanted to do something "cultural'' to show they were not despoiling the state. Hollywood wanted its own dream palace of the South. More movies have been made here than on Paramount's back lot. Susan Hayward and John Carroll are its proper tenants. Clint Eastwood, a Yankee deserter, unshaven but not ungallant, was hidden out here by Southern belles, a bevy of hoopskirted starlets from Sunset Boulevard . . .

Outside, between its far-flung wings, its famous twin staircases rise and curve as delicately as filigree between the columns of its slightly vulgar, thrusting Roman portico. The grounds are scattered with no less pretentious structures, garçonnières, pigeonnières, slave quarters, and even a columned Greek-revival privy.

Texaco, which didn't need it, gave the place to a private school, which had been founded to revive the traditional Southern academy founded on Greek ideals of virtue and to avoid the integration of the public schools.

Van Dorn holds out a hand to each of us. ''Old Br'er Possum Tom! Cud'n Lucy!'' He gives her a kiss, pulls us close, holds us off. ''Look at you two. I like. Splendid. Aren't y'all kissin' cousins too?'' Van Dorn looks good, his gray-green eyes glittering, his heavy handsome pocked face not pale but slightly flushed as if he had just waked. He's wearing old air force coveralls with knee pockets and loops for tools. He extracts a big Stillson wrench. ''Pardon the mess but guess who's the number-one handyman here. Have you tried to hire a plumber lately, Lucy? I've been up to my ass in cellar water. Come on in. Excuse me,'' he says, bowing to Lucy. ''Not Cud'n but Dr. Lipscomb, I believe. Nurse Cheney is expecting you.''

''I've come to pick up the kids, Van,'' I say, feeling better about him. ''I called Mrs. Cheney.''

''Sho now. Okay, come on in and I'll have 'em rounded up from the dorm or more likely from the stables.''

''Y'all go on in,'' says Lucy. ''I'll just go on over there to the rec room. I know the way.''

''Sho now. Tom—'' He opens a hand to me and the house.

Van Dorn doesn't mind Lucy striking out on her own. Inside,

232

he fixes his half-drunk drink and offers me one. I shake my head. We're in a splendid room, what I remember as an old-style living room but now turned into a sort of gaming room with a large round mahogany-and-rosewood poker table with red-leather inlay and slots for the chips, a Bokhara rug, a severe Derby mantel on which, however, are scattered half a dozen teal and pintail decoys. The plantation desk, stomach-high, so the busy squire, on the run between hunts, could write checks standing, has become a dry bar, with crystal decanters of whiskey and toddy glasses.

We are sitting at the poker table, Van Dorn gazing down at his bourbon, face grave. "I owe you an apology. I thought to be doing ya'll a favor, keeping the kids."

"Yes?"

"With Ellen headed for Fresno and you busy as a bird dog with your practice, I told her the kids were perfectly welcome to stay with us. She seemed quite worried. And she couldn't locate you."

"Thanks. I understand. But I've got Chandra to help me look after them. Is something wrong with Ellen?"

"I'm glad you asked, Tom." Van Dorn, still gazing at his drink, pulls back his upper lip. "I'm really glad you asked. Frankly I've been concerned, Tom."

"Is that so?"

"It's the mood swings, Tom"—he looks up, fine eyes glittering even in the soft light of the room—"which I'm sure you've noticed and which you certainly know more about than I do. But I've got news for you."

"Yes?"

"This trip is going to help her!"

"Is that right?"

"You better believe it."

"How?"

"I'll tell you how. She and Sheri are going to win the non-master pairs, she's going to go over one hundred MPs, become a master in her own right, and come home feeling great!"

"Oh, is Sheri going with her?" I feel better.

"I insisted on it. Sheri'll look after her. And Ellen will carry Sheri in the non-master pairs. Sheri's competent enough, though no super-lady like Ellen. Hell, Ellen would win it even with you, ha ha!"

"How do you know?"

"Like I told you, Tom, remember? She somehow knows the cards."

"How do you mean?"

"Tom." Van Dorn leans toward me, cradling his drink in both hands, elbows propped on the green baize. "I've tested her. After three rounds of play or two rounds of bidding, she knows the exact probability of distribution. I checked the math of it. She doesn't know how she knows, but she knows."

"How do you think she knows, Van?" I watch him curiously. He's exhilarated. He's still grave, but there's a fondness and a thrill in his gravity.

"I—don't—know, Tom! I've ruled out ESP. It's nothing supernatural. What she's doing is high-order math without knowing how she does it."

"Like an idiot savant."

Van Dorn gives me a single, steely look. "Don't hand me that, old buddy. That lady is not only not an idiot, as you well know, but is a great lady in her own right."

"Right. Is she on heavy sodium, Van?" I ask in the same voice.

He sets down his drink, eyes level, lips thin. "I'm glad you asked, Tom. Now that you're part of the team. If she is, old buddy, she ain't getting it here. You see that?" Picking up his drink, he holds it toward the French window. Beyond it, beyond the magnolias rises a silver bullet of a water tower. "You know where our water comes from? A ten-inch flow well, artesian water fifteen hundred feet straight down. More to the point, Doctor, where does yours come from?" He sits back, drinks his drink. "I knew you knew about Blue Boy. Seriously, where does your water come from?"

"Same as yours. The town has an artesian well."

We look at each other. He smiles for the first time. "You're a sly one. You didn't suppose, did you, that I didn't know that you knew about the boys' little Hadacol juice in the water?''

"I supposed that you knew. I talked to Bob Comeaux and he told me you were on the ACMUI team."

Van Dorn snorts and pushes back in his poker chair. "Me with those Rover boys? No way. No, I'm only a visiting fireman, consultant, no, those guys wanted some coolant—I'm the project engineer—I got the go-ahead from the guys at NRC. They had medical spread sheets from NIH, which looked promising to me. Hell, that's down your alley, Tom. You're the expert on the pharmacology of radioactive isotopes, especially sodium. You tell me."

"What do you think of that pilot, Van?" I ask, watching him.

"Blue Boy? Shit." He clucks, makes a face, pulls up close. "You really want to know what I think of those guys?"

"Yes."

"I think they're a bunch of Rover boys, eagle-scout mid-level bureaucrats, Humana airheads, Texas cowboys—hell, that's where I made my money, Texas, remember? I know those types—who ride into town and shoot up the rustlers and have a ball doing it."

"You don't approve of what they're doing?"

He gives a great open-hand Texas shrug. "Well, who's going to argue about knocking back crime, suicide, AIDS, and improving your sex life—any more than you'd argue about knocking back dental caries by putting fluoride in the water. But that's not the point."

"What's the point?"

"The point is, you don't have to throw out the baby with the bathwater. You don't treat human ills by creaming the human cortex. That's a technologist for you. Give a technologist a new technique and he'll run with it like a special-team scatback."

"Are you talking about Dr. Comeaux and Dr. Gottlieb and their colleagues?"

Van Dorn makes a face. "Max Gottlieb is unhappy with them too. He's a reluctant conspirator. But he's locked in—by his position at Fedville. But the rest of those guys, you want to know what they are?''

Not really. ''What?''

''Those guys are a bunch of ham-fisted social engineers, barnyard technicians, small-time Washington functionaries, long-distance reformers—you know who they remind me of? They remind me of the New England abolitionists, that bunch of guilt-ridden Puritan transcendentalist assholes who wanted to save their souls by freeing the slaves and castrating the planters. These guys—you know how they produce Olympic weight lifters in the U.S.S.R.? By steroids and testosterone—the same way they do football players and racehorses in Texas. These guys are running a barnyard. That's no way to treat social ills or to treat people. Those damn cowboys are killing flies with sledgehammers. Do you know the latest they're up to?''

''No.''

''Okay, so we've got a problem with teen pregnancy, children getting knocked up by the thousands right here. Plus a mean, demoralized, criminal black underclass. A real problem, right? But you don't cure it by knocking back all women in the pilot area into a pre-primate estrus cycle, do you? You don't treat depression by lobotomizing the patient anymore, do you? You don't treat homosexuals by dumping stuff in their water supply and turning them into zombies, do you?''

''What do you do, Van?''

But he doesn't need an answer. He's jumped up to fix another drink and is pacing up and down. He stops above me. ''You don't treat the ills of society by dumping stuff in the water supply, Tom.''

''Then why did you participate in the project? It was you who gave them the sodium isotope.''

''I'll tell you why, Tom.'' He's brooding now, eyes as brilliant as agates. ''Because it's war. In time of war and in time of plague you have to be Draconian.''

''Plague? War? What war?''

''Tom, we have, as you damn well know, three social plagues which are going to wreck us just as surely as the bubonic plague wrecked fourteenth-century Europe. If you'd been in London in 1350, wouldn't you have dumped penicillin in the water supply, even if it meant a lot of toxic reactions? Wouldn't you have quarantined the infected?''

"What three plagues are we talking about, Van?"

He counts them off with big referee arm strokes. "One: crime. We can't go out in our own streets, Tom. Murder, rape, armed robbery, up eighty percent. We don't have to tolerate that. Two: teenage suicide and drug abuse, the number-one and -two killers of our youth. Number three: AIDS. Now we're talking plague, Tom, five million infected, a quarter million dead.''

"So why are you complaining about this pilot project?"

"Tom, I have no quarrel with their short-term goals. Every society has the right to protect itself—even if it means temporary loss of civil liberties. But those cowboys—hell, they like what they're doing, and I think they want to keep on doing it. You want to know what their trouble is?" He leans over me. I can smell breathed bourbon.

"What?"

"Goals, Tom. They have no ultimate goals. They don't know what in the hell they're trying to accomplish. They're treating everything in sight, curing symptoms and wiping out goals. It's like treating a headache with a lobotomy. Tom, we have to leave the patient human enough to achieve the ultimate goals of being human.''

"What are the ultimate goals of being human, Van?" I look at my watch. I'm already sorry I asked. Where is Lucy?

Now Van is half-sitting on the poker table, swinging a leg, arms folded, at his ease, well-clad and graceful in his coveralls and—yes, exhilarated. He's nodding, eyes gone fine and far-away.

"I'll answer that by telling you what I tell the boys and girls out there. Incidentally, it's no accident, Tom, that since we took over this seg academy, we've got the highest SAT scores in the state and the most National Merit scholars. You know what the answer is, Tom, the only answer? Excellence. We give them the tough old European Gymnasium-Hochschule treatment. We work their little asses—''

"Right. Look, Van. I have to find Lucy. We have an appointment—''

"Sure, sure.'' He goes on but we're moving toward the door.

We're walking in the magnolia alley toward the parking lot, Van taking measured steps, sauntering planter-style, hands in pockets, gazing down at the fine pea gravel. No sign of Lucy.

"Tom, would you like to hear my own private theory of the nature of man?''

The nature of man. I can't stand theories about the nature of man. I'd rather listen to Robin Leach and watch *Barnaby Jones*.

"Well, actually I think we'd better track down Lucy—''

But he's got going on his theory of the nature of man. It has something to do with science and sexuality, how the highest achievements of man, Mozart's music, Einstein's theory, derive from sexual energy, and so on. "Didn't old Dr. Freud say it?'' he says triumphantly, stopping me and swinging around to face me.

"Well, not exactly—''

There are times when you can't listen to someone utter another sentence. This is one of them. Even shrinks run out of patience. Where is Lucy? I find myself looking attentive, either by frowning down at the pea gravel and presenting an ear or by maintaining a lively understanding eye contact meanwhile shifting around a bit so I can catch sight of Lucy, who, I calculate, should appear just beyond Van Dorn's ear.

Van Dorn is saying something about Don Giovanni, not the opera but the old Don himself being, in his opinion, a member of this company of sexual geniuses. "Wouldn't you agree?''

"Actually—'' I catch sight of Lucy behind the boxwood. She's converging on the alley from the service drive. I do not at first see the children but then, just above the hedge, two heads bob. She's in a hurry. She doesn't see me.

Van Dorn is talking but I'm not listening. I'm watching Lucy. There is something odd— She is perhaps two hundred yards away and could easily see us but she doesn't look. Her eyes are straight ahead. She walks with a curious stiff rapid gait.

"One thing," I interrupt Van Dorn.

"Yes?"

"You didn't know that Ellen had gotten a dose of heavy sodium?"

"No, I didn't."

"Why should I believe you?"

Van Dorn looks at me level-eyed. "If I had known it, would I have been so curious about her amazing talent for computing probabilities in bridge?"

"Well—no." He's right.

Van Dorn has seen Lucy. Her cheek is hard and high. I think she's seen us.

Van Dorn grabs me and pulls me playfully close—in men's style of talking at the approach of women and before they come within earshot. "Just suppose, Tom, we could combine the high sexuality of the Don and Einstein without the frivolity of the Don or the repressed Jewish sexuality of Einstein—who needs heavy sodium?"

"Right," I say. "Where's Claude Bon?"

Van Dorn turns. We watch the three approach. Lucy, Tommy and Margaret, the children moseying along rapt, regardless, normal; Lucy stone-faced and stiff, headed straight for the truck without looking at us though we're fifty feet away.

"Oh. I forgot to tell you. Claude's varsity now and they're playing Baton Rouge High, the state champs, and I kid you not, B.R. is in for the surprise of the year."

We meet Lucy at the truck. Van Dorn opens the door for her.

"Howdy, Miss Lucy."

She doesn't answer, but Van Dorn calls to me over the cab of the truck. "You can pick up Claude later tonight. Or I'll send him over. Let me know, folks."

I catch sight of Lucy's face as she stoops to get in. It is welted, almost ugly. A rope of muscle twists her black eyebrows. Her cheek is pulled back, freckles dark plum against pale skin. She says only, "Get in," to Tommy and Margaret, pushing them ahead of her, then backs up to let them in the middle, then gets in and slams the door. She's driving.

We leave. She looks straight ahead, face set. The pickup is old and big. There is room for the four of us on the broad front seat. In the rearview mirror I catch sight of Van Dorn. He has resumed his head-ducking, hands-in-pockets sauntering.

12. WE DRIVE DOWN THE RIVER ROAD IN SILENCE. THE Ranger four-door pickup passes, but the driver and passenger don't seem to notice us.

"Well," I say at last.

Lucy is still looking straight ahead. "Where are we going?" she says.

"To Popeyes to get my car."

"Could we get some drumsticks?" asks Margaret.

"I want a Happy Meal," says Tommy. "You get a baby transformer in it."

"Okay. Well, Lucy?"

"I'll tell you later."

"I think you'd better tell me now."

"Why?"

"I think we might be having company soon." I am watching the Ranger pickup.

"Yes, but—"

"There is not much time."

"How do you mean?"

"Did you see that pickup that just passed?"

"Sure. They were locals, a couple of good old boys, complete with gun rack."

"I'm afraid not."

"How do you know?"

"Good old Louisiana boys don't wear business suits like the

240

driver or bib overalls like the passenger. And they wouldn't be caught dead with an under-and-over in the gun rack."

"An under-and-over?"

"That was a new .410 shotgun with a .22 on top. It's a prop."

"You must have seen them before."

"I have. Locals might have a 12-gauge or a .30-.30 deer rifle, but not that."

"I see." She's gripping the wheel, frowning, knuckles white. "I think you'd better tell me now."

"I can't in present company." Lucy is relaxing a bit, but her face is still heavy and she has not looked at me.

"I want a Coke-cola too," says Tommy.

"They don't have Cokes at Popeyes, but you can get a diet Sprite," says Margaret.

"I don't want a diet Sprite," says Tommy.

"You're going to have to tell me. Tell me medically," I say. "Did you examine some kids?"

"Yes."

"How about this pair?"

"No, but I think they're all right."

"The others?"

"Yes, the others."

"Lucy, how many children did you examine?" She wants me to ask questions. She seems to be having trouble concentrating.

"Ah, about six. Yes, six." Again she falls silent.

"You shouldn't drink regular Sprite because it has sugar," says Margaret.

"Lucy, tell me about the examinations," I say patiently. "Tell me medically. Now. Do you hear me? Now."

"It was easy, since I had to do fecal smears for salmonella."

"I understand."

Silence.

"Well," I say.

She is gripping the wheel tightly, sighting the road, chin up, like a novice driver. Her voice is not steady.

"Well, it was in a sort of rec room that had a bathroom. I examined them in the bathroom. There was a Mrs. Cheney there,

241

and a spooky couple named Brunette came in later. And somebody they called Coach, an oafish type with a whistle who looked as though he'd gone to summer camp for ten years and finally made counselor.''

"The children, Lucy?"

"Yes, the children. I examined six children."

"A perineal examination, Lucy?"

"Yes, because I was taking smears for salmonella."

"I understand. Your findings?"

"Yes. Two girls, perhaps ten and twelve. One with recent hymeneal rupture, the other with marital introitus. You understand?"

"Yes. Any histories?"

"No time for histories."

"The boys?"

"Two had anal lesions. One, a recent laceration; the other, a fissure of some duration."

"I see."

"History?"

"No histories there either, but—"

"Yes?" Lucy's voice is more focused. She is using her doctoring to catch hold.

"There were two behavioral items." She has found her medical voice.

"Yes?"

"One of the girls made an oral advance to me."

"Oral to oral?"

"No."

"I see."

"It was as if she thought it was expected of her—in the bathroom, that is."

"I understand. And the other item?"

"One of the boys gave an unmistakable pelvic response to my digital examination, from the knee-chest position. It was quite startling. Do you understand?"

"I understand."

Lucy looks at me for the first time. "Tom, they were lined

242

up. They wanted to be examined. I could have examined twenty."

"I see."

"Tom, do you know what they reminded me of?"

"No."

"Do you remember that scene in the Alexandria Quartet where the child prostitutes were all reaching for him, clinging?"

"Yes."

We are silent. The road runs through a loess cut, twilit, worn deep as the Natchez Trace.

I look down at Margaret and Tommy. They are picking at each other and seem fine, Margaret her prim prissy self, Tommy pesky normal.

"Lucy, do you have any idea who was—culpable?"

"Mr. and Mrs. Brunette, who just happened to come in, seemed very agitated. They left, and then Coach What's-his-name came in—"

"Coach Matthews," says Margaret.

"Right," says Lucy. "I think the Brunettes called Coach Matthews to come over. He too seemed nervous."

"How do you like Belle Ame?" I ask the children.

"It's all right," says Tommy. "I like the horses but not treat-a-treat."

"Why don't you like treat-a-treat?"

"They play too hard."

"Who?"

"Coach. And I don't like sardines."

"What's wrong with sardines?"

"They play it wrong."

"How do they play it wrong?"

"When you're it and then somebody finds you in the attic, they're not supposed to close off the place with a trunk."

"Who closed off the place?"

"Mrs. Brunette."

"Did they do that to you?"

"No, I wasn't it. But Claude told me."

"What did you do?"

"I told Uncle Van."

"Uncle Van? What did Uncle Van say?"

"He said it was okay, that was the rule."

"Was Claude it?"

"Once, but he wouldn't play anymore."

"I see."

"What's treat-a-treat?" asks Lucy.

"You know," says Margaret. "First you go treat-a-treat on your knee, then gallop-a-trot, then hobbledehoy. It's all right for little kids, but later on it's dumb."

Lucy looks at me.

I explain. "You hold a kid on your knee and say, This is the way the ladies ride, treat-a-treat, starting off easy."

"I see," says Lucy.

Margaret cranes up to whisper something to me. She whispers the way children whisper, cupping my ear with her hand and not gauging her breath correctly. "They play it wrong. When you come to hobbledehoy you're not supposed to take off your panties, are you? That's dumb."

"Yes, it is. Did you do that?"

"No way, José!"

"Who wanted to play treat-a-treat that way?"

"Coach, Mr. Brunette, Mrs. Cheney."

"I see." After a moment I ask her, "Meg, where did you get your water when you wanted a drink?"

"Oh, Belle Ame has a deep well, Tom," says Lucy, quite herself now.

"I know that, but I was still wondering."

"You just get it out of the faucets, except in the rec room," says Margaret, losing interest.

"Where do you get it in the rec room?"

"They have a big upside-down bottle we have to drink from."

"Why do you have to drink from that bottle?"

"It's not from the bottle. The bottle is upside down and there is a little faucet."

"I understand, but why do you have to drink that water?"

"To get our Olympic vitamins."

"Sure," says Margaret, little Miss Smart. "The concentrated vitamins are up on the second floor with a little tube coming down. I've seen them change the bottles and put in a little from the tube."

"I see." I feel Lucy's eyes on my face.

We're at Popeyes. We back in under the live oak next to my Caprice.

Lucy and I look at each other. "Well?" says Lucy.

"Let's do this," I tell her. "Would you take the kids in and feed them. They're hungry. Meanwhile, may I use your cellular phone right here? I want to call Chandra to come pick up Tommy and Margaret."

"Yay!" says Margaret.

"Sure," says Lucy briskly. "Then we've got to get back to Pantherburn, remember?"

"Yes."

"I think you better get Claude as soon as you can," says Lucy.

"I will."

"I mean it. It is serious, I think."

"I will."

13. AFTER MAKING THE PHONE CALL, I WAIT IN MY CAR for Chandra. I can see a stretch of highway. It is getting on to early dusk.

Lucy and the children take a long time in Popeyes.

There are some tiny yellow birds high in the live oak. The last of the sunlight catches them. They blaze like fireflies in the dark rooms of the oak.

Lucy comes out at the same time Chandra drives up in her WOW-TV car. Tommy and Margaret are glad to see Chandra and like the idea of getting in a TV car.

Chandra relays my medical calls, briskly, efficiently. I thank
her and tell her I will call her later. She looks at me round-eyed
and alert. There's something going on, isn't there, she seems to
say, head cocked, but I'll go along with it.

I can count on her.

Lucy is waiting for me in the Caprice. I get in front at the
wheel.

Lucy looks at her watch. "Let's get over to Pantherburn right
away. I'll leave the truck."

"Why?"

"I want a word with you on the way."

"Maybe you'd better take the truck. I'll be there later."

She sits up and turns around to face me. "What do you mean,
later?"

"I have a call to make. Then I'll come over."

"A call! What do you mean a call?"

"It's a medical emergency. There is something wrong with
Father Smith. His friend Milton Guidry has been calling me all
day. Chandra took the message. He thinks Father Smith is dying. I have no choice."

"For God's sake. I mean, my stars, what can you— Look,
Tom, I—I'm afraid. Don't go. Look, wouldn't it be better for
Father Smith if we called an ambulance and got him to the
emergency room?"

"I'll be going along." The shaft of sunlight turns off in the
oak like a light in a room. "This won't take long. I'll call you
in an hour."

Lucy peers at me. "What's the matter with you? Are you
sleepy?"

"No."

"Don't you know they can't afford to have you on the loose?"

"Who? Oh yes. Don't worry."

Silence. There's a clatter of pots from Popeyes. Lucy sinks
back, hands shoved into the pockets of her lab coat, into the
already sunken Chevy seat. It would be difficult for anyone to
see us, or even the car, from the highway.

"What about Belle Ame?" she asks presently.

"What about it?"

"What are you going to do about it?"

"You're the public-health officer. What are you going to do about it?"

"I somehow have the feeling it's up to you."

"First, I'm going to get Claude. Tonight."

"I can send Vergil for him," says Lucy quickly. "There's no immediate worry."

"Why is that?"

"I learned from Margaret—what a dear!—that he really did go to Baton Rouge for a soccer game. She saw him leave on the bus. He's okay. We can go get him later tonight."

I don't reply.

Again she's up and turned around and looking back at me. "What's the matter with you?"

"Nothing."

"You're acting strange."

"Is that all you have to say?"

She's nodding. "Yeah. What are we going to do about Belle Ame?"

"You saw the children."

"You want to know what I think?"

"What?"

"I don't think Van Dorn even knew about it."

I am silent.

"Well?" she says.

"Well what?"

"What are you going to do?"

I am gazing at her. "What do you suggest?"

"I think we've got some sickos out there. I think they're in need of drastic treatment. What do you think?" She shakes me. "Well?"

"Right. We'll treat them. Starting tomorrow. We're going to the sheriff. You're going to report your findings and we're going to close them down. To begin with."

"Okay, Tom, okay. I'm on your side, remember."

"I have to go."

"Tom." She puts a hand on my arm.

"Yes?"

"If you don't come back with me now, they're going to be looking for you on the road."

"How do you know?"

She takes hold of my arm. "I called Carrie while the children were eating. Max and Comeaux are there. Waiting for you."

It is dusk-dark. A van passes on the road. Its headlights are on.

"Tom, listen! I think they know."

"I see."

"They can't afford to have you on the loose. Not now. If you don't come back with me, they'll be looking for you."

"Did you tell them I was here?"

"No. I told them you were coming from your office."

"Good. Don't worry about it. I know the roads around here and they don't. And they don't know where I'm going. Tell them the truth. I'm making a call."

"Tom, Max is on your side."

"Good."

"I don't know about Comeaux."

"Maybe you'd better go along now. May I borrow your bag?"

"What?"

"Your medical bag."

"Oh, sure." She turns to me, puts both hands on my arm, squeezes hard. "May I say one thing before you leave?"

"Sure."

"Two things. Here they are. First, Max and I agree on this. You ought to take Comeaux up on his job offer. Okay, so he's an asshole. But your best chance to change the system is to work within the system. Max's words! You and Max can be very effective. He needs you. And it will free you up for research. And guess what? Max wants you to move your office to his at Northshore Tulane and practice together. You both need each other. You belong in a research-academic setting, not in that jerkwater town. Max is worried about you, Tom."

She pauses, eyes on my face. I am watching the highway.

248

"Okay, Tom. Number two, and I'm going to tell it like it is. Ellen is in trouble, Tom. You know that. Max took it upon himself to tell me that he's seeing her professionally. He could not break confidentiality, but I did gather that he thought there was not much future in your and Ellen's relationship. I'm sorry. Ellen is a remarkable, gifted woman and we're all devoted to her, but she needs all the help she can get. I'm telling it like it is, whether you like it or not. Max of course thinks you're some kind of genius and that you've done remarkably well, but that you need a little space just now. What do I think? I'll tell you what I think. I think first of your kids—God, they're lovely kids, and believe me they're okay—ain't nothing wrong with those kids! So Max and I want the best for you and yours, but I've got news for you. I want something else. I want you around. I'm a selfish woman and I need— Sh!" She puts a finger to my lips. "All right. You better come on out to Pantherburn tonight."

She grabs my arm.

"What?" I look at her.

She's smiling.

"I think all of you better come on out to Pantherburn tonight."

"Well—"

"It seems natural, Tom."

"Well—"

"Like last night." She's smiling but serious.

"All right."

She touches my lips. "Don't say anything. You'd better get going. Be careful. Just be sure you get back to Pantherburn tonight. Your room is ready. Those guys mean business, Tom— I mean Comeaux and company. They're vulnerable and they don't know what you're going to do. Now get going. It'll soon be dark."

Dark is what I'm waiting for.

14. I TAKE OLD LA. 963 THROUGH SLAUGHTER, OLIVE Branch, through St. Helena Parish, past the Fluker fire tower, over I-55 and into the piney woods, to Waldheim and the old fire-tower road to St. Margaret's. Not a car in sight until the interstate.

The shed at the foot of the tower is dark. There is a full moon. I cannot make out if there is a light in the tower.

Milton Guidry has come up behind me. Now he too gazes up companionably.

"What's the matter with him, Milton?" I move around so I can see Milton's face in the moonlight.

"He had a spell yesterday and hasn't moved since." Milton describes Father Smith's symptoms in a lively fashion. He is worried, but he is glad to have company and takes pleasure in talking about it. "He is stiff as a board. When I helped him to the commode, his flesh was hard-like. Like that." He raps the shed. "What is that, Doc?"

"What happened? What kind of spell?"

"A spasm-like. He was sitting talking yesterday just as natural as you and me. Then he stopped and his hand went like this." Milton shows me, flexing his arm and curling his hand inward. "Since then he hasn't moved or done anything. I mean nothing." Milton cocks his head and watches me with a pleasant expression.

"What do you mean he hasn't moved?"

"I mean, he hasn't moved. He doesn't eat or drink or say a word."

"Did he fall down?"

"No, he just sits and looks at the woods."

"You mean he sat there at the table all last night and did not lie down in his bedroll?"

"You got it, Doc."

"How do you know?"

"I checked him every hour. You know how you can get worried about somebody."

"He doesn't talk to you?"

"He doesn't feel like talking."

"What do you mean?"

"He spots and I report on the phone."

"I see." I don't see.

Milton looks down. "I see you brought your little bag."

"Yes. I'm going up now. You stick around in case I need you. I'm going to have to take him to the hospital. I'll need your help to get him down."

"I be right here, Doc, don't you worry! You want me to help you with the trapdoor?"

"No thanks." I could use some help but don't want to fool with Milton.

Father Smith is sitting at the high table, temple propped on three fingers. He seems to be studying the azimuth. On a corner of the table, an old-fashioned kerosene lamp with a glass chimney casts a weak yellow light. Beside the lamp there is an open can of Campbell's chicken soup and a melted bowl of Jell-O.

"Hello, Father."

He seems to be looking at me, but his eye sockets are in deep shadow.

"Milton told me you were ill."

He is looking at me, I am sure, under his brow.

I sit on the stool opposite him. We gaze at each other.

"Milton said you had some kind of attack yesterday."

The priest says nothing. His head moves. Is it a nod? I try to make out whether his expression is ironic, but I can't be sure. I move the lamp beside me so I can see his eyes better. I like to see patients' eyes, unlike Freud, who looked at the back of their heads.

"He told me you had not eaten or slept."

No answer, but he is attentive. His eyes follow me.

"You've been sitting in that chair since yesterday?"

No answer, but his gaze is equable.

"How do you get over there to the toilet? Does Milton help you?"

A deprecatory pursing of lips, almost a shrug: No big deal.

"Milton also said you had some sort of spell."

Another near-shrug: You know Milton.

I set Lucy's medical bag on the table. His eyes follow it.

"Do you mind if I have a look at you?"

He doesn't mind.

"Give me your right hand. All right, squeeze. Your left. All right."

Milton is right. When I move his arm, there is a waxiness in the motion, like a stiff doll. But when I let go of his hand, it doesn't stay in the air like a catatonic but comes slowly back to the table.

"Can you stand?" He looks at me but doesn't move. Am I mistaken or are his eyes slightly rounded, even risible? I give him my hands. He stands. "Right leg. Okay. Left leg. Okay."

"I want to have a look." I open Lucy's bag, fish around, find her ophthalmoscope and reflex hammer. I look at his eye-grounds, tap a few tendons.

We sit in silence, the azimuth between us, like two diners at a lazy Susan.

I am beginning to get on to him. He knows it. He watches me with a lively expression, eyes rounded.

"I see that you are not moving around or talking or eating because you don't choose to."

He shrugs.

"I imagine that you feel depressed, that it doesn't seem worthwhile to talk, eat, get up."

A half-shrug, a downpull of lip.

"I'm half right? There's more to it?"

A nod.

"You chose to do this for other reasons?"

A nod.

"All right. Examination over. You don't need any help from me. I believe you are depressed. But if you have undertaken a fast for religious reasons, that is your affair. I don't have to tell you about the medical consequences. I need help from you, however, a bit of advice. But if you wish me to leave, tell me or otherwise signify. I do not wish to disturb you. Milton called me."

Long ago I discovered that the best way to get in touch with withdrawn patients is to ask their help. It is even better if you actually need their help. They can tell. They may be dumb but they are not stupid. Once, in trouble myself, I fell down in front of a catatonic patient who had not uttered a word for seven years. "You shouldn't be down there," he said in an ordinary voice. "Let me help you up." He helped me up.

"All right, Tom," says Father Smith in his ordinary voice.

"I'm not disturbing you?"

"No. What's the trouble? Would you get rid of those?" He nods toward the soup and the Jell-O.

"Sure. How?"

"Open the trapdoor and set them on the top step."

I do so.

I talk to him as if we were having an ordinary conversation, two fellows sitting at the lazy Susan in the Dinner Bell restaurant in Magnolia, as if there were nothing unusual about him perched on a stool like a wax doll atop a hundred-foot tower, not stirring for a day and a half. I tell him about my latest discoveries about Dr. Comeaux's and Dr. Van Dorn's Blue Boy project, about their offer of a job, about their threats if I don't take it to send me back to Alabama for parole violation. I mention the incidents of sexual molestation at Belle Ame Academy, but also tell him of Bob Comeaux's impressive evidence of social betterment through the action of the additive heavy sodium. "I'm not sure what I should do," I tell him, frowning, troubled, but keeping an eye on him. As a matter of fact, I do not know what to do. So I am doing my best therapy, killing two birds with one stone, asking for help and helping by asking. He may be depressed, but I'm in a fix too.

The priest listens attentively, his temple propped on three fingers. At first I fear he has lapsed into silence again. Finally he says in a low voice, as if musing to himself, "Social betterment"; then to me, "What kind of social betterment?"

"Well, for example, the effect on the catastrophic problem of social decay in the inner city, in the black areas of Baton Rouge and the poor rural whites of St. Helena Parish." I give him Bob Comeaux's figures on the dramatic reduction of street crime, teen pregnancies, suicides, drug abuse. "You must admit there is something to be said for his results, even if he's treating symptoms, not causes. And for his rationale."

"His rationale," repeats the priest.

I look at him steadily. "That every society has a right to protect itself against its enemies. That a society like an organism has a right to survive. Lucy agrees. So do I. My problem is—"

The priest is watching me with his peculiar, round-eyed, almost risible expression. "Society," he murmurs, and then, as if to himself, something I don't quite catch: "Volk—" Volk something. Volkswagen?

"What?" I lean forward, cock an ear.

With his free hand he is turning the azimuth slowly, inattentively, until the sights line up on me. He appears sunk in thought and I fear I've lost him again. But he looks up and says, "May I ask you a question?"

"Sure. You want to know what I think, right? Well, I must confess—"

But he is shaking his head. "No no," he says. "Not that." Wearily he rubs both eyes with the heels of his hands. "Could I ask you a professional question, a psychological question?"

"Sure sure," I say, but I fear I showed my irritation. He sounds like priests often do when they talk to psychiatrists about "psychological questions."

"Something wrong, Tom?" The priest asks, eyeing me gravely.

I have risen. Suddenly I don't want to talk or listen. I am worried about Belle Ame. "I'm sorry, but if there's nothing more I can do for you, I'd better be going. You eat something and you'll be all right. I have to pick up Claude Bon. Drs. Comeaux and Gottlieb are waiting for me." Besides, I feel a rising irritation. Did I come all the way over here to have a conversation about a "psychological question"?

"I'm sorry, Tom. I didn't send for you."

"That's all right. What's the question?"

"Something happened to me yesterday after you left." He is turning the azimuth. "No doubt it is a psychological phenomenon with which you are familiar. I know that you work with dreams. What I want to ask you is this: Is there something which is not a dream or even a daydream but the memory of an experience which is a thousand times more vivid than a dream but which happens in broad daylight when you are wide awake?"

"Yes." I am thinking of his "spell." It could be a temporal-lobe epilepsy—which often is accompanied by extraordinary hallucinations.

"It was not a dream but a complete return of an experience which was real in every detail—as if I were experiencing it again."

"Yes?"

"Is it possible for the brain to recapture a long-forgotten experience, an insignificant event which was not worth remembering but which is captured in every detail, sight, sound—even smell?"

"Yes, but I would question whether it was insignificant."

"Yes, I expect you would. But it was absolutely insignificant."

He speaks with some effort, in an odd, flat voice and in measured syllables, like a person awakened from a deep sleep. "Yes, I expect you would," he says again, rubbing his eyes. Now he moves the kerosene lamp, tries to focus on me.

"Well?" I say after a pause, feeling irritation rise in my chest like a held breath.

"I was dreaming of Germany. Germany! Why Germany? No, not dreaming. It happened. I was wide awake. I was lying down after you left yesterday. It was getting dark but the sky was still bright against the dark pines. It reminded me of—what? the

Schwarzwald with its dark firs? I've told you about it before. I don't know. Anyhow, it was as if I were back in Tübingen, where I'd been as a boy. I was lying in bed in my cousin's house. It was so vivid I could have been there. I stayed with them a year. I would wake every morning to the sound of church bells.''

He moves the kerosene lamp again, leans forward.

"Have I spoken to you about this?"

"About Germany? Yes."

"But not about—" He stops, rubs his forehead with both hands. "Yes, the church bells. They had a special quality, completely different from our church bells, a high-pitched, silvery sound, almost like crystal struck against crystal. Even the air was different. It was thin and clear and silvery and high-pitched too, if you know what I mean. It had a different—smell. Or was it lack of smell? Anyhow, nothing like our old funky, fertile South. No, it was a smell, a high-pitched sweet smell, almost chemical, yet sweet too, something like the cutting room of a florist's shop—like old geraniums? Of course it is impossible to describe a smell. But it came back! I would wake in the morning to that high silvery ringing and the chemical geranium smell. I slept in a narrow bed covered not by a blanket or a quilt but by a soft goose-down bolster, like a light mattress. It was like an old-fashioned Southern feather bed with the mattress upside down. There was also the vague but certain sense that something was about to happen.''

He stops. I say nothing. Now he's back propping temple on his three fingers, looking at me sideways, almost slyly. "How is such a memory possible? Many things have happened to me, but in this case nothing happened. Absolutely nothing. A boy lying in bed.''

I look at him for a while. The kerosene lamp seems to drizzle, sending out sprays of weak yellow light.

Presently I ask him, "Was it about then that you had your—ah—spell?"

"What spell? I didn't have a spell. Do you mean seizure? a fit? a convulsion? I didn't have a convulsion. Why do you ask?"

"Milton said you had a—what he called a spasm."

"No. It is true I have spells of dizziness, but what I had was this peculiar dream which was not a dream."

"Was Milton up here at the time?"

"Well, yes. He brought me something to eat."

"Was that before or after your—" I pause.

"My what? Go ahead and say it"

"I was about to say hallucination, because as you describe it, it was that vivid."

He's still eyeing me sideways, but now through almost closed lids. "Hallucinations are generally abnormal, aren't they? I mean, like a symptom of mental illness or something in the brain?"

"Sometimes." I rise and repack Lucy's bag. "I have to go now. I'm worried about the children, especially Claude Bon. I'd like you to come in for an ECG and a scan. I think you'd better come into the hospital for a general checkup. But if not, please call me or have Milton call me if you need anything." I look at his hand, which is still on the azimuth. It is as withered as Don Quixote's, yet, when he clasped mine, as strong as the Don's too. "As your physician I am obliged to advise you to resume eating and drinking. You're already dehydrated. Frankly, I cannot tell how much of your—ah—inactivity is due to depression and how much to a religious commitment. The latter is out of my territory. But you have my medical advice. Don't hesitate to call on me, even though I'm not certain I will be here tomorrow. If I'm not available, call Dr. Gottlieb. He's a good man."

He watches me with the same expression as I snap the bag and move past him to the trapdoor.

As I pass, he seizes my arm. I wait, expecting an affectionate goodbye squeeze, perhaps by way of thanks. But he doesn't squeeze and doesn't let go.

"Yes?"

He tilts his head even more, to see me. "I'm afraid I'm going to have to tell you something."

"Yes?"

"Something happened to me in Germany. I have never told anyone."

"I'm sure it's interesting. But I have to go. I'm worried about Claude Bon. I'm going to pick—"

"I'm afraid this concerns you. I didn't want to tell you, but I'm afraid I have to. There is something you need to know."

Father Smith's dry talon of a hand is still on my arm. Something stirs in the back of my head. For some reason I think of the time a priest came to get me out of a classroom to tell me my father was dead. There is in his voice and in the feel of his hand on my arm the same grave pressure, the same sweet urgency.

Then he gives a shudder, just exactly as one might for no reason at all, or as Negroes used to say, because a rabbit just ran over your grave. But then, to my alarm, the hand supporting his head falls away, pronates, the fingers bunching. It curls inward like a burning leaf. His head falls to one side. Fearing he might fall off the stool—his body slumps a little toward me, but not alarmingly—I catch him, ease him off and down to the floor. He makes no objection. I lay him out diagonally—the only way—prop his head on the bedroll. I sit beside him, watching him. No use to examine him. Mainly I'm casting about, wondering how best to get him down from the tower and to the hospital. Why didn't I get him down when I could? What a place to have a stroke. I hope it is a seizure. The moonlight falls on his cheek and forehead, leaving his deep eye sockets in shadow. One eyelid, the right, twitches, I think. Best to call for Milton to give me a hand. I could let him down—I begin to rise, but the old man is saying something. I lean close. His voice is different. Right hand bunched, I'm thinking, the geranium smell. A petit-mal seizure? Some seizures, especially in temporal-lobe epilepsy, are preceded by an aura, a strong resurgence of memory, of time, place, smell. But right eye twitch, speech altered? Left brain vascular accident, speech center affected?

But his speech is clear. His voice is thin and dry as dead leaves, but clear. He speaks in a rapid, dry monotone such as one might use in giving a legal deposition, not having much time.

"No no. Wait," he says, almost whispering. "Wait."

FATHER SMITH'S CONFESSION

In the 1930s I found myself visiting distant cousins in Germany. My father took me. They lived in the university town of Tübingen, where my cousin Dr. Hans Jäger was professor of psychiatry. He had two sons. One, Helmut, at eighteen, was older than I but became my friend. The other, Lothar, was a good deal older. I didn't like him. He was some sort of minor civil servant, perhaps a postal clerk, and also a member of the Sturmabteilung, the SA, the brownshirts. Not even his own family had much use for him. In fact, as best as I could tell, the entire SA had fallen into some sort of disfavor at the time. Sitting around in his sloppy uniform, he reminded me of a certain kind of American lodge member, perhaps a Good Fellow or Order of Moose dressed up for a lodge meeting. Helmut was something else. He had finished the Hitler Jugend and had just been admitted to the Junkerschule, the officer-training school for the Schutzstaffel, the SS. The one great thing he looked forward to was taking his oath at Marienberg, the ancient castle of the Teutonic knights. He already had his field cap with the death's-head and his lightning-bolt shoulder patch. What he hoped to do was to become not a military policeman like many of the SS but a member of an SS division and incorporated into the Wehrmacht, the German Army. Dr. Jäger had nothing to do with the Nazis. He was a distinguished child psychiatrist—did I ever tell you that at one time I was considering going into your profession?—a music lover, and, I remember, a dog lover—he had two dachshunds, Sigmund and Sieglinde, whom he was extremely fond of. When I think of him, I think of him as the "good German" as portrayed in Hollywood, say by Maximilian Schell or earlier by Paul Lukas in *Watch on the Rhine*—you know, sensitive, lover of freedom, hater of tyranny, and so on, certainly the courageous foe of the Nazis. Dr. Jäger was a composite of the two, better than both, not only a brilliant child psychiatrist but a fine musician—he had just played the Bruch concerto with the university orchestra, the ultimate expression of romantic German feeling—*Gefühl! Gefühl!* Toward Lothar, the brownshirt, he displayed an open contempt. But he was silent about Helmut. I could never make out what he thought of Helmut.

What were we, my father and I, doing there? I had just finished high school. My mother had died the year before and my sister had got married. My father decided it would be good for both of us if we went abroad. He had never been abroad. But he liked to say that we were both entitled to a *Wanderjahr*, as he called it. He was a romantic and a lover of music. In fact, he taught piano at the music school at Nicholls State Junior College. If you want to know the truth, he was second-rate, not really first-class at playing, not really first-class at teaching, not really a scholar. He was a certain type, quite common in the South, a lover of culture, books, the lofty things in life. Music of a certain sort moved him to the point of tears. In short, he was a romantic. His great ambition for years had been to make the grand tour of Europe, to see the cathedrals, above all to go to Bayreuth. It was natural that we should visit our cousins. The Rhine, the Lorelei, the cathedral at Cologne—they were as much a part of his dream of Europe as Chartres and Mont-Saint-Michel and Florence. I think he thought of Tübingen and Heidelberg as a sort of backdrop for *The Student Prince*. Do you recall that being a student at Heidelberg was as much a part of the Southern tradition as reading Sir Walter Scott?

It is important to understand that in the 1930s most Americans didn't have two thoughts about the Third Reich and Hitler. We were still in the grip of the Depression. Mussolini, in fact, was the object of more curiosity than Hitler. I remember my mother presenting a paper at her literary club entitled something like "Mussolini, the New Caesar." Mussolini, the strong man who made Italy work. Fascism was then thought of as a bundle of sticks, fasces, stronger than one stick and not necessarily a bad thing. Hitler seemed to be a German version of the same, another strong man whom the Germans had in fact elected, a matter of some, though not much, interest.

There was certainly no reason not to go to Germany then, if one was going to Chartres and Florence.

I must tell you how I felt about my father and mother, though it does me little credit. My father was, as I say, a type familiar in the South, not successful in life but an upholder of culture, lofty ideals, and the higher things. He was a practitioner of the arts, by turns a painter and a musician. And an author: he wrote occasional articles for the New Orleans newspaper about old Creole days, perhaps a humorous anecdote about Père Antoine or a historical sketch about a romantic encounter between a plantation belle and a handsome Yankee captain. As a young man he wrote poetry and was named poet laureate of Thibodaux by the mayor's proclamation. But he settled on music and gave piano recitals at places like Knights of Columbus halls or the Jewish Community Center. Later he became assistant professor of music at Tulane, not the university proper, but in the university college, which was a sort of night school for adults. As I've said, not first-rate.

We come from old Alsatian German stock who two hundred years ago were lured here by the thousands by a real-estate swindler named John Law who promised an idyllic life in a Louisiana paradise. So they landed in the swamps next to the west bank of the river, which is still known as the Côte des Allemands, the German coast, where they were engulfed by mosquitoes, malaria, yellow fever, and the French. My father's family, the Schmidts, became Smith. My mother's family, the Zweigs, became Labranche.

My grandfather had a hardware store in Thibodaux, but my father moved to New Orleans, where he lived in the French Quarter, wore a beret, and painted a bit, like an American on the Left Bank. He claimed to have been a confidant of Faulkner and Sherwood Anderson and Frances Parkinson Keyes.

My mother was a thin, hypertensive woman, perpetually worried by my father's airy improvidence, by his playing at *la vie de bohème*—I can still see him at the piano on students' nights-at-home, playing and singing *"Che gelida manina"* not quite accurately, fingernails clicking on the keys, head swaying, eyes closed at Puccini's melting melodies. But my mother had to make ends meet and keep up with New Orleans social life. She was both pious and hostile. She had it both ways. If someone offended her, she sent them holy cards, notices of Masses for their "intentions." What she was really saying was: Even though you've done this rotten thing, I'm having a Mass said for you. She had a mail-order hookup with some obscure order—I think it was the Palatine Fathers of Fond du Lac, Wisconsin—so that if, say, her own parish priest offended her by having a black altar boy, he would get a card of acknowledgment from the Palatine Fathers of Fond du Lac that thanks to the generosity of Mrs. Simon R. Smith ten Masses were going to be said for him. How to argue with that? The more somebody offended her, the more Masses he got. Once, an acquaintance of hers mortally offended her by contriving to have her daughter named queen of the Lorelei Carnival Ball—not one of the major balls, to be sure— when my sister was the obvious choice, what with my father being one of the founders of the Krewe of Lorelei. But money won out and my sister had to settle for being a maid in the court. My mother, white-lipped, blood pressure kiting over three hundred, of course said nothing. But after the ball both the queen and her mother received cards of acknowledgment from the Palatine Fathers of Fond du Lac that thanks to the generosity of Mrs. Simon R. Smith, thirty Masses were to be said for each, sixty Masses in all.

Honor thy father and mother. I didn't exactly. I am not proud of it. It sounds as if I'm saying that my father was a phony and my mother a shrew. Well, yes. On the other hand, no. To be truthful, I didn't exactly honor my father and mother. But no, it was sadder than that. I felt sorry for them. How many other people, I wondered, were messed up for life? Most, I later discovered. But yes, it's true, I was an ingrate. To tell the whole truth, I was a spiteful boy. I couldn't stand what my mother called religion. I couldn't stand my father's fecklessness and his everlasting talk about the loftier things in life, Truth, Beauty, Freedom, Art, the Soaring of the Spirit in the Realm of Music. Would you believe I couldn't stand all that Catholic business, holy cards, candles, rosaries, my mother's flying novenas and Nine First Fridays. I couldn't stand Holy Cross High School—

except for football. I played tackle and we beat Jesuit, who thought they were the hottest stuff in town. I liked to hit, as they say. And I liked the science courses—no bull, just the facts and verifiable theory, no praying for anyone's "intentions," no swooning over Puccini. Actually, I couldn't stand Louisiana, and New Orleans, with its self-conscious cultivation of being the Big Easy, its unbuttoned y'all-come bonhomie, good eats and phony French *laissez le bon temps rouler*, let the good times roll, which masked a cold-blooded marriage of moneymaking and social climbing, rotten politics and self-indulgence. Don't misunderstand me. If I was anti-Catholic, I was also anti-Protestant. They were, if anything, worse. Actually there was not much left of Protestantism except a dislike for Catholics and a fondness for their festival. For, though they had nothing to do with Ash Wednesday, indeed had not the faintest notion of what it was about, they took to Fat Tuesday like ducks to water, in fact took it over. Worst of all were the local village atheists, professor-philosophers, ACLU zealots, educated Episcopal-type unbelievers, media types, NBC anchormen, *New York Times* pundits, show-biz gurus. If one can imagine anything worse than Jerry Falwell governing the country, how about Norman Lear? Love your fellow man, the Lord said. That's asking a lot. Frankly, I found my fellow man, with few exceptions, either victims or assholes. I did not exclude myself. The only people I got along with were bums, outcasts, pariahs, family skeletons, and the dying.

What a background for a priest-to-be, you say. You say charitably, Well, at least you changed, became a priest, and ran the hospice here. I didn't change. Does anyone really change? I am still a spiteful man. The Lord puts up with all types. Look at his disciples. A sorry crew, mostly office seekers and social climbers. They could all have come from New Orleans's Ninth Ward. Down there in the world I had no use for my fellow priests or parishioners. I had use for the bottle. As one alcoholic to another, I'm sure I'm not telling you a secret—the secret of all alcoholics—when I tell you that the bottle enabled me to enjoy my spite. I despised TV, stereo-V, yet I watched it by the hour.

Do you know how I spent my evenings? Not exactly like St. Francis praising Brother Night. Watching reruns of *Dallas*, which I despised, despised every minute of it, despising myself, having six drinks and enjoying my spite. At every commercial I'd jump up and have a stiff drink—to stand *Dallas* and my fellow priests.

You're shaking your head: But you did run the hospice, you're saying, didn't you, and did a good job, before they took it away from you. You took in the dying and the unwanted, like Mother Teresa.

Don't kid yourself. I don't know about Mother Teresa, but I did it because I liked it, not for love of the wretched. Didn't your mentor Dr. Freud say that we all have our own peculiar ways of gratifying ourselves? Don't knock it. Yes, I took in the dying. Do you want to know why? Because dying people were the only people I could stand. They were my kind. Do you know the one thing dying people can't stand? It's not the fact they're going to die. It's other people, the undying, so-called healthy people. Their loved ones. And after a while of course their loved ones can't stand the sight of them, haven't a word to say to them, and they can't stand the sight of their loved ones. They liked me because I liked them and they knew it. You can't fool children and you can't fool dying people. We were in the same boat. They knew I was a drunk, a failed priest. Dying people, suffering people, don't lie. They tell the truth. Death makes honest men of all of us. Everyone else lies. Everyone else is dying too and spending their entire lives lying to themselves. I'll tell you a peculiar thing: It makes people happy to tell the truth after a lifetime of lying. The best thing I ever did for the living was, in a few cases, to make it possible for them to speak with truth and love to their dying father or mother—which of course no one ever does.

In the end, all they would send me out here were AIDS patients—God knows what they did with the others—because not even the Qualitarian Centers wanted to handle them. Now of course they've started the quarantine, so they can't come here. Do you think I'm setting up as another St. Francis or Mother

Teresa kissing lepers' sores? Certainly not. I liked them. They knew it. They told the absolute truth. So did I. I was at home with them. Did I try to convert them? Certainly not. Religion was never mentioned. Only if they asked. I knew I belonged with them, because I didn't have to drink. When they died or got quarantined, I came up here.

Germany. Let me tell you what happened to me. Well, my father of course was in a transport of delight. First, France: Notre Dame! Chartres! Mont-Saint-Michel! Then Germany: the Rhine! Beethoven! *Das Rheingold!* Heidelberg!

Well, he was half right, I thought. Right about Germany, wrong about France. Let me make a confession. I did not like the French. It took me years to discover their virtues. It was a prejudice, I admit, but for a fact France in the 1930s was fairly putrid and mean-spirited. Even I could tell. We stayed with my mother's cousins in Lyons. Our cousin was in the dyeing business. I recognized them on the spot. They were like my mother's family in Thibodaux. They knew nothing, cared about nothing except business and eating and politics—the latter with a passion which I could not quite fathom. They had their political party and favorite newspaper, which represented their views. I gathered there were many such parties and newspapers all over France, because our cousins spoke of them at length and with venomous passion. They only came alive in their hatreds. The French hated each other's guts. Only later did I realize that our cousins were what Flaubert called the bourgeoisie.

The Germans were a different cup of tea. I liked them. Dr. Jäger and his friends were charming and cultivated. They were accomplished amateur musicians. They invited my father to join their chamber-music group, welcomed him as Der Herr Musik Professor from New Orleans. I remember them playing Brahms and Schubert quintets, my father at the piano—and not doing badly. So happy he had tears in his eyes!

There were many distinguished German and Austrian psychiatrists in Tübingen that summer. It was some sort of meeting or convention—I can remember the exact name, isn't that strange?—the Reich Commission for the Scientific Registration of Hereditary and Constitutional Disorders. They were not Nazis, quite the contrary, had in fact been famous as psychiatrists and eugenicists in the old Weimar Republic. I remember them well! There was Dr. Werner Heyde from the University of Würzburg and director of the famous psychiatric clinic there—which had been famous for its humane care of the insane going back to the sixteenth century. Dr. Heyde, I remember, even mentioned Cervantes's description of the mental hospital in Seville, also noted for its humane treatment of patients. There was Dr. Karl Brandt, a great admirer of Albert Schweitzer, who had even planned at one time to work with him in Lambaréné. There was Dr. Max de Crinis, a charming Austrian, a very cultivated man, yet full of high spirits, who, I see I don't have to tell you, is still well known for his work on the social difficulties of children—he was even decorated by the West German government in 1950, came to Washington later, and participated in the White House conference on youth. And Dr. Carl Schneider, professor of psychiatry at the University of Heidelberg, successor to Dr. Kraepelin, founder, as you know, of modern psychiatry, and author of a pioneer work on schizophrenia—I see you recognize the name. And Dr. Paul Nitsche, director of the famous Sonnenstein hospital in Saxony, who, I learned later, wrote the best textbook on prison psychoses. And finally Dr. C. G. Jung, whom everybody admired and was supposed to come but couldn't—he was busy working as editor of the *Journal for Psychotherapy* with his co-editor, Dr. M. H. Goering, brother of Marshal Hermann Goering.

There was much lively discussion in Dr. Jäger's house after the meetings, laughter, music, jokes, drinking, horseplay, and some real arguments. They were excited about a book, a small book I had never heard of, not by your Dr. Freud, but by a couple of fellows I never heard of, Drs. Hoche and Binding. I still have the copy Dr. Jäger gave me. It was called *The Release of the Destruction of Life Devoid of Value*. I couldn't follow the heated argument very well, but it seemed to be between those who believed in the elimination of people who were useless, useless to anyone, to themselves, the state, and those who believed in euthanasia only for those who suffered from hopeless diseases or defects like mongolism, severe epilepsy, encephalitis, progressive neurological diseases, mental defectives, arteriosclerosis, hopeless schizophrenics, and so on. Dr. Jäger took the more humane side. Dr. Brandt, I recall, as much as he admired Dr. Schweitzer, maintained that "reverence for nation" preceded "reverence for life." Their arguments made considerable sense to me.

I must confess to you that I didn't warm up to those fellows, distinguished as they were. But I must also confess that I was not repelled by their theories and practice of eugenics—why prolong the life of the genetically unfit or the hopelessly ill? But I did admire German science—after all, it had been the best around for a hundred years—and in fact I was thinking of staying in Germany and going to the university at Tübingen and later to medical school. My father was all for it. And after all, none of these guys were Nazis, far from it—they joked about the louts. They might speak of Goethe but never of Hitler. And the little book they were excited about had been written in 1920, before anyone had heard of Hitler. Why didn't I like them better? Because they, like my father, were professors of a certain sort, and though they were certainly more successful than he, they had the Heidelberg smell about them, the romantic stink of *The Student Prince*. They even recited Schiller and Rilke, and sang student drinking songs—*Trink, trink, trink*—one of them even had saber scars on his cheek from student dueling and was very proud of them. Of course, my poor father was out of his mind with delight. Imagine: Saber scars! *Musik!*

One night in particular, I remember, was an occasion for celebration. Our cousin Dr. Jäger had just received news of his appointment to the famous hospital in Munich, the Eglfing-Haar, and there were congratulations all around, a great musical evening, piano quintets, much toasting of Dr. Jäger. Helmut even sang Schubert lieder with a wonderful voice.

Helmut and I became good friends. Imagine a friendship between two American boys of a certain sort, say, a sixteen-year-old starter on the varsity team being befriended by the eighteen-year-old all-state quarterback. It was like that but different, different because I was aware of a serious and absolute dedication in him which I had never encountered before. He was extremely handsome and strongly built. He showed me his SS officer's cap with its German eagle and death's-head. It dawned on me that he meant it. He was ready to die. I had never met anyone ready to die for a belief. His plan was to become an SS officer and then, as I told you, he hoped, not to become a military policeman, but to join an SS division and to be incorporated into the Wehrmacht—which in fact did happen. He was planning for war even then. Who can I compare him to? An American Eagle Scout? No, because even a serious Eagle Scout is doing scouting on the side, planning a career in law, insurance, whatever. Certainly death is the farthest thing from his mind. I can only think—and this may seem strange—of the young Jesuits of the seventeenth century who were also soldiers knowing they were probably going to die in some place like India, England, Japan, Canada. Or perhaps a young English Crusader signing up with Richard to rescue the holy places from the infidel.

He let me come with him to his last exercise in the Hitler Jugend before going to the Junkerschule, the SS officer school. It was a *Mutprobe*, a test of courage. He and the rest of the troop jumped in full battle gear from a sort of scaffold twenty feet high. Then they marched—and sang. The singing—! It made your blood run cold. I remember the *Fahnenlied*:

> *Wir marschieren, wir marschieren,*
> *Durch Nacht und durch Not*
> *Mit der Fahne für Freiheit und Brot*
> *Unsere Fahne ist mehr für uns als der Tod*

The flag and death.

After the *Mutprobe* and the ceremony, he took me aside and told me with that special gravity of his, "You are leaving tomorrow. I wish you well. I think I know you. We are comrades. I wish to give you something." He gave me his bayonet! It was the same as a Wehrmacht bayonet but smaller, small enough to

268

be worn on the belt in a scabbard. He withdrew the bayonet from its sheath and handed it to me in a kind of ceremony, with both hands. On the shining blade was etched *Blut und Ehre*. I took it in silence. We shook hands. I left.

So what? you seem to say. A valuable souvenir, the sort of Nazi artifact any G.I., any collector, would be glad to have.

No, that is not my confession. This is my confession. If I had been German not American, I would have joined him. I would not have joined the distinguished Weimar professors. I would not have joined the ruffian Sturmabteilung. I would not have matriculated at the University of Tübingen or Heidelberg. I would not have matriculated at Tulane, as I did, and joined the D.K.E.s I would have gone to the Junkerschule, sworn the solemn oath of the Teutonic knights at Marienberg, and joined the Schutzstaffel. Listen. Do you hear me? *I would have joined him.*

(At that point the old priest took hold of my arm and pulled me close. Through some illusion, no doubt a trick of shadow and light from the weak kerosene lamp above us, his withered face seemed to go lean and smooth, his eyes sardonic under lowered lids.)

I would have joined him. Do you find that peculiar? Then try to guess who uttered these words about them, the SS, that very year: *There is nothing they would not do or dare; no sacrifice of life, limb or liberty they would not do for love of country.* You do not know who said that? It was one Winston Churchill.

The Jews? How do the Jews come in, you ask. Believe it or not, they didn't. Not then. The Jägers never mentioned the Jews. The distinguished professors didn't mention the Jews. Not even Werner, who looked like a brown-shirted Kluxer, mentioned the Jews. This was before *Kristallnacht* when it became official policy to beat up Jews. I'm sure Werner did his part. But at the time it was bad taste. I remember one night when Hitler spoke on the radio. I watched the family as they listened. Hitler of course was a maniac and was rabid about the Jews even then. But extremely effective, even hypnotic. I understood enough German to understand such words as *alien, decadent, foreign body* in the pure organism of the *Volk*. It was always *Das Volk*. Werner was all ears, nodding, buying it all. Dr. Jäger was ironic, almost contemptuous—just exactly as my father had been listening to Huey Long. Mrs. Jäger was smiling and starry-eyed. The women loved Hitler! Helmut's face was expressionless, absolutely inscrutable. I asked him about the Jews later. He was not much interested. He shrugged and said only that there had been Jewish applicants to the HJ—Hitler Jugend—but they had been turned down. He added that anti-Semitic activities were forbidden in the HJ. Believe it or not, this was true at the time. I checked it. Then I asked him about Catholics. The Jägers were not Catholic, but there were many Catholics in the South and the Nazis were not as strong as they were in Prussia and Saxony. In fact, when I was there, the Catholic Center Party was the only opposition to the Nazis. He said only that the Catholic Church was part of the "Judaic conspiracy" and let it go at that. He was not interested.

I? I let it go at that too—though I didn't know what he meant. Catholics part of the "Judaic conspiracy"? I could not translate that into American or New Orleans terms, where there is, as you know, a kind of tacit, almost tolerant, anti-Semitism from Catholics and a species of ironic anti-Catholicism from Jews. Catholics and Jews go to a lot of trouble pretending there is no such thing, behaving toward each other with a sort of Southern Protestant joshing and jollification, like good old boys from Mississippi. But it's there. I remember a fellow telling me in the Lorelei Club that he had been bested in a business deal. By whom? somebody asked. By Manny Ginsberg. Nods, winks, looks all around, that's all. You know exactly what I mean.

Or: Once, before I became a priest, one night I was attending a symphony concert in New Orleans. I was talking to a friend of the family, a splendid old lady from a noble Jewish family and president of the symphony board—New Orleans Jews, God bless them, keep the arts alive. She was telling me about her recent trip to Italy. She'd been to Rome, where she'd seen the *pope* carried aloft around the square in a *throne*. She too winked. It was the way she said the word *pope* that was in itself outlandish. It made him sound like some grand panjandrum borne aloft by a bunch of loony Hottentots. As a matter of fact, she was right. I never did see why they hauled the pope around in that *sedia*—and I'm glad John XXIII put a stop to it. But it was the way she said the word *pope*—it made me think he was absurd too.

But Catholics as part of the Judaic conspiracy? Helmut said it. He took it as a matter of course. I couldn't make head or tail of it—then. Imagine hearing that from a young SS cadet, with his German eagle and death's-head on his cap and lightning bolts on his shoulder patch. Of course, in his own mad way he was right, but not quite in the way he meant.

I am ashamed to say that I did not question him or argue with him, at the time not having much more use for Catholics than he did. I thought of them as a lot of things but never as part of the "Judaic conspiracy." In defense I can only say that the expression would also have amazed both New Orleans Jews and Holy Name parishioners.

My father and I went on to Bayreuth. I remember hearing *Tristan and Isolde* with him. He had graduated from Puccini to Wagner. His eyes were closed during the entire second act. I confess I felt contempt for him and admiration for Helmut.

Do you know that I don't think he ever noticed the Nazis or Hitler or the SA or the SS that entire summer—any more than he noticed Huey Long when we got home?

I decided not to stay in Germany, after all. I came home and went to Tulane, tuition-free because of my father's academic connection.

15. DURING THIS STRANGE, RAMBLING ACCOUNT, I noticed with surprise that the old priest's voice grew stronger. Toward the end he pushed himself up to a sitting position and began gesturing vigorously—for example, holding out both hands, palms up, to show how Helmut had presented him with a bayonet inscribed with *Blut and Ehre*.

Now he is struggling to get up.

"Why don't you just stay here, Father," I suggest. "You need a good night's sleep."

"I'm fine! I'm fine!"

"But you suffered some sort of attack and I'm not sure what—"

"Oh, I've had those before. It's an allergic reaction."

"Allergic reaction? Maybe, but it may be something more serious." Like temporal-lobe epilepsy. Hence the vivid recall of smell, place, memory of Germany in the 1930s.

But he insists on getting up, back to his post, as he puts it, as firewatcher. I help him onto the stool, on condition that he come in for a CORTscan and an ECG. He agrees.

I am anxious to leave. I am worried about Claude Bon.

"One question, Tom."

"Yes?"

"What do you think?"

"Of what? The Nazis?"

"No. Your colleagues. The Louisiana Weimar psychiatrists," he says ironically.

"I don't understand."

"Never mind," he says quietly. "What do you think of my experience in Germany?"

There is nothing to do but answer truthfully, without saying

272

that I was more interested in his story as a symptom of a possible brain disorder than in the actual events which he related.

"Well, I see your German experience as a very vivid recollection of a youthful experience, not an uncommon phenomenon actually. It has happened to me."

"Is that all you see?"

"Very well. So you were attracted by Helmut and the esprit of the SS. You were very young. Many people were attracted, even Churchill, as you mentioned. I don't doubt you. As a matter of fact, I am familiar with some of the German doctors and eugenicists you mentioned. Very interesting, but—"

I must have shrugged. He shakes his head, makes a face, rounding his eyes in his earlier rueful-risible expression. He is fiddling with the azimuth.

"Okay," he says suddenly. "Except for—"

"Then I'll be going along."

"—one thing. A footnote."

I sigh but don't sit opposite him this time. I snap Lucy's bag shut.

FATHER SMITH'S FOOTNOTE

I'll make it short and sweet. You should pick up Claude as soon as possible. Believe me.

I did not stay in Germany. I came back to New Orleans with my father.

I went to Tulane for four years. I played some football.

The war came. I took OCS in Jackson, became a ninety-day wonder.

I ended up as an infantry lieutenant in the Seventh Army, General Patch commanding. Nothing very dashing about us, nothing like Patton's Third Army. I wasn't exactly a dashing lieutenant either, though I liked the army well enough. To tell you the truth, I was scared all the time. Scared of what? Of getting killed. To tell the truth, I never got shot at.

We were in the XV Corps that crossed the Rhine on the Mannheim bridge and took part in the final thrust in April of '45, down the Danube first, then struck south to Munich, which we captured on the thirtieth of April. Not much resistance. A single SS division tried to block our advance without success, but we lost a few. Our captain—we were in the 3rd Division—got himself killed, and I was acting captain for a few weeks, my highest rank in the military.

No, we didn't see Tübingen, but we liberated Eglfing-Haar, the famous hospital outside Munich. No, we didn't liberate Dachau, but I saw it later. There was no opposition at Eglfing-Haar, nobody in fact but the nurses and patients. Most of the doctors were gone. I asked about Dr. Jäger. The nurses knew him but said he had been "transferred" a few days before. But one nurse showed me where he worked. It was the *Kinderhaus*, the children's division, a rather cheerful place which had a hundred and fifty beds for child psychiatric cases. There were only twenty children there, most in bad shape, though nothing like what I saw at Dachau. I asked the nurse what had happened to the others. She didn't say anything, but she took me to a small room off the main ward. She said it was a "special department." It was a very pleasant sunny room with a large window, but completely bare except for a small white-tiled table only long enough to accommodate a child. What was notable about the room was a large geranium plant in a pot on the windowsill to catch the sunlight. It was a beautiful plant, luxuriant, full of bloom, obviously very carefully tended. The nurse said it was watered every day.

She was very very nervous, obviously anxious to tell me something, but either she was afraid to or didn't know how.

I asked her what the room was used for. She said that five or six times a month a doctor and a nurse would take a child into the room. After a while the doctor and nurse would come out alone. The "special department" room had an outside door.

It took me a little while to understand what she was saying. Then, as if I had understood all along, I asked her casually what they used. She said many drugs, Luminal, morphine, scopolamine, Zyklon B through a face mask. It was then a new gas manufactured by I. G. Farben which upon exposure to air turned to cyanide.

I asked her if she had ever gone in the room with the children.

"Oh no," she said. She would only see the doctor and nurse go in with the children and come out alone. She did not seem horrified, but only anxious that I get it straight. I couldn't be sure she was telling the truth, but she probably was, because she didn't have to tell me about the "special department."

"Was Dr. Jäger one of the doctors who went in the room?" I asked her.

"Yes," she said. "It was usually Dr. Jäger."

That's all, Tom. End of footnote. As a matter of psychological interest, I still don't know whether the smell I remember—part of the hallucination or whatever—is the smell of the geranium or a trace of the Zyklon B. I should add that there seemed nothing particularly horrifying about her showing me the "special department"—that is, she was not horrified nor was I, at the time. It was a matter of some interest. Soldiers are interested, not horrified. Only later was I horrified. We've got it wrong about horror. It doesn't come naturally but takes some effort.

But I've kept you long enough. Thank you for coming. I'm all right.

16. I LOOK DOWN AT HIM CURIOUSLY.
"What happened to Dr. Jäger?"

The priest, unsurprised, answers in the same flat, dry voice. "He disappeared. He was thought to have gotten across the Bodensee to Switzerland and eventually to Portugal and to Paraguay."

"What happened to the others you met?"

"Oh, that's a matter of record. You can look it up." He recites rapidly, as if he were a clerk reading the record. "Dr. Max de

Crinis, the 'charming Austrian,' who was responsible for sending retarded children to Goerden, one of the murder institutions, could not get out of the Russian encirclement of Berlin in 1945. He committed suicide with a government-supplied capsule of cyanide. Dr. Villinger, the eugenicist, was indicted in the euthanasia trial in Limburg. After questioning by the prosecution he went to the mountains near Innsbruck before the trial and committed suicide. Dr. Carl Schneider, respected successor to Kraepelin at Heidelberg, worked with the SS commission at Bethel and selected candidates for extermination. When he was put on trial after the war, he committed suicide. Dr. Paul Nitsche, author of the authoritative *Handbook of Psychiatry* during the Weimar Republic, was tried in Dresden for the murder of mental patients, sentenced to death, and executed in 1947. Dr. Werner Heyde, director of the clinic at Würzburg, where patients had been treated humanely since the sixteenth century, was also put on trial at Limburg for euthanasia. He committed suicide in his cell five days before the trial. He approved carbon monoxide as the drug of choice in euthanasia. At the time he was head of the Reich Society for Mental Illness Institution. Dr. C. G. Jung, co-editor with Dr. M. H. Goering of the Nazi-coordinated *Journal for Psychotherapy*, after the war became, I understand, a well-known psychiatrist.''

After he finishes, we sit for a while in silence. The moon is overhead. The sea of pines, without shadows, looks calm and silvery as water. There is a sliver of light in the south where the moonlight reflects from Lake Pontchartrain.

''No fires tonight,'' says the priest.

''No,'' I say absently.

''Would you do me a favor, Tom?''

''Sure.''

''Get me that soup and Jell-O. I'm hungry.''

He spoons up chicken soup from the can and drinks the melted Jell-O from the bowl.

''You seem to feel better, Father.''

''I'm fine.''

''Do you have these episodes often?''

"Mostly in winter. I think it's an allergy to the dampness."

"How long have you had them?"

"Since last year when we had all that rain."

"I see." I reach for the ring of the trapdoor, hesitate. "There is something I don't understand."

"Yes?" He turns up the wick of the kerosene lamp.

"I'm not sure I understand what you're trying to tell me—about your memory of—about Germany."

"What is there to understand?"

"Are you trying to tell me that the Nazis were not to blame?"

"No. They were to blame. Everything you've ever heard about them is true. I saw Dachau."

"Are you suggesting that it was the psychiatrists who were the villains?"

"No. Only that they taught the Nazis a thing or two."

"Scientists in general?"

"No."

"Then is it the Germans? Are you saying that there is a fatal flaw peculiar to the Germans, something demonic?"

"Demonic?" The priest laughs. "I think you're pulling my leg, Tom." He looks at me slyly, then narrows his eyes as if he is sizing me up. "Could I ask you a question, Tom?"

"Sure."

"Do you think we're different from the Germans?"

"I couldn't say. I hope so."

"Do you think present-day Soviet psychiatrists are any different from Dr. Jäger and that crowd?"

"I couldn't say. But what is the point, Father?"

Again the priest's eyes seem to glitter. Is it malice or a secret hilarity? "Of my little *déjà vu*? Just a tale. Perhaps a hallucination, as you suggest. I thought you would be interested from a professional point of view. It was such a vivid experience, my remembering it in every detail, even the florist-shop smell of geraniums—much more vivid than a dream. Some psychological phenomenon, I'm sure."

I look at him. There is a sly expression in his eyes. Is he being ironic? "No doubt." I rise. "I'm going to pick up Claude. Come

277

in tomorrow for a CORTscan. If you don't feel well, call me or have Milton call me. I'll come for you."

We shake hands. Something occurs to me. "May I ask you a somewhat personal question?" His last question about the Germans irritated me enough that I feel free to ask him.

"Sure."

"Why did you become a priest?"

"Why did I become a priest." The priest at first seems surprised. Then he ruminates.

"Yes."

"What else?"

"What else what?"

"That's all."

He shrugs, appearing to lose interest. "In the end one must choose—given the chance."

"Choose what?"

"Life or death. What else?"

What else. I'm thinking of the smell of geraniums and of the temporal lobe where smells are registered and, in some cases of epilepsy or brain tumor, replay, come back with all the haunting force of memory. And play one false too. I don't recall geraniums having a smell.

17. THE IRON GATE AT BELLE AME IS CLOSED. I GET out to open it, hoping it is not locked. It unlocks and opens even as I reach for it. In the same instant headlights come on beyond the gate not ten feet away. They are double lights, on high beam but close enough and low enough not to blind me.

It is the Ranger four-door parked, waiting.

"Okay, Doctor. You can hold it right there. That's fine."

It's the driver, the one dressed in the business suit. The other man is getting out of the Ranger. He is wearing a business jacket over the bib overalls.

"Please park your car over there, Doctor," says number one, opening the gate and pointing past the Ranger. He's Boston or Rhode Island, the *park* is almost *pâk*, the *car* almost but not quite *câ*. Not as broad as Boston. Probably Providence. Otherwise he's Midwest Purvis, old-style FBI, hair: crewcut; suit: Michigan State collegiate.

"Why?"

"We have a federal warrant, Doctor."

"For what? What's the charge?"

"We don't need a charge." He reaches for something under his jacket, behind him—cuffs?—but flips open a little pocket book, showing a badge. "ATFA, Doctor. Please park your car there."

"Take it easy, Mel," says number two. "The doctor's not going anywhere, are you, Doc?" He's upcountry Louisiana, strong-bellied, heavy-faced, not ill-natured, but sure, sheriff-sure. He could have been one of Huey Long's bodyguards. He's wearing a suit jacket over his overalls. Why bib overalls? Because he's too fat for jeans? "Doc, we got orders to hold you for parole violation. I'll park your car for you." He says *päk*, *cä*. They are not unfriendly.

"Where're we going?"

"Angola, right up the road."

"That's a state facility."

"We have very good liaison with state and county officers, Doctor," says Providence Purvis, picking up some Louisiana good manners. "I'm sure we can clear it up in no time. Don't worry. You're not going to the prison farm. We have a holding facility there, quite a decent place actually—for political detainees and suchlike."

"He's talking about parish, Doc," says Louisiana Fats, pronouncing it *pa-ish*. "I'm out of the sheriff's office in East Feliciana, on loan to the ATFA. It's the feds have the holding facility."

"Let's go, Dr. More," says Purvis.

"I want to pick up a patient here, one of the boys. It's an urgent medical matter."

"No way," says Purvis, turning Yankee again. "Move it."

18. THE FEDERAL HOLDING FACILITY IS UNDER THE levee, outside the main gate, and not really part of the Angola Prison Farm. It is a nondescript, two-story frame building which in fact I remember. It used to be a residence for junior correction officers. It looks like a crewboat washed up from the Mississippi, which flows just beyond the levee and all but encircles Angola like a turbulent moat.

It is not yet midnight. But the place is brightly lit by a bank of stadium lights. There are two tiers of rooms and a boatlike rail running around both decks. A couple of men, not dressed like prisoners, are lounging at the upper rail like sailors marooned in a bad port.

It turns out I know the jailer. He's a Jenkins, Elmo Jenkins, one of several hundred Jenkinses from upper St. Tammany Parish, sitting behind not even a desk but a folding metal picnic table in a passageway amidships which looks like the rec room of an oil rig with its old non-stereo TV, plastic couches, a card table, and a stack of old *Playboys*.

Officer Jenkins is uniformed but shirt-sleeved. When I knew him he was a deputy sheriff in Bogalusa. He is older than I and heavy. His thick gray hair, gone yellow, is creased into a shelf by his hatband.

He looks at me for a while. "How you doing, Doc," says Elmo mournfully, holding out his hand and not looking at me. He is embarrassed. He's expecting me. "What can I do for you fellows?" he asks the two federal officers in a different voice. He doesn't have much use for them.

"Just sign this, Officer," says Providence Purvis, taking a

paper from his pocket, "and the doctor will be out of our jurisdiction and into yours."

"He was never in yours," says Elmo, an old states'-righter.
He is speaking to Louisiana Fats, for whom he seems to have a
special dislike.

"I beg your pardon, Officer," says Purvis crisply, pronouncing it *perrdon*. Midwest after all? "If you will consult the federal
statute for ATFA detainees, I think you will find you're in er-
ror." *Errr*.

"Come back tomorrow and see the warden," says Elmo, not
looking at either one of them.

"But—" begins Louisiana Fats.

"Let's go," says Purvis.

They leave.

"Doc," says Elmo, "what in hail you doing here?"

"I don't rightly know. I'm tired. What time is it?"

"You look like you been rid hard and put up wet."

"You got a room, Elmo? I'm tired."

"I got the V.I.P. room for you, Doc. The one we keep for
political refugees. The last occupant was the ex-President of
Guatemala. You think I'll ever forget what you did for my
auntee, Miss Maude from Enon? You cured her after the best
doctors in New Orleans tried and couldn't."

I remember old Miss Maude Jenkins. She had shingles. I
often get patients after medical doctors and chiropractors strike
out. She was over the worst of the shingles but still had pain
which, with shingles, can be pain indeed. I perceived that she
was the sort of decent and credulous woman who believes what
doctors tell her. The other doctors had not bothered to tell her
anything. I did what I seldom do, used hypnosis and a placebo,
gave her a sugar pill and told her that the pain would soon get
better. It did. It might have, anyway.

"Here's what is going to happen, Doc," says Elmo. "It seems
you're being held for some sort of parole violation. Tomorrow
morning a Dr. Comeaux and a Dr. Gottlieb will come to see
you and you'll be taken care of one way or another. That's about
all I know. You going back to Fort Pelham?"

"I don't know. Could I go to bed?"

"Sho now." He takes me upstairs.

My cell could be a dorm room at L.S.U., except for the steel door and barred window. There's even a student-size desk with a phone on it.

"Can I use the phone?"

"Sho you can. I've authorized it. Just dial direct. If it's long distance, call me and I'll fix it up. There's some pajamas under the pillow. Left by the President of Guatemala. Silk. How about that?"

"That's fine."

"He jumped ship in Baton Rouge. Before him we had six Haitians. They were as nice as they could be. Highest-class niggers I ever saw. Three of them spoke better English than you or me. All spoke French."

"Thanks, Elmo."

"If you need anything, call me. Here's my number downstairs."

"I'm fine. Thanks, Elmo."

After Elmo leaves, I call Lucy.

"My God, where are you?"

"At Angola."

"My God, I thought so."

"Don't worry. It's not bad. Are the children all right?"

"They're fine."

"Lucy, did you get Claude out of Belle Ame?"

"No. I tried. They're not answering the phone and the gate is locked."

"I see."

"My God, where have you been all night?"

"Making a house call."

"Bob Comeaux has been looking for you."

"I know."

"He's been calling all evening. He wants to see you tomorrow. Before the wedding."

"He knows where I am now. What wedding?"

"At Kenilworth next door. You know. That fellow from Las

Vegas bought it—Romero? Romeo? He had in mind an English manor house, but it looks like Caesar's Palace. His daughter is getting married at noon. But Comeaux is mighty anxious to see you. He'll be there first thing.''

"I know.''

"What are they going to do with you?''

"Probably send me back to Alabama.''

"They can't do that!''

"They can.''

A pause. "You sound funny. Are you all right?''

"I'm fine.''

"I want you over here by me.''

"That may be possible later.''

"Is there anything I can do?''

"Yes. Can you be available tomorrow morning and have Vergil and your uncle available?''

"Sure. You mean—''

"I mean stay there. By the phone. We have to get Claude. It's no good calling the police. Wait by the phone until you hear from me.''

"Sure. I will. Are you—''

"What?''

"Are you sure you're all right?''

"I'm fine. A little tired.''

"You sound funny.''

"I'm fine.''

"Please—''

"What?''

"Take care of yourself.''

"I will.''

Sure enough, the pajamas are under the pillow. They are silk. The cot is hard but comfortable. The sheets and pillowcase are fresh.

I never slept better. There is something to be said for having no choice in what one does. I felt almost as good as I did in prison in Alabama.

IV

1. WEDNESDAY MORNING.

Bob Comeaux is striding up and down my cell. He is shaking his head mournfully.

"Son, you blew it. You really blew it."

"How is that, Bob?"

He is on his way to the wedding at Kenilworth and is dressed in a kind of plantation tuxedo, a formal white linen suit with a long-skirted jacket, scarlet cummerbund, ruffled shirt, and scarlet bow tie. He carries a broad-brimmed panama hat. His sideburns seem longer. He looks like an old Howard Keel in a revival of *Showboat*.

I am sitting at my little desk. He sets his hat on the desk and brushes back his sideburns. He stands over me, hands shoved deep in his pockets.

"Tom, you've not only violated your parole—by trespassing on the shunt compound. Hell, like I told you, we can live with that. But now you've blown your security."

"How is that?"

"We know that you and your friend, Mrs. Lipscomb—Dr. Lipscomb?—have accessed the NIH data bank on Blue Boy. We can't have the cover blown on Blue Boy until we're ready. Think of it as another Manhattan Project."

"All right."

"Now we have reason to believe you're trying to shoot down John Van Dorn. Tom, we can't afford to lose him. He's a bit eccentric, but he's our resident genius."

"He's a pedophile."

"Look, Tom"—Bob Comeaux picks up his hat and, spreading the skirt of his jacket, rests a haunch on my desk—"I know there've been some reports of irregularities in the staff out there. But I've got some news for you."

"Yes?"

"Belle Ame is closing down. Van is on his way to M.I.T. within the month. I knew we couldn't keep him. But we picked his brain while he was here and we've got Blue Boy on track. Exit Dr. Van Dorn. End of chapter. End of problem." He clears his throat. "I would think you of all people, Tom, would be glad of that."

"I am."

"Tell me one thing, Tom." Bob Comeaux puts a hand on my shoulder.

"What?"

"Were your kids molested in any way?"

"No."

"O—kay." He stands up briskly. "Look. I think I see a simple way out of this silly business."

"Yes?"

"Just to show you what we think of you, you old turkey, we're going to convene a little ad hoc meeting of the med-ethics parole board right here, today, in this room, and get this dumb-ass business squared away for once and all."

"Where is Gottlieb?"

"He'll be here. Two o'clock. Okay?"

"Sure."

"We're going to make you a proposition you can't refuse, ha ha."

"What?"

"You know, I think. We want you aboard. We're losing Van Dorn, but if we can sign you on as senior consultant in cortex pharmacology, we'll be ahead of the game."

"And if I don't?"

Bob is holding the panama at arm's length, eyeing it, evening up the brim. "That would be your choice. It would be out of our hands."

"Back to Fort Pelham."

"Look, Tom. Tom, please turn around and look at me."

I turn my chair around and look at him. He has put his hat on and is standing, feet wide apart, hands clasped behind his back.

"Hear this, Tom. I'll make it short and sweet. We're not talking about some bush-league medical project—fluoridating water to cure tooth decay. We're not even talking about curing AIDS. We're not even talking medicine, Tom. We're talking about the decay of the social fabric. The American social fabric. I'm not telling you anything you don't already know—all the way from the destruction of the cities, crime in the streets, demoralization of the underclass, to the collapse of the family. I don't have to tell you this, because you already know. What I'm telling you is that we'll be here at two o'clock and that we need you."

"All right. I'll be here."

He gazes at me, eyes going fine, then laughs. "Well, I'll be damned. Gottlieb said you'd give me static."

"No static. I'll be here."

He looks at me curiously. "Are you all right?"

"I'm fine."

"You seem—"

"I'm fine."

"Terrific!" He actually claps his hands. "I'll be on my way. A wedding of the daughter of an old friend right down the road. At Kenilworth. Tom, I got news for you. There is still grace, style, beauty, manners, civility left in the world. It's not all gone with the wind. You know who's coming up for the reception? Pete Fountain and his Half Fast Band. And Al Hirt. Both are personal friends of mine. I wish you could join me."

"So do I."

He taps on the door for the guard. When the door opens, he steps out, but then, bethinking himself, steps back and waves me toward him.

"Tom, I want you to see something. Okay, Officer? It's okay, Tom. Just step out here for a second."

Standing on the top deck of the stranded crewboat, we look out over the vast prison farm. Rows of cotton, mostly picked, stretch away into the bright morning sunlight. Hundreds of black men and women, the men bare-chested, the women kerchiefed, bend over the rows, dragging their long sacks collapsed like parachutes. Armed horsemen patrol the levee.

"Listen, Tom," says Bob Comeaux softly.

From all around, as murmurous as the morning breeze, comes the singing.

> Swing low, sweet chariot,
> Coming for to carry me home.

"Isn't that something?" Bob Comeaux almost whispers.

"Yes, it is."

"It beats Attica and Sing Sing, doesn't it?"

"Yes, it does."

"Why do you think they're so content with their lot?"

"I couldn't say."

"Yes, you could, if you thought of it—you of all people, with your knowledge."

"I see."

"They're not only making restitution for their crimes, paying their victims, they're enjoying it. Can you force anyone to sing like that?"

"No."

"I'll tell you another little secret of our success."

"What's that?"

"We allow—ahem—conjugal visits."

"Good."

"Would you believe that some of them don't want to leave

and go back to the streets of New Orleans and Baton Rouge when they've served their time?''

"Yes."

"Don't you love those colorful kerchiefs the women wear?"

"Yes."

We shake hands. He holds my hand in a firm grip for a second, gives me a final level-eyed look. He's quite handsome with his long sideburns, handsomer than Howard Keel. "Glad to have you aboard, Doctor. Guard!"

"Yes, sir."

"Lock this fellow up. He's a dangerous character."

2. I CALL ELMO ON THE DESK PHONE. "How you doing, Doc?"

"I'm fine, Elmo."

"What can I do for you, Doc?"

"Elmo, I need to get out of here."

Elmo sighs. "I'd like nothing better, Doc. But you know as well as I do we got to hold you for the ATFA. Doc, all you got to do is clear it with that doctor dude from Fedville and he can clear it with the feds."

"I know that. I'm meeting with them this afternoon. But I need to get out now for a while."

"Oh, I got you. No problem, Doc. We got exercise period coming up in a few minutes. You can walk the levee. No problem. It'll do you good."

"Thanks, Elmo. I appreciate it, but here's my problem." I tell him about Belle Ame, the Brunettes, and the sexual abuse, giving him all the technical details. I tell him dryly, as one professional to another, one cop to another cop. "The thing is, Elmo, I have a kid there and I think I'd better get him out. Now." I don't tell him the kid is Claude Bon.

There is a silence. I can hear the chair creak as he leans back.

"Goddamn, Doc." The chair creaks again. There is a soft whistling. "You know, I heard something about that from the sheriff over at Clinton. I thought they had turned them loose for lack of evidence."

"They did. But now Dr. Lipscomb has the evidence."

Another whistling of breath through teeth. "Well, I mean shitfire, Doc. Why don't I call Cooter Sharp over at Clinton and tell him to bust the whole gang? I mean all. I mean, when it comes to messing with chirren—"

"You can do that if you want. But they've tried that. And it will take time. And they'll probably be looking for you, ready with their lawyers, and you're going to run into problems of federal jurisdiction."

"Yeah."

"Elmo, I want to get the kid out of there. Now. We, you, whoever, can bring charges later."

"Yeah." The creaking becomes rhythmic. He's rocking. "Yeah," he says again and in a different voice. "Tell you what, Doc," he says in a musing voice. He's leaning back in his chair. "Tell you what. You go ahead and take your exercise. I'll send up an officer to let you out the back gate. That will put you on the levee and batture, which is fenced off. What we got here, Doc, is a minimum-security holding facility—for illegals, politicals, suchlike. We're not part of the high-security prison farm, you understand."

"I understand."

"Thing is, Doc, the fence is a joke. Anybody can get over it, under it. But the thing is, even the hard-timers know that nobody but a fool would try to make it out by the river. That's the Raccourci Chute out there, and ain't nobody, I mean nobody, ever made it out that way to live to tell about it. You understand."

"I understand."

"Now, what we got here, Doc, is a fenced-off exercise area for our detainees, about a quarter mile of levee. Just so you'll know where you'll be walking, the downriver end is fenced off. The patrol's not going to bother you—they know the people here are mostly politicals. The willows begin down there at the batture corner of the fence. You might recall an old jeep road that deer hunters use that runs up from old Tunica Landing. I know you know where that is.''

"Yes."

"That's about all I can tell you, Doc."

"I understand. Thanks, Elmo."

"For what? Enjoy your walk, Doc, but you be back here by two or my ass is in a sling. What I'm going to do now is send you up some breakfast. It's staff breakfast. After all, you been up here before on forensic business and are entitled to staff. You also looking a little poorly, Doc."

"I'm fine. Thank you, Elmo. Give my best to Miss Maude when you see her."

"I'll surely do that. She thinks the world and all of you."

"One last thing, Doc."

"Yes?"

"If you ain't back here by two, it's my ass."

"I'll be back."

"It's your ass, too."

"I understand."

Breakfast is at least four scrambled eggs, fried ham, a mountain of grits—the "big hominy" kind, which I haven't seen for years—and hot chicoried coffee.

I eat it all. There is a glass of water. It reminds me of something. I call Elmo.

"One little question, Elmo. I'll explain later."

"Sho, Doc."

"The breakfast was delicious. Where does the water come from?"

Elmo Jenkins laughs. "You noticed. Don't worry about it, Doc. You not drinking river water. That's Abita Springs water, right from our back yard, the best in the world, as you know."

"I know. What do the prisoners on the farm drink?"

"That's river water, treated so it's safe, but I can taste the chemicals."

"You mean from the Ratliff intake?"

"Right, Doc. Seems like you know this country around here."

"A little."

"Enjoy your walk, Doc."

I call Lucy. She picks it up on the first ring. "Yes?" she says breathlessly. She's ready. "Is that you?"

"Yes."

"You all right?"

"I'm fine. Is Vergil there?"

"Right here."

"Doc?" says Vergil. "You all right?"

"I'm fine."

"What are we going to do, Doc?"

"We're going to get Claude."

"Fine. How are we going to do that? I already tried. They're all locked up and don't answer the phone. You think we ought to call the police again?"

"No. Here's what we're going to do. You know where Tunica Landing is?"

"I surely do. That's where my daddy used to put in to cross over to Raccourci Island."

"Good. I want you to meet me there in forty minutes."

Pause. "Doc, you in Angola. How we going to do that?"

"Don't worry. I have a—like a pass. Does your daddy still have his pirogue?"

"No, sir. He got a new one, a light fiberglass one, just before he got sick. He only could use it once or twice. It's good as new."

"Will it hold three people?"

"Three people. Well, it will hold me and my daddy and two hundred pounds of nutria."

"Can you get it in Lucy's truck?"

"With one hand."

"Good. Is Uncle Hugh Bob there?"

"Yes, sir. You want to talk to him?"

"No, that's not necessary. Just tell him to come with you. He'll be glad to. And tell him one more thing."

"Yes, sir."

"You know that old long-barrel Colt Woodsman he's got?"

"I sure do."

"Tell him to bring it."

"Tell him to bring it," Vergil repeats.

"For dogs."

"For dogs," Vergil repeats.

"They might have guard dogs at Belle Ame."

"All right, Doc." He seems relieved.

"We not going to kill them. We probably won't even need it."

"Right, Doc."

"I figure it will take you forty-five minutes or so to get up to Tunica Landing. I'll probably be there by then. If not, wait."

"We'll be there."

"And, Vergil."

"Yes, sir."

"Don't worry about Claude. I feel sure he's all right. But I don't want my kids in that place and I'm sure you feel the same way."

"I sure do. But what—"

"We're just going to ease down the river to the old landing at Belle Ame and pick up Claude and maybe have a little talk with those folks. Later we'll call the police. But I want Claude out first. We can't go by car because the gate's locked and they'd be expecting us. They're not going to be expecting anybody from the landing. So we'll have a look around, and a little surprise won't hurt them. They can't lock the landing. But there might be some dogs."

"We'll be there in thirty minutes, Doc."

"Good. Let me talk to Lucy."

Lucy's voice is constricted and high in her throat. "What in the world—!"

I tell her the plan.

"Are you crazy? Don't fool around with those people. Let me call the police."

"We will. But I want to get Claude out now and there's something I need to find out."

"Yes, but they'll—"

"They'll what? Shoot me? No no. Van Dorn doesn't know what we have on him. He's mainly worried about the heavy-sodium connection. He'll want to explain, talk me into something. He's the one that's worried. They don't even know about your clinical findings with the children. You didn't tell anybody, did you?

"No, but—"

"But what?"

"Promise me that—"

"That I won't shoot anybody? I promise I won't shoot anybody."

"Promise me that you'll take care of yourself."

"I will."

"Good God."

"Now listen, Lucy."

"Yes?"

"Where is your truck?"

"Here. I've been here with the children, either on the phone trying to reach Gottlieb or waiting to hear from you."

"All right. Give the keys to Vergil. When we finish our business at Belle Ame, we'll either take my car if it's still there, or we'll drop on down to Pantherburn in the pirogue. I have to get back here by two. You can drive me up."

"After you finish your business." She's calmed down, is

breathing easier. "And what do I do if you don't show up or I don't hear from you?"

"If we don't show up by midnight, call the cops."

"Call the cops," she repeats. "Why do you need Hugh?"

"He knows the river."

"He knows the river."

"See you later."

"Sure," she says absently.

3. THERE'S A DIRT TRACK ATOP THE LEVEE BEYOND THE chain link fence. You can't see the river through the willows of the batture. There's another fence in the willows. The morning sun is already warm. A south wind from the gulf is already pushing up a dark, flat-headed cloud. It is like late summer. My nose has stopped running. Walking the levee in flatlands has the pleasant feel of traveling a level track between earth and sky.

There is no horse patrol in sight, only guard towers on the prison farm, but I'd as soon get off the levee and into the willows. The batture here has been cleared down to the fence. I quicken my stride. The smudge ahead under the cloud must be the loess hills. And here's the crossing fence, crossing the levee and squaring off the two fences running on each side. Beyond the fence a shell road angles up one side of the levee and down the other. The fence is maybe eight feet high, but it is not a good idea to climb it. I'm still in clear view of the near tower. Elmo mentioned the downriver corner. I see why. There's a washout just upriver from the corner, grown up in weeds, but a washout nonetheless, a space gullied under the fence. It is not hard to see. It can only mean that the fence is symbolic and the detainees have no reason to escape, or that the guards, both mounted and in the towers, keep them in sight. Or both.

I make my turn, look back toward Angola, see no one, widen the turn to carry over the brow of the levee to its shoulder, moseying along, hands in pockets like the bored ex-President of Guatemala, down and out of sight of the guard tower. The grass is ankle high, but the footing is good and it is easy to angle down the levee. On the steeper shoulder of the levee at the washout I roll down and under the fence the way you roll down the levee when you're a boy, elbows held in tight, hands over your face.

The willows of the batture are thick. It is good to be in the willows and out of sight. I figure to hit the shell road, which angles away from me, by keeping parallel to the river. The going is heavy, but after a hundred yards or so I hit not shells but a dirt track, hardly wider than a path. This must be Elmo's jeep trail. The soft dirt has three tire tracks, which puzzle me until I remember that deer hunters hereabouts use three-wheelers more than jeeps.

The trail angles toward the river. The batture is dropping away. The dirt is quiet underfoot, but presently there is a roaring. The top of a poplar moves fitfully as if it were being jerked by a human hand. It must be the river, high now and ripping through the batture.

I break out into a junkyard of rusty steel hawsers with caches of trapped driftwood cemented by dried whitened mud, chunks of Styrofoam, tires, Clorox bottles. A rusting hulk of a barge fitted with a crane conveyor is toppled and half sunk. This must have been a transfer facility, no doubt a soybean depot.

The river is on the boom. It's been dry here. They must have had late summer rains in the Dakotas or the Midwest. This stretch is the Raccourci Chute, which goes ripping past Angola even at low water. But now it's up in the willows and a mile wide, roaring and sucking and jerking the willows and blowing a cool, foul breath. A felon might imagine that if he could get over the levee and into the willows he could make it, but no. He'd get caught in the sucks and boils. There's nothing out there but roiled, racing, sulphur-colored water flecked by dirty foam from Dakota farms, Illinois toilets, and ten million boxes of Tide. Angola could just as well be Alcatraz. Looking across toward Raccourci Island, I could swear the river swells, curved up like a watchglass by the boil of a giant spring.

Old Tunica Landing is nothing but a rotten piece of wharf. The raised walk of creosoted planks is solid enough and high enough to clear the rising water in the batture. There's nobody here and the gravel road from Tunica is grown up in weeds. I pick out a dry piling I can sit against and from which I can see up the road without being seen. The landing was used first by the Tunica Indians and then to service the indigo plantations. I came here once to see the Tunica Treasure, a graveyard which somebody dug up and then found, not gold, but glass beads which the English, my ancestors, had given them for their land two hundred years ago. It is nine-thirty.

A little upriver and a ways out is Fancy Point Towhead, an island of willows almost submerged but long enough and angled out enough to deflect the main current and make a backwater. Foam drifts under me upstream. There's another noise above the racket of the current in the batture downstream. It's a towboat pushing fifteen or twenty rafted-up barges upstream. There's not enough room inside the island for him to use the dead water. He has to buck straight up the Chute and he's having a time of it. The current is maybe eight knots, and with his diesels flat out he's maybe making twelve. He sounds like five freight engines going upgrade, drive wheels spinning.

I watch him. There is so much noise that I don't hear Vergil Bon until the plank moves under me. He's carrying a pirogue by its gunwale in one hand, two paddles in the other. The uncle is right behind him, face narrow and dark under his hunting cap. He's carrying his old double-barrel 12-gauge Purdy in the crook of his arm and ambling along in his sprung splayed walk as if he were on his way to a duck blind. They both seem serious but not displeased.

"How you doing, Vergil, Uncle Hugh Bob?" The towboat is noisy.

"Fine."

"Fine."

We shake hands. They gaze around, not at me, equably. They are Louisianians, at ease out-of-doors. The uncle nods and pops his fingers. We could be meeting here every day.

"Did you bust out of there?" asks the uncle companionably, flanking me.

"I have permission. Don't worry about it."

We watch the towboat make the bend, creep past the concrete of the Hog Point revetment, which looks like a gray quilt dropped on the far levee.

"Uncle Hugh Bob, what are you doing with that shotgun?"

"You asked him about that little Woodsman." He nods toward Vergil as if he didn't know him well. "We brought it. But I didn't know what kind of trouble you're in." He's jealous because I asked Vergil.

"We're not going to have any trouble—beyond maybe a mean dog or a snake."

"I'm not going to shoot no dog with a .22. This won't kill him." He pats the shotgun. "What we going to do?"

"We're going to drop down to Belle Ame and pick up Claude. After that you and Claude can take the pirogue on down to Pantherburn. My car is at Belle Ame. I'll bring Vergil back up here to get the truck. We'll see."

That seems to satisfy him. "I brought along my spinning tackle, right here." He pats his game pocket. "Claude can go fishing with me." Then he thinks of something. "What you doing at Angola?" He screws up a milky eye at me.

"It was a misunderstanding. Some federal officers thought I was a parole violator. I have to be back up here at two to straighten it out. Nothing to worry about."

"They not looking for you?"

"No. It's like having a pass."

He nods, not listening. But Vergil is watching me closely. He says nothing.

"Vergil, how long will it take to get down to Belle Ame?"

He answers easily, gauging the current, without changing his expression. "It's not all that far. Just past the hills and where the levee begins again. And in that current—half an hour."

"Twenty minutes," says Uncle Hugh, willing to argue about the river.

"Do they still have a landing?"

Vergil and the uncle laugh. "A landing?" says Vergil. "Doc, that's where the new *Tennessee Belle* and the *Robert E. Lee* tie up when they bring tourists up from New Orleans for the Azalea Festival and the Plantation Parade in the spring."

"Do you think that pirogue will hold the three of us out in all that?"

"It took me and my daddy and two hundred pounds of nutria."

"Not out in that," says the uncle. He's offended because I didn't ask him.

"Yes, sir, out in that," says Vergil, telling me. I wish he would pay attention to the uncle. "Right over there on Raccourci Island is where my daddy used to run his traps."

"What do you think, Uncle Hugh Bob?"

The uncle considers, breaks the breech of the Purdy, sights through it. "Well, the trash will be going with us. All we got to worry about is getting run over or hit by a wake like that." The last of the towboat's wake is slapping and sucking under us.

"I tell you what let's do, Doc, Mr. Hugh," says Vergil, appearing to muse. "Mr. Hugh knows more about the river than anybody around here. Anybody can paddle. So why don't we put Mr. Hugh in the middle so he can judge the river, look out for snags, and tell us which way to go if something big is coming down on us. You know those sapsuckers will see you and still run over you."

Thank you, Vergil, for your tact.

"They will," says the uncle, mollified. "But what's he talking about, paddling in that thing? Y'all just worry about steering, ne' mind paddling."

"How much freeboard you reckon we going to have?" I am eyeing the pirogue, still in Vergil's hand. A pirogue is designed for one Cajun in a swamp, kneeling and balancing with a load of muskrat, nutria, or alligator. It can navigate in an inch of water and slide over a hummock of wet grass. It was not designed for three men in the Mississippi River.

"Enough," says Vergil.

"Two inches," says the uncle. "That thing supposed to be in a swamp."

"Not to worry," says Vergil absently, looking on either side of the wharf for a place to launch, and as absently: "What's going on at Belle Ame, Doc?"

"Did Lucy tell you anything?"

"She just said there was some humbug over there and that was why you took Tommy and Margaret out and why we ought to get Claude out." He appears to be inspecting the river intently.

"I don't think we have to worry about Claude, but I thought it better not to take any chances. We'll go get him. I also want to get a line on Dr. Van Dorn. As you know, he's involved in that sodium shunt and maybe in something else."

Vergil says nothing, after a moment nods. "All right, then."

"Something wrong with that fellow," says the uncle.

"Who's that?"

"That Dr. Van."

"What's wrong with him?"

"He's a little on the sweet side."

"Sweet? How do you mean?"

"He's slick behind the ears."

"Let's go," says Vergil. "Over here."

It's a trick getting into the pirogue. The water's a couple of feet below the planking. Vergil has no trouble, holding it steady with one foot and letting himself down, balancing like a cat. He holds fast to the wharf while I get in. We both hold for the uncle.

It's not bad in the dead water behind the towhead. The pirogue is new-style light fiberglass with two seats like a canoe. The uncle sits comfortably on the bottom amidships, arms resting on the gunwales, back against a thwart, like an easy chair. It's a big pirogue. There are perhaps three inches of freeboard.

The going is easy in the dead water, even downriver from the towhead. But there's a noise ahead like the suck of floodwater in a storm drain.

Then it takes us, the current of the Chute. Something grabs the bow at my knee. It's like starting out from the siding in a roller coaster car and being jerked by the big cable. A sluice of brown water ships over my paddle hand and catches the uncle. "Shit!" breathes the uncle. This isn't going to work, I'm thinking. But as soon as we're airborne, caught up in the current, it's better. We could be standing still if you didn't notice the green shapes of the batture slipping by like stage scenery.

It comes down to Vergil steering from the stern and me paddling some, mainly to keep heading up. Dark shapes, logs, scraps of dunnage nuzzle up, drift off, as friendly as dolphins.

"Look out for snags, Doc," says Vergil.

"The snags are going faster than we are."

"Shit, those are not snags," says the uncle at my ear. "Those are stumps, whole trees. Don't worry about them. Do what the man says."

We're settling down. It's even quiet out here. The current carries us close to the Pointe Coupée bank. The pale quilted concrete of a revetment shoots past like railroad cars.

The river turns. Sunlight glitters in the boils and eddies of the current. We're around Tunica Bend and at the foot of Raccourci Island. The levee runs out and the Chute slams straight into the dark hills of Feliciana. We find easier water near the inside of the bend. Now we're gliding along a pencil-size strip of beach on the Pointe Coupée bank. There is a break in the treeline and, beyond, what looks like a tufted lake. It's a hummocky swamp. We're out of the Chute. The racket is behind us. Now it's as quiet here as a bayou, but we're still making good time.

"You know what that is, Mr. Hugh Bob?" asks Vergil behind me. He must be pointing with his paddle.

"I ought to," says the uncle to me. "I been there enough. That's Paul's Slough."

"That's right," says Vergil. "It's also the western end of the Tuscaloosa Trend."

"I know that," says the uncle.

"You go another ten miles west and you got to drill forty thousand feet just to hit gas. This is where the Devonian fault takes a dip."

"That's right," says the uncle to me. "And that ain't all. I'll tell you something else about that piece of water that some folks don't know. I'm talking about that steamboat. Some people don't know about, but his daddy knows about it." His voice went away behind me. He must have jerked his head toward Vergil.

Vergil doesn't answer. We've got crossways of the current and are busy heading up.

The uncle, piqued by Vergil's showing off his geological knowledge, enlists me by tapping my shoulder. He knows some stuff too. "We heard it many a time when we were running our traps. Vergil Senior, his daddy, told me he heard it when he used to spend the night over there before a duck hunt."

"Heard what?" I say, thinking about Belle Ame. "How much farther to Belle Ame, Uncle?"

"Not all that far. Well, you know right here is where the old river used to come in. Right here. You know the Raccourci Cut happened one night during a June rise just like this. All it takes is one little trickle across the neck, then another little rise, a little more water, and before you know it, here comes the whole river piling across and ain't nothing in the world is going to stop it, not the U.S. engineers, nothing. If this river wants to go, it's going to go. Look out! The old river is still over there, you know, about twenty miles of the old river still looping around Raccourci Island, right there, blocked off, right across that neck where the swamp is. You can walk across to it in ten minutes. What happened was this. The night the river decided to come down the Chute, a stern-wheeler was working up the old river. They had a river pilot of course, and he was cussing. I mean, what with the fog and the rain and him fighting the current, he couldn't see bee-idly. It was taking him all night. Then he noticed the water was getting low. He began scraping over sandbars. He'd run aground. And he'd cuss. He didn't know the river had already made the cut across the neck and he was stranded. And he'd back off and head upriver and he'd run aground again. And he cussed. He couldn't get out. He cussed the river, the boat, the captain. He swore an oath. He swore: 'I swear by Jesus Christ I hope this son-of-a-bitching boat never gets out of this goddamn river.' And he never did. What he didn't know was that he was sealed off—the river had already come busting down the Chute. He couldn't get out. But the thing is, they couldn't find the boat. So they thought it had sunk in the storm. They never did find that boat. But I'm here to tell you that there's people, people I know, who have seen that boat in the old river on a foggy night during the June rise.''

"Have you seen it, Mr. Hugh?" Vergil asks him.

"I've heard it!" The uncle shouts. "And so has many another. Vergil, his daddy, and I heard it! We was camping out right over there across the slough by Moon Lake and the Old River and you could hear that sapsucker beating up the river through the fog, that old stern-wheel slapping the water like *whang whang whang*. Vergil Senior claimed he could even hear the pilot cursing. But we heard it!''

"I've heard that story," says Vergil behind him and talking to me past him. "It's part of the folklore of the river. You can hear the same story up and down the river wherever there's

302

been a cutoff. In fact, I've heard the same story from Mr. Clemens.''

Don't argue, Vergil.

''What I'm telling you is, I heard it,'' says tne uncle, still talking to me. They argue through me. I half listen. Here's a switch. Here's Vergil, the scientist, skeptic, the new logical positivist, and here's the uncle, defender of old legends, ghost ships, specters.

Let it alone, Vergil.

''The thing is,'' says Vergil, ''either that steamboat is there or it isn't. If it is there, then how come nobody has seen it in daylight or seen the wreck? If it was there and it sank, there would be some sign of it—the Old River is no more than twenty feet deep anywhere. The pilot house would be sticking out. It all reminds me a little bit of modern UFO sightings.''

''I'm here to tell you I heard that sucker,'' cries the uncle.

''Okay. Let me ask you both something.'' I'm not interested in hearing them try to upstage each other and don't like Vergil patronizing the uncle by talking about Mr. Clemens. To get them off it, I ask them where New Roads is, knowing it is off to the west and that we all have relatives there.

''You see right over there, over that cypress,'' says Vergil, his paddle coming out of the water. ''That's False River and just past it is New Roads and over there is Chevron Parlange Number One, the most famous gas well in history, twenty thousand feet, the discovery well of the whole Tuscaloosa Trend, came in August of '77, a hundred and forty thousand cubic feet per second, that's a million dollars a day. So big, in fact, it blew out.''

''You talking about Miss Lucy Parlange's place,'' says the uncle. ''And it couldn't have happened to a nicer lady.''

''My auntee lives there too,'' says Vergil. ''She still lives in the same little house on False River. But she had a piece of land over by Parlange when they hit that big well. My auntee leased her place for a hundred thousand.''

''That old Parlange house been in the same family for two

hundred and fifty years," says the uncle. "Through thick and thin. They never gave up."

"My auntee neither," says Vergil.

They tell stories about the big oil strike at False River, who got rich, how money ruined some.

"Blood will tell ever' time," says the uncle. "You take the Parlanges. They were aristocrats when they didn't have it, and when they got it, it made no difference."

"My auntee too," says Vergil. "She raised my daddy when his mamma got consumption and had to go to Greenwell Spring."

"How far is it?" I ask him.

"What?" asks the uncle.

"Belle Ame?"

"Around the bend. Watch out for the old oil fields and the tank farm."

We're back in the current, booming along past the great Tunica Swamp.

There is a double sun. The second sun reflects from a monolith mirror. It is the great glass pyramid of Fedville downriver. Beyond, in its shadow, the Grand Mer cooling tower looms as dark and spectral as the uncle's ghost ship.

We smell the old oil field before we see it. The loess hills have dropped away and the levee begins. Beyond are the tops of the tanks, which over the straight line of the levee gleam like steel marbles in a box. The scaffolding of the refinery, which used to hum and blaze away like the Ruhr Valley, is now gaunt and dark.

We ease into dead water behind a towhead of cottonwoods and there it is, the landing as fancy as ever it was in the great days of steamboats, three-tiered with heavy lashed piling, tire-bumpered, a heavy winched-up gangplank suspended in mid-air, ready for lowering onto the *Robert E. Lee*. A cotton bale stands at each end of the upper dock. The river laps over the lowest level and we slide right in.

"Upend it over that pile, out of sight, keep it quiet and we'll have a look," I tell Vergil.

There's a gazebo atop the levee with a booth where I reckon tickets are sold to tourists on the Plantation Parade. We sit on a bench inside the gazebo, in shadow and behind the booth.

Except for a man riding a gang mower, the grounds of Belle Ame are empty. The quarters, garçonnières, and carriage houses are dark. But there are movements at a window. The oaks look as dense and lobuled as green cabbages. Their shadows are short. Except for two lit carriage lanterns, the great house seems deserted. The soccer fields and tennis courts are empty. The flag hangs limply from its pole. A door slams. A black woman, long-skirted, kerchiefed, comes out on the upper gallery with a bucket and a mop.

We sit for a while.

The uncle breaks the breech of his Purdy, sniffs it, closes it with a click.

Presently the uncle says to Vergil, "What are we waiting for?"

They've made up.

"What we waiting for, Doc?" Vergil asks me.

"Just to have a look. What time is it?" I feel fixed-eyed.

"Ten-forty."

"Good." I am silent.

Vergil and the uncle look at each other.

"I want to see classes change. It should be at eleven."

At eleven the plantation bell rings, a solid peal of heavy metal. Classes change. Most of the children change from one room in the quarters to another. Some come and go from the rear of the big house. Nobody enters or leaves the garçonnière.

As we gaze, the dark green of the oaks seems to grow even darker, even though the sun is shining brightly. Then the dark whitens, just as if you had closed your eyes, the retinal image reversing, light going dark, dark light.

Vergil is watching me without expression, thumbnail touching his teeth.

"Well," says the uncle, opening and closing the shotgun.

305

"Let's go over there." I nod toward the garçonnière. "I think you better leave the shotgun here, Uncle Hugh."

"You think I'm going to leave a five-thousand-dollar Purdy out here for any white trash that comes along?" He snaps the breech a last time and hikes out.

We look at him. With his oversize hunting coat flapping around his knees, duck cap hugging his narrow skull, flaps down, seeming to sidle as he walks, one foot slinging, the barrel of the shotgun in the crook of his arm, he looks as loony as Ichabod Crane.

4. WE STOP IN THE SHADOW OF AN OAK NEAR THE garçonnière.

There is a movement in the window. It is a woman, standing, arms folded, looking out, but not at us. She seems to be smiling, but perhaps it is a shadow. No, it is Mrs. Cheney. I recognize the heavy dark eyebrows, rimless glasses, oval face still young-looking despite the heavy iron-colored hair pulled down tight.

Presently she turns away.

Several minutes pass. The uncle is as still as if we were in a duck blind. Vergil is watching me.

"Let's go over here." I move closer, into the shadow of the porch. Now we can see what Mrs. Cheney is doing. She is standing, arms still folded under her breasts, watching a boy playing cards on the floor. She is still smiling. She is often described as having a "sweet face" and she does. She has always been a sitter hereabouts, babysitter, sitter for old people. She is one of those women who have no other qualification than pleasantness and reliability. She used to sit with Meg and Tommy. Her best feature is her skin, which is like satin, smooth and dusky as a gypsy's. She has gained some

306

weight. Her forearms under her breasts are still firm-fleshed, but there is a groove along the bone separating the swell of pale underflesh pressed against her body from the dark outer arm.

"Well?" says Vergil, still watching me. He is worried about me, my silence. Do I know what I'm doing?

"Let's go say hello to Mrs. Cheney. Uncle, you're going to have to leave the shotgun by the door."

"There is no way—" he begins.

"Put it behind that sweet olive. You don't want to frighten Mrs. Cheney."

We knock and go in. Mrs. Cheney looks up, smiling. She seems no more than mildly surprised.

"Dr. More!"

"Hello, Mrs. Cheney. You know my uncle, Hugh Bob Lipscomb, and Vergil Bon, Claude's father."

"I surely do, and that's a fine boy. Hugh, that bluebird never came back. Hugh made me a bluebird box," she explains to me.

"That was a while ago," says the uncle, eyes somewhat rolled back. He's embarrassed and feels obliged to explain. "She had a bluebird nesting in her paper tube. I gave her the box but told her it would be better not to mess with the bird that season. But something ran it off."

"Is that right?"

"I first knew Mrs. Cheney when she used to sit with Lucy," the uncle explains to Vergil.

"They were all lovely people," says Mrs. Cheney. "All of y'all." Mrs. Cheney is nodding and smiling, eyeglasses flashing, as if nothing could be more natural than that the three of us should have appeared at this very moment.

While we talk, we are gazing down at the child. He is a boy, seven or eight. He looks familiar. He is picking up playing cards which are scattered face down on the floor. He is a very serious little boy, very thin, dressed in khaki pants and matching shirt like a school uniform. His narrow little butt waggles as he crawls around picking up cards. When he picks

307

up four cards, hardly looking at them, he stacks them awkwardly against his chest and makes a separate pile.

"Ricky, you speak to these nice gentlemen."

"Aren't you Ricky Comeaux?" I ask him.

Ricky doesn't speak, but he sits around to see us, large head balanced on the delicate stem of his neck. Finally he nods.

"What game are you playing, Ricky?" I ask him.

Mrs. Cheney answers for him. "Concentration. Y'all remember. I put all the cards on the floor face up. He takes one look. Then I turn them face down. You know. Then you're supposed to pick them up by pairs. You make mistakes, but you begin to remember where the cards are."

"I remember that," says the uncle.

"You know what Ricky does?" He picks them up by fours and in order, you know, four aces first, deuces, and so forth. And he doesn't make mistakes."

"I got to see that," says the uncle, eyes still somewhat rolled back.

"Do you want to see him do it, Dr. More?" Mrs. Cheney asks me.

"Yes."

Vergil looks at me: Why are we watching this child play cards?

Mrs. Cheney shuffles the cards expertly. Now she is on her hands and knees putting the cards down face up. She is agile and quick. A stretch of firm dusky thigh shows above the old-fashioned stockings secured in a tight roll above her knee. Ricky watches her but does not appear to be concentrating on the cards.

"Where are the others?" I ask Mrs. Cheney.

"Who? Oh, the children. Some are in class, some in rec. They're all over at Belle Ame."

"What are they doing in rec?"

"Oh, some watch the picture show, some play in the attic."

"Why isn't Ricky with them?"

308

"Ricky just came last week. He's still in our little boot camp, getting strong on vitamins in mind and body so he can join the teams. And he's doing so well!"

"We came to pick up Claude Bon. Do you know where he is?"

"Pick him up? What a shame! He's one of our stars. What a fine big boy. He's probably watching the movies or playing sardines."

"Where do they have the movies?"

Mrs. Cheney doesn't mind telling me. "They show the regular movies for the children in the ballroom and the staff watches the videos up there."

"You mean upstairs here?"

"You know, they take videos of the children and the staff sees them to check on their progress, you know, like home movies." Mrs. Cheney has turned the cards face down and now stands up, face flushed. "All right, Ricky."

Ricky starts picking up cards, first four aces, shows them to us in his perfunctory way, stacks them against his stomach then four deuces.

"Well, I be dog," says the uncle. "That's the smartest thing I ever saw."

"Where does he get his vitamins, Mrs. Cheney?" I ask.

"Right there." She nods to the bank of water coolers. "They all do. It's enriched Abita Springs water, for little growing brains and strong little bodies. You can see what it does."

"Enriched by what?"

"Vitamins and all. You know, Doctor."

"How much do they drink?"

"Eight glasses a day. And I mean eight, not seven."

Ricky picks up four sixes, shows them, stacks them.

"Do you drink it too?"

"Me? Lord, Doc, what's the use? It's too late for me. We are too old and beat-up."

"Why, you're a fine-looking woman," says the uncle, his

309

face keen, and begins blowing a few soft duck calls through his fingers.

Is Mrs. Cheney winking at me?

"Mrs. Cheney, call the big house and get Claude. Ask for Dr. Van Dorn or whoever, but I want Claude. Now."

"What, and interrupt sardines up in the attic. They would have a fit."

"I see. I'll tell you what, Mrs. Cheney," I say, changing my voice.

"What's that, Doctor?"

"I want you to go over to the big house and find Claude Bon and bring him back here."

"Oh, I couldn't do that, Doc!" cries Mrs. Cheney.

"Why not?"

"I'm not supposed to leave Ricky."

"We'll look after him."

"No, I'm not allowed to do that."

"Mrs. Cheney, get going. Now."

Both Vergil and the uncle look at me when my voice changes.

"All right, Doctor!" says Mrs. Cheney, smile gone, but not angry so much as resigned. "As long as you take the responsibility."

"I take it."

"It may take a while to find him."

"I'm sure you'll manage."

"All right!" Her voice is minatory, but she leaves.

"How can you talk that way to Mrs. Cheney?" the uncle asks me. "I mean she's one fine-looking woman."

I don't answer. We are watching Ricky pick up cards. Vergil is frowning.

"If that ain't the damnedest thing I ever saw," says the uncle. "That boy ain't even concentrating."

"He doesn't have to," I say. Somehow it is difficult to take my eyes from the back of Ricky's slender neck.

Ricky picks up kings, shows them, sits around cross-legged, evens up the cards against his chest to make a neat deck.

"Ricky."

"Yes, sir."

"Come over here and sit by me."

"Yes, sir."

Ricky sits on the plastic sofa close to me, legs sticking straight out. He's got a seven-year-old's guarded affection: You may be all right, I think you are, but— He hands me the deck, looking up, big head doddering a little. I flip through the deck, showing Vergil and the uncle. "That's very good, Ricky. Say, Vergil—"

"Yes, Doc."

"You notice anything unusual about the water fountains?"

"There's that tube coming down from the ceiling behind the drinking fountains."

"Yeah. It's clamped off with a hemostat, isn't it?"

"That's right."

"I'll tell you what let's do. You listening, Uncle?"

"Sho I'm listening. But you tell me how in the hell that boy did that. I don't think he knows himself, do you, Ricky?"

Ricky looks up at me but doesn't reply.

"Vergil, you go upstairs and take a look around. Look for the source of whatever is coming down that tube. Look for tapes, video cassettes, photos, transparencies, anything like that. Books, comics, and such."

"Okay." He starts for the iron stairs.

I look at my watch. "I think we've got about five minutes. Mrs. Cheney will bring Claude, all right, but the others will be coming too. Ricky and I are going to talk a little bit, maybe play a card game. Uncle, I think it would be a good idea for you to stand outside. When you see the others coming, give a couple of knocks, okay?"

"Don't worry about a damn thing," says the uncle, not quite sure what is going on but glad to do something.

"All right, Uncle. Do this. Keep your eye peeled on the big house. When you see anyone come out and head this way, knock twice."

"No problem," says the uncle, glad to get back to his shotgun.

"Ricky, where is Greenville, Mississippi?"

"That's"—Ricky is practicing some trick of ducking his big head rhythmically to make the sofa creak—"one hundred and thirty miles south of Memphis, one hundred miles north of Vicksburg, on the river."

"Where's Wichita, Kansas?"

He doesn't stop ducking, but I notice that he closes his eyes and frowns as if he is reading the back of his thin veined eyelids. "About a hundred and twenty-five miles southwest of Kansas City."

"Do you know your multiplication tables?"

He shrugs, goes on ducking.

"How about your sevens?"

"You mean going by the tables?"

"Yes."

"Sure." But he strikes out, doesn't know seven times three.

"What's the biggest sunfish you've caught?"

He shows me.

"What's eighty-seven times sixty-one?"

He doesn't stop ducking but closes his eyes. "Five thousand three hundred and seven."

"Do you know how to play War?"

"Sure. You want to play?"

"Sure."

We play War on the sofa. War is the dumbest of all card games, requiring no skill. High card wins. If there is a tie, it is a war. You put three cards face down and the next high card wins.

Ricky plays with pleasure, takes a child's pleasure in taking my cards, takes the greatest pleasure in double war, when there are two ties in a row and he wins nine cards. He evens up the cards against his stomach.

Vergil interrupts the second game of War. He comes down the stairs slowly. He is holding both rails as if he were unsteady. When he clears the ceiling and his face comes full into the fluorescent light, I notice that his skin is mealy. His eyes do not meet mine.

Without a word he sits on the sofa on the other side of Ricky and puts his hands carefully and symmetrically on his knees.

"Your turn," says Ricky.

I am looking at Vergil.

"Come on," says Ricky.

"Ricky, I have to talk to Vergil for a minute. Would you like to play that game over there?"

"Star Wars 4? It costs fifty cents."

"Here's three quarters. Vergil, you got any quarters?"

Vergil gives a start. "What? Oh, sure." He digs in his pockets, gives Ricky more quarters. He puts his hands back on his knees. His expression is still thoughtful, but his face is still mealy.

"Okay," says Ricky. "But leave the cards right here."

"Okay."

Presently lasers are lancing out into a three-dimensional cosmos. Satellites explode.

"Well?" I say to Vergil.

He opens his hands on his knees, inspecting them carefully, as if he were curious about the sudden change from the liver-colored backs to the creamy palms.

"Vergil?"

"They have a rocking horse up there," says Vergil, bending his fingers and inspecting the large half-moons on his nails. For some reason he is talking like his father.

"A rocking horse?"

"A rocking horse with a socket holder for a buggy whip."

"I see. What about tapes, cassettes, movies?"

"All that. There was a 3-D tape all set up. All I had to do was turn it on." He falls silent.

"And?" I ask, irritated with him.

"It was pornography."

"Pornography? What do you mean? Commercial? The stuff you can buy? Child pornography? What?"

313

"All that. I'm not sure. There wasn't time. What they had set up to roll was a local tape. It was like home movies. I mean a tape of folks here. But there were commercial cassettes. I brought three." He taps his jacket pockets.

"What did you see?"

The Star Wars 4 game stops. We wait while Ricky feeds new quarters and the laser explosions start up again.

"Vergil?"

Vergil hits on a way to tell me. Vergil is probably the most decorous man I know. He tells it as a report, as matter-of-factly as if he were reporting the soybean harvest to Lucy, number of bushels, price.

"In the home movies, that is, the 3-D videos, they had the children doing it with each other."

"You mean boys and girls having intercourse?"

"Yes." Vergil clears his throat. "And boys with boys. Going down, you know."

"And?"

"They also have the children with the grown people."

"I see. What grown people?"

"All of them. I didn't have much time. I fast-forwarded it, you know." He clears his throat, drums his fingers on his knees, looks around.

"Okay. What grown people?"

"Okay. Dr. Van Dorn, the Coach, Mr. and Mrs. Brunette."

"Mrs. Cheney?"

Vergil snaps his fingers softly, as if he had forgotten a soybean sale. "Mrs. Cheney? You're right. Mrs. Cheney." He nods in appreciation of the correction.

"What were they doing?"

"Let me see." Vergil is drumming his fingers and frowning in routine concentration. "Mr. Brunette was with Mrs. Brunette, but not in the regular way, and there were two girls with them. And—ah—Dr. Van Dorn was with a little girl—there was a lot more but I was fast-forwarding—there wasn't time—"

314

"I understand. And there's not time now."

"Don't worry. I have these cassettes. We can look at them later." He does not know how to tell me.

"I understand, but I need to know now what you saw. I'm afraid you're going to have to tell me directly. I know you have a great sense of propriety, but I have to know what you mean when you say that Mr. Brunette was with Mrs. Brunette but not in the regular way and about the two little girls. Ricky cannot hear us."

"Right," says Vergil, appearing to take thought, but falls silent.

"Goddamn it, tell me, Vergil. This is important."

"All right. Mrs. Brunette was sucking off Mr. Brunette with the two little girls placed in such a way that they could watch, don't you know."

"I see. And Dr. Van Dorn?"

"Oh. Well, he had this child and he was holding her like— Oh. I also picked up these stills." He is leaning over, fishing in his jacket pocket. "I had to grab what I could."

"Stills?"

In the space on the sofa where Ricky was sitting and out of sight of Ricky, Vergil carefully lines up half a dozen glossy 5 × 7 photographs, taking care to place them at an angle so I can see them easily and he has to slant his head. Vergil is finding it useful to be overly considerate. There is only time to catch a glimpse of the Coach and Mrs. Cheney, Mrs. Cheney on all fours, naked, the Coach behind her, also naked and kneeling, torso erect above her, and Mr. Brunette kneeling at a young man, not Claude, and Van Dorn lying on his back holding a child aloft as a father might dandle his daughter except that—when there are two knocks at the door, too sharp for knuckles, either boot heel or gun butt.

I sweep up the photos, slip them under the plastic cushion. Strange to say, what sticks in the mind about the photos is not the impropriety but the propriety: Mr. Brunette's carefully brushed hair, cut high over the ears and up the neck in 1930s style, the vulnerability, even frailty, of his pale, naked back; the young man's solemn, smartest-boy-in-the-class expression; the child's—perhaps a six-year-old girl—demure, even prissy simper directly at the camera.

"And I got these cassettes here," says Vergil helpfully.

"Never mind," I say quickly. "There isn't—" I see only the top cassette, *Little Red Riding Good*, showing Little Red Riding Hood without her hood astride the wolf in bed, who is dressed like Grandma in a bonnet and is arched up under her, in a cheerful opisthotonos, keeping her in place with his paws. "Just tell me quickly what the setup is with the additive, the source of the tube there."

He speaks rapidly, hands on his knees. He could be in his chemistry class at L.S.U. "They have metal canisters lined up. They're double-walled like a thermos. One was empty, so I could see that. One is upended right there in that corner and connected to that tube, rubber-stoppered, you know, like a chemical reagent. The reagent was stenciled on the side. Sodium 24."

"Concentration?"

"Molar."

"I see."

"They have a little card which gives the amount of additive per bottle down here. One cc. per ten gallons. What they must do is measure out the additive and add it to the Abita Springs water down here before they upend it on the fountain."

"I see."

After a while Vergil stirs uneasily.

"I wonder where they are."

"What?"

Vergil leans forward to see me better. "I said I wonder where they are."

"Don't worry. They'll be here."

"You all right, Doc?"

"Sure."

After another while Vergil gets up. "Doc, let's go get Claude and get out of here."

"Don't worry. They'll be here with Claude."

"Doc, what you got in mind?"

"We'll see. Here they are." There's a commotion outside and two more knocks.

5. IN THEY COME, A GOOD-HUMORED CREW: VAN DORN smiling and natty in his new-style long knickers and Norfolk jacket; Mr. and Mrs. Brunette in proper sober suit and dress, but by no means lugubrious; Coach in a clean scarlet warmup suit, heavy-shouldered and big-nosed—he's chipper, grips my hand warmly, is frank and forthcoming. He's the sort of rising young coach who would talk optimistically about his "program"—Mrs. Cheney, hugging her arms, giving me a special look, almost a wink: I got them here, didn't I? Claude is himself and of a piece, I see at once. Quickly he takes his place with Vergil. the two standing quiet and attentive, hands clasped behind them, as if they were attending a PTA meeting. There's a word and a nod between them. Vergil nods at me. He wants to leave. I shake my head.

Van Dorn, who has taken my hand in both of his, is shaking his head in mock outrage. "You old scoundrel beast," he says, and coming close: "I got some great news for you." He notices the uncle's shotgun propped by the door. "How do you like these guys?" he says to nobody in particular. "Probably poaching and shooting Belle Ame deer out of season. Mr. Hugh Bob, why don't you show the folks that Purdy? He's a hard man, Tom. Did you know I offered him five thousand for it?"

"I been offered ten thousand," says the uncle, who, however, is glad to show off his shotgun, walking from one person to another. They look politely.

"When you going to take me to Lake Arthur, Mr. Hugh Bob?" asks Van Dorn.

"Like I told you," says the uncle, "there ain't no ducks there. We'll have to go to Tigre au Chenier."

"You got a deal."

The uncle, pleased, blows a few feeding calls.

"How about that guy?" Van Dorn is still shaking my hand. "I don't know how you fellows got in here, but I'm delighted to see you."

"We came by the river. The gate is locked. We came to pick up Claude. His father was anxious about him."

Van Dorn lets go of my hand, grows instantly sober, paces.

"I know, I know. Would you believe we've had threats from some locals, Kluxers, fundamentalists, fundamentalist Kluxers; I mean, God knows. But we're not going to let a couple of rednecks scare us, are we, Claude?"

Claude says nothing, stands at ease, gazing at a middle distance.

"Mr. Bon," says Van Dorn to Vergil, "I understand your anxiety, but I can assure you we're delighted to have him and he's perfectly safe here."

"I think we'll be on our way," says Vergil.

"No problem," says Van Dorn. "A fine boy," he adds absently. "Make a world-class goalie."

Now we're sitting on the two bamboo lounges, with a scarred plywood table between marked out as a checkerboard and a Parcheesi game.

There follows a period of social unease, like a silence at a dinner party. But Van Dorn goes on nodding good-naturedly, as if agreeing with something. Vergil, hands on knees, shoots a glance at me. I am silent. The uncle, restless, stands at Mrs. Cheney's end of the couch, eyes rolled back.

Vergil opens his hands to me. What—?

Van Dorn claps his hands once. "Two pieces of news, Tom," he says in a crisp voice. "And I see no reason to keep either secret, since we're all friends here. As a matter of fact, it is serendipitous that you should have dropped by, since I couldn't call you—it seems the yahoos have cut my line. Number one: I'm going to be moving on. To a little piece of work at M.I.T., Tom," he says in a sober yet cordial voice. "I've paid my dues here. But the time comes— The school will be in good hands— in fact, no doubt better off without me—like my friend Oppie at Los Alamos, I seem to arouse controversy. Number two," he counts, leaning toward me across the table. "You're in, Doctor. You've got your grant from Ford: $125,000 per. Not great, not adequate compensation for your contribution, but you'll have time for your practice plus research access to Fedville—you can name it. They just want you aboard."

Ricky has left the Star Wars 4 game and is kneeling at the half-finished game of War, evening up the deck against his stomach and eyeing me impatiently.

I do not reply. As all shrinks know, it is useful sometimes to say nothing if you want to find out something. In the silence that follows, it is Vergil with his sense of social propriety who feels the awkwardness most. His expression as he looks not quite at me is worried and irritable.

"We'll finish the game later, Ricky," I tell him. "I'll tell you what let's do."

"What?"

"Uncle Hugh, my car is parked by the front gate. Here are the keys. Why don't you take these two boys out to the car and wait for us. We'll be along in a minute."

"Is that your car out there?" says Van Dorn, looking up in surprise. "For heaven's sake."

"But why—" Mrs. Cheney begins.

"But—" says the uncle, next to Mrs. Cheney.

"He's the best duck caller in the state," I tell Ricky. "He'll show you how to call ducks, won't you, Uncle Hugh?"

"Sure, but—"

"Get going."

"It's perfectly all right, boys," says Van Dorn. "No sense in them sitting around listening to us old folks discussing the state of the world," he explains to us. "Hold it, fellows. Let me give you a key to the front gate—I'm sure you understand my precautions, Tom."

"They're not going anywhere. Give it to me."

"Sure thing!" He hands me a key. He watches fondly as the boys leave with the uncle. "Good boys, both of them. I'll miss them. I'll miss them all."

After the door closes, Van Dorn claps his hands again. "Tell you what, Tom," he says, rising. "Why don't you and I walk over to my study and have a tad of bourbon by way of celebration."

"No thanks."

There is another silence. "Very well," says Van Dorn presently, fetching his pipe from a pocket of his Norfolk jacket. "What's your pleasure, Doctor? What can I do for you?"

"I'm curious about that water, Van." I nod toward the cooler. Both Van Dorn and Vergil look relieved. It is, I think, social relief. Not talking makes people uneasy.

"The water?"

"Do you drink it, Van?"

"No, I'm not in training. But it's no big deal." With a flourish, Van Dorn takes a Styrofoam cup, fills it from the cooler, drains it off. "Want one, Tom?"

I rise, go to the cooler, take a cup. Van Dorn watches me with a lively expression. I unclamp the hemostat, fill the cup not from the fountain but from the tube.

I hear Van Dorn shuffle his feet. "You're not going to drink that," says Van Dorn with genuine alarm.

"Why not?"

"Come on, Tom. Knock it off. You know what the additive is—Christ, it's no secret. And you've also seen what it does in minimal dosage—Ricky, for example. And his father does not object. But in micrograms, not molar. And as a matter of fact, I do drink a glass now and then. As a matter of fact, you could use a bit."

"Did Ellen drink any?"

"Not to my knowledge. If she did," says Van Dorn to Vergil for some reason, knocking out his pipe, "it was her choice.

After all she's one of our best volunteers and she may have seen me toss off a little cocktail." Now he turns to me. "Ricky was flunking math before he came here. Interesting, don't you think, Tom?"

"Then why not drink this?" I offer him the Styrofoam mug.

Van Dorn is embarrassed for me. He ventures a swift glance at the others. Vergil is embarrassed too, won't meet his eyes.

"Tom, that is molar sodium 24."

"I know."

Now he's stuffing his pipe from the leather pouch. "Tom, may I be frank?"

"Yes."

"Are you quite all right?"

"Yes."

"You seem—ah—not quite yourself. Mr. Bon, is our good friend here all right?" Pausing in his pipe-stuffing, he eyes Vergil shrewdly.

"He's fine," says Vergil, not looking up. He's not sure I am all right.

"Then it must be some kind of joke. Because he knows as well as I do—better!—that that's molar sodium 24. And he certainly knows what it would do to you."

"I wasn't intending to drink it," I say.

"I see." Van Dorn takes time to light his pipe. "Why don't I stop this stupid smoking." He appears to collect himself. "I see. Then who is going to drink it?"

"You."

"Me," says Van Dorn gravely, exchanging a glance with Vergil. "Anybody else?" No one replies. He shakes his head, rolls his eyes toward Vergil.

"Coach next, after you," I tell him.

Coach, who has been cracking his knuckles in his lap, looks up.

"Then Mr. and Mrs. Brunette. Then Mrs. Cheney."

"I see," says Van Dorn, nodding. "And you're not going to tell us what the scam is." He's nodding now.

"I would like for all of you to drink a cup of this."

Van Dorn becomes patient. "We hear you, Tom. And I suppose it is a joke of sorts. In any case, we are not going to drink it."

"I think it would be better if you drank it, Van."

"Oh my," says Van Dorn in a soft voice. "Well, that seems to leave us at an impasse, doesn't it, Tom?"

"I don't think so."

"He doesn't think so, Mr. Bon," says Van Dorn in the same patient voice, the voice I might use with a young paranoid schizophrenic.

But Vergil doesn't answer or look up.

I notice Coach, who is observing his knuckles. Looking at his head, which is covered by a thick growth of close-cropped blond hair, is like looking into the pile of a rug. At the proper angle one can see the scalp. His neck is as wide as his head, the sternocleidomastoid muscle so enlarged that it flares out the surprisingly fleshy lobe of his ear.

Mr. Brunette crosses his legs, not with ankle over knee but knee over knee, crossing leg dangling almost to the floor. His suit is not at all a preacher's suit, I notice, but the new Italian drape style, of charcoal silk, loose in the hips, tight in the cuffs. But he wears the sort of short thin socks with clocks fashionable years ago and loafers with leather tassels.

"Okay, gang!" says Van Dorn briskly, and would have clapped his hands, I think, if he wasn't holding his pipe. "I don't know about y'all but I got a school to run. If there's nothing else, Doctor?"—with a slight formal bow to me, eyes fond but distant.

The others are on their feet instantly, following Van Dorn to the door.

"Only these." I spread the photos on the plywood table between the sofas.

Van Dorn and the others are looking down at the glossies on their way out, heads politely aslant to see them better, as one might look at the photos of a guest fresh from a trip to Disney World.

I too have the first good look at them.

There are six photographs.

There are details which I missed in my earlier, cursory glance.

In the photograph of Mrs. Cheney on all fours, Coach at her from the rear, Mrs. Cheney's head is partially hidden between the bare legs of a young person who is supine and whose head and chest are not in the picture. It is not clear whether the young person is a boy or a girl.

In the photograph of Mr. Brunette kneeling at a youth, the youth has both hands on Mr. Brunette's carefully barbered head, as if he were steering it, and is gazing down at him with an expression which is both agreeable and incurious. Mr. Brunette's bare shoulders are surprisingly frail, the skin untanned.

In the photograph of Van Dorn dandling the child, the child is shown to have been penetrated but only by Van Dorn's glans and certainly not painfully, because the child, legs kicked up, is looking toward the camera with a demure, even prissy, expression. Her legs are kicking up in pleasure.

The fourth photograph depicts a complex scene: Coach penetrating, anally and evidently completely, a muscular youth, not Claude, upon whom Mrs. Brunette, supine, is also performing fellatio.

The fifth photograph depicts Van Dorn entering an older girl, perhaps eleven or twelve, again by holding her above him, again by no means completely. Again the girl is gazing at the camera, almost dutifully, like a cheerleader in a yearbook photo, as if to signify that all is well.

The sixth photograph, perhaps the oddest, depicts Van Dorn performing, it appears, cunnilingus upon Mrs. Brunette, he seated in a chair, she astraddle and borne high upon his folded arms, but not entirely unclothed, while on the floor behind them, sitting in a small semicircle, clothed, ankles crossed, arms around knees, faces blank—in the archaic pose of old group photographs—are half a dozen junior-high students. Two or three, instead of paying attention to the tableau, are mugging a bit for the camera, as if they were bored, yet withal polite.

6. FOR SOME MOMENTS THE BELLE AME STAFF GAZE DOWN with the same polite interest.

Then someone—it is not clear who—says in a muted voice: "Uh oh."

Someone else utters a low whistle.

The uncle is back. He whispers something to me about Claude and Ricky being in the car, playing cards, and all right.

"Jesus," says the uncle, who has come all the way around the table, the better to see the photographs of Mrs. Cheney. "I mean what—!" he says, opening both hands, beseeching first me, then the world around.

"What in the *world!*" exclaims Mrs. Cheney in conventional outrage, touching her tight bun at her neck with one hand. "Who—what is *that*? Ex-*cuse* me!"

"That's not you, Mrs. Cheney?" I ask her.

"Dr. More! You ought to be ashamed!" Her outrage, by no means excessive, seems conventional, almost perfunctory. Then she turns away from me and speaks, for some reason, to Vergil. "I for one do not appreciate being exposed to this material, do you?"

"Why no," says Vergil politely. He can't quite bring himself to look directly at the pictures on the table.

Van Dorn is still eyeing the photographs, face aslant one way, then the other, without expression.

Coach, who has been still until now, has put his hands on his hips and is moving lightly from the ball of one foot to the other. "This is a setup, chief," he says softly to Van Dorn; then, when Van Dorn does not reply, says loudly to one and all, "I can tell you one damn thing," he says to no one in particular. "I know a setup when I see it. And I for one am not about to stand for it. No way." He leans over, I think, to pick up one or more photographs, then apparently changing his mind resumes his boxer's stance. "This is rigged. I don't know who is doing it or why, but I can tell you one damn thing, I'm not buying in. No way!"

"Let me just say this," says Mr. Brunette calmly, shaking his head. His hands are in his pockets and he speaks with the assurance of one long used to handling disputes, perhaps a school principal or a minister. Though he is dressed like a TV evangelist and has a north Louisiana haircut, his voice is not countrified. Rather, he sounds like the moderator of an encounter group, reasonable, disinterested, but not uncaring. "I don't know who is responsible for this foolishness—though I have my suspicions—" Does he look in Van Dorn's direction? "It would not be the first time that photographs have been cooked for purposes of blackmail. Everyone here knows that photographs are as spliceable as tapes—and therefore signify nothing. In fact, this whole business could be a computer graphic. No, that's not what interests me. What intrigues me is the motive, the mindset behind this. Frankly I have no idea what or who it is. Is it a joke? Or something more sinister? And who is behind it? One of us? Dr. More? I've no idea. But let me say this—and I think I speak for my wife too, don't I, Henrietta?"

Surprised, Henrietta looks up quickly, nods. Her face is younger, more puddingish, less like a dragon lady than I thought.

"Just let me say this," says Mr. Brunette, taking off his glasses and rubbing his nose bridge wearily with thumb and forefinger. "As the fellow says, Hear this. I am notifying my attorney in short order to do two things: one, to employ a forensic expert who can testify as to the fakery of these phony photos and tapes— and two, to bring charges of libel against anyone who undertakes to use them for malicious purposes. That includes you, Dr. More. Frankly, though, I think it is somebody's idea of a joke— a very bad joke and a very sick somebody." Wearily he wipes his closed eyes. He puts his hands deep into the loose pockets of his drape trousers, clasps hands to knees, stands up briskly as if to leave.

"Did you say tapes, Mr. Brunette?" I ask.

325

Eyes still closed, he waves me off. "Tapes, photos, whatever."

"No one mentioned tapes," I tell Mr. Brunette.

Vergil still can't bring himself to look at the pictures or anybody. He sits perfectly symmetrically, hands planted on knees, eyes focused on a point above the photos, below the people.

The uncle, still on the prowl, stops behind my chair, gives me a nudge on the shoulder. "She's still a damn fine-looking woman," he actually whispers.

"Cut it out," I tell him. "Sit down. No, stand by the door."

"No problem," says the uncle.

Coach, who can't decide whether to go or stay, settles for a game of Star Wars 4.

Van Dorn sits comfortably on the sofa opposite me. He knocks out his pipe on the brick floor, settles back, sighs.

He makes a rueful face at Coach and the exploding satellites. "I sometimes think we belong to a different age, Tom."

"Yes?"

"Did I ever tell you what I think of your good wife?"

"You spoke of her bridge-playing ability."

"I know. But I didn't mention the fact that she is a great lady."

"Thank you, Van."

The plantation bell rings. Van Dorn puts his hands on his knees, makes as if to push himself up, yawns. "Well, I'll be on my way."

"Not quite yet, Van."

He pushes himself up. "What do you mean, Tom?" says Van, smiling.

"I mean you're not leaving."

"Ah me." Van Dorn is shaking his head. "I'll be frank with you, Tom. I don't know whether you're ill and, if so, what ails you. At this point I don't much care. I bid you good day." He starts for the door.

"I'm afraid not, Van."

"Move, old man," says Van Dorn to the uncle.

"No, Van," I say.

Van Dorn turns back to me. Now he's standing over me. "Do I have to spell it out for you?" he asks, shaking his head in wonderment.

"Sure. Spell it out for me." For some reason my nose has begun to run. My eyes water. I take out a handkerchief.

"I think you've got some sort of systemic reaction, Tom."

"You're probably right."

"You've been ill before."

"I know."

"You've harbored delusions before."

"I know."

"You want to know one reason I think you're ill?"

"Yes."

"You don't seem to realize your position. Isn't that what you shrinks call the breakdown on the Reality Principle?"

"Some of them might. What is my position?"

"Your position, Tom—which, as you know, is none of my doing—is that you either join the team—and as you yourself have admitted, you approve their goals, you just don't have any more use for some of those NIH assholes like Comeaux, nor do I— or you go back to Alabama. You're in violation of your parole. You know that, Tom. Come on! You don't want that! I don't want that. All I have to do is pick up that phone."

"I thought you said the phones didn't work."

"They work now. As for those phony photos—"

"Yes?" I am blowing my nose and wiping my eyes with a soggy handkerchief.

"There are two theoretical possibilities— Let me give you some tissues, Tom."

"Thanks. That's better. What are the two possibilities?" During the great crises of my life, I am thinking, I develop hay fever. There is a lack of style here—like John Wayne coming down with the sneezes during the great shootout in *Stagecoach*. Oh well.

"Consider, Tom," says Van Dorn gently, even sorrowfully. "It's a simple either/or. Either the photos are phony—which in fact they are—or they are not. Isn't that so?"

"Yes."

"If they are phony, which I'm sure a lab can demonstrate, then forget it. Right?"

"Right."

"If they are genuine, ditto."

"Ditto?"

"Sure, Tom. Once we get past the mental roadblocks of human relationships—namely, two thousand years of repressed sexuality—we see that what counts in the end is affection instead of cruelty, love instead of hate, right?"

"Yes." He gives me another tissue.

"Look at the faces of those children—God knows where they come from—do you see any sign of pain and suffering, cruelty or abuse?"

"No."

"Do you admit the possibility that those putative children—whether they're real or cooked up—might be starved for human affection?"

"Yes."

"Case closed," says Van Dorn, sweeping up the photographs like a successful salesman. "Tom, we're talking about caring."

"I'll just take those, Van," I say, taking them.

"Okay, gang," says Van Dorn, putting his pipe in his mouth and clapping his hands. "Let's go." He makes a sign to Coach, who has stopped playing Star Wars 4.

I nod to Vergil. Vergil understands, joins the uncle by the door.

Coach and Van Dorn face Vergil and the uncle.

"What's this?" asks Van Dorn wearily, not turning around.

"Before you leave, I suggest that all of you drink a glass of the additive," I say, blowing my nose. "Starting with Coach. You first, Coach."

Coach winks at Van Dorn, steps up to the cooler.

"I don't mind if I do."

"Not from the cooler, coach. From the tube."

"Shit, that's molar."

"That's right."

Coach looks to Van Dorn. "I can take them both." Smiling, he starts for the uncle. His big hands are fists.

The uncle looks to me. I make a sign, touch my ear. The uncle understands, nods.

"If he tries it, shoot him," I tell the uncle.

Coach looks quickly back at me, looks at the Purdy propped against the door behind the uncle, shrugs, and starts for the uncle. Meanwhile, the uncle, who has got the Woodsman from his inside coat pocket, shoots him.

A crack not loud but sharp as a buggy whip lashes the four walls of the room.

"You meant ear, didn't you?" says the uncle, putting the Woodsman away.

I am watching Coach closely. Part of his right ear, the fleshy lobe flared out by the sternocleidomastoid muscle, disappears. There is an appreciable time, perhaps a quarter second, before the blood spurts.

Coach stops suddenly as if a thought had occurred to him. He holds up an admonishing finger.

"Oh, my God!" screams Coach, clapping one hand to his head, stretching out the other to Van Dorn. "I'm shot! Jesus, he's shot me in the head—didn't he?"—reaching out to Van Dorn not so much for help as for confirmation. "Didn't he? Didn't he?"

Van Dorn stands transfixed, mouth open.

"My God, he's been shot!"

I look at Coach. There is an astonishing amount of blood coming between his fingers.

Coach turns to me. "Help me! For God's sake, Doc, help me!"

"Sure, Coach. Don't worry. Come over and sit right here by me. You'll be fine."

"You swear?"

"I swear," I say. "Mrs. Cheney."

"Yes, Doctor." Mrs. Cheney, who has sat down twice and risen twice, rises quickly.

"Please bring us two towels from the bathroom. Don't worry, Coach. We're going to fix you up with a pressure bandage."

"You swear?"

"I swear."

"My God, my brain is damaged. He could have killed me."

"I know."

He turns to show me. The blood running through his fingers and down his arm drips on me. My nose is also dripping. Every time I fool with surgery, my nose runs. This doesn't work in surgery. I think I might have chosen psychiatry for this reason.

I knot one towel, tie the other towel around his head, twist it as hard as I can. "Mrs. Cheney, you hold it here. Coach, you press against the knot as hard as you can."

"I will!"

"Don't worry, Dr. More!" cries Mrs. Cheney, taking hold of the towel.

"Meanwhile, drink this, Coach," I tell him, holding the towel against his head. "Vergil, fix him a glass of additive."

"Molar strength?" asks Vergil, still looking into his eyebrows.

"Right. Mrs. Cheney, twist the towel as hard as you can and he'll be fine. The bleeding has about stopped."

"I will!" cries Mrs. Cheney, twisting.

"Drink this, Coach." I hand him the glass with my free hand.

"You're sure?" asks the Coach, pressing the knot while Mrs. Cheney twists the towel. She is also pulling. Now his head is against her breast.

"I'm sure."

"I'll drink it if you say so."

"I say so. Vergil?"

"Yes, Doc?"

"Give a glass to Mr. Brunette."

"No problem." He fills a glass and sets it on the table in front of Mr. Brunette.

Mr. Brunette looks at it. "Let me just say this," he says, pushing up the bridge of his Harold Lloyd specs.

"All right."

330

"First, you're right about these people," nodding toward Van Dorn. "Accordingly, let me make sure the photos are safe. I'll just put them back in the file where they belong and where the proper authorities can find them." He scoops up the photos in a businesslike way and starts for the staircase.

"I think you'd better bring those back, Mr. Brunette. How're you doing, Coach?"

"I'm going to be fine, Doctor, since you said I would."

"Keep twisting, Mrs. Cheney."

"I am, Doctor!"

"There's a balcony up there and an outside staircase," says Vergil, taking notice for the first time.

"I really think you'd better come down, Mr. Brunette."

But he's halfway up and gaining speed. He's as nimble and youthful in his specs as Harold Lloyd and—do I imagine it?— grinning a wolfish little grin.

The uncle looks at me. I shrug and nod, but do not touch myself.

Before I can think what has happened, the uncle has picked up the shotgun and shot him. I find that I am saying it to myself: The uncle has shot Mr. Brunette with a 12-gauge shotgun held at the hip.

The room roars and whitens, percussion seeming to pass beyond the bounds of noise into white, the white-out silent and deafening until it comes back not as a loud noise but like thunder racketing around and dying away after a thunderclap.

My ears are ringing. Mrs. Brunette opens her mouth. I think I hear her say, no doubt shout, to everyone as if calling them to witness, "He's killed my husband!"

Everyone is gazing at Mr. Brunette. The ringing seems to be in the room itself. Mr. Brunette, blown against the far rail, comes spinning down the staircase, as swiftly and silently as a message in a tube, hands still on the rails, specs knocked awry but not off.

"Uncle Hugh," I say, but cannot hear my voice. Uncle Hugh has shot Mr. Brunette with a 12-gauge shotgun from the hip.

The room is filled with a familiar cordite Super-X smell I haven't smelled for years.

Mrs. Brunette covers her ears and says something again. Mrs. Cheney does not let go of the towel but pulls Coach's head close to hers, twisting the towel harder than ever.

"Don't worry about a thing," says the uncle beside me, and slaps at the seat of his pants. "I brushed him off right here is all. With number eight." He turns to show me, again slapping at his pants.

Mr. Brunette is struggling to get up. He gets up. It is true. The seat of Mr. Brunette's Italian drape suit, which is slack around the hips, has been shot out. There is no blood.

"But I mean, Uncle Hugh, even so, number-eight birdshot."

"Wasn't birdshot!" says the uncle triumphantly, lunging past me back to his post at the door, right shoulder leading. "Not even number ten. What that was what they call a granular load, little bitty specks of rubber like pepper, like if you wanted to run off some old hound dogs without hurting them. You remember, I told you I don't like to hurt a good dog."

"Yes."

"Here, I'll show you the shell."

"That's all right."

"Please help us, Doctor," says Mrs. Brunette, who has got Mr. Brunette to the couch, where he is kneeling, head in her lap.

"Certainly," I say. "Now let him lie across you, like that."

I examine him. The seat of his charcoal silk trousers has been shot away along with the bottom inch or so of his coattail. The exposed sky-blue jockey shorts of a tight-fitting stretch nylon are by and large intact, save for a dozen or so dark striae, as if they had been heavily scored by a Marks-A-Lot. Several of the scorings have ripped nylon and skin, and there is some oozing of blood.

Mr. Brunette adjusts his glasses, feels behind him, looks at his fingers. "My God," he says evenly, but not badly frightened.

"Don't worry. We'll fix you up." I turn to Vergil, who is

picking up the photographs. "Would you see if you can find a washcloth and dampen it with soap and water. Uncle Hugh, lend me your knife."

They do. I cut off the back of Mr. Brunette's jockey shorts, using the uncle's Bowie knife, which is honed down to a sliver of steel, clean him up, and instruct Mrs. Brunette to apply pressure to the two lacerations. Mr. Brunette is lying across her lap. She does so but in a curious manner, holding out one hand, face turned away, as if she were controlling a fractious child.

Van Dorn, I notice, is sitting back on the sofa, drumming his fingers on the cane armrest and by turns nodding and shaking his head. "Oh boy," he murmurs to no one in particular.

"Vergil, give everybody a glass of additive. There's a stack right there." The "glasses" are Styrofoam, Big Mac's jumbo size.

"Molar?" asks Vergil.

"Molar."

"All right."

"Very good. Drink up, everybody."

"Oh boy," says Van Dorn, shaking his head and murmuring something.

"What was that, Van?"

"I was just saying that I abhor violence of any kind."

"Right."

"The whole point of conflict resolution is to accomplish one's objective without violence. Conflict resolution by means of violence is a contradiction in terms."

"That's true. Drink up, folks."

Van Dorn is nodding over his drink. "Tom," he says in his old, fine-eyed, musing way, "can you assure us that the pharmacological effect of these heavy ions is reversible."

"I have every reason to believe it is."

A final nod, as if the old scientific camaraderie had been reestablished between us.

"The bottom-line question, Tom."

"Yes?"

"Knowing your respect as a physician for the Hippocratic

oath, I put you on the spot and ask you if any harmful pharmacological effect can occur?''

"None that you would not want."

"Done!" he says in his old "Buck" Van Dorn style, and drains the glass as if he were chugalugging beer back in the fraternity house.

Mrs. Brunette drinks and helps Mr. Brunette to drink, holding his glass.

Mrs. Cheney, still twisting the towel on Coach's head, leans toward me, her pleasant face gone solemn.

"Mrs. Cheney, you can let go now," I tell her. "He won't bleed." She accepts the glass from Vergil. Coach keeps his head on her breast.

"Dr. More, you and I have been friends for many a year, haven't we?''

"Yes, we have, Mrs. Cheney."

"You're a fine doctor and a fine man."

"Thank you, Mrs. Cheney."

"I knew your first wife and your second wife, and both of them were just as nice as they could be. Lovely people. Many's the night when you trusted me with your children of both ladies and yourself.''

"That's true."

"And you know I trust you."

"I'm glad you do, Mrs. Cheney."

"All in the world you have to do is tell me that drinking this medicine or vitamin-plus or whatever it is is the thing to do and I'll do it.''

"It's the thing to do, Mrs. Cheney."

"That's good enough for me. Hold the towel, Coach."

"You can take the towel off, Coach," I assure him.

Mrs. Cheney raises the glass and, with the other hand pressed against her chest in a girlish gesture, drinks.

Van Dorn puts a finger on my knee. "You want to know something, Tom?''

"Sure."

"I feel better already."

"Good."

"Listen," he says tapping my knee. "Do you mind if I add a footnote to history?"

"No."

"It has to do with the Battle of Pea Ridge and our kinsman, General Earl Van Dorn. I can prove this, Tom. I have the letters of Price and Curtis. He had pulled off the most brilliant flanking movement of the war—except possibly Chancellorsville. It could have changed the war, Tom. If only it hadn't been for those goddamn crazy Indians. Tom, I can prove it. Do you know what he had in mind to take and would have taken?"

"No."

"St. Louis!"

"St. Louis?"

"I'm telling you. Old Buck would have taken St. Louis. Except for those fucking Indians. St. Louis, Tom."

"Let me see. Just where was St. Louis in relation to Pea Ridge?"

"Hell, man, not as far as you think. Let me see." He closes his eyes. "Three hundred miles northeast—and nothing between him and it."

"What did the Indians do, Van?"

"Indians? Crazy. Whoops. Dance."

"I see. Uncle Hugh."

"Yeah, son."

I get the uncle in a little pantry where the phone is.

"Uncle Hugh, I think we better call the sheriff."

"You damn right. I've seen some white trash but I ain't never seen nothing like this. I mean, we all do some messing around"—he gives me a wink and a poke—"but we talking about children. I brought my gelding knife." He holds out the skirt of his hunting jacket to show me his Bowie knife.

"We won't need that now. The thing is, Uncle Hugh Bob, this charge has been made before and dropped and Sheriff Sharp is not going to be impressed by us registering the same complaint."

"Don't you worry about it. He'll come out. I know him. I'll call him."

"I know you know him. I know him too. He will come out, but he'll take his time. It could be a couple of hours. Or tomorrow. He talks about lack of evidence. We want him out here when there is evidence—I mean unmistakable evidence."

"When will that be, son?" The uncle's dark hatchet face juts close.

"It's beginning now. I'd want him and his men out here in no more than half an hour. It might get out of hand after that."

"Don't worry about it. Hand me the phone."

"How are you going to get Sheriff Sharp out here?"

"Who, Cooter? Don't worry about it. I've known that old bastard all his life. He first got rich on the Longs. Now it's the Eyetalians running cocaine from the gambling boats in the river. Shit, don't tell me. We still hunt a lot. Actually he's not a bad old boy."

"How soon can you get him out here?"

"How about twenty minutes?"

"That will be fine."

The uncle picks up the phone, cocks an eye at me. "What's going to happen between now and then? Maybe you better go over to the door by my gun."

"Don't worry. Make your call. Nothing is going to happen."

7. IN FACT NOTHING HAPPENS FOR SEVERAL MINUTES.
Everyone is sitting peaceably. I observe nothing untoward—except. Except that the persons present do not exhibit the usual presence of people waiting—the studied inwardness of patients in a doctor's waiting room, the boredom, the page-flipping anxiety, the frowning sense of time building up—how much longer?—the monitoring of eyes—I-choose-not-to-look-

at-you-and-get-into-all-that-business-of-looking—or the talkiness. None of that. Everyone simply sits, or rather lounges, out of time, as relaxed as lions on the Serengeti Plain.

Mrs. Cheney is still holding Coach's head against her breast and twisting the towel.

"Let's take a look, Mrs. Cheney. The bleeding should have stopped."

The bleeding has stopped.

"You did a good job, Mrs. Cheney."

"Oh, thanks, Dr. More!" says Mrs. Cheney, holding Coach close, patting him.

Coach's eyes follow me trustfully.

Mr. Brunette has got his pants up and is sitting at his ease, only slightly off center, next to Mrs. Brunette, giving no sign of his recent injury. Having got him dressed, zipped up, belted, Mrs. Brunette is busy straightening his clothes, smoothing his coat lapels, adjusting his tie. But now she is busy at his hair, not smoothing it but ruffling it against the grain and inspecting him, peering close, plucking at his scalp. I realize she is grooming him.

The uncle too is at his ease, having taken his place between door and shotgun, not out of time like the others, but passing time like a good hunter waiting, hunkered down, blowing a few soft feeding calls through his fingers.

Only Vergil is uneasy, shooting glances at me. I know that what worries him is not what the others have done but whether I know what I am doing. He takes to pacing. I motion him over.

"Vergil, why don't you go check on Claude and Ricky. But come right back. I might need you."

"Good idea!" he exclaims, as pleased to find me sensible as he is to leave.

To share his new confidence, he leans closer, almost whispering, yet not really whispering. Somehow he knows that overhearing is not a problem now. "Am I correct in assuming that you expect them to regress to a primitive primate sort of behavior as a result of the sodium 24?"

"Not primate. Pongid. Primate includes humans."

"Right. I had that in Psych 101. Did you know I was a psych minor?"

"No."

"So the reason you're doing this is not punishment or revenge but rather because, though they have not themselves received the sodium 24 earlier and are therefore entirely responsible for these abuses"—he pats the pocket holding the photos—"the only way you could be sure of convincing the sheriff of their guilt is to dose them up and regress them to pongid behavior, for which they are not responsible but which will impress the sheriff?"

"You got it, Vergil," I say gratefully. "The only thing is, we don't know if it will work. Otherwise the sheriff is not going to be impressed by this peaceable scene. The photos are probably inadmissible."

"That's ironical, isn't it?" muses Vergil, glancing around at our little group.

"Yes, it is, Vergil. But we don't have much time. Do you think you could check on Claude and be back here in five minutes?"

"No problem," says Vergil, and he's gone.

"How's Coach doing?" I ask Mrs. Cheney, who is sitting between me and Coach. Though she has removed the towel from Coach's head, she has her arm around his neck, her hand against his ear, pulling him close.

"Fine, darling!" says Mrs. Cheney, pressing her knee against mine. "You boys can both come by me!" Mrs. Cheney has suddenly begun to talk in a New Orleans ninth-ward accent.

I lean out to take a look at Coach. He has stopped bleeding and seems in a good humor, smiling and pooching his lips in and out.

"How are you, Coach?"

He too leans out in an accommodating manner and seems on the point of replying, but instead takes an interest in the leather buttons on the front of Mrs. Cheney's dress and begins plucking at them.

"Mrs. Brunette, how is Mr. Brunette?"

338

Mrs. Brunette says something not quite audible but pleasant and affirming. She is busy brushing Mr. Brunette's hair against the grain and examining his scalp. Mr. Brunette, head bowed in Mrs. Brunette's lap, is going through Mrs. Brunette's purse, a satchel-size shoulder bag, which he has opened. He removes articles and lines them up on the game table.

A glance toward Van Dorn, who is nodding approvingly.

"Van, what were the casualties at Sharpsburg?" I ask him.

"Federals 14,756; Confederates 13,609," he says instantly and without surprise.

There are two things to observe here. One: though we have both read the same book, Foote's *The Civil War*, he can recall the numbers like a printout and I cannot; two: he does so without minding or even noticing the shifting context.

"What is the square root of 7,471?" I am curious to know how far he'll go into decimals.

"Snickers," says Van Dorn.

"Snickers?"

"Snickers." He makes the motion of peeling and eating something.

"He's talking about a Snickers bar," says the uncle companionably from the door. "He evermore loves Snickers. You can get me one too."

I get them both a Snickers bar from the vending machine in the pantry. "Eight six point four nine," says Van Dorn, and begins peeling his from the top.

Mr. Brunette has removed, among other things, a good-size hand mirror from Mrs. Brunette's shoulder bag.

I hold it up to him. He sees himself, looks behind the mirror, reaches behind it, grabs air.

Van Dorn makes a noise in his throat. He has noticed something that makes him forget the Snickers.

Mrs. Cheney has risen from the sofa and is presenting to Coach, that is, has backed up to him between his knees. Coach, who is showing signs of excitement, pooching his lips in and out faster than ever and uttering a sound something like *hoo hoo hoo*, takes hold of Mrs. Cheney. But he seems not to know what

339

else to do. He begins smacking his lips loudly. Mrs. Cheney is on all fours.

"Now you just hold it, boy," says the uncle, rising, both outraged and confused. "That's Miz Cheney you messing with. A fine lady. You cut that out, boy. You want me to shoot your other ear off?"

But Coach is not messing with Mrs. Cheney but only smacking his lips.

Before anyone knows what has happened, before the uncle can even begin to reach for his shotgun, Van Dorn has in a single punctuated movement leaped onto the game table, evidently bitten Coach's hand—for Coach cries out and puts his fingers in his mouth—and in another bound landed on the bottom step of the spiral staircase. Van Dorn mounts swiftly, using the handrails mostly, swinging up with powerful arm movements. There on the top step he hunkers down, one elbow crooked over his head.

I wave the uncle off—he has his shotgun by now. "Hold it!" What he doesn't realize is that Van Dorn is only assuming his patriarchal role, establishing his dominance by cowing the young "bachelors," who do in fact respond appropriately: Coach flinging both arms over his head, palms turned submissively out. Mr. Brunette is smacking his lips and "clapping," that is, not clapping palms to make a noise, but clapping his fingers noiselessly. Both movements are signs of submission.

I glance at my watch. Where in hell is Vergil? Things could get out of hand. I know all too well that the uncle and I are no match for the new pongid arm strength of Van Dorn, and we can't shoot him.

"That's the damnedest thing I ever saw," says the uncle, not so much to me as to Mrs. Cheney, who, now sitting demurely, is casting an admiring eye in his direction. "Oh, Jesus, here he comes again," he says, eyes rolled back, and picks up the shotgun.

"Hold it, Uncle Hugh Bob!" Van Dorn has swung lightly over the rail. I pitch him the rest of his Snickers bar. He catches

340

it without seeming to try, resumes his perch. "Throw him yours, Uncle Hugh Bob."

"What?"

"Throw him your Snickers."

"Shit, he's got his own Snickers."

"Throw him your Snickers."

"Oh, all right." He does so.

Where is—

The uncle has replaced his shotgun and is opening the door.

"Where do you think—" I begin.

In walks Vergil and the sheriff, followed by two young deputies.

I experience both relief and misgivings.

The scene which confronts the sheriff is as peaceful as a tableau.

Coach is sitting aslant, one arm looped over his head, but no more hangdog than any coach who has lost a game. He is not even pooching his lips.

Mrs. Cheney, next to him, is plucking at one of her own buttons, eyes modestly cast down in the same sweet-faced, madonna-haired expression she is known for.

Mrs. Brunette is busy putting articles back in her purse, Mr. Brunette helping her with one hand, the other fiddling with her hive hairdo—just as any faculty husband-and-wife team might behave at any faculty meeting.

Van Dorn, seated on the top step, surveys his staff with a demeanor both equable and magisterial, a good-natured and informal headmaster munching on a Snickers bar, but headmaster nevertheless.

Sheriff Vernon "Cooter" Sharp is a genial, high-stomached, vigorous man who affects Western garb, Stetson, Lizard-print-and-cowhide boots, bolo tie with a green stone, cinch-size belt and silver conch buckle, and a holstered revolver on a low-slung belt like Matt Dillon. He is noted for his posse of handsome quarter-horses from his own ranch, which parade every year in a good cause with the Shriners, clowns, and hijinks rearing cars to raise money for the Shriners' hospital. He and his posse are famous statewide and are invited to many events, including Mardi Gras parades.

Now he's taken off his hat again to wipe his forehead with his sleeve, but left on his amber aviation glasses, and is looking around, surveying the peaceful scene with the same queer, for him, expression of gravity and solemnity and here-we-go-again rue. He's shaking his head, mainly at me.

"What we got here, Doc?" he asks, not offering to shake hands.

The two young deputies are standing at ease, hands clasped behind them, pudding-faced and bored.

"Sheriff Sharp, I want you to arrest Dr. Van Dorn, Mr. and Mrs. Brunette, Coach Matthews, and Mrs. Cheney for the molestation and sexual abuse of children."

"Oh me." The sheriff sighs and, nodding mournfully, catches sight of Mrs. Cheney. "Doc, we been that route."

"Do it, anyway."

"Hi, Lurine," he says to Mrs. Cheney, giving a little wave, hand at pistol level. "How you doing?"

"Hi, Cooter," says Mrs. Cheney, fingering buttons, eyes still downcast.

"We have evidence, Sheriff. Vergil, did you—"

"I showed him the pictures, Doc, but he wouldn't hardly look at them because he says they are not admissible." Vergil is taking the photographs out to show them again.

Sheriff Sharp waves him off. "They neither here or there. Y'all know we've had a regular epidemic of pictures like that all over the pa-ish. It's terrible. I hate to think of little children seeing stuff like that. But I'm here to tell you we're cracking down. On drugs too. And minority crime."

"You don't understand, Sheriff," I say patiently. "That's not the problem here. What we're talking about here are criminal molestation and photographic evidence."

"The thing is, Doc," he says, turning to face me but not looking at me, looking anywhere but at me—he can't stand the sight of me!—"we got a problem here." I'm the problem.

"What's the problem?"

"Doc, as I told you, we been this route before," he says wearily, pushing up his amber glasses and rubbing his eyes. "The same charges have been brought before against those same folks before—" He nods toward the Brunettes, a loving couple. "They were dismissed then for lack of evidence and they'll be dismissed again—those pictures ain't worth a dime, and now you're also wanting to charge Dr. Van Dorn here and Coach Matthews, who won state last year in triple-A—and even this little lady"—he stretches out a hand toward Mrs. Cheney—"who has done more to he'p people than anybody you can name, people you know, children, your children, Doc, old folks, Miss Lucy's mamma—I don't know, Doc." He is shaking his head in genuine sorrow. "To tell you the truth, Doc, you the only one we got a warrant for. We got a pick-up order on you from Dr. Comeaux yesterday. Now I wasn't going to bother you, Doc, since I been knowing you and your family for a long time. But it looks like you hell-bent on—"

"Now you listen here, Cooter," says the uncle, who, I see with some dismay, is hopping from one foot to the other in a peculiar fashion, coat flapping open, "I was here so don't tell me what I saw. These folks all crazy as hell. You know what that little lady and the Coach were—"

"You just hold it, Hugh Bob," says the sheriff, holding out a hand but not bothering to look at the uncle. "You just watch your mouth when you talking about Lurine—Mrs. Cheney. Ever'body knows you were pestering her when she was staying out at Pantherburn with Miss Lucy's mamma, your sister, before she died."

The pudding-faced, flat-topped deputy leans over to say something to the sheriff.

"Weapon?" says the sheriff. "What you talking about, weapon? You got a weapon, Hugh Bob?"

The uncle opens his mouth, but before he can say anything, the deputy simply lifts the uncle's coattails and extracts the Colt Woodsman from his jacket pocket.

The sheriff, again overcome with sorrow, accepts the gun, sniffs the muzzle.

"This weapon has just been fired, Hugh Bob."

"It sho has."

"Who at?"

"Him." The uncle nods at Coach, who appears lost in thought, studying his palms, which are open on his knees. The sheriff walks around him, looking him over. The other side of his head is not bleeding but is encrusted with a maroon clot.

"Coach?" he says, peering down at him. He stands up, hands on hips. "What in the hell did you do to him, Hugh Bob, shoot him in the head?"

"Just his ear," says the uncle, not displeased.

"What in the hell—check that shotgun, Huval," he says to the younger, balder deputy.

Huval checks the Purdy. "Two shells, one recently fired."

"Where else did you shoot him?" asks the sheriff, moving the game table back and stepping past Mrs. Cheney to get a good look at Coach.

"Hi, Cooter," says Mrs. Cheney, giving him a pat as he passes.

"Did that man shoot you?" he asks Coach.

Coach pooches his lips in and out and says, "Hoo hoo hoo."

"This sucker has brain damage," muses the sheriff. "Thanks to you, Hugh."

Across the table, Mr. Brunette begins to stamp with one foot.

"What in the hell did you do to him, Hugh Bob?"

"I had to shoot him," says the uncle, beginning to hop again. "He was coming at me and he would have gotten away."

"What—in—the—hell—" begins the sheriff, turning first to me, then, thinking better of it, beseeches Van Dorn, who is still sitting, rocking to and fro, on the top step.

"Sheriff Sharp," I say, rising, "I can explain everything. But right now I really think it would be a good idea if you would arrest all these people, examine the evidence, both these photographs and Dr. Lipscomb's medical evidence of abuse before any more children are harmed, in which case I hold you responsible. In fact, I insist on it."

The sheriff slowly rounds on me, stepping clear of the table—

Mrs. Cheney gives him another pat as he passes—plants feet apart, hand on hips. "You demand of me." He cups an ear. "Doctor, did I hear you say that you *demand* of me?"

"I didn't say demand." Now he does look straight at me, all the Western cantering-posse geniality suddenly sloughed—we're back to his old, flat-eyed, bulged-vein sheriff's anger. He hates my guts! We're back in the sixties, where we've always been, he the true Southerner, I the fake Southern liberal—the worst kind. He could be right.

"Let me just remind you, Doctor, of two little facts, one of which you may be aware of, the other you are evidently not."

"All right." Nothing is more menacing than an old-style, soft-voiced Southern sheriff.

"You're the felon here, Doctor, not them, you heah me? You're the one I arrested and convicted two years ago of selling drugs. You the one went to jail, not them. Two." He holds two not fat but big and long fingers in my face. "I have a telex in my office as of last night from the ATFA people to pick you up on the parole violation. You heah me, Doctor?" The cold rage of lawmen is never not present and never less than astounding. I've never seen even enraged paranoiacs get as angry as policemen. Slowly he folds his fingers, making a fist with a Masonic ring as big as a brass knuckle. He could easily hit me. Slowly the fist descends until his thumb hooks on to his Texas belt. "So I tell you what let's me and you do, Doctor. Let's you and me go on out to my car and go up the road a piece to Angola. Then we'll see about your old friend Hugh Bob here and take care these other good people—if I can find out what you done to them."

"Sheriff, I ask you for the last time and in your own best interests to arrest these people and hold them at least for investigation. Otherwise I fear I know what is going to happen. As for the warrant to pick me up, I've already been to Angola and am presently out on a pass. If you like, please call Warden Elmo Jenkins in the federal detention unit."

"If I like— You fear— You mocking me?" Smiling, he comes close. He hates everything I do. He hates my seriousness more

345

than sass, the hatefulness translating into a kind of familiarity. He comes up close as a lover, actually touching me with his stomach, like an enraged coach bumping an umpire—but more erotically. "If I like—I'll tell you what I like, Doctor. I'd like it if you would get going right through that door." He reaches for the door.

"Whoa!" says the uncle, not attempting to block the sheriff at the door but craning past him. "Look ahere, Cooter," says the uncle, hopping from one foot to the other. "Let me tell you—"

The sheriff, aware of a commotion behind him, slowly turns, holding out a staying hand to me.

Mrs. Cheney has meanwhile risen from the couch and, approaching the sheriff, turned her back, lifted her skirt, and now in one quick practiced motion, or rather, several in rapid succession, lifted her skirt, snapped down her panties—teddies? they're long, lavender, and loose-fitting—and presents to Sheriff Sharp, mooning him in the saucy way sorority girls do in certain film comedies, hands on knees, head cocked friskily around.

She backs into him.

"What?" says Sheriff Sharp, rearing a bit. "Hey!"

Mrs. Cheney reaches behind her and with a sure instinct and sense of direction takes hold of him. Then, finding him clothed, she seizes his hands in hers and places them on her hips, under hers, to assist her movements.

"What?" repeats the sheriff, looking right and left as if to call people to witness, but then thinks better of it, and in a lower voice, speaking to the top of Mrs. Cheney's head, "Jesus, Lurine," and in an even lower voice utters (I think): "Later, girl."

There is a growling above.

Coach and Mr. Brunette are still in their "bachelor" postures of submission—Coach, head bowed, studying his palms, contenting himself with a single stomp of his running shoe; Mr. Brunette, one elbow crooked over his head, laying it over to allow Mrs. Brunette to groom him.

"Would you look at that woman," whispers the uncle to Ver-

346

gil, the uncle at first rapt, then hopping and poking an elbow into Vergil's side.

But Vergil, arms crossed, eyes monitored, permits himself no more than a single unsurprised shrug. There is no telling what white people—

The two deputies, trapped between amazement and stoicism, both advance and retreat, stretch forth hands to help, pull them back. They cannot bring themselves to look at each other.

Mr. Brunette is exploring Mrs. Brunette's thigh with an unlewd finger, simply poking up the fabric of her skirt along her stocking as a child might look under a curtain in hide-and-seek, Mrs. Brunette simply allowing it through a lack of attention. The skirt reaches her waist and Mr. Brunette takes an interest in what is indeed a complex business—not panty hose, as one might expect, but stockings suspended by garters from a girdle of scalloped black lace at her waist—garter belt?—this rigging of straps and lace overlaying a bikini, that is to say, a single transparent tape and a small snug triangle of black lace.

Both Coach and Mr. Brunette have grown more excited but seem at a loss, like the two deputies.

Mrs. Cheney presents to the sheriff again.

From above comes the sound of hollow pounding, like kettledrums. The growling deepens to a roar ending in a sharp barklike sound, *aaargh*. Everyone looks up, even Mrs. Cheney. Van Dorn is lunging back and forth behind the balcony rail as if he were caged, then comes swinging down the staircase until, halfway down and with both hands on one rail, he vaults clean over and, projecting himself in an arc more flattened than not, clears Mrs. Cheney and lands squarely on Sheriff Sharp's back, bearing him to the floor, where he falls to biting the sheriff's head, thumping, shrieking, roaring all the while.

There are other screams, mostly from the women but also from the sheriff.

The two deputies leap to the sheriff's assistance, but succeed in little more than pulling and tugging at Van Dorn. Van Dorn is biting Sheriff Sharp's head and neck.

"Vergil, Uncle, come here!" I motion to them above the din.

One of the deputies, the older flattop, giving up, stands back, unholsters his revolver. He bumps into the uncle directly behind him. Vergil is on one side of him, I on the other. The deputy looks up at Vergil, then over to me.

"Put the gun up."

He puts the gun up.

"You want me to grab him, Doc?" says Vergil, nodding at Van Dorn, who is still atop the sheriff, biting and scratching but not doing him serious harm, I think.

"Okay, do this." I pull Vergil and the uncle close so they can hear over the din. "Vergil, you stay here to see that nobody gets hurt. Don't let Van Dorn put his arms around the sheriff and squeeze him. You're the only one strong enough to handle him. Uncle, you go get a dozen Snickers—shoot the machine if you have to. I have to get the women out of sight. Mrs. Cheney! Teddies up!"

Van Dorn has knocked off the sheriff's hat and is biting the top of his head.

Mrs. Cheney, who in fact has shrunk away from the fight, elbows looped over her head, arms flailing, is only too glad to have something to do, pulls her teddies up. I take her by the hand and Mrs. Brunette, who is no problem, who in fact is as docile as can be, her dress falling in place over her complex undergarments as she stands, take them both into the bathroom, reassuring them with nods and pats, close the door behind them. "Stay, ladies!"

Coach and Mr. Brunette are still excited, forgetting their submissive bachelor status. Coach is stamping with both feet, pooching his lips and making, I think, his *hoo hoo* sound, all the while looking around for Mrs. Cheney.

Mr. Brunette, standing, nattering, exposes himself, pulls down his mostly shot-away trousers, takes hold of himself, and starts for the stairs—looking for Mrs. Brunette? to become the new patriarch?

I grab Mr. Brunette, pull him toward the pantry, holler "Snickers!" to Coach as we pass. He follows willingly, loping along, stamping both feet.

The uncle has an armful of Snickers, having broken the glass of the dispenser.

The bachelors are content for the moment to gorge on Snickers in the pantry.

The women are quiet in the bathroom.

With the women out of sight, Van Dorn subsides, leaves off biting the sheriff, and instead cuffs him about in the showy, spurious, not unfriendly fashion of professional wrestlers. It is no problem to lure him away from the sheriff altogether with the Snickers. I tuck the candy in his coat pocket as one might do with a visiting child, head him for the pantry with a pat. Van is quite himself for an instant, noodles me around the neck with an ol' boy hug. "Thanks for everything, Tom," he says in husky, unironic, camaradic voice. "Thanks for everything, Tom." But before I can answer, he's clapping with his fingers, and off he goes, stooping and knuckling along to the pantry for more Snickers.

In no time at all, with the women out of sight, the sheriff is back in control, helped up and brushed off by his deputies, and has put on his hat to cover his bleeding head.

He too thanks me, shaking hands at length, with a sincerity which seems to preempt apologies. "I sho want to tell you, Doctor," he says, keeping hold of my hand without embarrassment, "how much I apprishiate your professional input with this case. I mean, we got us some sick folks here! I may be able to handle criminal perpetrators of all kinds and some forensic cases—I've done quite a bit of reading on the subject, in fact—but when you get into real mental illness such as this"—he nods toward the deputies, who are keeping an eye on the pantry and bathroom, from which issue no longer roars and great thumps but smaller, happier sounds, squeals, clicks, and a few stomps— "I leave it to you, Doc." He gives my hand a last pump.

"Thanks, Sheriff. I'll leave them to you."

"We'll need you and Miss Lucy—all y'all, in fact—to come down and give affidavits."

"Sure thing."

We part as co-defenders of the medico-legal and criminal-justice system.

I am always amazed and not displeased by the human capacity—is it American? or is it merely Southern?—for escaping dishonor and humiliation, for turning an occasion of ill will not only into something less but into a kind of access of friendship. Both the sheriff and Van Dorn, as they pass, transmit to me by certain comradely nods, ducks of head, clucks of tongue, special unspoken radiations.

Handcuffs and restraints are not necessary. The faculty and staff of Belle Ame troop past in more or less good order, even a certain weary bonhomie all too commonplace after too-long, too-boring faculty meetings.

The uncle, Vergil, and I watch in the doorway as the squad cars leave.

"You want to know what I think of that bunch of preverts and those asshole redneck so-called lawmen—I mean, which is worse?" asks the uncle.

"No," I say.

"Why don't I make sure Lurine, Mrs. Cheney, gets home safe." says the uncle.

"No."

Vergil says nothing, gazes speculatively at the sky as if it were another day in the soybean harvest.

I look at my watch. "I have to go. Here's what I suggest. I don't think anybody feels like fooling with the pirogue. Let's go to my car, take Claude and that other boy, Ricky, over to Pantherburn. I'll drop you. Tell Lucy the situation so she can call the Welfare Department, state police—she'll know—to take over out here until the parents can come get their children. Lucy can bring Vergil back to pick up his pirogue. Let's go."

* * *

There's time enough after dropping them off to stop at the driveup window of Popeyes to pick up five drumsticks, spicy not mild, and a large chocolate frosty before heading up the Angola road.

V

THE THANATOS SYNDROME

1. NO TROUBLE GETTING BACK TO ANGOLA IN TIME. NO trouble with Bob Comeaux.

I simply retrace my steps, drive up the Angola road, chewing Popeyes drumsticks, park at old Tunica Landing, take jeep trail to levee, climb under fence, and stroll along hands in pockets like a Guatemalan ex-President returning from his exercise period. Two horse patrols pass me and pay no attention.

Back before two o'clock! Stretched out on my cot as if I've been locked up all morning, when Bob Comeaux and Max Gottlieb show up. (What a pleasure to steal time, to do a thing or two while appearing to be idle, even incarcerated!) I report to Elmo Jenkins, thank him for allowing me my "exercise period." He asks no questions, thanks me again for my long-ago treatment of his auntee. Though he does not say so, I think he is really thanking me for not flying the coop. He has already heard from Sheriff Sharp, I can tell from his voice. We're all on the same side now, I, warden and sheriff. "Your visitors just walked in, Doc." What if I hadn't been there! "I'll send them up."

One look at Bob Comeaux and I know that he *knows*. He's still dressed in his white plantation tuxedo and he must have come straight from the wedding. But he gives me an odd, white-eyed look. Gone is his old Howard Keel assurance. For the first time he is at a loss. He doesn't even seem to notice the hundreds of blacks picking cotton on the prison plantation, stooped over their long, collapsed sacks and singing mournful spirituals. What does he know? He knows about Belle Ame. How does he know? He could have called his office or Sheriff Sharp, been beeped, used the cellular phone in his Mercedes Duck.

Max Gottlieb doesn't know. He only knows something is up. He's frowning, hot and bothered, shaking his head dolefully, even more dismayed than usual (what have you gone and done now?).

I sit at my little student desk, they side by side on my cot, Bob Comeaux holding his wide-brimmed hat between his knees, tuxedo somewhat worse for wear, shirt ruffles wilted. Max is very neat in his new Oxford-gray vested suit, which his wife, Sophie, must have bought for him, but his shoes are the same dried-up Thom McAns he's worn for twenty years. They are shoes no surgeon would be caught dead in.

"Well?" I say after a while.

Bob Comeaux jumps up and begins pacing back and forth as if it were he in prison. He explains he'd like to get back to the wedding reception. "Look, guys, let's make this short. After all, this is only a routine hearing, for the book. Let's spring our friend, the doctor here, sign the papers, vacate his parole status, and let's all go about our business. I got to get back—" He looks at his gold wafer of a watch. "Jesus! Let's get this show— So he's had a couple of violations—but what's a little kinkiness among shrinks, ha ha—right? Say, Tom—" He pulls up in front of me. "I was just wondering. Were the hell-raisin' and hijinks at P&S as dumb in your day as they were in mine?"

"Well, I remember we dropped water bombs on pedestrians."

"Hot damn! We did too!" He socks himself. "Can you believe it?" he asks Max, and instantly sobering: "Okay, guys, let's get this show on the road"—and heads for the open door.

But Max, worried as usual, likes to have everything squared away and kosher. "Yeah, right. Hold it. Let's just hold it. I never had any use for this parole foolishness, anyway. But what's this business about some incident this morning—'disturbance of the peace'?—out at Belle Ame involving Dr. Van Dorn? And some arrested? What is all that about?" Max opens his hands, first to Bob Comeaux, then to me.

Bob Comeaux waves him off, speaks quickly to both of us.

In a word, Bob simply wants shut of me. He assures Max the "incident" was not of my doing, is still willing to take me on at Fedville at consultant's salary plus Ford grant money, is willing for me to do what I'm doing, or throw in with Max in Mandeville—whatever I want to do—but mainly move, move out from here, from him. Let's go. He's at the open door. "Come on, Tom, I'm signing you out, okay?"

But Max is scratching his head, one eye screwed up, trying to make head or tail of it. "Well. He sure doesn't belong here." Sighing, he's pushing himself up from the cot. He can't quite get hold of it.

Bob Comeaux, relieved, relaxes in the doorway and, gazing out at the prison plantation, shakes his head elegiacally. "God," he says softly, "would you listen to those darkies!"

We listen.

> *Nobody knows the trouble I seen,*
> *Nobody knows but Jesus*

"Well, Tom?" He holds out hand-with-hat to me. Let's go.

I do not rise from my student desk.

Max gives me his quizzical eye. "Well?"

"There're a couple of things," I tell Max.

"What's that?" asks Bob quickly, as if, what with the singing, he couldn't hear.

"I think there're a couple of things that need to be settled before we go any further."

"Right," says Max, still feeling unsettled.

"By all means," says Bob, putting his hat on.

"Well?" says Max, giving me his curious eye.

"I think it would be a good idea to discontinue the Blue Boy pilot immediately, today."

"What's that?" asks Bob Comeaux, cupping an ear.

I repeat it.

"What do you mean?" Bob asks me "What does he mean?" he asks Max.

"What do you mean, Tom?" Max asks me.

"I mean turn off the sodium shunt at the Ratliff intake and dismantle it, today."

Max's worries are back, worries now about me weighing him down. He sinks to the cot.

"Tom," he says, screwing up an eye, "I was aware you knew about the sodium pilot. We've never discussed it, for obvious reasons—since it was Grade Four classified. But since you do—to tell you the truth, I've never been too happy with it—I prefer individual therapy, as you well know—to this sort of mass shotgun prophylaxis. But how can you argue with success? I mean, the numbers from NIH are damned impressive, Tom. I mean, it may not do much for our egos if they can reduce street crime, drug abuse, suicides, and suchlike by a simple sodium ion—but what are you going to do? We weren't too happy with lithium either. But zero recidivism at Angola. How do you argue with success? If it ain't broke—" He trails off.

"So I thought at first, but you don't know, Max," I tell him.

"I don't know what?" he says absently, distracted. He's worried, I know, less about Blue Boy than about me.

"Max, NIH doesn't even know about Blue Boy, the heavy-sodium pilot program. They never heard of it. The FDA never heard of it. ACMUI never heard of it. Dr. Lipscomb even spoke to Jesse Land, the director whom she knows. He says it could only be what he calls an instance of 'aberrant local initiative'—that is, some ambitious regional NIH people using their discretionary funding to run a pilot which might otherwise not be funded and then present them with a *fait accompli* which they can't turn down. It's been done before— and sometimes with good cause—to get around bureaucratic hassle—until the election next month.''

"Wait." Max has risen again, this time with both hands out, palms up. "Hold it. Are you telling me that Dr. Comeaux here and Dr. Van Dorn cooked up this sodium additive without even telling—''

"Just as Dr. Fred McKay did with an equally simple ion, fluoridating water," says Bob Comeaux from the doorway, facing us now, arms folded, eyes level and minatory. "If he'd waited for D.C. bureaucracy, children's teeth would still be rotting out. And as both you doctors know, every kook and Kluxer in the country accused him of everything from mind control to Communist conspiracy.''

Silence. Max sighs. "Well—" He is speaking to me.

"Max, Blue Boy was not a pilot involving Angola. It covered the entire parish, in fact, all of Feliciana. Moreover, I'm afraid what we've got here are some side effects which in fact you are aware of and which I can show are related to the additive—''

"Such as? What do you mean, the whole parish?''

"Such as regression of some subjects, especially children, to pre-linguistic pongid levels of behavior, regression of some women from menses to estrus, the sexual abuse of children—''

Bob Comeaux has taken off his hat, placed his hand on his forehead, closed his eyes. "Dear God, do you hear?" He speaks softly. "Where have we heard this before? Do I hear echoes? Of men descended from apes? Who was accused of this? Of corrupting the youth of Athens? You know who was accused of that. But I will confess that tampering with the sexuality of women is a new one." He's shaking his head sorrowfully at me. "From the local yahoos I would have ex-

356

pected it. But from you? *Et tu*—'' He turns to Max. ''Well, I suppose it always happens in a scientific breakthrough—''

''I wasn't speaking of science, Bob. I was speaking of you and Dr. Van Dorn. It was you who made the decision to enlarge the pilot to the entire Ratliff water district—exempting Fedville. And it was your colleague Van Dorn who used the additive on the students at Belle Ame for purposes of the sexual gratification of himself and his senior staff—''

''Hold it, Doctor!'' Bob Comeaux now stands against the door, hands behind him on the knob. He has entirely recovered, not only himself and his old assurance, but his old anger. ''Hear this, Doctor. In the first place, I put my money where my mouth was. I sanctioned a dosage of additive for my own son—and hear this: he is doing brilliantly. And finally, Doctor, you know damn well I'm not responsible for Van Dorn's behavior. But apparently this is the way you want it.'' From his pocket he takes a paper, slowly tears it once, and again, drops it into my student wastebasket. ''That was your release. After what you pulled at Belle Ame this morning, what is going to happen is that we're packing your ass right back to Alabama. I'm sorry, Doctor. I came up here to get you out of here. I had the door open. I did everything but pull you out bodily. Max,'' he says.

I look at Max.

Max is standing over me, hands deep in his pockets, staring down at the curled-up toes of his Thom McAns. ''He can do it,'' says Max softly. ''Look, Tom. Here's what's let's do. Why don't you—and I'm sure Bob here would accept this— why don't you and Ellen— Look, there's no reason to, ah, go to Alabama—instead, why don't you and Ellen do what I've been trying to get you to do, move down to Mandeville, into Beau Rivage with us—there's a condo on 12 just below us available—and I need a partner—I'm tired of clinical work, want some time for writing. You know we always did well together, especially in group. I know you've had some problems, ah, at home, that is, adjusting. Tom, we could do well together, and economically too—'' He breaks off suddenly, eyes widening.

While Max is talking I'm spreading the Belle Ame photos on the floor, plus Lucy's printouts and graphics from the NIH and Public Health mainframe in Baton Rouge and the local Fedville data bank showing not only the distribution of Louisianians dosed up on Na-24—the starry galaxy over Feliciana—but the procurement order from Fedville, signed by Dr. Comeaux, exempting Fedville from the Ratliff water district and ordering a second intake upstream from Ratliff. The photographs, I can't help but notice again, exhibit the same Victorian propriety, the decorous expressions, every hair in place, bobbed in the women, old-fashioned 1930s high haircuts in the men, a British sort of nakedness, white-as-white skins and vulnerable backs, unlike tan-all-over U.S. California nakedness, and the children above all: simpering, prudish, but, most of all, pleased. It is the proper pleased children—

For a while both Max and Bob gaze, at first politely, heads aslant, as people will attend to other people's photos. Max's cheek is even propped reflectively on three fingers.

In my clinical voice—doctor showing slides at a medical conference—I explain the exemption of Fedville from treated water, the sodium-additive arrangement, the presenting behavior of Mrs. Cheney, the anal lesions of this child, her curious linguistic regression, the extraordinary I.Q. of that child—not omitting Ricky's perfect score in Concentration.

"Ricky?" says Bob, not comprehending.

"Ricky is all right, Bob. He's at Lucy's house."

"What?" says Bob. "Ricky?"

"I understood you wanted to have him in the program, Bob."

"Yeah, but at first-level minimum dosage, to improve his— he was flunking math—Jesus, they didn't— Is he all right?"

"He's fine. He's not injured. He's with Claude at Lucy's house. You can pick him up anytime."

"Thank God," says Bob. "Thanks, Tom."

"That's okay, Bob. He's with Claude at Lucy's house."

"Jesus," says Bob.

Max seems not to be listening. His attention seems to be caught by one photograph, the one depicting Van Dorn supine, bearing the child aloft and impaled between his knees, the child's expression, demure, as pleased as if she had just won the spelling bee, legs kicking up happily. The child is facing the camera and therefore appears to be looking at the viewer of the photograph.

As Max examines the photographs he falls into an old habit, hissing a tune between tip of tongue and teeth, which I remember him doing as house physician standing with a patient's chart in the nurses' station—a sinister, amiable hissing, the attending intern casting about: How did I screw up this time?

Max is also nodding in his old abstracted way. "So," he says to no one.

Bob Comeaux has come alongside, head medically-comradely aslant, like the attending physician co-inspecting an X-ray with the chief on grand rounds. He too is nodding, hands in pockets, upper lip folded against his teeth.

"Bob," he says in his old ominous-gentle, grand-rounds voice, head back, looking along his cheek. "Just what are we doing here?"

Bob is clucking back-of-tongue-from-teeth *tck tck tck* meditatively, resident considering case: it's amazing how everything you do, even late in life, you did in school.

Silence, except for the spirituals.

"What are we doing here?" Max asks again.

"We are listening to the darkies singing," I say.

"All I can say is this," says Bob Comeaux. He's squinting into the afternoon sunlight, hat in his hands, head leaning back against the jamb. "I don't know about those, whatever they are"—he nods toward, without quite looking at, the photographs—"but I will say this, you try the best you can to help folks. And what do you get? I'll tell you what you get. You get the same thing Lister got, Galileo got, Pasteur got.

Ridicule. Did that son of a bitch use Ricky?'' he asks in a different voice.

"Ricky's okay, Bob."

Silence, except for the singing.

> I looked over Jordan and what did I see,
> Coming for to carry me home.
> A band of angels coming after me,
> Coming for to carry me home.

"Don't tell me that's not beautiful," says Bob absently.

"Right, Bob," I say. "Now here's what we ought to do." I exchange glances with Max—one of our "group" glances. We understand each other. We know something movies and TV don't know. Here's where movies and TV go wrong. You don't shoot X for what he did to Y, even though he deserves shooting. You allow X a way out so he can help Y. X is going to have enough trouble as it is. Max already recognizes a tone in my voice, the clinical-helper voice of the "resource person" in group therapy. He and I have run many a group. It's like two cops playing tough cop and softy cop.

"What's that, Doctor?" asks Max in his tough cop voice.

"This is just an idea to kick around. I was thinking: Now that Blue Boy is closed down, wouldn't it make sense to use the NIH discretionary funds and the Ford money to help Father Smith reactivate the hospice? The good Father is a nut, as we all know, but his place can be useful as a facility for your terminal cases—for one thing, save you an awful lot of money. He's going to need all the help we can give him. I'm thinking of giving him a couple of afternoons a week." Group strategy: Don't shoot Bob Comeaux, use him.

We all appear to consider.

"Well, I don't know," muses Max, who is just beginning to grasp what has happened, is astounded, and is not showing it.

Bob Comeaux, still martyred, eyes still closed elegiacally, is actually attending closely. He almost nods.

360

"I was thinking too," I say, not to Bob, but to Max. "You know, we've not only got a lot of toxic-abused children, overdosed on sodium 24, thanks to Van Dorn's hapless experiment"—blame Van Dorn for now—"who've been knocked back to a cortical deficit, a pre-linguistic level like a bunch of chimps and are going to need all the help Father Smith and the rest of us can give them. I think it would also be a good place to transfer the euthanasic candidates and quarantined patients from the Qualitarian Center."

Max rolls his eyes. Things are moving too fast. It's all right for resource persons to fall out in group, stage mock warfare. But this! *For Christ's sake, Doctor*, Max is saying, eyes rolled back, *you're pushing him too far.*

"I for one," says Max, switching to his nice-cop-versus-mean-cop voice, "don't think Dr. Comeaux should take that to mean you're suggesting the transfer of all infants who are candidates for pedeuthanasia for one reason or another—hopeless retardation, Down's syndrome, AIDS infants, status epilepticus, gross irreparable malformations, and suchlike—who have no chance for a life of any sort of acceptable quality—you're not suggesting that they too should be transferred from the center to the hospice?"

"That's what I meant. The hospice will take them all."

Bob Comeaux has recovered sufficient footing to lever himself away from the doorjamb and face us both.

"You're talking about violating the law of the land, gentlemen," he says quietly. "*Doe v. Dade*, the landmark case decided by the U.S. Supreme Court which decreed, with solid scientific evidence, that the human infant does not achieve personhood until eighteen months."

Max's eyes are in his eyebrows. If his junior resource person insists on screwing up, he's on his own.

"Not only that," I go on in the same sociable tone, non compos but not hostile either, "we want all the so-called prepersonhood infants at St. Margaret's by next week, plus all the terminal cases of any age, including adult AIDS patients

361

who've been quarantined—plus your nursing staff until we can get organized.''

Why am I saying all this? Father Smith is a loony and can't even take care of himself.

"Shit, Max!'' Bob Comeaux, now altogether himself, collected in his anger, has squared off with Max. "He's talking about shooting down the entire Qualitarian program in this area. No way.''

Max now, dropping group voice: this is serious. "Tom, we don't want to get into a legal hassle. It is, after all, the law of the land.''

"Max, the law of the land does not require gereuthanasia of the old or pedeuthanasia of pre-personhood infants. It only permits it under certain circumstances.''

"I know, but—'' says Max.

Group falls silent.

"No way,'' says Bob Comeaux softly.

"Very well,'' I say, picking up the photos and Lucy's printouts from NIH's mainframe. "I'll be going.''

"What you got there?'' asks Bob Comeaux quickly, eyes tracking the printouts like a MacIntosh mouse.

"You know what these are, Bob.''

"What you going to do with them?''

"Return them to Dr. Lipscomb. They're her property. She in turn will be obliged to notify NIH, ACMUI, and the Justice Department.''

"But we haven't signed you out!'' exclaims Bob Comeaux, actually pointing to the torn paper in my student wastebasket.

"In that case I'll just hand them to Warden Elmo Jenkins, who is familiar with the case and will pass them along to Lucy.''

"Ah me,'' muses Max.

I'm halfway to the door. "Hold it, old son,'' says Bob Comeaux, uttering, in a sense, a laugh, and clapping a hand on my shoulder. "As L.B.J. and Isaiah used to say, Let us reason together.'' And, to tell the truth, he looks a bit like

L.B.J. back at the ranch, in his Texas hat, smiling, big-nosed, pressing the flesh.

2. ELLEN LOST OUT IN FRESNO. CUT OFF FROM VAN Dorn and heavy sodium, she got eliminated in Mixed Doubles and came limping home.

We were all glad to see her. She wouldn't talk to anybody but Hudeen. They exchanged a few murmured syllables which no one else could understand.

The children, out of school, stood around either picking at each other or moony and cross as children are when something is wrong. But Chandra is good with them, playing six-hour games of Monopoly. Between times they're on the floor in front of the stereo-V, as motionless as battlefield casualties, eyes glazed: back to six hours of *Scooby Doo* and *He-Man*.

My practice is almost nil. People are either not depressed, anxious, or guilty, or if they are, they're not seeing me.

I begin dropping by the Little Napoleon and having a friendly shooter of Early Times with Leroy Ledbetter.

Ellen is puzzled, distant, and mostly silent. At night we lie in our convent beds watching Carson without laughing and reruns of *M*A*S*H* and *Lifestyles of the Rich and Famous*.

What to do?

Leroy makes his usual suggestion, after one of his all-but-invisible knockings-back of a shot glass as part of the motion of wiping the bar and leaning over to tell me.

"Why don't y'all take my Bluebird and go down to Disney World? Y'all will like it. There is something for all ages."

I thank him as usual, hardly listening, since Disney World is the last place on earth I would choose to go.

But as I look at the moony, fretful children and puzzled

silent Ellen lying in the silvery glare of the tube watching cockney Robin Leach and Carson and Hawkeye between her toes with exactly the same dreamy, unfocused expression, the thought occurs to me: Why not?

As it turns out, it is a splendid idea, and Leroy is right: Disney World is for all ages.

We find ourselves in the Bluebird parked in Fort Wilderness Resort next to the Magic Kingdom. Fort Wilderness is a pleasant wooded campground with hookups for motor homes. Our campsite is on Jack Rabbit Run.

The Bluebird is a marvel. It cost Leroy over a hundred thousand dollars secondhand, and he's spent another ten on it. He lives in a room over the Little Napoleon. It is like giving me his house.

We go spinning along the Gulf Coast in the fine October light as easily as driving a Corvette, but sitting high and silent as astronauts. The children are enchanted. They spend days exploring the shiplike craft, opening bunks, taking showers, folding out tables and dinettes, working the sound system and control panel and the map locator, which shows us as a bright dot creeping along I-75.

The four-speaker stereo picks up the *Pastoral* symphony. We're a boat humming along Beethoven's brook. I would be happy, but Ellen, in the co-pilot seat, is still abstracted, brows knitted in puzzlement. I take a nip of Early Times both in celebration and for worry.

Ellen gets better the second night out in a KOA campground in the pine barrens.

While I'm hooking up, figuring out where the plugs go, Ellen disappears.

Oh, my God. But the kids are not worried. They've already found the playground. Neighbors come ambling over, offering a beer, inspecting the Bluebird. They think Meg and Tom are my grandchildren. They show me pictures of theirs. The American road is designed for children and grandparents. Oh, my God, where is Ellen? Have a drink. I have a drink, three drinks. Nobody else is worried. Neighbors assure me she has gone to the commissary.

She has. She's back with groceries. No more Big Macs and Popeyes chicken.

Now in the violet October light after sunset, the air fragrant with briquet and mesquite smoke perfumed by lighter fluid, there is Ellen at the tiny galley cooking red beans and rice, not my favorite boudin sausage but Jimmy Dean sausage and—humming!

I do not dare signify to her that anything is different, let alone approach her from the rear, as I used to. Instead, in celebration and gratitude I step outside in the violet dusk and take three nips like a country man.

We sleep aft in a kind of observation bedroom—Meg has discovered how to slide back the roof, making a bubble under the stars—the kids amidships in complex fold-out astronaut pods. The bed is king-size, bigger than Sears Best. I am having bouts of nervousness and so take a nip for each bout. To keep the key low—no grand epiphanies, thank you—I turn on the tube. Leroy's stereo-V is a pull-down screen big as a movie. There's Hawkeye and Trapper John back in Korea. I never did like those guys. They fancied themselves superdecent and super-tolerant, but actually had no use for anyone who was not exactly like them. What they were was superpleased with themselves. In truth, they were the real bigots, and phony at that. I always preferred Frank Burns, the stuffy, unpopular doc, a sincere bigot.

But if Ellen likes them—

But Ellen turns them off.

There we lie in the Florida barrens in a bubble of a spaceship as close to the stars as Voyager V, I not quite drunk but laid out straight as an arrow, feet sticking up, hands at my side, eyes on Orion.

She too.

Presently her hand comes down lightly on my thigh, stays there.

"Okay then," says Ellen.

"Yes, indeed."

"I—good."

"Sure."

"Soon—better."

"Right."

Ellen is still too stoned on sodium ions to talk right.

I am too drunk for too long to make love.

But it's all right. Soon she'll talk better and I won't have to drink.

Disney World is indeed splendid—though I could not stand more than one hour of it.

After one day of the Magic Kingdom, Tomorrowland, Adventureland, Mickey and Goofy, Spaceship Earth, the World of Motion, the Living Seas, I take to the woods.

The children love it. Ellen seems to like it in an odd, dreamy way. Tommy and Margaret are the only kids around—everybody else is in school. They're laid out, paralyzed by delight, when they shake hands with Mickey and Goofy (though they don't really know who Mickey Mouse is).

But it is splendid. The kids run free and safe, catch the tram, launch, monorail, quasi-paddle-wheeler in a quasi-river, go where they please.

Ellen makes friends with other ladies in Jack Rabbit Run, plays some bridge, not too well, no better than they.

We're there a week.

I am quite happy sitting in our private little copse in Fort Wilderness reading Stedmann's *History of World War I*. A little vista affords a view of the great sphere of spaceship earth and the top of the minaretlike tower of Cinderella's Castle.

It is easy to make friends. Sometimes I catch the Conestoga tram up to Trail Blaze Corral or down to the Ole Fishing Hole. Though we are hedged off from our neighbors by a brake of cypress, pine and palmetto, they are only a few feet away. A haze of perfumed briquet smoke, friendly talk, laughter enlists us in a community of back yards.

We meet on the tram or strolling about Jack Rabbit Run or Sunny Sage Way or Quail Trail.

Most of my neighbors are from Canada or Ohio. They are very pleasant fellows, mostly retirees who have done well and are cruising America in their Bluebirds and Winnebagos and Fleetwoods. The Ohioans are recognizable by their accents, not their license plates, which are mostly Florida, for they have settled down in places like Lakeland or Fort Myers or Deerfield Beach and have hopped over for a few days.

Native Floridians look down their noses at the Ohioans. The saying is: An Ohioan arrives with a shirt and a five-dollar bill and never changes either. But it isn't true. My Ohio neighbors in Jack Rabbit Run couldn't be nicer. It is quickly evident that I know nothing about motor homes and they spend a great deal of time demonstrating electrical and sewerage hookups and even the features of my own Bluebird, which they know better than I (they marvel at the modifications Leroy has made, especially the map locator).

The Canadians are as affable but standoffish—though not as shy as the English.

But both, Canadians and Ohioans, are amiable, gregarious, helpful—and at something of a loss. Here they are, to enjoy the rewards of a lifetime of work, to escape children and grandchildren, and they have. They stand about nodding and smiling, but looking somewhat zapped.

Ellen gets along splendidly with them too. She talks to the women by the hour, especially the Canadians, about the queen of England and Princess Di. Like many American women, she loves British royalty even more than the Brits.

Their expressions are fond and stunned.

The Ohioans looked zapped but keep busy.

The Canadians looked zapped but also wistful.

Every time I talk to a Canadian, either he will get around to asking me what I think of Canada or I will know that he wants to.

I realize that I do not have many thoughts about Canada. Reading Stedmann, who mentions the heroic role the Canadians played in World War I, I realize a curious fact about Canadians: When you hear the word *Canada* or *Canadians*, nothing much comes to mind—unlike hearing the words *Frenchman* or *Englishman* or *Chinese* or *Spaniard*—or *Yankee*. I realize this is an advantage. The Canadian is still free, has not yet been ossified by his word. (Why am I beginning to think like Father Smith?)

I read Stedmann about the Battles of the Somme and Verdun for a while, then step out into my tiny plantation fragrant with hot palmetto palms—it is like summer here—walk over to Quail Trail, and have a Coke with my amiable, stunned neighbors.

Like my cellmates at Fort Pelham and unlike folks at home, they want to talk about current events, politics, Communism, Democrats, Negroes (their word), terrorists, and such.

I listen attentively and with interest.

After reading Stedmann in the Bluebird and stepping out into the fragrant Florida sunshine and discussing current events with my knowledgeable, up-to-date neighbors, who even with their knowledgeability—unlike me they're up to date—still look fond and stunned even as they speak, I experience the sensation that the world really ended in 1916 and that we've been living in a dream ever since. These good fellows have spent their entire lives working, raising families, fighting Nazis, worrying about Communism, yet they've really been zapped by something else. We haven't been zapped by the Nazis and the Communists. On the contrary. It is a pleasure to fight one, worry about the other, and talk about both.

We stand about in the Florida sunshine of Jack Rabbit Run, under the minaret of Cinderella's Castle, they fresh from the wonders of Tomorrowland—Tomorrowland!—We don't even know what Todayland is!—fond, talkative, informative, and stunned, knocked in the head, like dreamwalkers in a moonscape.

* * *

Ellen wants to stay on the road, head for Wyoming and Jenny Lake in Jackson Hole. But I have to get back to testify in the trial of John Van Dorn and company. We'll go later.

3. VAN DORN AND HIS STAFF WERE NOT CONVICTED OF child abuse, after all. The presence of heavy sodium in their bloodstreams (they'd been taking a cocktail now and then for one reason and another) compromised the case against them. In a plea-bargain agreement with the district attorney they were confined to the State Forensic Hospital in Jackson until their bizarre symptoms and behavior abated, whereupon they were paroled into the custody of Sheriff Vernon "Cooter" Sharp and sentenced to five years of community service. Sheriff Sharp, after consulting with me and Max, assigned them to St. Margaret's Hospice.

Meanwhile, Father Smith had come down from his fire tower and the hospice was reopened.

Mr. and Mrs. Brunette were assigned to the Alzheimer's patients, old addled folk who could not take care of themselves and in whom no one, not even the Brunettes, could take the slightest sexual interest. It was a hunch, mine and Father Smith's, and it paid off. The Brunettes went to work willingly and in good heart. Father Smith says they are a caring couple. What he actually said was: "Paroled murderers are the most trustworthy aides but sex offenders and child abusers are also excellent, once occasions of sin are removed."

* * *

Mrs. Cheney works as a nurse's aide in a ward of malformed infants, formerly candidates for pedeuthanasia. An excellent babysitter for twenty years—I so testified—she was and is never otherwise than her old motherly and solicitous self toward the children. And even though she persisted for some weeks in her odd rearward presenting behavior as the effects of the sodium ions wore off, there was no one to present to on the children's ward.

Coach also found his talents put to good use. He was assigned to the AIDS wing, which housed not only dying adult patients but also, in a separate cottage, a little colony of LAV-positive children, that is, children who harbored the virus but were not sick. Neither I nor any other physician considered them a threat, but since federal law requires quarantine, what to do with them? Coach did plenty. He is, after all, an excellent coach. His sexual preferences were no problem. The dying adults were too weak to bother him, and he was too terrified to bother them. In a word, he was good with them, didn't have to feign sympathy, was willing to talk and listen. He organized card games, skits, and sing-alongs. But the children were the challenge. He formed a soccer team which, since soccer is not a contact sport, was eligible for Little League competition. His Jolly Rogers (smiling death's-head insignia) are undefeated, have every prospect of winning the league and being invited to the Special Olympics in San Francisco.

Van Dorn, however, was a difficult case. He did not recover as rapidly as the others. Perhaps he ingested a more massive dose of sodium additive and suffered brain damage.

Anyhow, he had to be detained in the Forensic Hospital. When anyone approached, he would at first rattle the bars, roar, and thump his chest. Then, after this ruckus, he would knuckle over to the toilet and cower behind it. He became abject. What to do, legally or medically? No statute could be found to fit his case. Nothing in the Louisiana Civil Code seemed applicable. No medical or psychiatric diagnosis could be arrived at.

What to do with Van Dorn?

Months passed. Van Dorn gave up roaring and thumping, instead knuckled across his cell, crouched behind the toilet, and gave up eating.

I had an idea. It came to me by luck and happenstance— like most good scientific ideas.

It came to me one day while I was making my weekly visit to the Tulane Primate Center, where I earn a few needed dollars—my practice having gone to pot—by doing CORT-scans on the primates housed therein. It is part of an FDA program to test for toxic side effects of new drugs on brain function.

The director, Dr. Rumsen "Rummy" Gordon, old friend and classmate, was showing me around the place, a pleasant compound of piney woods and oak groves which housed colonies of rhesus monkeys, chimps, orangutans, and a single gorilla.

The gorilla, a morose female named Eve, was a special case. She was the last of the so-called talking apes, the famous chimps and gorillas who were supposed to have learned sign language but had been given up on and so had lapsed from fame to obscurity. It was not clear whether they had learned sign language after all, or whether, if they had, they had grown weary of it, even abusive, and stopped talking, and their teachers weary of them. At any rate, in the end for lack of funding these world-famous apes were either packed off to zoos or to the wilds of Zaire, where, it was hoped, they might be accepted by their native cousins.

Only Eve remained, and only Rummy Gordon persisted in his conviction that apes could be taught sign language—not merely to signal simpleminded needs like *Tickle Eve, Eve want banana, Eve want out, Rummy come play*—but to learn to tell stories, crack jokes, teach language to their young, and so on.

But Eve, like the others, fell silent, no longer greeted Rummy with a happy hopping up and down and a flurry of signs, and took to her bower in the low crotch of a live oak.

"She won't sign, not even for bananas," sighs the disconsolate Rummy as we gaze up at Eve, supine and listless on her bed of bamboo leaves, one arm trailing down, one leg sticking straight up, for all the world like a catatonic patient on a closed ward. "In fact, she won't eat bananas, period."

"Rummy, I've got an idea."

He thinks I'm joking at first. "Cut it out, Tom," he says with a wan smile. "I'm serious."

"So am I. Look. This is a lovely spot and enclosed—you'd be taking no chances." It is a lovely spot, a half acre of live oaks and pines, and even a brooklet. If it were listed by any realtor in Feliciana, it would be called a ranchette and go for at least $300,000.

"You've got to be kidding—" But I see he's taking it seriously. "How do you know they would get along. She could kill him. Eve weighs in at about 250."

"I have a hunch, Rummy. A strong hunch. I think it would work. To be on the safe side, we'll watch them at first."

"My God." But he's thinking. "Let me look into the insurance." He's shaking his head. "No way."

In the end he's convinced by a single argument: It's his only chance to revive Eve's language. I know his weak spot. "Don't you see, Rummy? As Van Dorn recovers, they can communicate."

"How? He doesn't know sign language, let lone Ameslan." Ameslan is the special sign vocabulary apes are taught.

"That's the point," I say, watching him. I think I've got him.

"Oh. You mean—" He's got it! His eyes are alight. "She teaches him!"

He's got it: *she teaches him!*

372

"It hasn't been done before, not even ape teaching ape, has it? Isn't that the big breakthrough you've been trying for? Wouldn't it prove your detractors wrong once and for all?"

He's tapping his lips, casting ahead. I've got him. "Why not," he says finally. "We could put a metal hut in there in case he doesn't take to the bower. He might even get her into the hut," he muses.

Why not?

To make a long story short, he did it. They did it. Van Dorn joined Eve in her idyllic ranchette. After a good deal of wary knuckling and circling, baring of teeth, they made friends. For of course mountain gorillas, the species *Gorilla gorilla*, are gentle creatures despite the chest thumping and roaring, which are mainly for sexual display by males and for scaring off predators. And Van Dorn was no predator. Eve smacked her lips, a good sign. Presenting often follows. They, Eve and Van Dorn, spent the brisk fall days playing, romping about the compound, or taking long siestas in the live oak. She gave him a hand up to the crotch. On chilly nights she allowed herself to be led into the hut, which she converted to a proper bower by weaving bamboo shoots over it. They were observed signing to each other in Ameslan, the sign language of the deaf, Eve signing first, Van Dorn watching closely, then venturing a tentative sign in return.

It lasted two months—in a word, until Van Dorn recovered. Having recovered his humanity, become his old self, his charming, grandiose, slightly phony Confederate self, he summoned Rummy Gordon in ordinary Mississippi English and expressed his desire to rejoin his own kind, was released to Sheriff Sharp, examined, found competent to stand trial, was tried, convicted, and sentenced to Angola for ten years.

As resilient as ever, however, he was soon running the prison library, giving bridge lessons, and writing a book. *My Life and Love with Eve* was an immediate and sensational best seller, serialized with photos in *Penthouse* and eventually made into a six-hour mini-series for stereo-V, the Playboy channel. It made such a hit with the Louisiana governor that he pardoned Van Dorn, who has since been busy on the talk-show circuit and making appearances on the *Donahue* show, often with Dr. Ruth.

Dr. Rumsen Gordon prospered as well. He wrote a land-mark scientific paper, ''The Interspecies Acquisition of Ameslan Small Talk by an Na-24 Intoxicated *Homo sapiens sapiens* from a *Gorilla gorilla*,'' which became celebrated in academic circles and led to his appointment as Emeritus Professor of Semiotics at Yale at twice his former salary.

Eve did not fare as well. Having lapsed into silence upon Van Dorn's departure, she was returned to Zaire, where it was hoped she would be accepted by other mountain gorillas, who, however, were members of an endangered species on the verge of extinction. She was last seen squatting alone on a riverbank, shunned by man and gorilla alike.

4. BOB COMEAUX AND MAX AND I REACHED A GENTLE-man's agreement. Instead of turning Bob over to the Justice Department for prosecution for defrauding the federal government, specifically in his misuse of both discretionary NIH funds and Ford Foundation grants, we suggested that it might be in his interest to stay long enough to dismantle the sodium shunt and to divert next year's funds to St. Margaret's Hospice—and then to leave town. Max, who knows every-body, made friendly telephone calls to the directors of both NIH and ACMUI and let drop not even a hint but only an intimation that even though they were not legally responsible for the Blue Boy pilot, it might be prudent—politics being politics, and we know about politicians, right, Doctors?—not only to dismantle the sodium shunt for environmental reasons but to terminate the local Qualitarian Center at Fedville—for fiscal reasons.

The center was closed, quietly. Bob Comeaux left town even more quietly. I have not heard from him. There are rumors. Some say that he returned to Long Island City, resumed the family name Como—Huguenots being in short supply in Queens—and is running a Planned Parenthood clinic on Queens Boulevard.

He bears me no malice. In fact, the last time I saw him, in the A&P parking lot, where he'd had to park to get to the post office because his Mercedes was pulling a two-horse trailer, he greeted me in his old style, with knowing looks right and left as if he meant to share a secret. The secret was that he'd been invited to the People's Republic of China to serve as consultant to the minister for family planning, who wanted to enlist his expertise in the humane disposal of new-born second children—Chinese families being limited, as everyone knows, to one child.

"You want to know something, old buddy," says Bob Comeaux, hitching up his pants, hiking one foot on the bumper of the horse trailer just below the long gray tails of two splendid Arabians. He hawks and spits, adjusts his crotch, casting an eye about, Louisiana style.

"What?"

"You and I may have had our little disagreements, like Churchill and Roosevelt, but we were always after the same thing."

"We were?"

"Sure. Helping folks. Our disagreement was in tactics, not goals."

"It was?"

"You always did have a genius for the one-on-one doctor-patient relationship—for helping the individual—and you were right—especially about Van Dorn and that gang of fags and child abusers—for which I salute you."

"Thanks."

"But I was right about the long haul, the ultimate goal, as you must admit."

"I must?"

"We were after the same thing, the greatest good, the highest quality of life for the greatest number. We were not a bad team, Tom. Between us we had it all. We each supplied the other's defect."

"We did?"

"Sure." He pats the round rump of an Arabian, and his eyes go fond and unfocused. "We've never argued about the one great medical goal we shared. And you still can't argue." His eyes almost come back to mine.

"About what?"

"Argue with the proposition that in the end there is no reason to allow a single child to suffer needlessly, a single old person to linger in pain, a single retard to soil himself for fifty years, suffer humiliation, and wreck his family."

"I—"

"You want to know the truth," he says suddenly, giving me a sly sideways look.

"Yes."

"You and I are more alike than most folks think."

"We are?"

"Sure—and you damn well know it. The only difference between us is that you're the proper Southern gent who knows how to act and I'm the low-class Yankee who does all these bad things like killing innocent babies and messing with your Southern Way of Life by putting secret stuff in the water, right? What people don't know but what you and I know is that we're both after the same thing—such as reducing the suffering in the world and making criminals behave themselves. And here's the thing, old buddy"—he is smiling, coming close, but his eyes are narrow—"and you know it and I know it: *You can't give me one good reason why what I am doing is wrong.* The only difference between us is that you're in good taste and I'm not. You have style and know how to act, and I don't. But you don't have one good reason—" He breaks off, hawks, eyes going away in his newfound Southern style. He smiles. "You all right, Doc."

"I—" I begin, but he's gone.

5. TWO GREAT HAPPENINGS TO LUCY LIPSCOMB WITHIN the month. Exxon brought in a gas well at Pantherburn and her ex-husband, Buddy Dupre, divorced his second wife and came home.

Acquitted of charges of grand theft and malfeasance in office by the Baton Rouge grand jury, mostly Cajuns, he returned to Feliciana exonerated and something of a hero. He is said to have political ambitions. Many friends, he reports, have urged him to seek higher office. What with his extended family—he's kin to half of south Louisiana—and Lucy's high-Protestant connections in Feliciana and his own advocacy of a "scientific creationism" law in the legislature—which helped him in Baptist north Louisiana—he has a political base broad enough to run for governor. And now Lucy has the money. Louisianians, moreover, have a fondness for politicians who beat a rap: "Didn't I tell you that ol' boy was too damn smart to catch up with?"

Lucy, to tell the truth, would not in the least mind being first lady of Louisiana and presiding over the great mansion in Baton Rouge. She is one of those women who can carry off being wife, doctoring, and running a plantation—doing it all well, albeit somewhat abstractedly.

It is just as well. I'd have gotten into trouble with Lucy for sure, lovely as she is in her bossy-nurturing, mothering-daughtering way, always going *tch* and fixing something on me, brushing off dandruff with quick rough brushes of her hand, spitting on her thumb to smooth my eyebrows. The one time she came to my bed, coming somewhat over and onto me in an odd, agreeable, early-morning incubus centering movement, I registered, along with the pleasant centered

377

weight of her, the inkling that she was the sort who likes the upper hand.

It is just as well Ellen came home and Buddy came home. She, Lucy, gave signs of wanting to marry me, and how could I not have, lovely large splendid big-assed girl that she is, face as bruisy-ripe as a plum, with a splendid old house and Ellen having run off with Van Dorn? An unrelieved disaster it would have been, what with the uncle calling ducks night and day and what with Ellen coming home eventually. I'd have ended up for sure like our common ancestor, Lucy's and mine, with one wife too many in a great old house, sunk in English Tory melancholy, nourishing paranoid suspicions against his neighbors, fearful of crazy Yankee Americans coming down the river (Como and company) and depraved French coming up the river (Buddy Dupre and the Cajuns)— in the end seeing no way out but to tie a sugar kettle on his head and jump into the river.

What a relief all around.

Lucy deserved her good fortune, restored Pantherburn without prettying it up, replaced rotten joists and moldings, hung her English landscapes for the first time since the War, replaced the silver stolen by the Yankees and General Benjamin F. "Silver Spoons" Butler.

Vergil Bon was toolpusher for the Exxon well, and made enough money to return to L.S.U. for his graduate degree in petroleum geology.

The uncle won the Arkansas National Duck Call for the eleventh time.

6. THE EFFECTS OF THE HEAVY-SODIUM ADDITIVE ARE gradually wearing off in Feliciana.

In the universities, for example, one sees fewer students lying about the campus grooming each other.

There are fewer complaints from parents about "human fly" professors scaling the walls of the women's dormitories. Fewer professors complain of women students presenting rearward during tutorials.

L.S.U. football had a losing season.

Writers-in-residence, as well as local poets who for years have been writing two-word sentences like the chimp Washoe and during readings uttering exclamations, howls, and routinely exposing themselves, have begun writing understandable novels and genuine poetry in the style of Robert Penn Warren, formerly of Feliciana.

But my practice is still dormant. Still, no one complains of depression, anxiety, guilt, obsessions, or phobias. People hereabouts still suffer from physical illnesses, mainly liver damage and arterial clogging, but, mentally speaking, appear to have subsided into a pleasant funk, saying very little, drinking Dixie beer, fishing, hunting, watching sports on stereo-V, eating crawfish and sucking the heads thoughtfully.

I report this state of affairs to Leroy Ledbetter at the Little Napoleon over a drink of Early Times. Taking his invisible drink during a wipe, he replies only, "So what else is new, Doc?"

7. MY TWO OLD FRIENDS, EX-JESUIT KEV KEVIN AND ex-Maryknoller Debbie Boudreaux, who had long since abandoned belief in God, Jesus, the Devil, the Church, and suchlike in favor of belief in community, relevance, growth, and interpersonal relations, have now abandoned these beliefs as well.

They went their separate ways.

Debbie works quietly as full-time bookkeeper at her father's new Nissan agency in Thibodaux.

Kev has given up writing political tracts and now writes commercially successful paperback novels about nuns and ex-nuns, priests and ex-priests who engage in a variety of political and sexual activities, both heterosexual and homosexual, gay and lesbian, Marxist and Fascist.

We remain friends. They are in fact quite solicitous of me and my troubles. They call regularly. In turn I call on them to help me out at the hospice. I need them. They are good. They willingly volunteer and often spend a day with me in the AIDS wing or the Alzheimer's pavilion. All you have to do, I discover, is ask people. They do it because they're generous and, I think, a bit lonely. I work with them because I need their help and I've nothing better to do. In return, I give them couple's counseling, no charge. They might get back together.

8. CHANDRA IS A BIG SUCCESS ON LOCAL STEREO-V. SHE didn't make anchorperson as she had hoped, but eventually did become weatherperson, where she was an immediate hit, her pert manner and general sassiness contrasting with the bland Indiana style of the other members of "NewsTeam-7." She became a "personality"—"Watch Chan on Channel 7" went the promo.

During the minute or so of happy talk at the end of a newscast, when other members of NewsTeam-7 are smiling and making pleasantries and semi-jokes as they stack their papers, Chandra will have none of it: no grins, no banter. Instead, she often challenges the anchorman: "What you talking about, have a nice day—what's nice about that?"—socking the weather map with her pointer.

9. WHILE I WAS TALKING TO BOB COMEAUX AND MAX Gottlieb in my cell at Angola, I asked the former casually what drugs they used in the pedeuthanasia program at the Qualitarian Life Center. He answered as casually, without thinking about it, as one doctor to another, "Amobarbital and secobarbital, IV."

"That's peaceful, isn't it?"

"They go to sleep like the babies they are."

"How about the adults?"

"Secobarbital IV and"—he rouses, showing interest—"do you know what I hit on more or less by accident and what is now state of the art?"

"No."

"Secobarbital plus THC."

"THC?"

"You know, tetrahydrocannabinol, the active constituent of marijuana—and you want to know something, Tom?"

"Yes."

"There is an exaltation, a joyousness, a sense of acceptance and affirmation you would have to see to believe."

"I believe you."

Max Gottlieb is frowning uneasily and moving toward the door. Bob detains him.

"I don't mind telling you guys that for the first time we have actually achieved the full meaning of the Greek word *eu* in euthanasia. *Eu* means good. I may be simpleminded, but I think good is better than bad, serenity better than suffering. You know what you ought to do, Tom?"

"What?"

"You ought to tell Father Smith about THC."

"I will."

"I mean as a therapeutic agent."

"I understand."

He looks at me curiously. "Why is your friend Father Smith so dead set against us?"

After a pause—actually I don't know how to answer him—I think of an answer which might also satisfy my own curiosity. "He thinks you'll end by killing Jews."

"What's that?" Bob asks sharply; then, for some reason, also asks Max, "What's that? What do you mean?"

Both Bob and Max are embarrassed, Bob for me and Father Smith—I've exposed his nuttiness. Max is embarrassed because he is one of those Southern Jews who are embarrassed by the word *Jew*.

"What does he mean?" asks Bob, opening his hands to both of us.

Max, frowning, is having none of it.

"Tom?" asks Bob Comeaux.

I shrug. "He claims it will eventually end as it did with the Germans, starting out with euthanasia for justifiable medical, psychiatric, and economic reasons. But in the end the majority always gets in trouble, needs a scapegoat, and gets rid of an unsubsumable minority."

"Unsubsumable?" asks Max, who, I think, wouldn't mind being subsumable.

"Unsubsumable."

Bob Comeaux is shaking his head mournfully. "Ah me. I thought I had heard it all. Sorry I asked. Does he think I'm anti-Semitic, for God's sake?"

"No."

"Let me tell you something, Tom. I mean, hear this, loud and clear, Doctor!" He is standing arrow-straight, hat held over his heart, addressing me, but for Max's benefit. "Some of my very dearest friends—"

But Max has had enough of this, of both of us. "Let's go, Doctor," he says wearily, holding out one hand to the door, handing along Bob Comeaux with the other.

10. ELLEN IS QUITE HERSELF.

She's given up tournament bridge—actually she's not much better at it than I. We play social bridge with Max and Sophie Saturday and Sunday afternoons.

It is pleasant to gaze out over Lake Pontchartrain from Max's high-rise condo. The bright mazy sun whitens out the sky into a globe of pearly light into which the causeway disappears like a Japanese bridge into a cloud. Between hands Max goes out on the little balcony and focuses his telescope on a coot or a scaup bobbing like corks on the light, vapory water. Once, a memorable day, he put on the high-power lens and we saw a vermilion flycatcher perched on the bridge rail, pooped, taking a breather on the long voyage from Venezuela.

Later Ellen experienced a religious conversion. She became disaffected when the Southern and Northern Presbyterians, estranged since the Civil War, reunited after over a hundred years. It was not the reunion she objected to but the liberal theology of the Northern Presbyterians, who, according to her, were more interested in African revolutionaries than the divinity of Christ. She and others pulled out and formed the Independent Northlake Presbyterian Church.

Then she became an Episcopalian.

Then suddenly she joined a Pentecostal sect. She tells me straight out that she has had a personal encounter with Jesus Christ, that where once she was lost and confused, seduced by Satan and the false pleasures of this world, she has now found true happiness with her Lord and Saviour. She has also been baptized in the Holy Spirit. She speaks in tongues.

I do not know what to make of this. I do not know that she has not found Jesus Christ and been born again. Therefore I accept that she believes she has and may in fact have been. I settle for her being back with us and apparently happy and otherwise her old tart, lusty self. She is as lusty a Pentecostal as she was a Southern Presbyterian. She likes as much as ever cooking a hearty breakfast, packing the kids off to school, and making morning love on our Sears Best bed, as we used to.

She loves the Holy Spirit, says little about Jesus.

She is herself a little holy spirit hooked up to a lusty body. In her case spirit has nothing to do with body. Each goes its own way. Even when she was a Presbyterian and I was a Catholic, I remember that she was horrified by the Eucharist: *Eating* the body of Christ. That's pagan and barbaric, she said. What she meant and what horrified her was the mixing up of body and spirit, Catholic trafficking in bread, wine, oil, salt, water, body, blood, spit—things. What does the Holy Spirit need with things? Body does body things. Spirit does spirit things.

She's happy, so I'll settle for it. But a few things bother me. She attributes her conversion to a TV evangelist to whom she contributed most of her fortune plus a hundred dollars a week to this guy, which we cannot afford, or rather to his Gospel Outreach program for the poor of Latin America. I listened to this reverend once. He'd rather convert a Catholic Hispanic than a Bantu any day in the week.

She has also enrolled Tommy and Margaret in the Feliciana Christian Academy, which teaches that the world is six thousand years old and won't have *Huckleberry Finn* or *The Catcher in the Rye* in the library.

At least it's better than Belle Ame, and the kids seem happy and healthy.

But I worry about them growing up as Louisiana dumbbells.

I might have held out for the parochial school, which was good, but it folded. The nuns vanished. The few priests are too overworked to bother. Catholics have become a remnant of a remnant. Louisiana, however, is more Christian than ever, not Catholic Christian, but Texas Christian. Even most Cajuns have been converted, first by Texas oil bucks, then by Texas evangelists. The shrimp fleet, mostly born again, that is, for the third time, is no longer blessed and sprinkled by a priest.

Why don't I like these new Christians better? They're sober, dependable, industrious, helpful. They praise God frequently, call you brother, and punctuate ordinary conversation with exclamations like Glory! Praise God! Hallelujah! I've nothing against them, but they give me the creeps.

Ellen often invites me to a meeting of her Pentecostals, who hug and weep and exclaim and speak in tongues. She wants to share her newfound Lord with me, especially the Holy Spirit.

"No thanks," I say, after one visit.

"Why not?"

"I'm afraid Marva will hug me." Marva, her mother, has converted too.

"I'm serious. Why not?"

"I don't want to."

"Why don't you want to?"

"I can't really say."

"I know why."

"Why?"

"You're still a Roman." There's nothing new in this. While she was an Episcopalian, she began calling Catholics "Romans."

"I don't think so."

"At heart you are."

"What does that mean?"

"That that priest still has his hooks in you."

"Father Smith? Rinaldo? He doesn't have his hooks in me."

"He got you to do Mass with him."

Do Mass? "That was back in June. It was my namesake's feast day. I could hardly refuse."

"Namesake's feast day. What does that mean?"

"The feast of Sir Thomas More. June twenty-second."

"And he got you again last month."

"He didn't get me. It was the fiftieth anniversary of his ordination. I was the only one he asked. You wouldn't want me not to go."

"Do you know what he does now?"

"Who, Rinaldo? What?"

"When he calls you and I answer the phone, he won't tell me what he really wants. He'll make up another excuse like being sick and needing a doctor."

"He's a sly one."

"And how about you taking the children to Mass last week?"

"It was Christmas."

"We don't think much of Christmas. The word means Christ's Mass."

"Well, after all Meg and Tom are Catholics."

"I don't care what you call them as long as you admit that neither you or Tom or Meg will be saved until you are born again of the Holy Spirit and into the Lord."

"Okay."

"Okay what?"

"I thought I was born again when I was baptized."

"How can a little baby be born again right after it has been born?"

"That's a good question, Nicodemus."

"What did you call me?"

"Nothing bad. Come over here by me."

But she keeps standing, hands on her hips.

"Why don't you go to the fellowship meeting with me to-night? The children are going."

"I think I'll stay home. But right now—"

"I know exactly what you're going to do."

"What?"

"Have five big drinks and watch another stupid rerun of *Barnaby Jones*."

386

"That's so. But for now, why not come over here by me? You're a very good-looking piece."

She sighs, but takes her hands off her hips, holds them palms up, looks up to heaven: what to do? Actually she's quite content to have it so, as am I.

"Come by me."

"All right." She sighs again, comes by me—a wife's duty—then smiles.

We get along well. It is my practice which is shot.

11. HUDEEN KEEPS WELL, STILL REIGNS, SEATED ON her high stool, in her tiny kingdom bounded by sink, stove, fridge, counter, and stereo-V.

She still keeps an eye on the soaps, mumbles amiably in a semblance of conversation, making sounds of assent and demurrer. But once she made herself clear.

It was Thanksgiving. Ellen had quit her bridge tour and was home for good. The children had quit Belle Ame Academy. Chandra had landed her new job as weatherperson, and even as we watched, there she was! On TV! Slapping the black Caribbean with her stick, she as black as the Caribbean.

"Bless God!" cried Hudeen, who can't believe it, a person, someone she knows, Chandra herself, up there on the magic screen. "Bless Jesus!"

"It's a good Thanksgiving, Hudeen," I said.

"And you better thank the good Lord!" cried Hudeen, clear as a bell.

"We will," said Ellen, who says a blessing indistinctly, speaking in tongues, I think.

Hudeen is not speaking in tongues. "I say bless God!" said Hudeen, looking straight at me. "Bless his holy name!"

"All right."

"You be all right too, Doctor," said Hudeen straight to me.

"I will?"

"Sho now."

"How do you know, Hudeen?"

"The good Lord will take care of you."

"Good."

12.

THE LITTLE CEREMONY WHICH WAS SUPPOSED TO celebrate the reopening of the hospice turned out to be a fiasco.

Father Smith, who I had understood from Max to have come down from the fire tower in his right mind ready to take over St. Margaret's, behaved so strangely that even I, who knew him best, could not make head or tail of what he was saying. To the others he appeared a complete loony, or, as Leroy Ledbetter put it, crazy as a betsy bug. To make matters worse, he also managed to offend everyone, even those most disposed to help him and the hospice.

It was doubtful at first that the hospice was going to succeed, after all.

Local notables gathered to welcome the staff, a civic and ecumenical occasion, not only other priests, ministers, and a rabbi, but many of my fellow physicians both federal and local— good fellows who were ready to donate their time and services— the mayor, a representative from United Way and the Lions Club. Even our Republican congressman showed up and promised his support of legislation to divert at least some of the federal funding of the Qualitarian program to the hospice movement.

Chandra had even arranged for a NewsTeam-7 remote unit

to tape the highlights for the "People and Places" segment of the six o'clock newscast. It was one of those occasions, Chandra assured me, which has "viewer appeal," like helping old folks, flying in kidneys and hearts for dying babies. Americans are very generous, especially when they can see the need in their living rooms. And NewsTeam-7 had 65 percent of the market in the viewing area.

It, the hospice, couldn't miss.

There was to be a Mass in the little chapel at St. Margaret's, a few words from Father Smith, followed by a televised tour of the facility, with perhaps short interviews with a malformed but attractive child, a spunky addled oldster, and a cheerful dying person.

It couldn't miss.

But one look at Father Smith as he comes up the aisle of the crowded chapel and I know we're in trouble.

He's carrying the chalice, but he's forgotten to put on his vestments! He's still wearing the rumpled chinos and sneakers he wore in the fire tower for months, plus a new sweatshirt. It is a cold January day.

People turn to watch, as a congregation watches a bride enter church for her wedding. I am sitting in the front row with Max. There is a stir and a murmuring at Father Smith's appearance. But it is not his clothes I notice. Something else: a certain gleam in his eye, both knowing and rapt, which I've seen before, in him and on closed wards.

The chalice is held in one hand, properly, the other hand pressed on the square pall covering, but there is something at once solemn and unserious about him, theatrical, like my daughter, Meg, playing priest.

Oh my.

Well, at least he is going to say Mass, where it's hard to get in trouble. Perhaps the friendly crowd will take his old clothes as a mark of humility, albeit eccentric—but you know what a character he is!—or maybe they'll see him as a worker-priest or a guerrilla priest.

But instead of mounting the single step to the platform of

389

the altar, he turns around in the aisle, not two feet from me, exactly between me and Max, and faces the little crowd, which is still well disposed if somewhat puzzled.

"Jesus Christ is Lord!" he says in a new, knowledgeable, even chipper voice. Then: "Praise be to God! Blessed be his Holy Name!" A pause and then, as he looks down at the upturned faces: "I wonder if you know what you are doing here!"

Well then, I'm thinking, what he's doing is what Catholics call pious ejaculations, which are something like the Pentecostal's exclamations—Glory! and suchlike—that plus a bit of obscure priestly humor.

But no. They are uttered not as pious ejaculations but more like a fitful commentary, like a talkative person watching a movie.

All is not yet lost. Sometimes priests say a few words before Mass, especially on a special occasion like this, by way of welcome.

No one is as yet seriously discomfited.

Father Smith begins to make short utterances separated by pauses but otherwise not apparently connected, all the while holding chalice and covering pall in front of him. They, the utterances, remind me of the harangues delivered by solitary persons standing in a New York subway or in the ward where I was committed by Max and later served as attending physician.

But his remarks, though desultory and disconnected, are uttered in a calm, serious voice. During the pauses he seems to sink into thought.

"The Great Prince Satan, the Depriver, is here."

Pause.

"It is not your fault that he, the Great Prince, is here. But you must resist him."

Pause.

"I hope you know what you are doing here," he says.

Pause.

"The fellows at Fedville know what they were doing."

Pause.

The audience is trying to figure out whether the pauses are calculated, as some preachers will pause, even for long pauses, for purposes of emphasis. They listen intently, heads inclined, with even a tentative nod or two.

"True, they were getting rid of people, but they were people nobody wanted to bother with."

Pause.

"Old, young. Born, unborn."

Pause.

"But they, the doctors, were good fellows and they had their reasons.

"The reasons were quite plausible.

"I observed some of you.

"But do you know what you are doing?

"I observe a benevolent feeling here.

"There is also tenderness.

"At the bedside of some children this morning I observed you shed tears. On television.

"Do you know where tenderness leads?"

Pause.

"Tenderness leads to the gas chamber."

Pause.

"This is the feast day of my patron saint, Simeon the Stylite.

"Simeon lived atop a pillar forty feet high and six feet in diameter for twenty years.

"He mortified himself and prayed for the forgiveness of his sins and the sins of the world below him, which was particularly wicked, being mainly occupied by the Great Prince Satan.

"I don't see any sinners here.

"Everyone looks justified. No guilt here!

"Simeon came down to perform good works when his bishop asked him to, but when the bishop saw he was willing, he let him go back up.

"I'd rather be back up in the tower, but I do know what I'm doing here.

"Do you think it is for the love of God, like Simeon? I am sorry to say it is not.

"I like to talk to the patients here.

"Children and dying people do not lie.

"One need not lie to them.

"Everyone else lies.

"Look at you. Not a sinner in sight.

"No guilt here!

"The Great Prince has pulled off his masterpiece.

"These are strange times. There are now two kinds of people.

"This has never happened before.

"One are decent, tenderhearted, unbelieving, philanthropic people.

"The other are some preachers who tell the truth about the Lord but are themselves often rascals if not thieves."

During one of the pauses Chandra and the NewsTeam-7 crew turn off their lights, fold their cameras, and quietly creep out.

"What a generation! Believing thieves and decent unbelievers!

"The Great Depriver's finest hour!

"Not a guilty face here!

"Everyone here is creaming in his drawers from tenderness!"

Long pause.

"But beware, tender hearts!

"Don't you know where tenderness leads?" Silence. "To the gas chambers.

"Never in the history of the world have there been so many civilized tenderhearted souls as have lived in this century.

"Never in the history of the world have so many people been killed.

"More people have been killed in this century by tenderhearted souls than by cruel barbarians in all other centuries put together."

Pause.

"My brothers, let me tell you where tenderness leads."

A longer pause.

"To the gas chambers! On with the jets!

"Listen to me, dear physicians, dear brothers, dear Qualitarians, abortionists, euthanasists! Do you know why you are going to listen to me? Because every last one of you is a better man than I and you know it! And yet you like me. Every last one of you knows me and what I am, a failed priest, an old drunk, who is only fit to do one thing and to tell you one thing. You are good, kind, hardworking doctors, but you like me nevertheless and I know that you will allow me to tell you one thing—no, ask one thing—no, beg one thing of you. Please do this one favor for me, dear doctors. If you have a patient, young or old, suffering, dying, afflicted, useless, born or unborn, whom you for the best of reasons wish to put out of his misery—I beg only one thing of you, dear doctors! Please send him to us. Don't kill them! We'll take them—all of them! Please send them to us! I swear to you you won't be sorry. We will all be happy about it! I promise you, and I know that you believe me, that we will take care of him, her—we will even call on you to help us take care of them!—and you will not have to make such a decision. God will bless you for it and you will offend no one except the Great Prince Satan, who rules the world. That is all."

Silence.

"Oh, there is something else of the utmost importance I must tell you—"

But suddenly he breaks off, frowns, touches his lip as if he has forgotten what he was going to say. Then, frowning all the harder, he appears to sink into thought. Seconds pass.

This time the pause does not end. Perhaps ten seconds pass. Already there is consternation, exchanged glances, murmurings, shifting about in the seats. Ten seconds is a long time. Then perhaps twenty seconds pass. Now there is anxiety.

When a speaker who is supposed to speak and then make an end to the speaking, stops speaking inadvertently, like an actor going up in his lines, or a young preacher who has a lapse, his audience at first grows restive, is embarrassed for him. Perhaps there are a few titters. Then the audience develops pure anxiety. The anxiety is worse than any offense the speaker may have given.

Behind me, two doctors and the representative of United Way and the Chief Leo of the Lions Club are offended. One says to the other, "Church is out." Another replies, "For us too."

All four leave.

Other people begin to murmur and stir about anxiously.

Only Father Smith, lost in thought, does not appear anxious.

Max and I exchange glances. There is the slightest upward movement of his eyes. We understand each other. We have exchanged such a glance in group, past a patient. I rise and hunch over toward the priest with the air of a deacon or usher who knows what he is doing.

"Father," I say in a low but ordinary voice, "let's get on with the Mass." There are patients, one learns from experience, who will simply do what they are told, never mind Freud and his "non-directive" therapy, and there are times when it is better to tell them.

"Of course," replies the priest, giving a start. "You assist me."

"What?"

"I said, you assist me."

"But, Father, you know very well—" I am looking around for Milton Guidry, his crewcut assistant. No sign of him.

"Sure, I know," says the priest. "But assist me, anyhow."

"All right. But I only remember the old Mass."

"That will do."

He turns and kneels on the platform step. I kneel beside him like an altar boy.

394

"I will go up to the altar of God," says the priest, holding the chalice.

"To God who gives joy to my youth," I reply.

13. ELLEN IS RIGHT AND WRONG ABOUT FATHER Smith. He did not "have his hooks" in me. He only asks me to assist him when he's out of it, needs help, Milton is sick and can't bring him the bread and wine.

The hospice opens and down he comes from the fire tower in his right mind and very much in charge. Very much his old wiry, vigorous self, he jokes with the children, listens to the endless stories of the senile, talks at great length with the dying. He calls on me only when the depression and terrors of his AIDS patients are more than he can handle. We do little more than visit with them, these haggard young men, listen, speak openly, we to them, they to us, and we to each other in front of them, about them and about our own troubles, we being two old drunks and addled besides. They advise us about alcohol, diet, and suchlike. It seems to help them and us. At least they laugh at us.

But when he invited me to serve Mass routinely, because I was visiting the hospice early every morning, I refused. It is easy to say no at the hospice, because honesty is valued above all. I told him the truth: that since I no longer was sure what I believe, didn't think much about religion, participation in Mass would seem to be deceitful.

He nodded cheerfully, as if he already knew.

"Don't worry," he said, doing a few isometrics in the hall, pushing and pulling with his hands. "It is to be expected. It is only necessary to wait and to be of good heart. It is not your fault."

"How is that, Father?" I ask him curiously.

"You have been deprived of the faith. All of us have. It is part of the times."

"Deprived? How do you mean?"

"It is easy enough to demonstrate," he says, shrugging first one shoulder high, then the other.

"Yes?"

"Sure. Just consider. Even if the truths of religion could be proved to you one, two, three, it wouldn't make much difference, would it? One hundred percent of astronomers have discovered that the universe was created from nothing. The explanation is obvious but it does not avail. Who can handle it? It does not signify. It is boring to think of. Ninety-seven percent of astronomers are still atheists. Do you blame them? They are also boring. The only thing more boring would be if the ninety-seven percent all converted, right? It follows that there must be some other force at work, right?"

"Right," I say, noting with alarm the same brightness of eye and chipper expression he used to have in the fire tower.

But before I can escape, he has taken me by the arm and drawn me aside, as if some poor dying soul might overhear.

"Do you recall what happened in Yugoslavia a few years ago?" he asks in a low confidential voice.

"Yugoslavia," I say, wishing I had not gotten into this.

"The six little children to whom the Mother of God appeared?"

"Oh. I do recall something of the sort, yes. Now if you will excuse—"

"What she told them has been much publicized, doubt-lessly exaggerated by the superpious—who knows?—but one little item has been largely overlooked."

"Is that so?"

"Yet I think it highly significant—one of those unintentionally authentic touches which make a story credible."

"Very interesting. Well, I—"

"I'd like your professional opinion on this," he says in a low voice, drawing me still closer.

"Certainly," I say, glancing at my watch.

"The story of the apparitions is well known. Of course, no one knows for certain whether the Virgin appeared to them. The Church does not know. Many pious people believe that she did. That is not what interests me. It is one small detail which they related about one of the many apparitions which seemed so outlandish that no one could make sense of it and either laid it to childish fantasy or overlooked it altogether. You recall that though she identified herself as the Mother of God, one of the children related that she appeared not as the Queen of Heaven with a serpent under one foot and a cloud under the other, crowned with stars and so on—but as an ordinary-looking young red-cheeked Jewish girl, which of course she probably was. But what she told them on this one occasion and which they related without seeming to understand what they were saying was this: Do you know why this century has seen such terrible events happen? The Turks killing two million Armenians, the Holocaust, Hitler killing most of the Jews in Europe, Stalin killing fifteen million Ukrainians, nuclear destruction unleashed, the final war apparently inevitable? It is because God agreed to let the Great Prince Satan have his way with men for a hundred years—this one hundred years, the twentieth century. And he has. How did he do it? No great evil scenes, no demons—he's too smart for that. All he had to do was leave us alone. We did it. Reason warred with faith. Science triumphed. The upshot? One hundred million dead. Could it be a test like Job's? Then one must not lose hope even though the final war seems inevitable as this terrible century draws to a close. Because almost everyone has lost hope. Christians speak of the end time. Jews of the hopelessness of the mounting Arab terror. Even unbelievers, atheists, humanists, TV anchormen have lost hope—you've heard how these commentators speak in their grave style which conceals a certain Ed Murrow delectation of doom. Do you think that there is a secret desire for it? But you must not lose hope, she told the children. Because if you keep hope and have a loving heart and do not secretly wish for the death of others, the Great Prince Satan will not succeed in destroying the world. In a few years this dread century will be over. Perhaps the world will end in fire and the Lord will come—it is not for us to say. But it is for us to say, she said, whether hope and faith will come back into the world. What do you think?''

"What? Oh. Do you mean about Yugo—about the ah predictions. Very interesting. Well, Father, I really must be—"

"So don't worry about it," says the priest. He has let me go and is absently doing a few calf isometrics, balancing on the ball of one foot, then the other.

"And to be specific in your case, Tom."

"Yes?"

"Do what you are doing. You are on the right track. Continue with the analysis and treatment of your patients."

"All right," I reply, somewhat ironically, I fear. "But I don't have many patients."

"You will. You are on the right track. I have watched you. Carry on. Keep a good heart."

"All right."

"I will tell you a secret. You may have a thing or two to add to Dr. Freud and Dr. Jung, as great as they were."

"Thank you." Did he wink at me?

We shake hands. He gives me his old firm Ricardo Montalban handshake, turns, throws a punch or two and is gone.

14. SITTING ON THE FRONT PORCH OF MY OFFICE sailing paper P-51s at the martin house.

A fine warm Louisiana winter day, my best time: the morning sun booming in over the live oak, the air yellow and clear as light, oak leaves glossy, bottle-glass green. Pollen gone. My nose clear as a bell. The white-throated sparrows are back, kicking leaves under the bushes like chickens.

In the next few minutes I must make a decision and phone Max.

I must tell him either/or.

Either take him up on his offer, join him in Mandeville, do group work and divorce facilitation with his aging yuppies, crisis intervention with their stoned-out teenage children. It's good work and I need the money, but I'd rather do my old-fashioned one-on-one therapy with depressed and terrified people.

Or take the directorship at the hospice. Low-paying but steady. No one else wants the job. Father Smith had had to be let go after all. In fact he became a patient. He wanted to go back to the fire tower for good. Max diagnosed Alzheimer's, pointing out his strange harangues, his memory loss and disconnected speech—more and more now he is given to short gnomic utterances which grow ever more gnomic and disconnected, as if he cannot remember what he said five seconds ago. I disagreed, pointing out that his CORTscans showed no loss of cerebral tissue and his PETscans no loss of cerebral function, and other tests were negative. And he is too old. Alzheimer's dementia usually sets in in the fifties or sixties. But there was no denying his strange behavior. Perhaps it is presenile dementia. I agreed to co-sign his commitment—on one condition: that he be allowed to stay in the tower as long as he wanted. For he remains quite agile and can scramble up like an old mountain goat. He watches the horizon, mainly in the east, like a hawk, and at the first sign of a smudge he'll line up his azimuth, call another tower, crisscross his fishing-line coordinates, report the fire as precisely as you please, talk at length and in the peculiar ham lingo to Emmy in the Waldheim tower. He did not object to being committed, seemed quite happy in fact. Max is pleased. Our treatment of Father Smith accorded well with new ideas in geriatrics—which boil down to making the elderly feel useful.

Only occasionally does he seem confused. Then it is not clear whether he is speaking of locating brushfires or God by signs and coordinates. Milton Guidry looks after him, assists at Mass. But Milton's emphysema is worse. When he can't make it up the tower, Father Smith calls me and I substitute—when I can.

* * *

I must make up my mind about the future. We're in debt. Tuition at the Pentecostal school is high and Ellen has given away all her money to the Baton Rouge evangelist.

A doctor needs patients to make a living. What happened to the sort of patients I used to see, the lonely-hearts, the solitary aching consciousnesses—they were my kind of people—the fears, the phobias, the depressions? Have these symptoms been knocked out for good by the heavy sodium? Or are they being treated by GPs prescribing pills? Or by pharmacists? In any case, who needs me?

One good sign. Ellen is back as my secretary-nurse-receptionist.

She'll be here any minute. Better go inside. Wouldn't do to be caught out here sailing P-51s.

She's canny, cheerful, businesslike. It's like the old days, having her back, hearing her nimble voice in the outer office, weeding out undesirable patients, charming the desirable ones. She's already got referrals from her bridge crowd, her Episcopalian book-review group and her big Pentecostal church. The Pentecostals are decent folk, honest and forthright, no crazier than liberal unbelievers and a good deal less neurotic, but perhaps a bit paranoid, given to suspecting godless conspiracies under every sofa. But if I keep them off the couch, don't mention sex, wear a white coat like a TV doctor, speak to them face to face, take their blood pressure—they tend to hypertension—examine their eyegrounds, they'll tell me their troubles.

The telephone is ringing inside. A patient? There is still no Ellen but I needn't hurry. The answering machine clicks on during the third ring. I can hear my voice and a woman's which I almost recognize. There is a familiar overtone of hushed urgency.

Go inside. Play the message.

It is Mickey LaFaye. She's not asking for an appointment or even for a return call. She speaks in the hushed-mouth-in-the-phone voice of a woman hearing a prowler and calling the police.

"I'm coming in—now," she all but whispers. Click. The silence of the machine roars.

It is as if even the machine could grasp the urgency and reach me.

Ellen arrives before Mickey. I try to tell her about Mickey, but she's excited about something.

"That priest called you at home, said he couldn't reach you here—" She pauses for an explanation.

"Probably hadn't arrived. I walked." I'm not about to tell her about sitting on the porch and flying P-51s.

"For once I think he's being helpful."

"How's that?"

"He's got an important referral for you."

"Who?"

"It may be royalty." Ellen lowers her voice.

"Royalty." Is Princess Di—I almost say, but decide not to joke.

"He wouldn't give names—it's all very hush-hush—but do you know who I think it is?" Royalty really lights her up, and her an American Pentecostal. I'll never understand it.

"You know that the new king and queen of Spain are in New Orleans paying a state visit to commemorate Spanish rule in the Vieux Carré—which is in fact more Spanish than French."

I am nodding, mystified, more puzzled by the change in Ellen than by the Spanish king.

"The priest wants you to meet them out there. Tomorrow."

"I see."

"Now get this," says Ellen. She's in her chair and I sitting on her desk in the outer office.

"All right." She's got it figured out.

"He only gave me three hints. Royalty, a visit, gifts and— a Jewish connection."

"That's four."

"Right. Now get this. I happen to know that the new queen,

Margarita, has Jewish blood—a noble old Sephardic family from Toledo.''

"Ohio?"

"And you know what?"

"No, what?" I don't know what, but I'm pleased to see her so pleased.

"I happen also to know that your friend Rinaldo has a Spanish connection, is highly regarded in certain circles over there—which would account for him being called in in case of some trouble—and I also happen to know that Queen Margarita has a psychiatric history. I think she might be your patient.''

"I see."

"Tomorrow morning at eight—why eight I don't know." She's briskly writing down the appointment. "Out there."

"Very good," I say as briskly, frowning to keep from smiling. "Why don't you call him and tell him I'll be there."

"Don't you worry." She's already on the phone.

What Father Smith has told her and she me without knowing it is that he needs me tomorrow morning. Milton must be sick again. It's a little code. Neither of us likes to upset Ellen. Tomorrow is the Feast of the Epiphany. A Jewish girl, a visit from royalty. Gifts.

"He says fine." She's pleased. "I think it's a valuable connection for you."

"You may be right."

In blows Mickey LaFaye, brushing past me and Ellen in the outer office without a word, headed for the sofa in the inner office.

Ellen and I exchange looks, shrugs. She's still pleased.

Mickey's back on the couch as she used to be, facing the window. No Duchess of Alba she now. She's almost Christina again. She's quite beautiful actually, but beginning to be ravaged again, thin, cheeks shadowed under her French-Indian cheekbones, but not yet too thin, not yet wholly Christina. I wonder if she has stopped eating.

"Mickey, please come over here and sit where we can see each other."

She does.

She doesn't mind looking at me.

"Well, Mickey?"

"I—" She breaks off, nods as if nodding could finish the sentence.

"I'm—"

"Yes."

"I'm having an—"

"You're having an attack."

"Yes."

"Of—"

"I'm— Driving over I was terrified—of killing someone."

"Well?" Well.

Her great black eyes, as rounded as a frightened child's, are full on me. One hand is holding the other. She is actually wringing her hands, something you seldom see.

"Are you afraid, Mickey?"

"It's— It's not like anything I ever had before. Something is about to happen. I dread something, but I don't know what it is—" Her eyes fall away, unconverge, as if she saw something, someone, behind me, far away but approaching. Now she's nodding, reassuring herself. "Now isn't that something?"

"What?"

"My life is fine. Durel is fine. My kids are fine. My horses are fine. My painting is fine. But—" She stops, eyes coming back to me, focused, seeking out. She gives a little laugh.

"Well?" Well.

"Could I talk about it?"

"Yes."

"Do you remember that dream I had, about being in the cellar of my grandmother's farmhouse in Vermont and the smell of winter apples and the stranger coming?"

"Yes."

"Could we work on that?"

"Sure."

"I had it again. Last night and the night before."

"I see." Well well.

"Did I say or did you say that perhaps the stranger might be someone trying to tell me something?"

"I don't remember. It doesn't matter what I said. What do you think now?"

"You know what I think?"

"No."

"I think the stranger is trying to tell me something."

"Yes?"

"I also think the stranger has something to do with the terror."

"I see. How?"

"He is not someone to be terrified of, yet I am terrified."

"I see."

"Do you know who the stranger is?"

"Who do you think he is?"

"I think the stranger is part of myself."

"I see."

"I am trying to tell myself something. I mean a part of me I don't really know, yet the deepest part of me, is trying to—"

"Yes?"

"Could I talk about it?"

"Yes."

She falls silent, but her eyes are softer, livelier, are searching mine as if I were the mirror of her very self. She lets go of her hand. She almost smiles. She ducks her head and touches the nape of her neck as she used to.

"Well?" I say.

She opens her mouth to speak.

Well well well.

About the Author

WALKER PERCY himself went to medical school and interned at Bellevue, intending to be a psychiatrist. After a three-year bout with tuberculosis, he married, converted to Catholicism, and became a writer, first of essays, then of fiction. His first novel, THE MOVIEGOER, won the National Book Award and has never been out of print since its publication in 1961. His other novels are THE LAST GENTLEMAN, LOVE IN THE RUINS, LANCELOT, and THE SECOND COMING. His nonfiction books are THE MESSAGE IN THE BOTTLE and LOST IN THE COSMOS. He and his wife, Mary Bernice, live at Greenwood Plantation, 100 miles up the Mississippi from New Orleans.